INNOCENT BLOOD

INNOCENT BLOOD

ELIZABETH CORLEY

First published in Great Britain in 2008 by
Allison & Busby Limited
13 Charlotte Mews
London W1T 4EJ
www.allisonandbusby.com

A CIP catalogue record for this book is available from
the British Library.

10 9 8 7 6 5 4 3 2 1

ISBN 978-0-7490-8096-9 (Hardback)
978-0-7490-8062-4 (Trade Paperback)

Typeset in 11/16 pt Sabon by
Terry Shannon

Printed and bound in Great Britain by
MPG Books Ltd, Bodmin, Cornwall

ELIZABETH CORLEY was brought up in West Sussex. Married with a stepdaughter, she manages to balance her passion for crime-writing with a successful position as Chief Executive, Europe for a global investment company, dividing her time between London, Germany and France. A one-time committee member and vice-chairperson of the Crime Writers' Association, Elizabeth is an active member of the organisation yet still finds the time to pursue her outside interests of travel, gardening and music.

Available from
ALLISON & BUSBY
Requiem Mass
Fatal Legacy
Grave Doubts
Innocent Blood

For Jane and Neil,
with love always,
because family matters.

PROLOGUE

He edged back into a dusty seat on the last train from London to Harlden and let go a sigh that he seemed to have been controlling for the whole of his life. Andrew Fenwick was emotionally and physically drained. All he wanted to do was lay his head back and close his eyes but he couldn't and it wasn't the greasy cushion that stopped him, but his conscience. Earlier that evening he had finally found the answer to a neglected crime that had remained unsolved for more than two decades. Instead of feeling elated, success had left him facing the worst dilemma of his career.

As a result of what he now knew, a good man's fate lay in his hands, and while his duty as a police officer was clear, it was, uniquely, at war with his sense of what was right. The unexpected conflict was eating into him, making him feel too old for his job. He closed his eyes and tried to think calmly about his dilemma but it was impossible. The burden was his alone and no amount of wishful thinking could make it vanish. He had no choice but to decide a man's future and only the breathing space of his journey home in which to do so.

He blinked hard to keep himself awake and his gaze fell to his hands where they lay loosely on his thighs. For a fanciful moment he imagined the man's liberty in his left hand and the sentence that society would pass on him were the truth ever known in his right. Revealing it would be a boost to his career at a time when he was being considered for promotion despite a singular lack of sponsorship from the powers on high. The fingers of his right hand started to curl subconsciously as if he were plucking his advancement from the stale air. Then he clenched both fists tight and relaxed his muscles slowly as he acknowledged the futility of his thoughts. His problem remained and the decision he made would be a defining moment in his life.

The train rattled on as it gathered speed, swaying over points, flashing past stations already closed for the night, taking him towards a time in the future when the decision would have been made and fate decided. He stared ahead, trying to discern what that resolution might be but it was a pointless exercise, a way of wasting time and he despised himself for it.

He'd always considered himself a man who could make difficult decisions, had even thought it one of his strong points but now, when he was really tested, he realised that he was no Solomon. So he resorted to a familiar remedy when his mind became recalcitrant and dry; he pulled out a notepad and opened his pen. At the top of a fresh sheet of paper he wrote down the question that had been circling in his mind like a child's riddle without answer ever since he'd discovered the truth: *When is a murderer not a murderer?*

The words confronted him. The crime he had solved was murder after all, not some petty misdemeanour. With an audible grunt of frustration he ripped the page from the pad and screwed it up, stuffing it into his pocket so that his thoughts wouldn't join the litter on the carriage floor. His watch ticked past midnight as he smoothed his palm across a fresh page, preparing himself.

He wrote down the man's name – his real one. Beneath it he drew a line down the centre of the page. On one side he listed the harsh facts of his guilt; on the other he wrote out the case for the defence, so strong he needed more paper. Then he stared at his work, imagining he was judge and jury. There were so many reasons to grant a lenient sentence but he had no right to make that decision. Could he betray his years of dedicated, scrupulous law enforcement because – in this instance – he couldn't trust the law to be merciful? Slowly, the pen moved across the virgin paper, staining it with his thoughts. Even more slowly his decision began to reveal itself. And finally, he arrived at his destination.

PART ONE

On the last day that his parents saw him alive Paul Hill cycled from home on a new bike that he was proud to claim he'd saved up for himself. It was the first day of the school year. He was fourteen but looked twelve, a reality that had begun to eat into his shaky self-confidence over the summer until his customary bravado had worn thin. It was enough to see him through the first day of school though, despite the jealous reaction to his bike and the sniggers behind his back, which he pretended not to hear.

He was on his own when he left the school gates, his sometime friends having run on ahead, shouting snide comments over their shoulders. He hadn't been inclined to join them anyway, he told himself, as he turned his bike downhill, stroked the elaborate gear mechanism with a fleeting smile of pleasure and raised himself up in the saddle. Before he reached the road he braked suddenly. He had forgotten that he was meant to be meeting someone, despite all the trouble he had gone to constructing careful lies for his teachers and parents in order to give himself the excuses he needed to miss choir practice but still be late home from school. These meetings, which had started as a glorious exciting secret, had become a source of deep anxiety. He wanted them to stop but that idea scared him too. Without consciously making a decision, he turned the bike around and started to pedal towards home, pumping more quickly the closer he drew.

When he got there he would pretend that he had a stomach ache. His mother would have one of her fits and send him straight to bed and his dad would call him a wimp but it would be worth it. If he really played up he might even be able to stay home from school for a few days.

He was taking his usual short cut when a familiar red car overtook him and pulled in to the lay-by ahead. He slowed obediently and watched the driver wind down his window.

'Where are you going, Paul?'

'Home.' He wasn't in the mood for a detour today.

'But we had an agreement. I was expecting you.'

'Don't want to, not today.'

'Go on, it's early; you'll not be missed.'

'I've got homework and extra reading.' He shifted his duffle bag between his shoulder blades and refused to meet the man's eye.

'Nice bike.'

Paul grunted, a monosyllabic sound that meant 'So?'

'Cost a lot I imagine.'

The reminder of how he'd earned his money made Paul's insides burn.

'Go away.'

'Don't be like that. We're friends, remember, and friends are nice to each other.'

Paul shut his eyes, then opened them again and stared stubbornly at the dirt beneath his wheels. He didn't have proper friends, not any more, and it was all this man's fault.

'I never want to see you again.'

The man laughed dismissively, as if Paul had made a bad joke.

'Don't be silly, of course you do; you can't stop now.'

The words made him shiver.

'But I don't want to.' He forced his mouth into its sad look, the one that always worked on his mother.

'Look, Paul,' the man said in a firmer voice, 'it's not as if you have anywhere else to go. I'm the best friend you've got. I've never shared our secret, or showed anybody those photographs, have I? Because friends don't betray each other.'

'I've got tummy ache.'

'Really.' The man stepped out of the vehicle slowly, as if he hadn't a care in the world. With a glance down the empty road he walked around to the rear of the estate car and opened the door.

'But...' Paul could feel real tears in his eyes. 'I don't want to do this any more.'

'Pop your bike in, go on.'

The man smiled. It was the first friendly face Paul had seen since leaving home. Reluctantly, he dragged his bike through the gravel and let the man lift it into the car. When he saw the blanket he took an involuntary step back but the man rested his hand comfortingly on Paul's shoulder and gave him that smile again, the one that was meant to make him feel special.

'You can ride up front with me today, at least for the first bit. Get in. There's some chocolate in the glove compartment. We can talk more on the way.'

And, now that the decision had been made for him, Paul did talk, almost non-stop. In the car he didn't feel so bad; it was familiar, and although he now hated what he was about to do, it no longer scared him quite so much. He told the man about the bad things his friends were saying, the names they called him and how he'd tried to tell them they were wrong.

'Have you told them about me?'

Paul shook his head.

'And have they ever mentioned my name?' The man asked the questions casually but Paul was careful with his answer.

'No, never.' He took a bite of chocolate so that he couldn't talk anymore. The man patted his knee.

'Don't worry, I'll sort things out. Now, it's time to hop in the back.'

Fifteen minutes later Paul told himself he wasn't scared even though the drive was taking a lot longer than usual and the smell of exhaust was making him sick. He clutched his duffle bag to his chest and drifted into a familiar fantasy world where he was brave, and tall and above all popular. Within its comfort he drifted asleep.

CHAPTER ONE

Castleview Terrace was tucked economically beside a remnant of Harlden's ancient city wall, the houses designed to resemble almoners' cottages with mellow stone and decorative brickwork. Each cottage had an element of individuality, though not so much as to disturb the pleasing regimentation of the sweeping crescent which sheltered beneath the remains of the Norman stonework.

The dark blue front door of the end cottage gleamed in the sunlight. Terracotta pots, overflowing with alyssum, lobelia and scarlet geraniums, flanked the step and gave the house a feminine touch that belied its solitary male occupant. He was taking advantage of the fine morning to edge a handkerchief of perfect green lawn, manipulating the shears skilfully around the picket fence which bordered his property. A rose had started to colonise its woodwork, white blooms mingling with red honeysuckle to fill the air with a welcoming fragrance for the too-occasional visitor.

'Morning, Major Maidment.'

The man looked up and nodded to the postman.

'Good morning, George.'

'Just a bill today.' George's hand stretched out respectfully over the fence.

'How is your lady wife? Quite recovered I hope?'

'Fit as a fiddle, Major. She said to thank you for the flowers.'

'My pleasure.'

Maidment waved the postman on his way and popped inside to make himself a cup of coffee. He measured semi-skimmed milk into the pan, regretting that he was no longer allowed the Cornish full-cream variety that had been his favourite since he was a boy. It seemed strange to take such care to extend this solitary life, but his doctor was conspiring to do so and he felt it would have been impolite to ignore his best intentions. He was rinsing his cup and saucer when the phone rang.

'Maidment.'

'Oh, Major. Good, you're home.'

His expression settled into resignation as he pulled a chair closer to the phone and placed a cushion against his back.

'Miss Pennysmith, how are you?'

It was not an empty enquiry. He knew that news of her ailments would now be described in detail, saving only those of a feminine nature deemed too sensitive to discuss. Ten minutes later Miss Pennysmith finally reached the purpose of her call.

'I wonder if I could trouble you for a lift to church tomorrow?'

'Of course.' His heart sank. 'I'll be round at oh-nine-hundred hours.'

'Well, I wonder if you could make it a little earlier. I have two lightbulbs that need changing and I can't reach them.'

He agreed to see her at half past eight.

Preparing, eating and tidying away after lunch took him through to two o'clock without a problem, though his eyes misted briefly as he dried the single plate, a precious remnant of the dinner service that had been a wedding present. Inevitably he thought of Hilary, even though nearly three years had ticked by since she had passed away. At the end he'd been grateful for that final soft breath. Such suffering as she had endured was surely the invention of the devil himself. He missed her terribly. Her quiet

companionship and interest in the minutiae of his day had gone
for ever leaving a vacuum that was at times almost unbearable.

He shook himself. This wouldn't do; he was growing maudlin.
Weekend afternoons were the worst. After a brief moment's
deliberation he determined to walk around the castle and then
down to the river. It would be busy on a Saturday but that
couldn't be helped. The only other alternative was a round of
golf but he rationed the number of times he played to prove to
himself that he had not become dependent on the club and all it
stood for. Besides, he was inclined to drink too much when he
went there and then risk the short drive home.

The next morning, Maidment was adjusting his trilby and
checking the trim of his moustache when his doorbell rang. He
removed his hat and set it back precisely on the peg before
opening the door.

'Good heavens!' He covered his mouth in embarrassment. 'I'm
sorry, it's just that—'

'I know, I'm the spitting image, except that he would be
considerably older than I am by now.'

The amiable young man extended his hand, which Maidment
shook automatically.

'Luke Chalfont. How do you do?'

'What can I do for you, Mr Chalfont?'

'I specialise in energy cost saving. Now, I know that's not at
the forefront of people's minds in June but, as I'm sure a prudent
man such as yourself will realise, it's always better to plan
properly and be prepared.'

The man's eyes wandered from the major's face for a moment as
if scanning the hall but he returned his attention quickly. His patter
continued as smooth as butter and it took Maidment some while to
realise that he was a salesman touting an alternative gas supply.

'I'm sorry, Mr Chalfont, but I was on my way out when you

called and I have no interest in your company's services.'

'I quite understand. However, I have a small dossier containing facts and figures comparing our supply with others. Perhaps I could leave it with you to study at your convenience? If you decide that you are interested, just call me.' He extended his hand. 'My card.'

The salesman left with a cheery wave and was walking up the neighbour's path as Maidment double-locked his front door.

Miss Pennysmith was a young-looking 67-year-old with an appetite for life that was being tested by the recent onset of arthritis, but she remained optimistic, believing equally in the healing powers of prayer and a positive mental attitude. She was living, as Jane Austen would have said, in reduced circumstances following the near collapse of the pension fund that was to have been her income in retirement. The one-bedroom flat, in a neighbourhood she would once have walked far to avoid, was all she could now afford following the sale of her house to realise additional capital on which to live.

For church she had chosen to wear a floral dress in pinks and greens that she felt complemented her complexion and strawberry-silver perm. Fresh coffee and home-made scones were ready on the table next to crisp linen napkins. Her sitting room smelt of baking and lavender from the polishing she'd completed the day before. Had it not been for the church her life would have been even harder but friends helped her with invitations to meals that were always over-catered and to shared outings towards which her contribution was reduced in a conspiracy she did not suspect and would have resented had she known.

The major arrived punctually and stood to attention on her doorstep.

'Major Maidment! Would you like some coffee and a scone perhaps?'

'I think I should see to the lights first, Miss Pennysmith.'

'Oh, don't worry. Someone did them for me yesterday shortly after I called you. We have plenty of time.'

Maidment valued politeness above free expression so followed his hostess into her sitting room without comment. She was a silly woman and the little-girl dress she was wearing was unsuitable for someone her age, but in the fresh baking and recent evidence of cleaning he recognised an echo of his own loneliness. Consequently, he endured her chatter and schooled his face to amiability as he drank her excellent coffee and nibbled a scone.

After church, he declined her invitation to lunch and took his customary walk to the municipal cemetery and Hilary's grave. He bought fresh flowers on the way, despite his lingering scruples against Sunday trading, and spent frustrating minutes trying to tease the white chrysanthemums and pink lilies into the pretence of an arrangement. His eyes grew moist as he thought again about how unfair life could be. Hilary had been ten years his junior, healthy and cheerful until her sudden, shocking illness. She would have been far more adept at coping with this business of grief; he should have been lying here. He should have gone first.

Maidment felt guilty for such selfishness immediately and chided himself for wishing this pain on her. God had a purpose in keeping him alive and God alone knew that he had sins enough to expiate before his soul was judged. Perhaps that was why he was still here, though he knew no amount of good works in the winter of his years would atone for the sins of his lifetime. The idea of hell terrified him and the cemetery suddenly became an awful place. Chastised, scared, he headed for his car and drove resolutely to the golf club where he would attempt to silence his conscience with excellent claret and the distraction of convivial company.

CHAPTER TWO

'This is the second identical burglary this month.'

'Let me see.' Bob Cooper passed the report over to Detective Inspector Nightingale, fresh back from training at Bramshill and wearing her new rank with care. 'A con man; good too. How does he persuade the old dears to trust him?'

'He's patient,' Cooper explained, 'doing odd jobs and never asking for payment. All the time he's building up their trust then, *bang*, he's gone and so have all their valuables.'

'What's NCS got on him?'

Cooper passed her a computer printout from national criminal records.

'Plenty; he's been working his way down the country for the past two years. Never does more than three to five jobs in an area. It was only a matter of time before he reached Sussex.'

'Is this the e-fit? Good grief, he looks just like—'

'Lord Lucan, I know but no one's been able to catch him.'

'It's because each incident is treated as a minor crime – never gets to us – but if he runs to form we'll have a chance to nail him before he moves on. Why don't you go out to this one rather than leave it to MCS? I'll arrange to have his likeness put in the local papers and distribute information to places pensioners are likely to visit.'

Nightingale perched on the side of his desk, swinging a long leg in an absent-minded gesture which would have been flirtatious in another woman. Cooper thought it bizarre that the most attractive woman in Harlden Police Station also managed to be the most remote.

She had no idea of the effect of her looks, or of the fact that a fair majority of the detectives considered her a hard-nosed upstart who had been over-promoted. Cooper returned his attention to the burglary report in front of him and to his new boss's suggestions.

'Seems like a lot of work for two minor crimes.'

'I don't call stealing the mementos of a person's life for scrap value minor. Let's catch the bastard before he does any more harm.'

Cooper picked up his keys, suitably chastened.

He parked his car in front of a poorly maintained block of flats and walked up to the fifth floor as the lift was out of order. A WPC in uniform greeted him at the door, her face pink with the July heat.

'She's inside, very tearful. I haven't been able to get much from her but I'm hoping the sherry will help.'

Cooper stepped into the hall and recoiled from the ambush of chintz. Three different patterns collided in their demand for attention. It was worse in the cramped sitting room where frills and lace joined in the full-frontal assault. As a beige-and-tweed man it took him a moment to recover, not that the well-preserved lady, sitting among cushions festooned with plump peonies, was in a fit state to notice his discomfort.

'I'm Detective Sergeant Cooper, Harlden CID, Miss Pennysmith.'

She dabbed at her eyes, but brightened visibly in the presence of a man, even one as unprepossessing as Cooper. Over a pot of tea he coaxed a familiar story from her. She had been robbed of everything of value: some costume jewellery, her only valuable ring left to her by her mother, her father's medals and some silver picture frames containing portraits she missed more than the frames themselves. Almost two hundred pounds in cash was missing, the result of a year's careful saving towards a much longed-for holiday. The proceeds of the theft would be considerably less than a thousand pounds but she had been robbed of more than possessions.

'He was such a nice young man.' She sniffed fresh tears away and took a sip of tea.

Her description confirmed that the thief Cooper had nicknamed Lucky had first visited Miss Pennysmith three weeks before when he'd successfully sold her a fictitious new gas supply. The next day he had returned and ripped up the contract before confessing, in tears, that it was a terrible deal and she should never have signed the papers.

Over tea and biscuits he had explained that his young son was ill and he needed to pay for private medical treatment. The commission on the contracts he sold would make the difference between his son's recovery and a life of crippling illness. She had persuaded him to take a little cash in exchange for doing odd jobs about the flat. Within weeks he was a regular visitor, almost a trusted friend.

Cooper shook his head in frustration. Throughout that time Lucky had been learning her routine. The night before, he had gained entry using a duplicate door key that he'd had the cheek to leave behind after robbing her. Miss Pennysmith had been left feeling betrayed and a fool.

'Is there anyone we can call on your behalf? Some family?'

'I have a nephew who works in Hong Kong and my sister lives in Scotland but there's no point calling either of them.'

She was persuaded to accept the company of a female neighbour, someone Miss Pennysmith had previously tried to avoid. As Cooper left, he heard the woman start a lecture against trusting strangers, which he thought unnecessary as he doubted Miss Pennysmith would ever trust someone she didn't know again.

Jeremy Maidment pulled up outside Miss Pennysmith's flat at

oh-nine-hundred hours sharp the following Sunday. While he waited for the door to open, he rehearsed his excuses for not being able to join her for lunch. When it did, he was quite unprepared for the make-up-less, strained face that peered over a newly fitted safety-chain. Her eyes filled with confusion.

'Jeremy, what are you doing here?' A fluttering hand strayed to her untidy jumble of pink-white curls.

'It's Sunday, Miss Pennysmith. We are to go to church. Margaret, are you all right?'

His concern brought forth a flood of tears. Some time later, church forgotten, he assembled the fragments of her story into a more or less coherent whole. He was filled with indignation and a desire to take action but none of his feelings showed in his face.

'Why don't you stay with your sister for a few days? Scotland will be lovely at this time of year.'

'I don't think she'd welcome me. She and her husband lead busy lives.'

'Nonsense. When she hears what's happened she's sure to want to help.'

'I doubt it.' She sniffed loudly. 'Mary's always telling me "three's a crowd".'

Maidment understood. He could picture Margaret flirting at the breakfast table in Perth, while her sister bit her lip and her brother-in-law swallowed embarrassment with his coffee. But she couldn't stay here to mope around the flat, too scared to step outside her front door.

'Let me speak to her. I'll explain what you've been through.'

He retreated to the hall to place the call. The conversation lasted a long time but when he returned he was smiling.

'That's sorted. She's looking forward to seeing you. I'm going to arrange your train tickets and call her to say when you'll be arriving. Now, I know it's early but I think we could both do with a sherry.'

* * *

Special prayers were said for Miss Pennysmith at the evening service and the major was pressed for news. He made a point of speaking to every woman in the congregation whom he knew lived alone, to urge them to be on their guard.

The matter stayed at the back of his mind until he was queuing to buy stamps the following week. The police poster by the counter brought him up with a start. Errand forgotten, he walked home briskly.

'A Major Maidment on the phone, Bob. Wants to talk to the officer in charge of the Pennysmith case. Says he has information that might be helpful.' The duty sergeant put the call through.

'Detective Sergeant Cooper. How can I help you?'

'Jeremy Maidment here, Briar Cottage, Castleview Terrace, Harlden. I think I've met the man who robbed Miss Pennysmith. He called at my house three weeks ago.'

'I see. I don't suppose you've seen him since, have you?'

'No, but he did leave his card. I wondered whether I should invite him round so that you might arrest him.'

Cooper stifled a laugh. Whoever heard of a thief leaving a calling card?

'Jolly good idea, sir. Why don't you do that and call me back with the appointment details?'

He was telling his mate George Wicklow the latest joke when the front desk called.

'Major Maidment's down here. Says he's arranged a meeting with a thief for oh-nine-hundred hours tomorrow and wishes to discuss your plans for deployment.'

The laughter had disappeared from Cooper's face by the time he reached the dowdy interview room on the ground floor that they kept for walk-ins. Maidment was standing with his back to the window, at ease. He was shorter than Cooper and many pounds lighter, despite broad shoulders beneath an immaculate blazer. His face was weathered by foreign suns and the ruddy skin contrasted with sandy-white wavy hair, moustache and pale blue eyes.

His handshake was firm but not overpowering. On the table between them he had laid out a hand-drawn plan of his house with access points marked. Before Cooper had a chance to speak, he tapped it.

'I thought three men upstairs, two in the garden to the rear, three plainclothes outside plus two downstairs with me.'

Cooper noted the scale of the drawing and completed some surprisingly quick mental arithmetic to deduce that they'd be falling over each other.

'An interesting suggestion, Major, but that many officers would attract attention. I think we need something more "covert", shall we say.' He was rather proud of his subtlety.

They agreed that four officers, plus Cooper, would take up position in and around the house by seven-thirty.

'You're absolutely sure that you won't be armed, Sergeant?' Maidment looked disappointed.

'No, sir. We don't have grounds to request armed back-up. There's no mention of a weapon being used in his many previous crimes and no one has been hurt during his break-ins.'

'Hmm; one can never be too careful. You think they're harmless then, BANG! they're shooting up the place and you've lost a good man.' His eyes stared back briefly into a past beyond Cooper's experience. 'Still, it's your operation. I won't second-guess the officer in charge. I'll see you and your men at oh-seven-thirty sharp tomorrow.'

That evening, as he watched an unconvincing documentary on the Falklands War, Maidment unlocked the case that held his service revolver and cleaned the gun with care. He loaded six rounds, ignoring Hilary's sceptical voice in his mind. It took him some time to decide where to conceal the weapon, before he chose the bread bin. If the blighter made a run for it, he'd be more likely to go through the kitchen to the back door than out of the front, which he would make sure was bolted. If that crook tried anything, he'd be ready for him, oh yes.

He slept well, as he always did before a mission. None of the enemy he had killed rested heavily on his conscience. When he did have nightmares, and they were thankfully rare, they were triggered by the memory of private transgressions and of one gross sin. But that balmy July night, the major slept the untroubled sleep of a child.

The dawn chorus woke him. He was showered, shaved and dressed before six. His shoes were already polished to a mirror finish, his trousers pressed. The prospect of seeing some action again excited him. He was about to help the police arrest a serial criminal and he was invigorated by a sense of purpose.

That Sergeant Cooper seemed solid enough, though he had never liked elbow patches, and a Prince of Wales check jacket was most unfortunate given the man's build. But he was old for a policeman, which gave Maidment added confidence despite the shabbiness of his clothes.

Against his best intentions he started to fret about the arrangements. The gun was where he had left it – oiled, cleaned and loaded. He tested putting it in his jacket pocket, but of course it was far too big and he no longer had his holster. So he replaced it in the bread bin, finally deciding that he was ready.

Cooper cast a critical eye over the team he'd been given. The two uniforms, Perkins and Lee, were all right – he'd worked with them before and knew he could rely on them – but he'd drawn the short straw with the detectives who would be undercover outside. DC Partridge was a twenty-year veteran with a drink problem that remained a secret only to the superintendent in charge of Harlden Station. DS Rike had been good until a knife incident the previous year, but he'd only been back at work two months, most of which had been spent safely behind a desk.

Operations must have decided that this was a low-risk arrest, which would help their work records without being too difficult. They were going to confront a non-violent con man with no history of assault. Just the same, Rike looked pasty so Cooper assigned him to cover the service alley that ran behind the terrace gardens.

He watched as the detective donned a council worker's green overalls and yellow reflective jerkin, before wheeling a cart and broom behind Maidment's cottage garden. Partridge he consigned to a car parked up the road at the front, where he opened the day's paper and promptly pretended to fall asleep; at least Cooper hoped it was an act.

The major was waiting for him inside, impeccably dressed in jacket and tie despite the early heat. He looked calm but Cooper sensed a tension about him that caused him a moment's concern. The last thing he needed was a case of citizen's heroics.

Cooper, Perkins and Lee drank fresh coffee and waited. There was no small talk; it wasn't Maidment's style and Cooper had never mastered the art. Shortly after eight, the two uniformed men disappeared – Constable Perkins upstairs and Lee to the dining room, while Cooper sneaked into the downstairs cloakroom and perched on the lowered toilet seat. He heard Maidment washing their cups and clearing away. Rike and Partridge called in by radio on cue and he was relieved that they sounded alert.

At half past eight Partridge announced Chalfont's arrival over the radio, which was followed seconds later by a ring from the doorbell. Cooper heard voices, loud in the small house.

'Ah, Mr Chalfont, come in. You're rather early.'

'Never like to leave a potential client waiting.'

'Would you like some coffee? I'm just making some.'

'Thought I could smell it, but don't go to any trouble on my account.'

The plan was that Maidment would close and lock the front door and then lead Chalfont into the sitting room before retreating to the kitchen on the pretext of making coffee. Cooper, backed up by the two uniformed constables, would then arrest the suspect while he was waiting for Maidment's return.

Unfortunately, things didn't go according to plan, as Cooper was later to put in his report. Instead of sitting down Chalfont followed the major into his kitchen.

'Please, I can do this; go and make yourself comfortable.'

'No problem, I need to see the appliances anyway. Where's your boiler?'

There was silence. Cooper looked up from his seat on the throne and stared at the appliance in question.

'Ah…' The confusion in Maidment's voice was obvious. 'I've only just moved in. Let me see, it's—'

'Don't worry, I'll find it. I'm an expert. I bet it's in the cloakroom.'

The door opened before Cooper could hide. For a moment the two men stared at each other then Cooper gathered his wits and said firmly:

'Police! You're under ar—'

The punch knocked the breath from his body and he doubled over. Wheezing, he heard the sounds of a scuffle in the narrow hall and look up to see Lee land painfully on his behind. There was a clatter of footsteps on the stairs as Perkins hurtled down, slamming into Cooper, who was in the process of hobbling along the hall. Perkins tripped and almost fell. Cooper squeezed past him into the kitchen in time to see Chalfont land another punch, this time on Maidment's nose. Blood spurted out, spattering both men's jackets. Instead of giving way, Maidment squared up to his attacker and landed a solid right to the side of Chalfont's jaw.

Cooper struggled to stand straight and rushed at Chalfont but the man picked up a bread knife and started waving it wildly in front of his face. DC Partridge was banging on the bolted front door while Rike hovered white-faced outside the kitchen window. Perkins and Lee were backed up in the hall behind Cooper.

'Let's all calm down, shall we?' Cooper's voice was laboured and his stomach felt on fire. 'Take it easy there – Luke, isn't it? There are five officers here and more on the way. There's no point making matters worse with threatening behaviour. Put the knife down.'

Both he and Maidment were within striking distance of the blade. Cooper told Perkins to stay out of the room, hoping the lad would have enough sense to obey an order. He heard Lee unlock the front door but there was nothing they could do with the advantage of numbers as the kitchen was too small. In the sudden silence Maidment, Chalfont and Cooper eyed each other warily.

'I won't go to prison.' Chalfont's voice held a tremor of panic.

'Who's said anything about prison? Let's not jump to conclusions, but wielding that knife won't help you. Put it down, son.'

'I'm not your son and who do you think you're kidding?' Cooper heard the rising note of hysteria and watched with growing concern as Chalfont's hand started to tremble. 'I'm going to leave now and you're not going to stop me. Open that door.'

Chalfont turned to Maidment and gestured with the knife, then swung back to Cooper, who had risked a step forward.

'Keep away!'

In the instant the two men confronted each other, Maidment opened the bread bin, pulled out a gun and pointed it at Chalfont's chest.

'I don't think you're going anywhere, sonny.'

Chalfont's mouth dropped open. Cooper became aware that

his own was agape in shock.

'Put the gun away, Major. That isn't going to help.'

He stared at the two armed men and wondered who looked more dangerous. Chalfont was shaking all over as he backed away, while Maidment remained calm except for a small tic at the corner of his eye. Cooper had the horrible impression that he might actually be enjoying himself.

'Don't worry, Sergeant, I have the situation under control. I'm not going to let that bastard get away, not after what he did to Miss Pennysmith.'

His words drove Chalfont even further away, unaware of how close he now was to Cooper. The man with the gun was the only thing he was focused on. Cooper lunged for the knife and locked his right hand around the man's wrist. Chalfont swivelled in his grasp and jerked his left elbow sharply into Cooper's aching stomach. His hold weakened and Chalfont swung the knife up to Cooper's neck.

There was a deafening report. An expression of confusion covered Chalfont's face, then he started to scream. The knife fell as he grabbed his thigh and tried to stop the flow of bright arterial blood that was pumping out over the kitchen units and walls to puddle on the floor.

Maidment kicked the knife away and pulled a tea towel from the drawer to apply pressure expertly on the wound. Chalfont screamed louder.

'Hold this, Sergeant Cooper, while I call an ambulance.'

'If you'll just give me the gun first, sir.'

Cooper stretched out his hand and took the pistol delicately between thumb and index finger before folding a towel around it and passing it back to Perkins.

'Ambulance is already on its way, sir,' the constable said, 'and back-up.' Perkins was staring anxiously at the growing pool of blood.

'That compress is already soaked through,' Maidment observed, still unnaturally calm.

He found another freshly laundered tea towel and applied it to the thigh himself. Chalfont shrieked and passed out.

'Best way. Blighter would have been in agony. At least now he won't know a thing until he's comfortable in hospital.'

He spoke without a trace of emotion, causing Cooper and Perkins to exchange a bewildered look. Cooper cleared his throat.

'Major, do you have a licence for that gun?'

'Licence? Hmm.' Maidment scratched his chin with his free hand. 'Do I need one? It's my service revolver. Had it years. Never even thought about it. No, I don't suppose I do.'

'You should have cautioned him first, sir!' Perkins hissed.

The reality of the situation slowly settled on Cooper. His shoulders sagged and he noticed the splashes of crimson about his trouser legs for the first time. Dot would be livid, he thought, and wished for a moment that he was at home with her now having a nice cup of tea. Instead, he forced himself to stand up and address the major.

'Jeremy Maidment, I am arresting you on suspicion of attempted murder. You are not obliged...'

'Attempted murder? Good heavens, Sergeant, he was less than eight feet away. I was aiming to disable him, which I did successfully. Had I wanted to kill him, I can assure you—'

'...to say anything but...'

'Sergeant! Didn't you hear me? I disabled a man who was about to slit your throat. I can understand you being a little concerned about my overlooking the need for a gun licence, but to suggest I tried to murder someone is utter nonsense.'

Cooper finished the caution, feeling the blood rise in his face to match the purple in Maidment's. He was sorely tempted to explain the situation, even to apologise, but he knew that would be very unwise. Instead, they awaited the arrival of reinforcements in silence.

Ten minutes later, Constable Lee helped a still speechless Maidment into the back of a waiting police car while Cooper watched as paramedics strapped Chalfont to a stretcher, before speeding him away beneath the clamour of a siren. The sense of shock that had enveloped him since Chalfont had picked up the knife slowly gave way to foreboding that solidified as an ache in his injured stomach. He had cocked it up. A routine arrest had turned into a life-threatening incident as a result of which a man was bleeding to death and he had been forced to arrest a pillar of the community. There would be hell to pay but meanwhile he had more important concerns.

DS Rike was leaning against the kitchen wall sucking on a cigarette. There was a smell of fresh vomit beneath the smoke.

'All OK?'

Rike nodded and took a long drag. Cooper noticed that his hand was shaking.

'Back door was locked; I couldn't get in.'

'Right. The kitchen was crowded enough and he could have broken out. You needed to cover the exit.'

Rike nodded but was unable to meet Cooper's eye.

'Let's go.' Cooper rubbed his face, looking older than his fifty years.

'What do you want me to say?' Rike hadn't moved.

'Pardon?'

'What shall we say? Who are we going for – Chalfont or Maidment? I reckon we could put it all on Chalfont; say he jumped the major, forcing him to defend himself. He'll still have to cough to no licence but that will be a minor charge.'

Cooper realised where Rike was heading and held up his hand.

'Don't say any more, Richard. We're going with the truth. There'll be an inquiry; it'll be bloody, but all you need to do is make a statement explaining exactly what you saw.'

Rike stared at him as if he were mad but shut up as instructed and followed him to the car.

Maidment spent a night in the cells and was released the following day after a call by an enraged Assistant Chief Constable Harper-Brown, who tore into Cooper for holding him in custody in the first place. No sooner had the call from the ACC finished than he was summoned upstairs to see the head of Harlden Station, Superintendent Quinlan.

Quinlan didn't ask him to sit down.

'This is a bloody farce!' Quinlan hardly ever swore and use of the mild expletive had a disproportionate effect on Cooper. He felt very sick indeed and looked down at his shoes. 'What the hell were you thinking of, taking so few men?'

'I honestly don't think having more officers there would've made any difference, sir, and Maidment gave no clue that he would turn the vigilante on us.'

Quinlan stared at him and shook his head.

'The arrest of Maidment was poorly handled. We're lucky that he's not the sort of man to issue a complaint against us.'

'He hasn't?'

'No, but the ACC has been on the phone and he's very upset. Have you seen the papers?' It was a rhetorical question. 'Even without a complaint we're going to have some very negative PR. Harper-Brown has insisted on an inquiry.'

'Oh, no.' Cooper felt his knees sag. The look on his face must have been pathetic because Quinlan took pity on him.

'It will be by another force and low key; quite a smart move. Should he come under pressure he can say that an investigation is already underway, and by staffing it from outside he can demonstrate independence.'

'What should I do in the meantime, sir?'

'Type up your reports and make sure that your team cooperate fully. And I don't want you involved in the Maidment case in any way. Nightingale can take it forward. Pity you didn't get her involved in the arrest.'

'Yes, sir.'

The thought had already occurred to Cooper but the arrest had seemed routine, or so he told himself. At the back of his mind lurked the hint of suspicion that he'd wanted the credit for himself, not shared with the newly appointed inspector, even though he was one of her few fans.

After possibly the worst morning of his police career, Cooper retired to the canteen and sought comfort in food that was as bad for him as possible.

'Fish 'n' chips followed by treacle sponge and custard. What's happened to your diet, Bob?'

Nightingale was standing by his table with a tray of food he just knew would make him feel worse.

'Mind if I join you?'

He did mind but gestured to the empty seat opposite with his knife, then remembered his manners. He glanced at her plate. As he'd suspected, lots of green stuff. Look at her, glowing with health. He wondered who she was seeing these days. There were rumours that it was Andrew Fenwick but he couldn't quite bring himself to believe it.

As they ate he waited for her to mention the Maidment debacle. He had his defence ready but she just chatted about a film she'd been to see the night before. Eventually, he said, 'You could make a bloody film out of my life right now.'

'I heard. Do you want to talk about it?'

He opened his mouth to say no but found himself reliving the previous thirty-six hours instead. She listened without interruption. Skin formed on his custard.

'I don't think you did anything wrong, Bob. Perhaps you could've had an officer in the kitchen but what good would that have done? Chalfont would only have threatened him instead. What sort of inquiry is it going to be?'

'Internal.'

'That's about as good as it gets. Your guardian angel must be working hard.'

She smiled at him encouragingly as he finished his last chip, chewing on it determinedly, despite the fact that it was stone cold. He refused to be comforted.

'I'm deep in the doo-doo, trust me. Harper-Brown's baying for blood...'

'Unfortunate turn of phrase. Quinlan's furious now but he's a fair man. He won't allow you to be a scapegoat.'

Cooper just shook his head, took a spoonful of congealed custard and then dropped it in disgust.

'It's not going to be up to Quinlan, is it? I'm already being tried in the press. There'll be so much pressure on the ACC to "do something" that I'm dead meat. You wait, I'll be lucky if I escape unretired.'

'So you thought you'd eat yourself to death first.' She laughed to take the sting out of her words and Cooper tried to join in. Despite his determination to be gloomy, Nightingale had made him believe in the possibility of a positive outcome and the flicker of hope brightened his day.

CHAPTER THREE

Andrew Fenwick stared down at the pungent mixture of earth and leaf mould beneath his feet and brought his emotions back under control. The fragments of bone that had been recovered so painstakingly were finally being transferred into rigid containers that would have looked more at home on an archaeological dig. The remains were too small to require a body bag. Despite his years of practised detachment, the grave site moved him deeply.

'Boy or girl?'

'I can't tell you that with certainty until I've completed my analysis but I think it's a boy given the pelvis.' The forensic anthropologist spoke without rancour despite the premature questioning.

Fenwick didn't know him other than by reputation; a supposedly exceptional professor who went by the unexceptional name of Grey, who had travelled from London to stand in while Sussex's only expert was away on holiday.

'Age?'

'From the state of the teeth I'd say about twelve or thirteen, but I'm sure you know better than to quote me at this stage.'

Chris, Fenwick's son, was almost nine.

'But it's not Sam Bowyer.' It was a statement. Fenwick didn't need a post-graduate medical qualification to work that out. He said it only to relieve some of the sadness that had rooted itself in his eyes and throat since he'd stared down at the top of the child's skull earlier that morning.

'Who?'

Fenwick looked at Grey in surprise. Sam Bowyer's disappearance had been on the news for days but perhaps it had only been a local sensation. Eleven years old, from a good home but a terror at school, Sam had disappeared on Monday, last seen boarding a train to Brighton when he should have been in assembly. That was four days ago and he hadn't been seen since, despite intensive work by Brighton Division.

'Never mind. Can you tell how long the body's been in the ground?'

'At least two years but frankly it could be a lot more. Look, your best way forward will be to check through missing persons' records as soon as I send you dental impressions. There's very little for me to work with; the body's completely skeletised and there are no obvious signs of trauma on the remains.'

'Did you recover them all?'

'Most, not all. Some of the small bones of the feet are missing.' Grey stood up and removed his gloves with a snap. 'You'll have my preliminary report in twenty-four hours; detail will take a lot longer. If I do find anything interesting, I'll make sure you're informed.'

A brief shake of hands and the man was gone, threading through trees towards his black BMW parked on the narrow road above, already thumbing his phone and apparently unmoved by the contents in the sterile plastic boxes. Fenwick watched him go, hesitating at the scene though there was no need for him to linger, reluctant to return to the noise and distraction of his base in Burgess Hill.

Around him, the white-clad shoulders of crime scene technicians rose and fell as they subjected the immediate area to fingertip scrutiny. Perhaps they were speculating about why he was committing so much time and money to a search when the crime scene would have been degraded by the passage of time and the impact of the seasons. He didn't care what they thought, or what his boss would say when he saw the bill for the work.

The thought of HQ made his mouth twist in distaste. The chatter and infantile humour in the team room were driving him mad with irritation, despite his best intentions. The banter seemed to go on non-stop, seasoned with crass jokes that failed to raise a ripple of amusement on his mirror-calm surface. He told himself to relax as he walked downhill to the bed of a stream that split the undergrowth. The casual working atmosphere was his own doing, the result of his experiment with a more 'personal' leadership style he had been advised to develop. But the attempt wasn't working. How could he pretend to be someone he wasn't, even for the benefit of his career?

He wasn't considered one of the boys, never had been, never wanted to be and never would be. Having reached the rank of chief inspector without that nicety, it annoyed him that he was now supposed to affect some sort of chumminess so that his team would 'relate to him more as a human being'. He could remember the words on his year-end performance review even after all this time and was unaware that he sneered whenever he recalled them. *Relate.* Well, he knew who's stupid idea that had been.

His new boss, Assistant Chief Constable Harper-Brown, was unfortunately punctilious about assessing performance thoroughly. After years of benign neglect while working for Superintendent Quinlan, Fenwick hadn't been prepared for the hour and a half interview he'd had with Harper-Brown, nor for the coruscating dissection of his personality that had passed for his assessment. Thinking about the meeting made his face burn with indignation.

He had half listened to H-B's opening monologue with his customary knowing smile, the one that said, 'OK you've got to go through this, so have I, let's make it quick'. Unfortunately the

ACC had other ideas. After ten minutes, when he was showing every sign of continuing strong, Fenwick tried to make an excuse and leave.

'You have another meeting, Andrew? Then cancel it. You should have known better than to book something back to back with your review. We'll need at least another hour.'

Fenwick had been too shocked to respond and started to listen properly for the first time. Naturally, he took the compliments for granted. He knew that his detection rate was excellent, that he inspired people to do their best, had integrity and drove his team to work hard and achieve results. Of course he did, that was his job. It was irrelevant, in his view, that he didn't 'nurture' them even though he could have been 'an exceptional role model'. So what? Those who had the gumption to learn from him did, and the others didn't deserve to. What's more, the good ones wanted to continue working for him and he had no interest in the others. So he'd shrugged H-B's words aside, crossed his legs and kept his mouth shut. The less he said, he figured, the sooner the wretched meeting would be over.

Perhaps if he had managed to keep to his rule they wouldn't have argued, but how was he supposed to sit there and listen to the garbage that the ACC moved on to next?

'Try to celebrate success more, Andrew.' It sounded like a phrase he'd picked up from one of the management textbooks that filled his bookcase.

'What do you mean? I take them to the pub when we make a good arrest and I don't charge the round to expenses like some I could mention.'

'Yes, but you don't linger there, do you?'

'Trust me, the last thing my team wants is some stuffed shirt breathing down their necks trying to be pally after they've had a few. I always stay for a couple of hours but after that they'd rather be left well alone; I know I would.'

'A quick visit to the pub is hardly an appropriate celebration, is it? This constant need for alcohol to play a part in team building is detrimental to the moral fibre of the force and bad for our image with the public.'

Fenwick couldn't believe what he was hearing and had started to explain to his boss why he was so wrong. Big mistake.

'Sir!'

One of the technicians was standing, waving something at him. Fenwick ran back up the hill, ignoring the twinge in his knee and pleased that he wasn't breathless at the top. His jogging routine must be paying off; perhaps it was worth the tedium.

'What have you got?'

'A key. It was in the spoil from the grave and there's some sort of identity tag with it.'

Fenwick peered but of course the scrap of metal meant nothing. It would take days of work to try and identify what the key was made of and from that to produce a list of manufacturers. But the discovery pleased him; it vindicated his insistence on a fingertip search of the ground in and around the grave.

'Excellent,' he said, and his spirits lifted.

He had respectful confidence in the Sussex Forensic Laboratory and real hope that the key would turn out to be significant. The advances in the science of crime fascinated him; they complemented his fundamental approach to detection: the belief that detailed, rigorous investigation would yield success in time. But he had to admit that most other aspects of modern policing bored him. The obsession with the latest management theories; the politics local and national; the need to be a statistician just to cope with the never-ending hunger for analysis: did they result in one more conviction? Answers on the back of a postcard, he thought. No, make that a postage stamp.

His problem was that for the past thirteen years he'd ignored the need to identify what it now took to work the way up the ladder, relying on his compulsion to solve crimes to see him through. Beyond that, he'd barely given his career a thought. His marriage, the arrival of two children in quick succession, his wife's illness and then her slow decline had meant that there'd been no place left for ambition. When Monique had eventually died the year before, it was a blessed release for her and essential for the children, allowing them to grieve properly and move on. But turning off the life support machine had been the hardest thing he had ever had to force himself to do and the personal impact had been more devastating than he would have believed possible.

At first he'd simply been exhausted. Then the hunt for a serial killer – a particularly complicated and deadly case – had consumed him. But once he had the murderer in custody, the grief he had unknowingly been holding at bay engulfed him, though no one, not even those closest to him, would have known. Despair and fury had almost overwhelmed him, would have done probably had it not been for the children, who needed him more than ever. He couldn't let them down. For more than three months, as the previous autumn declined into winter, he had withdrawn into himself, maintaining a pretence of engagement by swinging violently between the extremes of immersing himself in the children and working too hard.

How long he would have stayed in his semi-vegetative state was anybody's guess but he had been jolted back to reality by the offer of a transfer to head up West Sussex Major Crimes' Squad, reporting directly to ACC Harper-Brown. It wasn't exactly a promotion – his rank remained unchanged – but the previous incumbent had been a superintendent and it was clear from the way the opportunity was presented that promotion might follow if he did well.

At first Fenwick had declined the opportunity, claiming that he couldn't risk the impact on his family, but his old boss Superintendent Quinlan had refused to accept the decision. He'd dragged him away from the station to a pub in the backwoods of Sussex where they wouldn't be recognised and proceeded to get the pair of them drunk. In his cups, Fenwick found it impossible to maintain his façade. Once he started talking it all came out. Quinlan had listened without interruption, suddenly sober and wise, an unsentimental man moved by what he heard.

'You have to take this chance, Andrew. You're in a rut and going deeper. And you're too good to give in to this. I remember you when you first arrived in Harlden. You were so ambitious you didn't care that it showed. You were also bloody good, the best detective I've ever worked with. But there comes a point in a career when being good at solving cases isn't enough; even I know that though I despise half the management gobbledy-gook we have thrust on us.'

'But the ambition's gone; I told you, I'm no bloody good anymore. I'm just a faç...faça...a show.'

'You still want to win; I see it in you every day. You care about justice and you're the most tenacious person I've ever known. Look at what you did with the Smith case.'

Quinlan was referring to his arrest of a serial killer the previous year. It had earned him a commendation. 'Your instinct is uncanny. I know you resent the word intuition but that's what it amounts to, like it or not.'

Fenwick had been too drunk to argue. Deep down he knew that he possessed a rare skill that was as elusive as it was valuable. His mind had a way of sucking in apparently useless pieces of information and then allowing them to fester and combine randomly in his subconscious until, seemingly from nowhere, an idea came to him that would push an investigation on with a lurch in an apparently random direction. The thoughts that came to him were fragile. If he concentrated on them too hard or too soon, they vanished. So, over the years he had become superstitious about sharing his thinking with others, preferring instead to cogitate in private. When finally the ideas solidified, they weren't always coherent, sometimes just a feeling or else the lingering cobweb of a dream on awakening, but he'd learnt to persist in coaxing them out no matter how elusive.

Recalling the conversation as he delayed his return to his new responsibilities at MCS he hoped that Quinlan had been right and that he did have the personal resources to do this job. He would need every skill he possessed to find the killer of the boy in the grave on the hill. With a case this cold it would take more than luck and good police work to produce a result.

A male pheasant rose up in front of him, squawking and clacking in alarm as if it had been beaten out of cover into a line of guns, but there was over a month yet before it would have to run that gauntlet. After the bird flapped heavily through the trees, the woods settled quieter. Still pines, silver birch, their bark glowing eerily in the shadows, and enormous beeches surrounded him. On the other side of the stream, the pale root ball tombstones of conifers, blown down in previous season's gales, punctuated the gloom, with foxgloves and nettles garlanding the impromptu clearings they had created.

His preoccupation with his career brought a moment's guilt. Then the macabre sense of excitement he'd felt on his way to the scene that morning returned. Maybe the discovery would be the breakthrough he needed on an investigation that was proving resistant to every line of inquiry he tried, one that had defied resolution for months before it was handed to Fenwick, with a mixture of relief and reluctance, by the out-going head of MCS.

'This one's a sod, Andrew,' he'd said. 'We've got nowhere but it wasn't for want of trying. We had a strong tip from the Yanks that a sophisticated paedophile ring is operating somewhere on our patch. A Brit they've arrested in Florida is talking as part of a plea bargain. Before moving to the States he claims he was part of a ring in Sussex that was extensive and had been running for a long time. The only name he could give them was Joseph Watkins, and sure enough they were able to track him using one of the child porn sites they'd infiltrated.

'But when we raided Watkins' home his computer was clean. Don't ask me how he knew we were coming but he did. We put surveillance on him – cost a bloody fortune and I had to drop it after a month. All that time he was as good as gold – I was never able to pin a thing on him.'

Even when other investigations had taken priority Fenwick had kept a small team on the investigation, codenamed Choir Boy. It wasn't a popular assignment, deemed a lost cause by those who worked on it and a joke by those who didn't.

Joseph Watkins was fifty-five, married, retired with a good income – all of it clean. Rumour was that he'd been a mercenary and before that in the services but that was all they had. Fenwick had put a watch on him and his acquaintances. None of the men visited any of the known areas of child prostitution in West Sussex and they all had respectable backgrounds, but even so Fenwick refused to give up. After a month, he had narrowed the list down to Watkins and one man – Alec Ball. There was nothing unduly suspicious about Ball's actions but everyone on the team agreed that he looked guilty, didn't like him and refused the idea to drop the surveillance on him. Over the following weeks they'd come up with a list of places that Watkins and Ball visited – though never together. They included a club in Burgess Hill and, to his surprise, Harlden's golf club – The Downs.

He didn't have enough to request warrants, only suspicions, so he was now concentrating on building a log of activity. It was painstaking work but Fenwick could be patient when he needed to be and the MCS department was large enough to cover his semi-official work.

In parallel, he had another of his team collate missing persons' files and then review all cases involving sexual abuse against Caucasian boys between the ages of nine and fifteen. So far none of the men's names had been mentioned in any way.

Then Sam Bowyer had disappeared and the theoretical work had taken on a new urgency, though the search for the boy had criss-crossed the county without success for the past four days.

As he'd watched the child's remains being removed, and realised with relief that it wasn't Sam, Fenwick had wondered which of the cheeky faces in the ageing school photographs in the missing persons' files had once clothed the skull that was on its way now to a morgue in London to be measured and probed in the search for justice.

Fenwick bent down and picked up a handful of dirt, squeezing it tightly into a ball in his palm. It was light and friable, a superficial skin on the bones of chalk that made up the North Downs. He opened his hand, scattering the earth as if into a grave, and brushed his palms clean. He sighed deeply, thinking of the boy who had been left to rot here in an unmarked grave, leaving his parents to mourn in a vacuum, perhaps hoping against hope that he might still be alive. If he was able to match the dental records from the well-preserved jaw to those on a missing persons' file he would have to destroy their hope. He felt his melancholy returning and decided it was time to leave the scene.

He walked up the hill slowly, lost in his thoughts, and didn't notice a green Peugeot pull up behind his car, so he was surprised when a voice close by called out his name.

'Chief Inspector Fenwick!'

He turned to see Blake Bowyer, Sam's father, standing by the Peugeot, his wife strapped into the front passenger seat, her window wound down to hear their words. Bowyer's face was marked by signs of unbearable pain that yet had to be endured, the lines around his mouth deep cuts in his badly shaven skin, the hollows beneath his eyes so dark they looked bruised. But his visible agony was nothing compared to his wife's. Fenwick almost winced when he met her eyes and the dread in them lanced through him.

The men shook hands quickly and Fenwick walked over to the car, resting his hand briefly, gently, on Mrs Bowyer's shoulder.

'It's not Sam,' he said at once, not asking how they knew about the body, not blaming them for being there at the scene.

'Thank God.' Bowyer kept repeating the words, an incantation, as his wife wept silent tears of relief.

Fenwick had no news for them, had used up all his words of sympathy in their first meeting and had nothing left to say. He walked away to his car.

CHAPTER FOUR

'I'm glad all that nasty business is over and done with for you, Sergeant.'

Cooper tried to back away but a sturdy oak support beam hemmed him in. It was bad enough bumping into Major Maidment in the Hare and Hounds, worse still to have had a fresh pint of beer thrust into his empty palm before he could say no. He'd been in the pub since five with Dave McPherson, the Police Federation representative who had stood by him throughout the inquiry that was dragging on for the worst weeks of his career.

He was already light-headed and had been trying to reach the Gents before leaving for home, having bought Dave three large whiskies as a thank you. He'd matched him drink for drink, ending up tipsy with the excess and too slow to think of a way to extricate himself from the major's company, despite the fact that he shouldn't have been within a mile of the man. Maidment sensed his embarrassment.

'Of course, you can't discuss it. I perfectly comprehend. I stand accused – by you!' He laughed as if the idea were nothing more than a shared joke.

Cooper wanted to tell him that he was in serious trouble. Chalfont, real name Henry Luke Carter, had almost died. The medical reports showed that the bullet had nicked a major artery. Only prompt first aid and excellent medical care had prevented him from dying of shock because of loss of blood. That it was

Maidment who applied first aid was irrelevant to the Crown Prosecution Service, who saw it as a poor attempt to minimise the original crime. As he gulped his pint, Cooper reflected that he'd never arrested a less guilty man. Perhaps it was remorse that prompted him to try and finish the oaty brew.

'I have one question, Mr Cooper. I understand why I had to be fingerprinted but the swab they took from my mouth...was that for DNA?'

'It's routine.' Cooper squirmed at the return of the conversation to the case. 'There's a national database of millions of people so you're not alone, Major. Still, if you were found innocent—'

'*When*, not if. Anyway, it doesn't bother me, I just found it curious. Now, what do you think of England's performance yesterday? Eighty-one for five, I ask you...'

Cooper breathed a sigh of relief at the change of subject and started to taste his pint, but he declined the invitation to lunch with Maidment at his golf club that weekend.

'Once this is all over I'll look forward to it but right now, well, I shouldn't even be talking to you.'

'Oh I see, of course. But you won't be investigating my case, will you, given all the fuss?'

'No.'

'Pity, you'd have done a thorough job. Please tell me they haven't put an imbecile in charge.'

'Inspector Nightingale is one of the best officers in Harlden. I think you'll be very impressed.'

'Good. I look forward to meeting him.'

Cooper smiled. Nightingale was going to enjoy this.

She stood in front of the door and noted the pristine paintwork and freshly polished brass. Everything about the house and garden was immaculate. The major was going to be a challenging man to prosecute, the sort who would appeal to a jury no matter how guilty. She was pleased to have been asked by Superintendent Quinlan to take the case regardless of its sensitivity. Perhaps it demonstrated his growing confidence in her despite her problems the previous year. He said that he trusted her to 'dig deep with diplomacy' and she was determined to do just that.

'Yes?'

'Major Jeremy Maidment?'

Nightingale had expected a taller man. She extended her warrant card but he was too busy scrutinising her to notice. Nightingale found her eyes drawn to the bald spot on his crown, carefully concealed by the abundant silver waves around it to everyone save those taller than himself. She tried not to smile. Bob Cooper had told her that she'd find the interview interesting. 'Nice bloke,' he'd said, 'but a little bit old school if I'm not mistaken.' He hadn't been.

'I think you must have the wrong house. And if you're selling something I'm not interested.'

He made to close the door on the tall woman who looked at him as if they had already been introduced, then noticed a man lurking behind her and squared his shoulders as if for an assault.

'I'm Detective Inspector Nightingale, from Harlden CID. This is Constable Watson. Might we come in?'

He completed a perfect double-take, then studied her warrant card carefully.

'Humph. Very well, but I wasn't expecting—' He broke off suddenly.

As she stepped into the hall, Nightingale was surprised to see a modern still-life hanging on the wall. She stepped closer and noted that it was an original. Her father had bought one quite similar at an auction she'd been forced to attend as a teenager.

'Do you like it?'

'A Peploe, isn't it? An early one too; lovely colours.'

Maidment's surprise was obvious. He was still struggling with the concept of a female police inspector and clearly found the idea that she might be cultured as well too much.

'My wife loathed it. She couldn't cope with what she called my abstract rubbish.'

'Hardly rubbish.'

'I know. What do you make of this one?'

He was pointing to a startling picture above the faux Adams fireplace in the sitting room.

'I'm not so sure... Is it a Crosbie?'

'Yes, painted by William Crosbie.'

'I'm amazed the insurance company lets you hang them in full view like this.'

'Oh, I'm not insured. The premium was ridiculous and I wouldn't have had the pleasure of seeing them, so what would be the point?'

'No wonder Luke Chalfont risked a second visit when he accepted your invitation. We now know that he was quite an expert and had links to a number of well-connected dealers.'

'So he's cooperating, is he?'

'Let's just say that our interviews with him have been productive.'

'And I'm still under investigation, am I?'

There was a suggestion of belligerence in his manner that she doubted would have been there with a male officer. It made her think that despite his confident demeanour he was more worried about the pending prosecution than he was willing to admit. Good.

'Shall we sit down, Major?'

Without waiting for a reply she took the seat she judged to be his favourite and pulled out her notebook. The young constable who'd followed her into the house stood unnoticed by the sitting-room door.

'I'd like to start by reminding you that you were cautioned on your arrest and that anything you—'

'Yes, yes. I know all that! For heaven's sake, get on with it.'

After completing the caution anyway and reminding him again of his right to have a solicitor present, which he waved aside impatiently, she questioned him for over half an hour, going over his original statement in painstaking detail. Within minutes she could see that he was finding it hard to accept her authority. Had she been in need of his protection there was no doubt she would have experienced a different man but instead it was obvious he resented having to submit to her questions. There were times when her own irritation almost surfaced because of his behaviour but she held her temper, determined to make him condemn his actions with his own words.

As the interview progressed she succeeded in finding minor inconsistencies in his statement but he was too defensive for her to gather anything really useful. Whilst continuing to pay attention to his answers, another part of her mind was calculating how to adjust her style and open him up. He'd be mistrustful of her because of her sex but after half an hour, she decided to opt for a ruse that was an old favourite. She stumbled over her questions a few times and then raised a hand to her forehead.

'I'm so sorry, Major, but I have a terrible headache. Could I trouble you for a glass of water so that I can take some aspirin?'

He was unsure how to respond to this shift in roles.

'We could stop for today and arrange another appointment for later in the week?'

That was the last thing she wanted. She turned her mouth down in a small moue of regret.

'Oh, I'd love to but my superintendent is a stickler for deadlines. He'd be very cross if I went back with my job half done.'

By making herself appear the mere instrument of a man, she might reassure Maidment that power lay in the hands of the appropriate gender and perhaps offset his distrust in her. Nightingale told herself that the end justified the means and avoided the constable's eyes. She was brought water, then tea and dutifully took her medicine.

'I've only a few more questions.' She made it clear that she was as keen to be gone as he was to see her go. They rushed through her checklist, fellow conspirators now, eager to go through the motions in as short a time as possible. Imperceptibly, he started to relax. When she asked him to describe the way he'd spent the evening before the incident he told her about finding, cleaning and loading the gun. At her prompting he explained the difficulty he'd had in deciding where to hide it before deciding that the bread bin would be most accessible.

The more he said the stronger the case against him grew. By the time he'd made a second pot of tea Nightingale almost felt sorry for him. Almost.

'But why did you aim at him and not fire a warning shot?'

'He was a dangerous man, my dear, I had little choice. If I'd warned him he might have killed Bob Cooper.'

'Did he threaten Bob's life?'

'Not with words, no, but he looked very menacing and he was holding that knife.'

'Right, I see. Now, how close was he holding it to Bob?'

'I'm not sure I can remember exactly.' He creased his brow in thought. 'He didn't hold it still. In fact, yes, I recall now.' He slapped his thigh, pleased with himself. 'Chalfont was waving it about, quite wild.'

'So not right up against him then?'

'No, I suppose not.'

'What happened next?'

'I shot him. I aimed for his leg. It was bad luck that the bullet nicked the femoral artery. Twenty years ago he'd have suffered the flesh wound I intended.'

'Were you a good shot when you were in the army then, sir?'

'Excellent!'

He beamed at her. For a moment she saw the man his wife had fallen in love with but as she returned the smile she reminded herself that he had almost killed a man.

'And now, how is your aim?'

'Inevitably not quite as good as it once was, I suppose.'

'Only I noticed a slight tremor when you poured my tea. Did you realise that might affect your aim?'

It was asked so gently that Maidment nodded yes automatically (as noted by the constable at the door) before he realised the significance of her question. There was silence, into which fell the chagrin of an old fool and the fleeting shame of the young pretender. The mood was broken. His expression closed. Nightingale stood up.

'Thank you for your time, Major Maidment. We may need to ask you further questions so please don't leave Harlden without checking with us first. And thank you for the tea. We can see ourselves out.'

He watched her go, her black hair, straight back and long legs reminding him of an American girl with whom he'd had an affair during his posting to Washington. She'd been almost as beautiful and certainly as devious; Hilary had never suspected, but then, why should she? He had always been adept at covering up his indiscretions, the consequences of his appetite as a younger man. His spirits were heavy as he cleared away the teacups and untouched biscuits. What a fool he'd been to trust those beguiling green eyes and listen to the nonsense from lips that looked as if they had been made for kissing, not deception.

His revised statement was damning but he couldn't take it back and he would no doubt have to sign it as a true record the following day. Ironically, he was a man conditioned by upbringing and environment to aspire to follow his own moral code of right and wrong, so he would be unable to deny it. If only he had been more careful and kept his mouth shut. By his own rules silence did not count as a lie, particularly in a good cause. He could no more lie to save his skin than he could tell the truth if it would breach an oath given to a friend or one of the elite band of men with whom he'd served.

No civilian would ever understand the power of shared experience: waiting through slow nights expecting death with the morning; fighting shoulder to shoulder through the blur of action; burying the dead with inner tears that calcified into the guilt of survival over the years. And then there were the compensating spells of recreation when the reality of being alive had been the most powerful drug of all, an aphrodisiac that compelled men, married or not, to satisfy their most basic desires in ways they would never have dared at home.

Although it was early he poured himself a whisky, sipping steadily during televised coverage of the cricket. It was a long game and the bottle emptied as the evening progressed and a televised Prom concert replaced the match. He woke up in the early hours of the morning, slouched in his chair and stiff in every joint. It was the first time since the night of Hilary's funeral that he'd fallen under the influence in his own home and the sense of degradation was almost as bad as the memory of the policewoman's cunning. Groaning into the empty room, he rose and made his way slowly to bed.

CHAPTER FIVE

'Oh that's lovely, just there.' Nightingale groaned as his fingers found a knot of muscle in her shoulder and kneaded gently.

'Bad day?'

'So-so. A piece of cake in some ways but it's one that's left a bad taste.' She told him about Superintendent Quinlan's new-found confidence in her and the case she'd been given as a result. When she described her interview with the major he laughed and kissed the back of her neck.

'That's why you're good and why you're going to have a great career. You can be so devious.'

'Thanks!' Her back stiffened and she pulled away to rise up out of the bath.

'Don't stalk off just because you know it's true.'

'That I'm good or that I'm devious?' She wouldn't look at him as she rubbed herself dry.

'Both, they go together. Talking of your career, has Bob Cooper adjusted to your promotion yet?' The man lay back in the hot water and stretched his legs until his toes pushed against the taps.

'Getting there. He's easier to work with but I think he preferred things as they were last year – everything, I mean.'

'That was predictable. Just don't let it get to you.' She came back to the edge of the bath, her skin pink and fragrant within the white towel and looked down at him, her face serious. 'I mean it; you're a great detective but you're young and people are going to resent you for a while. But you'll win them over. Relax;

don't let them cramp your style.'

He jerked the plug out and stood up, wrapping a towel around his waist.

'How are you doing?' She dropped her towel and hugged his back. 'There's a rumour going around that you're up for promotion.'

He shrugged in answer and turned away from her with reluctance, to pick up his clothes.

'Well, is it going to happen? If anyone deserves it, you do.'

'It might. I've got widespread support but there's a lot of competition and the whole process still to go through. I'll know in the next few months whether it's this time or if I have to wait. A lot will depend on my boss's recommendation.'

'If you were promoted, would it mean you going away?' Her face was studiedly neutral.

'I don't know. I hope not but I might not have much say in the matter.'

He watched her closely but she betrayed no emotion. Her constant self-control was astonishing. It made him want to get under her skin as she had managed to slide under his, and to make her as hungry for him as he was for her. Their affair was dangerous. If it became known it would damage her career and potentially his own, but she appeared not to care about the risk and he was so addicted to her by now that it would have been impossible for him to distance himself even if he wanted to.

'Do you have time for coffee?' Her question was casual, as if she were indifferent to his answer. He paused in the act of buttoning his shirt and smiled at her.

'Why not?'

Andrew Fenwick's house was in a private road on the outskirts of Harlden, in a location normally beyond the means of a policeman who had resisted the temptation of extra-curricular earnings. He wouldn't have been able to afford it had it not been for a legacy from his mother's brother.

When he arrived home from work on Saturday, Nightingale's car was parked in front of the garage. In the sitting room, she was wedged firmly between Chris and Bess on the sofa, watching a cartoon. Bess's hand was on top of Nightingale's and Chris had relaxed his cheek against her arm. As the door slammed shut three heads turned towards him and he smiled.

'I'll be down as soon as I've changed,' he shouted.

As he walked up the stairs he called out a cheery hello to Alice, his housekeeper, but was ignored. When he had changed into a clean shirt and jeans he went to find her in the kitchen. She was fussing over some potatoes.

'Hi. Sorry, we're one extra for dinner – I meant to tell you,' he said.

'Is she staying the weekend?'

'No, she never does.' Fenwick was confused by her aggression. 'That smells good. What is it – your home-made quiche?'

Alice was not to be mollified and merely gave him a curt nod. Her attitude towards Nightingale confused him. There was no threat to Alice's tenure and he couldn't understand why she resented Nightingale's occasional visits so much. They'd started at Easter when Nightingale had surprised him by accepting an invitation to join his family for lunch. It had been an off-the-cuff suggestion prompted by the realisation that she would be on her own for the holiday weekend, and he had immediately regretted it.

Alice had been away visiting her brother but on her return it hadn't stopped her taking against the much younger woman. Unfortunately, the children had spoken of nothing else but the lunch and Nightingale for days afterwards. Looking back he realised that that had been the start of the problem and things hadn't improved since.

'Would you like a glass of wine, Alice?'

'If you're having red I'll join you.' Nightingale normally drank white.

He opened a bottle of both, confident that they wouldn't be wasted over the weekend. When he took Nightingale's glass of Sauvignon through to the sitting room Bess jumped up and hugged him about the waist, almost spilling the wine. He could remember when she'd barely reached his knees, now look at her. She was ten, almost a young lady, with her own opinions and preferences. Unaffected and popular at school, she excelled at games and had a growing love of drama that was starting to worry him.

Fenwick kissed the top of her head and sat down on the arm of the sofa next to his son.

'Hi Chris. Do I get a hug?'

Chris nudged his head against his father's hip as an animal might butt its feeder. Where Bess was tall for her age, dark and confident, Chris was slight, fair and painfully shy. He was supposed to wear glasses but, despite Harry Potter's example, he hated his specs and only wore them when nagged. It meant that he was poor at sports and had to sit at the front of the class. Fenwick's heart ached for his son's seclusion but he remained at a loss to know how to offer any practical help.

Chris liked Nightingale though. She was quiet, not showy and had surprising patience, which meant she waited for as long as it took him to read from one of the books he'd been set to improve his English.

'Have you had a good day?' Fenwick threw the question out to whoever chose to answer.

'Ssh!'

'This is good.'

'You'll get more out of them when the programme's finished.'

Nightingale looked at him sympathetically and raised her wine glass in silent salute. When the programme concluded she asked Bess to switch the television off and ignored Chris's protests.

'If you want to eat with Daddy it's time to go and wash your hands.'

To his amazement Chris shut up and both children left obediently. When they had disappeared she explained.

'Last time I was here you said that you saw very little of them so I asked Alice if they could stay up and eat with you as it's the weekend.'

'And she said yes?' Alice was a stickler for bedtime discipline.

'Well…' Nightingale winced, 'let's just say that the three of us managed to persuade her.'

'Supper!' Alice's shout prevented him asking more and he decided that ignorance might be better than knowing the truth.

'It's on the plates going cold.' Alice turned away from the table despite Fenwick's invitation for her to join them and headed upstairs for her evening's television.

After the meal and a bedtime story for the children, Fenwick and Nightingale took the rest of their wine onto the terrace where moths were beating themselves to death against the outside light. It was a blissful summer evening, one in an unbroken line since Whitsun. The air was filled with the noise of watering systems scattering fine sprays in neighbouring gardens and the scent of honeysuckle and roses from the trellis. A few birds were chirping a sleepy evening chorus. In the darkening twilight the garden almost looked cared for.

'How are you? I haven't seen you for ages.' Nightingale settled back into the swinging seat that Bess and Chris usually fought over. She looked beautiful in the twilight and Fenwick was surprised by the thought.

'I'm in good shape; you?'

She shrugged in a gesture he recognised. Now that he had moved on to Major Crimes she rarely talked about Harlden, where they had previously worked together.

'What's up? Want to talk about it?' He leant over from his chair and poured her more wine.

'It's the usual: politics, paperwork and petty-mindedness.'

'Oh, you mean the three Ps of police work. You forgot the others – piss-poor pay.'

She laughed, then sighed.

'You're right. It's nothing out of the ordinary but a number of people are upset by my promotion.'

'That was inevitable; just don't let it get to you.'

A shadow crossed her face, as if his words were an unwelcome echo.

'I know, I should forget about them. Now,' she said, with an obvious effort to change the subject, 'tell me all about MCS; word at the station is that you're doing well.'

'Really? Truth is I'm busier than I've ever been. I like being in charge of something and I can still get involved in the complex operations if I want, so I don't feel cut off.'

'You've always been a sucker for complication. Give me a straightforward life any time.' Again the trace of shadow in her features. 'Can you tell me about any of the work? I need a distraction.'

'Not much.' The Choir Boy investigation was strictly need-to-know and Fenwick felt uncomfortable in confiding, even to her. 'But there's something you might be interested in. It'll be in the papers tomorrow. A boy's body was discovered on the Downs, not ten miles from here, earlier this week.'

'Why don't we know at the station?'

'It's being kept quiet for now. Part of the hillside had crumbled, it's chalk and the ridge is eroding. When workmen went in to clear debris from a minor road, one of the JCBs came off the tarmac and slid down a slope into a tree, partially uprooting it. The boy's body was underneath.'

'How did it get under a tree?'

'It was a small one, a birch. They grow fast at the edges of woodland. Either the person who buried him put a sapling on top or it self-set. Either way, we would never have found him had it not been for the carelessness of the JCB driver.'

'A burial; so it's murder?' He nodded. 'Then why aren't Harlden involved?' she asked, instantly alert.

'There's a possible connection with a case MCS has been working on for months. We've been given first crack at it.' He stared at her in a way that made it clear there was no room for argument and, credit to Nightingale, she let the matter drop. Fenwick rewarded her with a blow-by-blow account of the work the forensic team had been doing since the discovery.

'The body was skeletised so the first job was to estimate approximate date of death, age and sex of victim, the usual. While that was going on I asked the lab to find a dendrologist to analyse wood from the tree that had been growing on top of him and that gave us a minimum burial time – the tree was at least twenty years old, you see. Grey, the pathologist, did an exceptional job in less than twenty-four hours, confirmed that the bones were those of a pre-pubescent boy, probably aged between ten and thirteen. Using the lab's analysis and dating from the dendrologist, we were able to produce a shortlist from missing persons; that's why I'm so late back. We recovered a skull complete with upper and lower teeth so they were cross-checking dental records all morning. They identified him just after lunchtime as Malcolm Eagleton. His parents still live locally so I had to see them.'

She grimaced in sympathy; Fenwick merely sipped his wine.

'Bad luck. Were they expecting it?' For all his taciturn, emotionless style, Nightingale suspected that Fenwick loathed breaking bad news to a family as much as any officer.

Fenwick sighed and poured them both more wine.

'I'm not sure you can ever expect to hear that your child's dead, even after more than twenty-five years, which is how long he's been missing,' he said heavily. 'And of course they had questions that I couldn't answer, including cause of death. There were no marks of injury on any of the bones we discovered, including the hyoid—'

'So he wasn't strangled.'

'No. Anyway,' he heaved another sigh, 'enough of that.'

Nightingale wasn't ready to give up.

'With a murder from so long ago, why is MCS interested?'

It was a good question and one that the ACC would be bound to ask as soon as he heard how old the case was. But Fenwick didn't want to relinquish control. MCS had been set up for large, complex and sensitive investigations, not to dig over cold cases, but he had to be absolutely sure there was no link to his Choir Boy investigation. He planned to ask H-B's indulgence until the end of the week and thought he would succeed.

'Well?'

'There's still the ongoing analysis of items we found in the grave with him. Until that's complete I don't want to pre-judge.'

'How long will it take?'

'A week perhaps. Why so interested?'

'I'd like the case, of course. It would be my first chance to be SIO on a murder and even one this old will be good experience.'

'Do you think Quinlan would give it to you?' Not that he intended to let the case go that easily.

'If I ask for it, maybe... But you're right; it's more likely to go to Blite, particularly if the press is involved. Quinlan's only allowing me to stay at Harlden as long as I maintain what he calls a low profile. But if I had a head start on the case, knew what was coming, I'd be able to impress him with a strategy before it goes to someone else.'

On two of her previous cases Nightingale had become the

subject of unprecedented press attention and Quinlan had threatened to transfer her. That she was still at Harlden said a lot for her powers of persuasion. Her shoulders sagged, forcing Fenwick to smile in sympathy.

'All, right – wait a minute.'

He disappeared into the house and was back quickly carrying a file that he passed to her.

'I trust you not to say a word of this to anyone. This is the file on the boy who died.'

'Of course.' Nightingale was on the edge of her chair already, reading. 'Malcolm Eagleton, aged twelve when he disappeared from Crawley swimming baths on 16th August, 1981.' She looked up. 'He lived in Pease Pottage, that's only a few miles away.'

'Look at his photograph.'

She did. He noticed that she stroked the edges with her fingertips and her expression softened briefly before she brought it back under control.

'A lovely child. He reminds me of someone.' She paused, searching her memory. 'But maybe it's just that old Sussex colouring, dark hair, blue eyes, fair complexion. A lovely boy,' she repeated.

'"Like angels' visits, short and bright, mortality's too weak to bear them long",' Fenwick murmured, staring out into the dark garden at the children's swings.

Nightingale looked at him in surprise but he was too lost in his thoughts to notice.

'Were there any leads at the time he disappeared?' she asked, to break the mood.

'None that led to anything; a few reports of him disappearing with a man no one could describe.'

'And what did you recover from the grave?' He looked at her in surprise. 'You mentioned that the lab was still working on something.'

He tried to decide how much he should divulge. He trusted her of all people but he was a poor sharer of secrets.

'Some scraps but they might be promising.'

It was all he was willing to say and they finished their wine in silence, punctuated by the soft strains of Debussy that was playing on the CD inside. When the piece finished he called her a taxi.

First thing Monday morning he asked to see ACC Harper-Brown in an attempt to buy himself time. The lab and his team had worked around the clock to try and give the 'scraps' substance.

'Go on, Fenwick, you have five minutes to persuade me. After that I have another meeting and if I don't like what I hear the case goes straight to Harlden.'

'We found something in the grave.' He reached over and took Malcolm's file from his briefcase. 'Here.'

He pushed it over the polished mahogany of H-B's desk and tapped some evidence photographs at the front. One of them showed part of a femur poking up out of the ground and a piece of what looked like nondescript rubbish in the same depression.

'What is it?'

'A plastic car-parking permit. Unfortunately it's aged badly where the laminate was cracked and only a piece of it remains, but see here.'

'It looks like a logo of some sort but only part's left.'

'What you can see is the top of the letters T, D and G in a stylised script. On the next page is the crest for The Downs Golf Club, just the initials arranged in an inverted triangle with the C at the bottom. It's a permit for their car park. We also know that it's from an old permit because the club redesigned their crest in 1984, so it has to be older than that.

'What's more,' he leant over and turned a page for him, 'a

wider search of the area found this.' He didn't wait for Harper-Brown to try and guess this time.

'A metal locker key.'

'From Crawley swimming pool?'

'No, they never issued keys like this. See, there's a distinctive manufacturer's mark stamped on one side. We've been able to trace the maker. Fortunately they were local though they're part of a bigger firm now. The original list of clients has long gone but we tracked down the previous proprietor and he still remembers some of his biggest customers. One was in Harlden – The Downs Golf Club.'

'Hence your continuing interest in the Eagleton boy. But was it dropped at the same time the body was buried? You said you found it in a wider search, not in the grave.'

'We can't be certain because the JCB tracks disrupted some of the surrounding soil but it was lying in spoil a few feet away.'

'So you think Malcolm was abducted and killed by someone from my golf club.' Harper-Brown played off a handicap of nine and had been a member for twenty years; his uncle had been a club president. 'Half the great and the good of Harlden play there.'

'I appreciate that this is going to have to be handled with sensitivity but we'd already identified the club as a potential link in the Choir Boy investigation.' Harper-Brown raised an eyebrow in surprise and Fenwick hurried on. 'I don't think we can ignore this connection. Whoever's been organising the paedophile ring in Sussex is very clever and has got away with it, according to the American's witness, for at least ten years. Who knows how long it's actually been going on? Malcolm's murder is all I have to work on at present. Please give me a week to look into it more fully.'

The ACC stared at Fenwick, his expression unreadable.

'Very well.' The chief inspector breathed an inaudible sigh of relief but Harper-Brown hadn't finished. 'I appreciate that you will handle the investigation with delicacy, but Fenwick...'

His heart sank.

'If you find out anything, I expect you to probe as fully and as thoroughly as for any other case. There are to be no special privileges just because of the club's membership. Do I make myself clear?'

Fenwick was too surprised to speak but nodded his understanding, forced to admit that at least some of his prejudices against the ACC were proving to be unfounded. Maybe he should push his luck.

'There is just one other thing, sir.' Harper-Brown looked up, almost benign, and he rushed on. 'I'd like to excavate the terrace at the club.'

'No; preposterous!'

'It was reconstructed around the time Malcolm Eagleton disappeared. We need to find his clothes, potentially other belongings. Given the other connections with the club—'

'I said no. Parts of that bloody terrace have been rebuilt almost every year to my knowledge and this coincidence is no grounds to authorise something so expensive and disruptive.'

'But—'

'The answer remains no.'

CHAPTER SIX

Sometimes it was easy to forget how fortunate he was but all it took was a trip to Mount Ellingham Hospice to remind him. He went once a week, dreading the visit for days beforehand and guilty afterwards that he'd left it so long.

As one of the few fit survivors of his old regiment it had fallen to Maidment to act as unofficial liaison officer with others in the area. One of them, Stanley Elthorpe, was spending his last days in the Mount. A widower like Maidment, his only son had emigrated to Canada and he never saw his grandchildren. On the previous visit Maidment had learnt to his surprise that Stanley also had an estranged daughter. Stanley had never mentioned her before and the major sensed a gulf of hostility between them.

But Stanley was dying and dying quickly. The cancer his doctors thought eradicated seven years before had returned, this time in his lungs. At least palliative care saved him from the worst pain.

The faint institutionalised smell hit Maidment as he walked through the entrance. It wasn't exactly unpleasant, the carers made sure of that, but there was an inevitable miasma of medication, disinfectant and hospital meals that lay in corners and among the cushions in the lounge. He had to wait for a nurse to leave Stanley and spent his time looking at some watercolours with ridiculous price tags that served the dual purpose of decoration and commercial opportunity. He couldn't imagine living with any of them.

A strip of carpet softened the impact of the corridors but to his exacting eye it clashed with the paisley chairs that lined the walls. Two elderly women, one no more than skin and bone, sat side by side in the lounge holding hands, locked in mute companionship as they waited for the inevitable parting. The thin one plucked at the wool of her cardigan and he could see the beginnings of the hole she was making. The other looked on but said nothing, perhaps recognising that the garment would outlast its owner so any counsel was an irrelevance. He bade them too hearty a good morning and walked back to Stanley.

His old friend was sitting up in a chair beside his bed, looking brighter than he'd seen him for weeks. Were it not for the intravenous drip snaking its way into the vein on the back of his bruised left hand, he would have thought him in better health.

'Stanley, old chap, you're looking well!'

They shook hands, the major careful not to squeeze the papery skin too tight.

'Spot of remission, Major. It's taken us all by surprise. The poor old priest was hopeful that my imminent departure would prompt a conversion so it's quite a setback for him.'

Maidment flinched slightly at the words and covered his discomfort by depositing a bottle of Glenfiddich malt whisky on the side table.

'Had I known, I'd have bought you Bells as usual but I thought this might be your last bottle.'

Stanley enjoyed the gallows humour and laughed until a choking fit returned both men to the practicalities of finding him a glass of water. He was still purple in the face when he pulled another tumbler from the bedside cupboard and poured them two fingers of malt apiece.

'Steady, I'm driving. Don't want any more trouble with the Old Bill, thank you very much.'

'I read about that. You're a hero in here. There's some will want your autograph if they find out you're visiting. Surely the police are going to drop the case?'

'Oh, bound to.' Maidment hid his misgivings behind convincing bluster. 'But they have to go through due process. You know the law.'

'Waste of taxpayers' bloody money, if you ask me. The bugger was set to do you and murder that copper.' It wasn't clear from Stan's tone which aborted crime appalled him more.

With practised skill, Maidment steered the conversation gently away from his predicament towards safer subjects. They had exhausted cricket, politics and regimental gossip by the end of the allotted hour and Maidment started a well-rehearsed ritual of departure. It was carefully orchestrated so that at the right moment Stanley would suggest it was time for his nap and his guest would rise to collect his hat. In that way they avoided the embarrassment of his visitor being so impolite as to say that he had to leave.

On this occasion, though, Stanley missed his cue. Maidment coughed, shot his cuffs, stood and looked out of the window but Stan remained lost to his own thoughts. Maidment had reached the point of contemplating a glance at his watch when the other man blurted out.

'Major, I need you to see my daughter.' He was staring down at his veined hands, toying with the IV needle in a way that made the major look away. 'We haven't spoken in over twenty years. I know she's alive because the vicar tells me.'

'Easy to drift apart in these times...'

'There was no drifting. It was a rift. We argued and we were both too damned proud to bend afterwards.' It was as if he wanted the brutality of their parting to be understood. 'But in these last days, since the remission started, I've been wondering why I've been given this extra time.'

'And what is your answer?'

'I think I've been granted a last chance to put my life in order.' The glance he gave the major was almost menacing and Maidment looked away.

'Why not ask the vicar to do the honours? He'd be far better.'

'No. She holds no truck with religion, though she was a believer once until her faith was broke. You'd be ideal. You have a way with the ladies. Don't look like that, we both know the truth.' Again the look. 'She's only a few miles away.'

'But why me?'

'She respects authority, you've got that, and you're well spoken. Bless her heart; she always was a terrible snob. Besides,' there was an ominous pause, 'I reckon you owe me.'

Maidment didn't need to ask why. He could feel himself weakening. After all, could he really claim that a dying man's wish to be reunited with a long-lost daughter who lived nearby was unreasonable? No; in good conscience he could not deny Stanley's request.

'I can't guarantee success, old boy.'

'I'm only asking you to try. Just get her to read this.'

He thrust a sealed envelope towards him. Maidment noticed how Stanley's hand trembled and the last of his reservations disappeared.

'Very well, I'll do it.' He put the envelope in his pocket and Stan sank back in his chair, suddenly exhausted.

'Tell me, why did you fall out?'

'Best not to talk about that. If you don't know you won't be tempted to take sides. She's tough, my Sarah. If she thinks you're with me she'll shred you in a minute. But if she wants to tell you, that's fine by me.'

'Her exact address?'

'On the envelope. Thank you, Jeremy.' He looked up and Maidment was embarrassed to witness the tears in his eyes.

'I'll call you to let you know how it goes.'

'Good. Well, I think I need my nap now. Perhaps it's the daily snoozes that are doing me so much good; them and decent whisky!'

Maidment didn't look at the envelope until that evening. Never one to put off a difficult task, he decided to call round and visit daughter Sarah the next day. When he turned the envelope over and saw the name and address he had to sit down. At first he thought that Stanley was playing a cruel trick on him but dismissed the idea immediately. This wasn't a joke; it was his worst nightmare become reality. Sweat broke out on his forehead.

'Oh my God.'

He could barely breathe as he read the few words in Stanley's spidery hand:

Sarah Hill
26, Penton Cross
Woodhampstead
Nr. Harlden
Sussex

He knew that name, that address. He even knew what her face would look like. There had been photographs of her aged beyond years by emotions no woman should have to face. Semi-digested baked haddock rose up at the back of his throat and he washed it away with a mouthful of wine. If only his sins could so easily be dealt with.

He was bound by his promise and Stanley's implied threats to see this woman. Yet in doing so his terrible disgrace would become real again. A lesser man would have cursed and wept but one of the many ironies in his life was that he'd been born strong.

Only God could have devised such justice.

* * *

The house was set back from the road as if seeking obscurity. An old Ford Fiesta was parked in the drive. Someone, children probably, had written in the dust on the rear window: *'don't clean me, grey is my colour'*; *'Angie luvs Greg'* and some obscenities he pretended not to see. Where there had once been a square of garden, weeds now consumed every scrap of soil. It was impossible to tell where the gravel of the path ended and what had once been a lawn began. The air of determined abandonment and the desire for solitude oppressed the major as he locked his pristine Corsa and opened a gate that creaked in protest against the unwelcome intruder.

He'd timed his journey for late morning when there was a strong possibility that she would be out at work, or with friends, or doing her shopping, so that he would have an excuse to post the letter through the door. But one look at the house told him this woman had no job, no friends and was an infrequent shopper. As he walked up what he took for the path, a grey-green curtain twitched in the front bedroom window. By the time he reached the front door a shadow was hovering beyond the frosted glass. A thought assailed him that perhaps she was still waiting, after all these years.

The door opened before he could knock and the look on her face confirmed his fears. He saw there a dreadful mixture of anguish and hope and he thought he could almost see the words *'my son'* stretched onto her open mouth. But it was her eyes that almost unmade him. Even though they were washed out from too many years of tears, they unmistakably belonged to Paul's mother. At one time she must have been a beauty but grief and self-neglect had aged her cruelly.

'Mrs Hill?' It was an unnecessary question but he knew of no other way to begin.

She just stared at him as he held out the letter, her eyes fixed on his face with a look of expectation that broke his heart. Then there was an inward collapse. She had become expert at reading the expressions of strangers in her long years of waiting and saw nothing in his that answered her need.

'What do you want?'

If a ghost could speak it would sound like this, he thought, and shuddered. For an instant he was afraid that merely by meeting her he might share her doom but then his common sense reasserted itself.

'I have a letter for you.' The rekindling of hope in her eyes made him rush on. 'Not from…ah…may I step inside?'

He was loath to enter her grimy house on that hot July day but realised she might shut the door in his face if he so much as mentioned her father's name. Sarah Hill turned without a word and walked along the short hall into a sitting room of browns that had faded to the colour of dust. The fetid smell that wafted from her as she moved caught in his throat, forcing a coughing fit. When he recovered, he wiped his face with a brilliant white handkerchief that flickered as a bright flash in the gloom. She was staring at him without expression, the diminishing blaze of her eyes at odds with everything else about her.

Behind her, set on the wall where whatever faint rays from the sun that managed to filter inside would light up his face, was a shrine to Paul. He had been a beautiful child. His smile was cheeky, engaging and so bright it would have been infectious. One large portrait photograph had been reproduced as an oil painting, an effect popular in the 1980s. Beneath it was a sports trophy that had been polished to a smoothness that disguised its origins. A certificate of commendation for a swimming gala hung next to it, beside a child's drawing framed as if it were a priceless work of art – which to her it was. She caught him staring and he looked away.

'You're of an age to remember,' she said, as if this simple statement exempted their conversation from explanation.

'I remember very well.' The sincerity in his voice had an

immediate effect on the woman before him. Her stoniness melted and she smiled briefly.

'Would you like something to drink?'

The odour in the house was making it hard for him to breathe and the idea of something from her kitchen passing his lips made him want to retch. But he'd made a promise to Stanley and gaining the woman's trust might help him succeed in his mission.

'Just a glass of water, thank you. It is a very hot day.'

She was gone for a while, too long for his peace of mind. Paul looked at him with a knowingness that forced him to blink hard to clear his eyes. By the time she returned he was wiping his face again and the letter in his hand was damp with perspiration.

'Would you like a biscuit?'

He declined, certain that he would have choked on the crumbs.

'This letter,' he began again, 'is from an old friend of mine whom you used to know. He wants to see you again.'

She stared at him blankly as she nibbled on a chocolate digestive covered with white bloom.

'Mrs Hill, Sarah, this letter is from your father. He's dying,' he added because he could see rejection already in her face.

'I'm surprised he's still alive. He is nothing to me. Go away.'

'I can't, not without giving you this. I promised him I would and I'm a man of my word. We served together, you see. It creates a certain bond of obligation.'

'I could tell you were army the moment you got out of the car. My Paul was a cadet once, when he thought that he wanted to go into the services. Do you think he would have made a good soldier?'

'I'm sure he would have done.' Maidment was suffocating in the tiny sitting room as Paul looked on, enjoying the torture.

'He would have been good at anything, my Paul. He had so much potential.'

The major took a tiny sip of the tepid water so that he could speak.

'I must give you this letter,' he repeated, insistent now, but she refused to take it from him. 'I'll leave it on the coffee table then.'

'Did he tell you?'

'I beg your pardon?'

'Why we argued.'

'No. He said I didn't need to know.'

She barked a laugh, a sound so devoid of humour that it made his eyes ache.

'Oh, how like him; but you should know.'

He shrugged helplessly, pinned by the sharpness of her stare.

'It was long after Paul disappeared.'

She paused and drank her coffee in an unfussy way, not enjoying it but not grimacing either. Her neutrality characterised this as it did everything else about her. He waited.

'The police had stopped looking though they never told us that of course. They didn't have family liaison officers in those days, not like now.'

She rose with a jerky movement, like a pre-programmed robot, and went to a cupboard at the bottom of a built-in bookcase from which she lifted a heavy box file.

'This is a recent case.' She passed him the file. 'Another boy. Look at the coverage and all the fuss. Fascinating what the police do these days. We had none of that.'

Sarah Hill bent down and opened another door. The file she passed him this time was much smaller, a bare half inch across.

'That's Paul's file. See how tiny? And half of that is from references to him during other investigations. Criminal science has progressed wonderfully, at least in its vocabulary. Doesn't save the children though.'

He winced at her words and looked up expecting tears, but she was dry-eyed.

'Do you follow many cases?'

'Every one. The loft is full of past files. The ones down here are only those from this year. On New Year's Eve I take the old year's files upstairs and put the new ones ready in the cupboard.'

'New ones?'

'Of course, empty, ready for use. I think of all those mothers on the 1st January each year, singing "Auld Lang Syne" as if tragedy were going to apply to someone else and not to them. I make the files ready, stick on blank labels. Then I drink a toast to the New Year's victims and their parents. I don't know who they'll be and neither do they, but there hasn't been a year yet that I've put a file away empty on the 31st December. Usually I have to buy more. 1992 was a bad year. I ran out of filing space down here in July.'

He realised then that she had become deranged by grief.

'I write to them all. Letters of hope at first because I really appreciated those. Then the prayers. I was sent some lovely ones. They mean nothing to me but they might help the others. And, eventually, I send them condolences. I've improved the wording over the years and I'm quite pleased with the latest letter. Would you like to see it?'

'No, thank you, Mrs Hill. I'm sure it is very fine.'

His skin crawled and he wanted to be gone. He stood up.

'Wait! I haven't told you about my father, what he did to me and Paul. He came around one evening, months after Paul had disappeared. My husband was still living with me then, just...'

Her concentration drifted away into an echo of remembered conversation and he waited. He understood grief and remembrances.

'He told me that Paul had to be dead, that I should give up hope and start to grieve. That it would be good for me. Good for me!' Her shriek made him jump and he almost dropped his water.

'He was murdering Paul with his words. I had to shut him up. Every sentence he uttered was death for Paul; I couldn't allow it. I hit him. He didn't defend himself. The more I punched the more he seemed to want it. Eventually, my husband pulled us apart. I told them both to get out, that I never wanted to see them again.'

'And they stayed away?' He was fascinated despite himself.

'Not at first. It took a long time but I finally made them leave me and Paul alone. No one comes to disturb us here now.'

He tried not to stare at the dowdy woman in front of him who had shaped her personal madness from hatred born of grief.

'He's dying, your father.'

'Of course he is. Why else would he send you here after all these years?'

'He wants to see you.'

'No. I will never forgive him for wishing Paul dead.'

The hatred in her face made him frightened for Stanley. It was better that his old friend never saw his daughter than be forced to confront this dangerous wreck. But still he argued, loyal to the last.

'I don't think that your father wished Paul dead. He was probably trying to help you, as well as finding a way to cope with his own grief.'

She shook her head in denial but he continued, endeavouring to do his best.

'I'm sure that your father was as desperate for Paul to be found alive as you were. He just couldn't hold on to hope for as long as you were able to. He never wished Paul dead.'

Sarah Hill bent forward and picked up the letter, weighing it in her hands as if it were her father's soul on the scales of Judgement. Abruptly she ripped it across the middle, the noise as loud as a pistol shot in the silence of the room. She kept tearing at it until the pieces littered the carpet like confetti. He had his answer.

'I'll see myself out.'

'Wait!' She ran up behind him as he opened the front door and inhaled fresh air. 'You're a man of the world, you have experience. Tell me, do you think he's still alive, my Paul?'

Her eyes held him. Their plea for something, anything, to keep her hope alive humbled him.

'Yes,' he said and felt his gut churn with guilt at the lie, 'yes, I do.'

CHAPTER SEVEN

Based on his revised statement and on the authority of the Criminal Prosecution Service, with Quinlan's approval, Nightingale rearrested Jeremy Maidment for attempted murder on 25th July at ten o'clock. She took him into custody on her own authority knowing that she had until four that afternoon to gather sufficient evidence to persuade Quinlan that they could hold him for the full twenty-four hours. That was all the time she would have to prepare a case strong enough to convince a magistrate that Maidment should be remanded in custody and not released on bail. It was what the Crown Prosecution Service wanted and they had made it clear that they were relying on her and her team to achieve it.

It was a tough order. Maidment looked an unlikely criminal or flight risk. While she understood all about someone being innocent until proven guilty, and their right to liberty until trial except in extreme circumstances, she could not help but wish that the law cut the police some slack once in a while. Twenty-four hours was so little time, particularly with Bob Cooper and the other original arresting officers tied up in the inquiry.

She needed their detailed statements double-checked; the report on the gun and bullet from ballistics (which still had not arrived); information from Maidment's doctor about his tremor…the list went on. The one thing she did not actually need was a lot of time with the major himself but as he was only supposed to be in custody to help her gather evidence, or prevent him from hindering her investigation or committing another crime, she had to go through the motions. One of her small team was re-interviewing him at that moment as she struggled to complete her work.

When the phone rang she ignored it but the team secretary interrupted her anyway.

'It's the assistant chief constable,' she said white-faced. 'He's not best pleased at having to wait to talk to you.'

Nightingale grimaced.

'Put him through – oh, and close the door, would you?'

The phone rang and she picked it up at once.

'Inspector Nightingale.'

'About time. Don't you answer your own phone since you've been promoted? Too grand for all that now, are we?'

'No, sir, not at all. I was just up against a deadline and—'

'Never mind that. What's this I hear about you rearresting Major Maidment? I gave an order only last week for him to be released on bail. The man's a pillar of the community.'

After her interview with Maidment she had known that there were strong grounds for a renewed charge of attempted murder. It had only been a matter of time before the ACC found out and called her.

'I was aware of the reasons for Maidment's release, sir, but subsequent evidence has come to light that has led CPS to prefer a charge of attempted murder.'

'Preposterous! Whose evidence? I demand to see it.'

'It was mine and I'll arrange for a copy to be sent to you as soon as Superintendent Quinlan has reviewed it.'

In the silence that followed she could feel the fury directed towards her but when he spoke Harper-Brown's voice had returned to its normal smoothness – and that worried her even more.

'I shall expect your report immediately, Inspector, and if I find that you have been motivated in any way by the mistaken desire to elevate the charge in order to somehow alleviate the situation in which the ridiculous Cooper now finds himself, you will be in serious trouble.'

He broke the connection without another word and she replaced the receiver carefully. Her heart was pounding but she was pleased to see that her hand was steady and her voice normal as she asked the secretary to email a copy of her interview to the ACC. It was a full record of their conversation and CPS had congratulated her on its clarity and value. She doubted Harper-Brown would have the nerve to go up against the prosecutors but far from vindicating her, that would only serve to deepen his resentment.

Fenwick hadn't been warned of Harper-Brown's mood before he saw him later that morning in another attempt to excavate the terrace at The Downs Golf Club, which had been undergoing reconstruction at the time of Malcolm Eagleton's disappearance in 1981. It had been a frustrating meeting. Harper-Brown again refused to grant permission and had ended up ordering Fenwick out of his office.

Drinking a foul but strong coffee from the canteen before he drove back to MCS, Fenwick calculated the damage he had inflicted to his prospects by pushing his demands so hard. On the Richter scale of career suicide he thought he was moving up over a seven. Serious structural damage, economic disruption and potential loss of life. The ACC was not the shock-absorbent kind.

As he dashed across the busy car park Fenwick cursed his lack of an umbrella for the second time that day. The heat wave they'd been enjoying for ten weeks had been broken without warning by a storm that started before dawn and showed no sign of easing. In the steamy shelter of his car, he turned on the air-conditioning to clear the windows and hung his jacket on a coat hanger. The worst of the creases should fall out by the time he arrived but there was no hope for the trousers. It did nothing to improve his mood.

The ramp out of the car park was flooded. With the earth baked hard and drains cluttered with debris, the water had nowhere to go but onto the roads. His journey to Burgess Hill took an hour, double the normal time and his desk was covered with new reports when he finally reached it.

He was reading the last of them when Nightingale rang. Although they now saw more of each other in their spare time, it had not become a habit – at least not as far as he was concerned. She was calling to invite him out for a drink and he almost said no on principle as he'd seen her for dinner at his house the Friday before. But it had been a frustrating day and he felt in need of company before he faced Alice and the children, so he said yes. They agreed to meet at the Bull and Drum, a pleasant village pub overlooking a cricket field that was on his way home. It also served some of the best bitter in the county.

Her car wasn't in the car park when he arrived, making her late again. It was becoming a habit and it was one that annoyed him. He expected punctuality in others even though he achieved it infrequently himself. The rain was, if anything, heavier and he took his pint into the cosy snug bar where an arrangement of dried flowers took the place of a fire in the grate.

Nightingale was a puzzle to him. The previous year they had come very close to having an affair but he'd stopped it. In the aftermath though they had gradually become friends; he corrected himself, they had become very good friends. They saw each other once, at the most twice, a month, sometimes at his house where her presence was exerting a subtle influence over his children. She was careful not to seem in any way like a replacement mother. It was friendship that she offered and easy, undemanding companionship. Because she wasn't looking for anything from them they naturally loved her.

Bess was obsessed with Nightingale's slenderness, style and sleek hair, so different from her own curls and puppy-fat chubbiness. Recently he'd even noticed Chris curling himself up against her like a kitten, content to feel her warmth without any other demonstration or contact. It was strange behaviour from his detached and difficult son. Some of his irritation towards her faded as he acknowledged to himself how sensitively she managed their affections.

As to her present feelings towards him, he'd been left to fathom them out for himself. Once he'd made it clear that he didn't want a relationship she had never raised the subject again. If anything, over the past few months it was she who was becoming more detached. As a result, he was starting to find her more interesting. He loathed clinginess in women, a lasting consequence of his doomed marriage. Overt dependency had the same effect on him as bromide, killing any sense of lust. When Nightingale had declared her love, part of him went into hiding. The more distant she became the more attractive he thought her, though fortunately she seemed unaware of the fact. Or perhaps, he thought with a jolt as he spotted her walking towards him with a small glass of wine, she had found someone else and no longer cared. The idea upset him.

'Sorry,' she waved him down as he started to rise from his seat in an automatic gesture of politeness. 'The main road out of Harlden is flooded underneath the railway bridge. I had to find a route through the back roads. This rain is terrible.'

'You shouldn't have bought your own drink.'

'Why not? It saves time and as I drink white wine I knew that you wouldn't have got me one in case it went warm. Am I right?'

It was obvious that she was.

'Are you hungry? Only I missed lunch and I don't want to drink this on an empty stomach.'

'Alice will have something for me,' he said, shaking his head, 'but let me get you a bite to eat.'

'I wouldn't dream of it.'

She was gone before he could protest but was back in minutes with a cheese and pickle sandwich. No matter how busy a bar she always seemed to be served quickly.

'So, good day?' His opening line was always the same, nice and neutral.

'Awful.' They were on their own in the snug but she still lowered her voice. 'I heard from CPS on the major. His revised statement means that they've raised the game to attempted murder again. You can imagine H-B's reaction to that.

'I think they're being a bit ambitious but they're in charge. It's going to be a difficult case because he has public sympathy and he's a likeable old man. Everyone we've interviewed can't speak highly enough of him. Apparently he sold the family house after his wife died and bought somewhere much smaller. The proceeds were split between his son and a couple of charities and now he lives a very modest life. On top of that, he's a regular churchgoer, does charity work, helps out those less able than himself and he's well connected. His time as secretary of the golf club was one of the most effective in the club's history according to a number of people, and his service record is distinguished. He's not the sort of man one would ever expect to see in the dock.

'But frankly that's irrelevant; he shot and almost killed a man. Chalfont could have died.' Nightingale's hushed voice held the outrage only a truly logical person could feel.

'It was the major's presence of mind that saved him.'

'From his own bullet,' she hissed.

'How is the ACC coping? He must have known Maidment well.'

'He's deeply pissed.' Fenwick blinked in surprise at Nightingale's uncharacteristic choice of language. 'Now that his attempt to have Maidment released on a minor charge has failed he's said that his involvement will be at purely arm's length. He wants to be kept informed of any developments with CPS but he's made it abundantly clear that I'm on my own if it starts to get rough. I think his strategy is to maintain a low profile and hope that he isn't called as a character witness!' Nightingale's laugh at the idea of Harper-Brown in the dock faded quickly.

'I've got to build enough of a case against Maidment to persuade the magistrate to keep him in custody tomorrow; no bail for attempted murder as far as CPS is concerned.'

'The press will have a field day.' He thought but didn't say: *particularly with you as SIO*. They knew to their cost that her face was good for sales.

'Right but what choice is there? I still have a job to do. How about you?' she asked, changing the subject that was obviously unpleasant to her. 'Any nearer to going public on Malcolm?'

He told her about his failure with the ACC. To his surprise she was unsympathetic, almost critical of his desire to push for an excavation in the first place. He found himself having to defend his position and didn't like it.

Nightingale put the last of her sandwich in her mouth and chewed with obvious delight. 'I might take another of these with me; they're better than the canteen's.'

'You're going back to work?' It was gone seven.

'Yes. I have to try for remand tomorrow so I've got more work to do.'

'I'm sorry, if I'd known I would have suggested a different pub.'

'Well, I did try to call you to rearrange once I realised I was going to work late but all I got was your answering service. Never mind, I needed the food and the drive has cleared my head.'

She picked up her handbag, obviously ready to leave, forcing

Fenwick to down the rest of his beer. He'd been going to suggest another drink but that clearly wasn't an option. They left the pub together, Fenwick walking in her wake watching the eyes of every man follow her to the door. If she was aware of the effect she had on them she gave it no heed.

CHAPTER EIGHT

The following morning Fenwick pushed yet more reports to one side and went to find himself a cup of coffee. Somewhere between the broken vending machine and the staff restaurant he became lost in thought and found himself at the main entrance. He had his pass and a fiver in his pocket so decided to go out to buy a decent espresso. As he left the building he wondered whether it was what he'd intended all along.

It was still raining but there was a local Italian café close by and he ran there in less than two minutes. Inside, the atmosphere was warm and steamy, the coffee as excellent as always and he bought a second after the downing the first in one gulp.

Although the owner said his name was Giuseppe, Fenwick knew he was Polish and that his brother, who now called himself Leonardo and was an expert with the coffee machine, had done time for stealing cars. He didn't care though, as the man had served his sentence and now served the best coffee in Burgess Hill.

'Another, Chief Inspector?' Giuseppe insisted on using his rank and he'd given up asking him not to.

'I should be getting back.'

'On the house.' A small white cup and saucer appeared in front of him. 'And biscotti too; you look a little thin today.'

'*Grazie*, Giuseppe.' Fenwick laughed inwardly at himself for playing his part in their façade.

He was running out of time. The investigation into Malcolm's death was making little progress. His team had compiled a list of members of the golf club in 1981 and were steadily interviewing those that were still alive, so far without any success. It was looking inevitable that he would have to cede the case to Harlden and concentrate again on the crumbs of evidence he'd been able to gather in following up the Choir Boy ring. He dunked the biscuit and forced his thoughts into a semblance of order.

Joseph Watkins hadn't appeared to put a foot wrong in all the time he'd been under surveillance. His acquaintance, Alec Ball, had now been watched for ten weeks, going about his life without a hint of suspicion. Fenwick pulled out his notebook and turned to a fresh page, forcing himself to recall the few details that had emerged from recent surveillance.

Alec Ball was sixty; a short square man who ran a market stall that sold old books, LPs and other bric-a-brac. He looked a bruiser, with his bald head and tattoos, but hadn't been in any trouble according to police records since he'd been a bouncer at a Brighton club where he was once arrested for GBH. The prosecution had collapsed when the key witness and victim withdrew their statement. It smelt nasty but had nothing to do with pimping or using young boys.

Joseph Watkins was a retired sports coach who still did occasional supply work. He lived well, in a house way beyond his salary, with his wife and a grown-up son who showed no sign of wanting to leave home. His only daughter had just made him a grandfather. So far, so innocent, but he and Ball had an unlikely friendship, even travelling abroad for weekends together despite their very different backgrounds. Joseph was a member of the club in Harlden, although his golf wasn't great and he played rarely.

The cost of watching these two men was horrendous. Finding the manpower to keep up the surveillance was also putting a strain on the MCS team, which was under strength because Fenwick had encouraged three officers to seek transfers when they didn't live up to his exacting standards. Yet he didn't want to give up. If there were a paedophile ring here in West Sussex – and the FBI was convinced that they had evidence one existed – he was determined to find it. Ball and Watkins would become his only leads once he was forced to pass over Malcolm Eagleton's file. Fuelled by the coffee he decided that he would keep the Choir Boy team live for another week and then he'd be forced to decide whether to suspend further work.

The doorbell jangled and there was a rush of cold air as a boy about Chris's age ran in. In looks he was the opposite of Fenwick's son: tall, maybe as much as a stone heavier and very dark, with beautiful eyes that would devastate the girls in a few years. Billy, Guiseppe's son, was in Chris's class at school and a bit of a tearaway by all accounts. Fenwick stared at the boy's retreating back as he ducked under his uncle's outstretched arm and grabbed biscotti from the jar by the till.

'Hey!' his father called, then shrugged indulgently, including his customers in his conspiratorial smile. But Fenwick didn't notice.

Sight of the boy had triggered something in his memory and he felt an urgent need to return to his office and look again at the missing persons' files he kept as a constant reminder that there were real victims as a result of the Choir Boy ring, perhaps growing with each fruitless month that passed.

'*Arrivederci,* Chief Inspector,' Leonardo called out as he opened the door and turned up his jacket collar against the rain.

'*Domani,* Leonardo,' he replied and dashed outside.

He didn't spot the stationary green Peugeot until it was too late to avoid it. Blake Bowyer leapt out of the car and intercepted Fenwick before he could reach the station entrance. Oblivious to the rain that was soaking them both he put a restraining hand on Fenwick's arm, removing it quickly as he realised he had caused offence.

'Chief Inspector, please...' Bowyer stared at him, his eyes beseeching him for news, words of comfort, anything. It had been two weeks now since Sam's disappearance.

Fenwick noticed that the car was parked on a double yellow line.

'Let's get out of the rain,' he said and went towards it. At least this way if a traffic warden did brave the weather in search of a ticket Fenwick would be able to prevent a fine. Out of the rain he turned to the distraught father.

'Mr Bowyer, I'm not the senior investigating officer on your son's case, you know that. It's being handled with every effort and care by a colleague of mine in Brighton. I came to see you in case there was a connection to another investigation, that's all.'

'And is there?' Bowyer stared at him with eyes so red they looked as if they would bleed if he blinked.

Before he'd had his coffee Fenwick would have said no but the realisation that had come to him as Guiseppe's son ran into the café made him pause. Bowyer noticed.

'There is, isn't there! You're keeping something from me.' He grabbed Fenwick's arm, creasing his jacket where it was already a mess from the rain. Fenwick loosened the man's fingers gently.

'I'm not, Mr Bowyer, really. My case is complex, years old and there is absolutely no proven link to your son's disappearance.' He wondered if his qualification would be spotted but Bowyer was too devastated to notice.

'It's killing Jenny,' he said. 'She barely eats, won't leave the house in case Sam comes home and...oh God!' He buried his exhausted face in his hands. 'I can't talk to her but that's all she does, talks and talks and talks about it all the time. What if she'd taken him to school; what if she'd given him an extra hug that morning; what if I hadn't shouted at him not to tease the cat...it goes on and on. She's reliving the last hour we had with him over and over again looking for a way we might have changed the future; blaming us for letting him leave the house, blaming me for just watching him go.'

'Are you receiving any help – from the church or friends or family? I can recommend a very good victim support group—'

'WE'RE NOT FUCKING VICTIMS!' Bowyer wiped his face; his nails were bitten down to raw skin. 'We're *not* victims.' His anger subsided as suddenly as it had arrived and he added, in a voice that made Fenwick look away, 'not yet.'

He spent another half hour with the man, just listening. When a patrol car cruised by and stopped to order them on he waved his warrant card at them and, when they looked inclined to argue, told them to bugger off. They did. Bowyer didn't notice, barely interrupting his monologue. When he finished, Fenwick wanted to give him a lift home, worried that he was driving in his distressed state, but the man refused and he had no choice but to watch him drive off into the indifferent traffic, his own heart heavy with an echo of the man's sadness and guilty that he was unable to help him.

Back in his office, in no mood for small talk, in fact in no mood for company at all, Fenwick pulled out the photograph of Malcolm Eagleton and tacked it carefully to the cork board that covered half the wall opposite his desk, old-fashioned but effective. Then he picked up a copy of the *Brighton Argus* that he'd been keeping and cut out the picture of Sam Bowyer from the front page, pinning it next to Malcolm's. The resemblance was marked despite the difference in hairstyles caused by the passing of more than twenty-five years.

As he was backing away to take in the similarities Angela Marsh ambled into his room to collect his filing. A member of the civilian support staff on the team, she'd been nicknamed Jell-O as soon as she'd arrived, much to Fenwick's annoyance. He thought, given her complexion and build, it was too cruel but she seemed to like it so he'd kept quiet.

'Sorry, sir, thought you were still out. I'll come back later.'

'No, go ahead, you're not disturbing me.'

She gathered the papers from the casual bundle he'd left in the usual place and was about to leave when she noticed the new material on the board and stopped. Fenwick looked up, frowned and nodded her away but she didn't move.

'Strange,' she said, staring at the two boys. 'Very odd.'

'Thank you, Angela, that will be all for now.'

'Right.' She nodded but stayed where she was.

'Angela!' He was growing impatient.

'What? Oh, sorry, it's just that, seeing them there, I wondered why you hadn't put the other one up.'

'What are you talking about?' Fenwick asked, irritated by her intrusion into his thoughts.

'The other lad, the one who disappeared after Malcolm. I was only filing him away last night when they'd finished with the box.'

A chill spread over Fenwick's arms, raising the small hairs and it had nothing to do with his damp clothes.

'Get the file, would you, Angela,' he said softly, and waited.

She was back in less than a minute.

'You're lucky, I was about to send it down to archive. I know I shouldn't have been nosing in it,' she glanced at him anxiously but seeing his abstraction carried on, reassured, 'but I remembered the case, see. I was in the year above him at school. Didn't know him of course, didn't even notice him until he disappeared, but he was friends with a friend of mine, Wendy.'

Fenwick wasn't listening. He thanked her without noticing the words he used and she left. In the new silence of his office he noted the name on the cover of the file, leafed through it and pulled out a school photograph. Carefully, he pinned the picture of missing schoolboy Paul Hill squarely between that of Malcolm and Sam. It was as if he had found a missing link. Even in the garish technicolor of the old film, even when compared with the attractiveness of the other two boys, Paul Hill stood out with film-star beauty.

He combined the best of both boys: Malcolm's pale complexion; Sam's girlish neck; his own extraordinary eyes that seemed to invite the observer to share in a secret joke.

Fenwick sat down. There was a link, had to be. Someone somewhere had a predilection for pretty, pre-adolescent boys of a certain look and when he found them, they had a way of disappearing. He was suddenly very afraid for Sam Bowyer.

CHAPTER NINE

'I'll take the files over myself, sir; it's on my way home. That way I'll be able to brief Superintendent Quinlan personally.'

'Who do you think he'll assign as SIO, Fenwick? It will be Inspector Blite, I imagine, but I'd like to be sure. Can you suggest it?'

There was an infinitesimal pause.

'That might be tricky. I understand that he has two important cases coming to trial in the next three weeks plus four current investigations including a fatal stabbing last Saturday night.'

'You're well informed for someone who left more than six months ago. No, this case is perfect for Blite.'

'How about Inspector Nightingale, sir?' Fenwick suggested.

'Far too green.' Harper-Brown shook his head dismissively. 'This is murder after all, albeit an old one.'

Fenwick opened his mouth to argue but the ACC picked up a set of papers, a sure sign that he was dismissed. Then abruptly, he put them down again and removed the half-moon reading glasses he wore perched on the end of his nose.

'Fenwick, a word. I've been quite impressed by how you've handled your new role so far.'

'Thank you, sir.'

'But, and I mean this in a helpful way, you should pay attention to the way you offer preferment to certain officers.'

'Sir?'

'Do I have to spell it out for you?'

'I'm afraid so as I have no idea what you mean.'

Harper-Brown looked at him with exasperation.

'Very well, let me give you an example. Louise Nightingale. There is a suggestion that you showed her favouritism when you were in Harlden and that part of the reason she made such rapid progress to Inspector is because of this.'

'That's nonsense! I don't single people out for special treatment, never have done. If they get praise or opportunities it's because they've done a good job and I trust them. And besides—'

'Spare me the lecture, Andrew. I have no opinion of the veracity of what has been said, I am merely repeating it for your own good.'

'I'll bear it in mind, sir.'

'Make sure you do and be particularly careful whom you favour in your new role. It wouldn't do to get a reputation for...shall we call it, reverse sexual discrimination. That will be all.'

Fenwick managed to hold his tongue until he'd reached his office and shut the door. Then he delivered a stream of profanity that would have earned him a clip round the ear from his mother whatever his age, before counting to twenty and deciding it would take more than that for him to calm down. Two coffees later he stalked into the detectives' room, his bad mood obvious to anyone who knew him. There were three of the team at their desks and three heads suddenly dropped as if the files in front of them had become fascinating reading.

'Where's Alison?'

Sergeant Alison Reynolds was the head of the Choir Boy investigating team. A twenty-year veteran of the force who had worked in Vice and CID before transferring to Major Crimes, she was rumoured to live with three cats, was nobody's fool and disparaging enough of male advances to be called a lesbian behind her back. Fenwick had good reason to suspect that she wasn't, as he knew she had up until recently been married and had a son of twelve. He had found out by accident on a rare occasion when he'd gone to pick up Bess from school. Alison had seen him and introduced him to James and a wheelchair-bound man she said was her father. They'd neither of them mentioned the incident since, nor expressed any interest in the other's family life but Fenwick had asked around and discovered she was the sole wage-earner, her husband having left her the year before.

'Here.' The voice came from behind a filing cabinet.

'Got a minute?'

She followed him back to his office in silence, not being someone who employed small talk. Fenwick had found in Reynolds a good substitute for Cooper's diligent common sense and he had every confidence that she was the right officer to oversee the surveillance of Ball and Watkins, whatever the ACC might say about women.

'Push the door to and take a seat.'

'I hear we've lost the Eagleton case to Harlden.'

'Afraid so; we gave it our best shot but there's no obvious link to Choir Boy. But I've found another missing boy with the same looks as Malcolm Eagleton: Paul Hill, he's on the board behind you. Unfortunately, I can't connect him to Malcolm or any of our suspects, so it means nothing. Has there been anything interesting from surveillance in the last couple of days?'

'Ball went up to London yesterday but we lost him on the tube. He took the Victoria line north and jumped on the train at the last minute; we were left behind on the platform.'

'Who was tailing him?'

Reynolds squirmed in her chair. 'It was Clive but it wasn't his fault.'

'Hmm.' Fenwick still hadn't decided whether Clive was up to scratch and this was a black mark against him, whatever Alison said. 'Was the trip relevant?'

'It's his first break with routine for two months so it might be.'

'Or maybe he was visiting the latest exhibition at the Tate!' A trace of Fenwick's exasperation slipped into his tone and he saw her wince. 'Look, I'm not getting at you; I'm just bloody frustrated.'

'You and me both. So's the team. We've all tried our hardest to make something stick against Ball or Watkins but it's just no good.'

'Do you think we should stop watching them? It must be demoralising for you all.'

'It's as dull as any work I've ever done to tell you the truth and I know the others feel the same but,' she gave him a rare lopsided grin, 'and they'll kill me if they know I've said this, I think we should give it a week. If Ball makes another trip out of the ordinary we'll be ready for him and, who knows, he might just get careless.'

Fenwick looked down at his hands and exhaled slowly. The cost of the surveillance was becoming an embarrassment, impossible to hide from the ACC much longer, but she might be right and he hated the idea of simply giving up.

'Very well. Let's give it one more week and then we'll have to call it a day. Meanwhile, can you get a room set up with boards of all the photographs you've taken of Ball and Watkins? I want one last look at them to see if we've missed anything.'

'We've been through them again and again, sir. There are hundreds of them!'

'I know but maybe we're not seeing the wood for the trees.'

'Perhaps,' she sighed. 'We're all too close to this. I'll get it set up over the weekend for Monday morning.'

'Aren't you taking any time off?' Fenwick stopped short of making the obvious comment that her son would be home from school.

'I need the overtime and I'll make sure I'm home for Sunday but thanks for asking.'

* * *

Nightingale was trying to concentrate on catching up with the paperwork she'd let drift while preparing evidence for Maidment's remand hearing but her heart wasn't in it. Less than an hour before, the major had walked out of custody thanks to some excellent work from his lawyer who had convinced the magistrate that there was no chance he would break the conditions of his bail. It was an outcome she should have expected but it hurt anyway. She was thinking of leaving early when her phone rang.

'Nightingale.'

'It's me, Andrew. I'm in Harlden to see Quinlan. Thought I'd let you know.' He was in a bad mood, she could tell, and probably wanted cheering up. Tough; he'd picked the wrong day and the wrong person.

'Good for you.'

'I heard about Maidment.'

'Who hasn't?'

'What I heard is that CPS was completely satisfied with the job you did. They never really expected to have him remanded.'

'Oh?' Despite herself she perked up at his words, then suspicion bit her. 'You're not just saying that?'

'Hardly. Not my style.'

'True. Look, thanks; I appreciate the call.'

'Do you want a quick drink? I'm going home early so I could be ready in half an hour.'

'Twice in as many days, Andrew. What's got into you?'

'No, idea, but I need to unwind before I see the kids and you're as good as anybody.'

'That's better; indifference I can cope with. Sure, give me a call when you're ready.'

Cooper stopped by her office while she was reading the *Police Review* having given up any pretence of constructive work. He still looked drawn from the internal investigation. Dave

McPherson, the Police Federation rep, was with him, a surprising combination as she thought that the two of them disliked each other.

'I've just been telling Bob not to worry,' McPherson said, wandering into her office uninvited behind Cooper.

'Quite right,' she agreed, mildly irritated by their hovering. 'What Bob needs are a couple of decent cases to get his teeth into, that's all.'

'Nah, what he needs is a pint!' Dave slapped Cooper on the shoulder. 'We were just off. Want to join us?'

'Thanks, guys, but I'm busy tonight.' Her phone rang as if on cue. 'In fact...hello? Yes, I'll meet you downstairs. Don't forget your umbrella.' She picked up her bag and coat and encouraged them out of the door. 'Gotta go.'

Dave and Bob Cooper hovered by the plate-glass window that looked out onto the car park. They watched as Nightingale pulled on a hat and raised an umbrella with a distinctive matching check – well, distinctive to anyone other then the two fashion dinosaurs watching. Moments later, Fenwick emerged at a run from the side entrance, his collar up against the rain. She saw him and went over to share her brolly. After a moment they split up and dashed to their respective cars.

'Whatdya reckon?' Dave tapped the glass as the cars left the station in convoy. 'They at it or not?'

Cooper bristled, not just at his choice of words but also because he had been thinking the same thing and didn't like to find himself on the same level as McPherson. He shrugged.

'Odds are 2 to 1 on if you're interested.'

'In what?'

'Placing a bet. I'm keeping the book. It was 7 to 1 but then George saw them in town together a couple of weeks back. Had the kiddies with 'em and all. So, you know them both, yes or no?'

'I've no idea, Dave and I'm not that interested.'

McPherson gave him a knowing look and chuckled.

'Well, you know where to find me if you change your mind about the bet.'

'I think I'm going to pass on that drink tonight after all. I've just remembered that Doris wants me home pronto.'

'Suit yourself, Bob, the offer's always open. We'll be in the Dog and Duck if you change your mind.'

Cooper watched him go with relief. He'd almost gone for a second drink with Dave McPherson, the lowest of the low. What had he been thinking of?

At the Dog and Duck they were forced into a corner because the pub was busy with commuters fortifying themselves before completing the journey home.

'I'm fed up with this rain.' Nightingale looked at the pale skin of her arms and felt miserable.

'It's not like you to let the weather get you down.'

'Oh I know. It's this damned case.' She paused. It was too crowded to talk openly.

'Why does it bug you so much that he's...' he leant forward and whispered the words, '...out on bail?'

'I don't like him, Andrew. He's a sugar-coated phoney.'

They were talking in murmurs, heads close together.

'Hardly phoney to give most of his wealth away to his son and charity.'

'But he shot and almost killed a man,' she argued. 'I tell you, he's proud of what he's done and I think it excites him somehow.'

'He saved Bob's life and helped you arrest a vicious bastard who some would say deserved what he got.'

'Yes, but Maidment's not a decent old codger. Trust me!'

'OK, OK, calm down. I was just trying to make you feel better.'

'I realise that but I don't want to.' Nightingale sounded like a spoilt brat and he was about to tell her so when the same thought must have occurred to her because she looked embarrassed and then tried a laugh. 'Ignore me. I'm being a pain. So what brought you to Harlden?'

He told her, keeping his voice low so that it wouldn't carry over the loud buzz of chatter in the pub. They were standing so close together that neither of them noticed the arrival of Messrs Blite, McPherson and Wicklow on the other side of the bar, to be joined shortly afterwards by three other veterans of Harlden CID.

'So, do you reckon I'll get a look in as SIO on the Eagleton case?'

'You need to ask Quinlan, he's the one who's going to decide.'

'Yes, but you might've put a word in for me.'

Fenwick took a long, slow sip of beer and concluded that, on balance, it would be better not to tell her about the exchange with Harper-Brown that morning.

'Well?'

'The most obvious course of action isn't always the best,' he said cryptically. 'Come on, drink up, it's my round.'

'No thanks. I should be going.'

'Going out this evening?'

'No, staying in,' she replied but her cheeks coloured. 'I've a lot to do.'

It was still pouring with rain as they made a dash for their respective cars. There was nothing in their parting to suggest a relationship between them but that was irrelevant to the men at the bar. Dave McPherson had just shortened his odds and was limiting the size of individual bets. The only question still exercising his mind was how to gather substantive proof of their affair. If only he chose to apply the same diligence to his police work he would have been, in Quinlan's customary phrase, 'a damn fine officer'.

PART TWO

Paul woke up and they were still driving. The journey was taking for ever. He opened his mouth to shout at Bryan to stop but years of conditioning kept him quiet under the blanket. His resentment, simmering all day and stoked by the merciless teasing he had received at school, slowly hardened into a familiar hatred for Bryan and the disgusting things he made him do.

His formal sex education had been limited to an embarrassing lesson involving anatomically correct plastic models of the human sexual and reproductive organs the previous term, a mumbled conversation with his dad about 'protection' and a clip round the ear and a few stern remarks from his nan when she'd caught him kissing a girl after school near the local café. He knew more about sex than they could ever imagine and their coy words and assumption of his innocence had once made him feel superior. But now he knew that what he was doing with Bryan was very wrong and if his family and friends ever found out he would become an outcast.

He had a recurrent nightmare about his secret being discovered in which he was in the showers at the swimming baths with Bryan. They were naked and doing what Bryan liked best, except that Paul was trying to explain that this was a public place and someone might walk in. Bryan ignored his pleas and carried on but Paul could hear voices outside. They grew louder and he recognised his dad, then his best friend Victor, calling for him. There was a blue plastic curtain across the shower with a gap at the bottom and he could see feet coming nearer and nearer but Bryan still wouldn't stop.

The nightmare always shocked Paul awake as the curtain was pulled aside. He would lie in his bed in the creakily silent house trying to work out how to end it all. But Bryan had photographs, dozens of them. Paul's face was in full view though Bryan's was blacked out and it was obvious what they were doing.

The first time he saw the pictures he'd cried and Bryan had called him a sissy. At their next meeting Bryan had shown them again and talked about what it had been like the first time, when Paul was a 'little boy'. Looking at them added a new twist to their ritual. Paul hated it; he hated what he was made to do and the person he had become, but most of all he hated Bryan.

Sometimes he fantasised about killing him. He had started to carry a knife, a sharp one with a wooden handle that his mum had bought from Woolworths years ago. A steak knife she called it. In his fantasies he would stick it into Bryan while he screamed like a pig, or chop bits off him slowly. But in reality Paul cut himself, little nicks on his arms and legs that he passed off as scratches, the result of falls from his bike.

At night he put the knife under his pillow so that it was there when he woke from his nightmare in a sweat with the long hours to dawn stretching ahead of him. That morning he had put the blade at the bottom of his school bag and packed his holiday project, reading list and sports kit on top.

A smile twitched his lips upwards as he slipped his hand down the side of his duffle bag and touched the familiar wooden handle. He let his fingers rest there, comforted despite the jolting of the car and smell of exhaust fumes that were making him feel sick. He closed his eyes and tried not to think about what was going to happen next. Paul drifted into a daydream where he forced Bryan to leave him alone by using photographs of his own, taken with the Instamatic camera he'd bought on holiday. It was packed in his duffle bag next to the knife but, confronted now with reality, he didn't know whether he would have the courage to use it.

The car slowed and his stomach tightened. There was a familiar sound of large gates being opened and he realised then that Bryan had lied to him. They weren't just driving somewhere deeper into the woods. He'd been brought to Nathan's house, though Paul knew that wasn't his real name. The idea made him want to cry. He hated 'Nathan' even more than Bryan because despite his small build and polished manners, he was a sadistic bully. The gates clanged shut behind them. As Bryan eased the car forward Paul sneaked his hand out from beneath the blanket and aimed the camera blindly through what he hoped was the rear window. He pressed the button, wound the film on and pressed again.

Bryan stopped the car, climbed out and walked away without letting him out. Paul heard a distant murmur of voices and sat up in a half crouch. Without looking he aimed the lens through the side window towards the house where he imagined the men to be standing. He snapped a picture and risked another just before Bryan returned to the car. By the time the back door was unlocked the camera was safely back in his bag.

'Leave that bag with your bike.'

'Can't I bring it with me? It's got all my homework and stuff.'

Bryan shrugged as if he didn't care one way or another and Paul lifted the duffle bag onto his shoulder, his right hand casually draped inside the half-open top. The house was large, with a landscaped garden and swimming pool. The first time he had come here he'd been eleven and in awe of his surroundings; now it was familiar and he was conscious only of the locked gates and high walls around him.

Paul followed Bryan along the terrace and over an expanse of neat lawn to the pool. It was screened by a trellis that acted as a windbreak while providing privacy. Within its shelter three men were leaning against the poolside bar. Two were tanned and already in swimming trunks. The third was their host. He recognised Paul and gave him a welcoming wave.

'Paul. I'm so glad you could find time to come and join us. I'd like you to meet my friends – Alec and Joe. They live abroad but

are visiting for a few days. I've told them all about you and they really wanted to meet you. Say hello.'

Paul looked at the strangers. Joe was tall and looked like a film star. He had very white teeth and a friendly, foxy smile. Alec obviously thought himself a tough guy. He was short and square and ignored him.

'Here's your drink, a Coke with ice – that's right, isn't it?'

He saw the men exchange glances and knew that there would be a large shot of vodka in it. It was meant to be a secret but he'd worked it out years ago. The alcohol no longer made him woozy unless they gave him more than one drink but it did help him to relax.

'Come over here, Paul.' Joe raised an arm and then dropped it lightly on his shoulder as he came to stand between the two men.

'You can put that bag down; no time for homework now!'

Everyone but Alec laughed and the strap was eased off his shoulder.

'Bloody hell, it weighs a ton!' Alec's voice was coarse and he swore, which Nathan never did.

Paul sipped his drink and searched – without success – for signs that there would be other boys joining them. He started to panic. Surely they couldn't all want him. That had never happened before. He looked around nervously for his bag and saw it lying on a sun lounger. It had fallen onto its side and he was worried in case the camera fell out.

'Drink up; that's it, then you can have a swim. It's a hot day.' Nathan sounded like a kindly uncle. Perhaps he didn't want him today. Perhaps he only wanted to show Paul off to his friends, like a curious specimen.

'I haven't got my trunks.'

They thought that very funny. Joe lifted his hand from his shoulder and ruffled Paul's hair.

'No need to be shy,' he said, 'you're among friends. I tell you *what, why don't we all go skinny-dipping?'*

He put his drink on the bar and pulled down his trunks. Paul saw a flash of white buttocks as he sprinted to the edge of the pool and executed a perfect dive. Bryan joined him. They stood in the pool, water up to their chests, their legs foreshortened, and looked expectantly at Alec, Nathan and Paul.

'Come on!'

Alec jumped in with his trunks on creating a tidal wave that washed over the terrace and splashed Paul's blazer and school trousers.

'Now you're wet anyway. Why don't you take off those damp clothes and spread them out. They should be dry for your journey home.' Nathan came up close to him, hands raised to touch him. Paul backed away until his calves hit the sun lounger and he sat down abruptly next to his bag.

'I don't want to.' He could feel tears in his eyes.

'It's not like you to be shy.' Nathan still sounded kind. 'Is it because there are four of us? You don't need to worry about that. You know I wouldn't let anyone hurt you, not here in my house.'

Paul shook his head as his mouth turned down and a tear escaped onto his cheek.

'Oh, don't cry.' Nathan knelt in front of him, a hand on his knee, stroking. 'Everything's going to be fine. You'll love being in the water; it'll make it all so easy. You wait, you'll really enjoy yourself.'

'Come on, Purse, for fuck's sake! I thought you said he was ready and willing.' Alec shouted from the pool and Nathan turned on him angrily.

'It's Nathan, remember? Keep it clean and keep quiet. He's only startled but he's a good boy, aren't you, Paul? Ah, I know what you like – here.'

Nathan took two crisp ten pound notes from his wallet and placed them carefully on his leg. Paul's right hand had strayed into his school bag and he refused to pick up the money. He'd grown used to the availability of so much easy wealth but it meant little to him now because he'd realised too late that it had never been easy money. What was about to happen would be horrible and embarrassing, not least because he could no longer stop his body from reacting. He was mortally ashamed.

Nathan took the money and folded it into Paul's blazer pocket.

'There'll be more later.'

'There'll be more now.'

Joe lifted himself easily from the pool and went over to a nearby chair. He wiped his hands dry and reached into a sports bag.

'Here. Have you ever seen one of these before?' He lifted up a large note. 'It's twenty pounds.'

Paul kept his eyes away from the man's naked body.

'I know. I had one from my nan when I won the first year prize.' Paul didn't know what he was boasting about, the money or the school prize.

'Good for you! How about this one, then?' Joe passed him a note with $50 on it.

'Is it real?' Paul held it up to the sky to check for the metal strip, his school bag momentarily forgotten.

'Oh yes. It's what Alec and I are paid in where we come from, and there's more...if you're a good boy.'

Paul turned the money over in his hands for a long time then looked up at Nathan and Joe, tears still wet on his smooth cheeks.

'Adorable,' Joe murmured, 'just like you said.'

'And a very good boy too,' Nathan agreed, wiping the wetness away from Paul's face with a clean white handkerchief. 'Come on, my dear; let's swim while it's still warm.'

Paul put the money away and started to undress. Behind him in the depths of the pool Alec leant across to Bryan and muttered in a low voice.

'You found us a fucking expensive whore. He'd better be worth it; you know how I hate to be disappointed.'

Bryan tried not to look concerned.

CHAPTER TEN

The phone call was worrying.

As he replaced the receiver, the man in the immaculate white shirt with diamond-studded cufflinks reflected that it had been years since he'd heard anything of Alec. Although he knew he was living on the south coast less than thirty miles away, they had no reason to contact each other, quite the opposite. The secrets they shared were better left dead and buried and they both knew it. But now one of the men who worked for him had been approached by Alec, who'd used their historic association to try and put pressure on him for help. It was unexpected and particularly unwelcome as, since Joe had got religion and told him he could no longer handle Alec, he had assumed the responsibility himself. He had thought it would be simple.

But Alec hadn't changed with age. The man was still a risk-taker with appetites he found hard to control, rather like the Maidment of old really but with a predilection for a different type of flesh.

Thinking of the major made him frown. The man was too principled to be trusted and were it not for his own knowledge of certain...how to describe it...indiscretions in his youth, Maidment would have been a difficult man to control. As it was, he'd found it surprisingly easy to encourage him to push his scruples to one side when it mattered.

No, Maidment had given his word and was aware of what would happen to his precious reputation if he so much as whispered a hint of what he knew. Alec was another matter. The man who was so proud of his diamonds couldn't understand how he had once allowed Alec to get so close. Of course they had interests that some might consider shared but Alec's tastes were gross whereas his own were refined. It was a relationship that he deeply regretted. There was no such thing as a code of honour where Alec was concerned. The law of dog-eat-dog governed his little world, which meant that if he ever ended up in the wrong hands he would be a liability.

What to do about Alec? The thought preoccupied him as he ate the supper his housekeeper had prepared for him before going home to continue whatever moribund life she led. He imagined it to involve back-to-back TV soap operas interspersed with trips to the pub with that tub of lard husband of hers. Still, she was a discreet and efficient worker and her husband managed the limited work required of him outside without breaking anything or getting in the way, so he allowed them to manage his household needs.

He left the tray with his dirty crockery next to the sink to be dealt with in the morning, even though it would have been easy to stack the dishwasher himself. He didn't stoop to menial tasks, having lost the habit after years in the Far East. His fingernails were manicured, the skin on his hands soft and perfectly kept, rather like his life.

His ordered existence was exactly to his liking, with interference from no one. He had power and was known, by those who needed to know, to be ruthless if crossed. Over the years he'd done precisely as he wanted, and had even grown rich on the back of it. But now Alec had surfaced and made contact; he really should have known better.

William had rung him two days before with the news that Alec was in town asking for a favour. Apparently his regular supplier had let him down and he needed goods urgently. William had sent him off with a warning to keep away but had then wondered whether it wouldn't have been better to help Alec out; at least that way they'd know what he was up to. It was an interesting thought and the man mulled it over as he sipped his iced whisky, so cold that it numbed his lips, just the way he liked it.

There were only three choices really: to get rid of Alec once and for all – tempting but very risky. He could humour him, give him enough to keep him away from other contacts, but that had risks and would strengthen their connection. Or he could ignore him; after all what sort of a threat was he really? A tiny cog in a machine of which he had limited understanding. Except that Alec had been involved in one of his very few lapses of judgement and that made him a liability.

He decided to leave things alone for a few days and see what happened; there was no rush. He knew where Alec was and could arrange for him to be dealt with however he chose, whenever he chose. In the meantime, he had his own needs to consider. William's call had awoken in him desires of his own and it was time he paid him a visit. He owned the house William ran and enjoyed owner's perks. Yes, he could definitely hear London calling.

CHAPTER ELEVEN

Sam stood in the corner of the room and shivered. It was his turn next. The other boys were all occupied so whoever came through that door would be his. Or rather, he'd be theirs. He stared fixedly at the handle, waiting for it to turn, silently begging it not to but knowing such thoughts were fanciful. It was only seven o'clock. The wash from the early commuter rush had peaked and flowed over the margins of the establishment and now it waited for the evening wave.

That Sam hadn't been chosen was both good and bad. Good because it meant that he was still fresh, his mouth tasted of toothpaste, his skin was clean. Bad because in the few days he'd been in the house he had already learnt that it was never a good sign to be last. He sniffed, his nose raw from his recent addiction. Mucus was a constant problem and one of his frequent nightmares involved suffocation as he choked.

At least he still looked good. His skin was clear, hair glossy, body slim and smooth. Unlike some, his eyes remained bright, the whites shiny. The customers that came here liked his looks.

He shuddered again, thinking of the world outside that door and the way of life he'd touched during chilling nights hanging around King's Cross station before William had found, fed, washed and clothed him. He'd been grateful at the time. Only later had he realised there was a price and what it was.

Despite the realities of life on the streets, Sam had run away twice on the first day. Once by breaking a fanlight in the upstairs bathroom, the second time by dashing through a punter's legs before anyone could stop him. That seemed a long time ago, although it was hard to keep track of time in this place. He'd been behaving like a kid back then he told himself; he was smarter now. It didn't pay to run away. William always found you and had ways of hurting you so that it never showed. He'd learnt his lesson the hard way, just as he had all the tricks of the trade after that; how to please, how to pretend to be pleased and, most importantly, how to sham pain before it became real.

Some of them really liked you to scream and, for a reason he didn't understand, he seemed to appeal to men like that. William called it a speciality and made sure he was cared for especially well after sessions that went bad. They weren't meant to leave marks on him, that was the rule and they had to pay extra if they did, but some of them couldn't help themselves once they started. They were barred if they did it more than once, even if they offered to pay for the privilege, because William didn't like his property damaged; it put you out of action for too long. Sam closed his eyes and hugged himself in an unconscious gesture.

Why hadn't he been picked tonight? It was bad news. The last boy who'd ended up the regular tail-ender, as William called the last one standing, had been Jack. It was a while since he'd seen Jack around. Rumour was that he'd been pushed out. No one knew what happened to you when you were finished here, only that you didn't come back.

'Sam!'

He jumped as William's hand landed heavily on his shoulder.

'Stop huddling, you look like a whipped puppy.'

'I'm cold, that's all,' Sam said and rubbed his bare arms briskly to prove it.

'Here.' William threw him a jumper. 'No, don't put it on, you daft twit, just wrap it round your shoulders. Not long to wait now. He said he'd be here at seven as long as his train was on time.'

Sam did a look. It was one of several he'd perfected since arriving that were meant to convey various permutations of innocence, cheekiness, arousal and curiosity. This was his innocent/curious look, which usually worked.

'What?'

But not this time. William stared at him blankly.

'You said "he",' he ventured timidly, aware that the question might cost him. William knew endless ways to inflict pain.

'Oh.' He shrugged indifferently and Sam relaxed. 'The man we're waiting for. I've promised you to him. He's our most important customer so you'd better be on your best behaviour.'

'Course!' Relief flooded Sam. He wasn't last, he'd been reserved.

A smile transformed his face and William nodded approvingly.

'Good boy. You're his type. Make sure you behave, not like that chump Jack. He really disappointed him last time.'

He reached over and squeezed Sam's left cheek hard, leaving a pink impression on his white skin. Sam didn't so much as blink.

'Better even you up,' William said and pinched the right side with his other hand. 'He likes dark hair with a pale complexion.' He bent down so that his nose was an inch from Sam's. 'You're to tell him you're new, got it? He won't like it if he knows I've been keeping you a secret. And he's very, very particular, so be nice.'

'Promise,' Sam said.

At that moment the door opened and William shot upright, his customer smile on his face.

'Nathan!' he boomed with ingratiating good humour. 'Welcome, it's been too long.'

'What do you expect, Bill? You let me down last time. There are plenty of other places only too happy to please.'

'A small misunderstanding. The boy concerned has been dealt with. Believe me, you won't be disappointed this time.'

'We'll see. Where is he?'

Nathan sounded angry and Sam's smile faltered. With a heroic effort he corrected his expression.

'Just here. Samuel, come forward, my dear, and meet Nathan.' He removed the jumper from around Sam's shoulders with an irritable flick.

Sam shivered in his vest and stepped out of the shadow into the pool of light at the centre of the room, his smile firmly in place.

'Hmm,' was all Nathan said as he walked slowly around Sam, inspecting him. He reached out a finger and prodded one of his arms. 'More muscle than I like.' The finger lingered on him. 'But the skin's good. Bend,' he instructed. Sam folded at the waist.

Nathan barked a laugh as frightening as any snarl.

'No, I meant your head, boy; I want to see your neck. Bloody obedient, Bill – I like that.'

'He's the best,' William said and Sam's cheeks flushed.

He hung his head. The man's fingers touched the back of his neck, slipped down his vertebrae slowly as if counting them. Without warning he gripped Sam's throat fast as a snake, choking him hard.

William didn't say a word. Sam's eyes watered as he tried desperately not to moan and gasp for air. After a long moment Nathan let go and Sam gulped in oxygen, keeping his breathing as silent as possible.

'Yes,' said Nathan, 'he'll do.'

Sam put on his smile.

The house appeared deserted when Fenwick walked in. It was the end of another long day. His children had eaten their tea, watched as much television as his housekeeper would allow and must have been sent upstairs early to get ready for bed. Alice heard him close the front door and came to the top of the stairs, a pile of laundry on her arm. He could tell from her face that she'd had a tough day. With the children home from school for the holidays her workload more than doubled and he felt a twinge of guilt that he'd not managed to return at a decent hour at all in the past week. At least his mother would be coming to stay shortly to give Alice a well-deserved break.

'I'm not sure where Bess is, in her bedroom I think. Chris is still in the bath; he just won't come out and I've had enough of his moods for one day.'

'I'll go and have a word.'

He walked into the steamy bathroom to find Chris dive-bombing a plastic boat with a dinosaur. His son's back was towards him. At eight he still had the soft skin of a baby. Inevitably, Fenwick thought of Malcolm Eagleton and Sam Bowyer. As his son and daughter grew from babies into small people he was finding crimes against children increasingly hard to deal with, though no one who worked with him would have guessed.

Across the force he was known for his self-control and his absolute views of right and wrong. They called him the Zebra behind his back because he was so black and white but he was also acknowledged to be rigidly fair.

He looked at Chris's slender neck, the bones of his spine visible beneath the perfect brown skin, and shuddered. Such innocence. If anyone ever soiled his son's simple beauty he felt that he would kill them. The unexpected depth of his emotion caught him off guard and he reacted with typical bluntness to compensate.

'Boo!'

'Dad! You made me jump.' Chris flashed him one of his looks.

Fenwick removed his jacket and squatted beside the bath.

'So, how are you?'

'All right.'

Chris beat the water with his stegosaurus and splashes went

everywhere. Fenwick ignored the spreading damp on his shirt sleeves and kissed the top of his son's head.

'How was your swimming lesson?'

'Boring. I don't like Mr Sells, he's not nice.'

'You'll get used to him.'

'He made my friend Nick cry.'

'Oh dear,' Fenwick ruffled Chris's sticky wet hair, 'how did that happen?'

'He made us put our faces in the water and Nick doesn't like that.'

'But you didn't mind?'

Something approaching pride flickered on Chris's face.

'I can swim underwater for three strokes now.'

'That's very good.'

Chris beamed at him and Fenwick bent forward to kiss his forehead again. It was so rare for Chris to excel at anything that it was a double delight when he did.

'You'll be better than your sister soon, even though she's older than you.'

Chris nodded decisively and returned his attention to making his giant lizard do things that no palaeontologist would have believed possible.

'What else was good about today?'

Chris had to think hard.

'We had sausages for lunch and I went round to Gary's 'cos he got a new computer for his birthday.'

'He's only eight.'

'Nine. Can I have one for mine, Dad? I'll be nine soon.'

'We'll see. Now, about your birthday, we haven't got long to organise something. What would you like to do?'

In previous years his withdrawn son had refused to have a party and they'd gone to McDonald's as a family instead. Chris's face scrunched up in thought.

'I'd like a party,' he said eventually, to his father's delight. It meant that he was making friends at last.

'That's great...'

'...As long as it's better than Tony Easter's. He's always going on about how much money his dad has, and about their holidays, and his mum always makes brilliant costumes for school.' Chris's face twisted with dislike. 'He's a real show-off.'

Fenwick was shocked at his son's naked envy and disappointed by the desire to show off that was behind his wish for a party.

'What sort of party did Tony have?'

'It was awesome! He had a bouncy castle, a clown that'd been on TV and we got brilliant presents at the end.'

Chris pulled a plastic basket of toys from the side of the bath into the scummy water and began to sink them as Fenwick's mental image of a picnic on the lawn followed by games of hide and seek and blind man's bluff faded. He didn't want to let his son down but he refused to pander to one-upmanship. He blamed the parents; look at what it must be doing to their children's sense of values. Heaven help them when they discovered real materialism as teenagers.

'What if we had a party, a nice one, but without a bouncy castle?'

Chris shook his head savagely and drowned a pterodactyl under a doll that Fenwick realised belatedly belonged to Bess.

'Hey! That's not your toy. I've told you before about taking Bess's dolls; you know she gets upset when you spoil them.'

He pulled the sodden Barbie, complete with drooping bridal veil, wedding dress and disintegrating bouquet, from under the water. His son's ears went bright red, a sure sign that he was about to make a fuss. Fenwick bit the inside of his lip in frustration. He should have known better than confront Chris directly as it brought on his worst behaviour.

'Look, if you promise not to do it ever again, I'll dry Barbie off in the airing cupboard and hopefully Bess won't even notice.'

Chris refused to look at him. As he grew older, whenever he was caught doing something wrong, his defence was to become angry. His teacher had taken Fenwick to one side at a parents' evening to suggest that Chris was a confused and sad little boy, still deeply affected by his mother's death. She thought the anger that was starting to replace his moody silences was really directed inwardly against himself and had suggested family counselling. Fenwick had told her bluntly that her well-intentioned remarks were unnecessary and that he could take care of his own children, thank you. He'd then avoided her for the rest of the evening.

Looking at his son now he wondered for the first time whether she'd been right. Was his determination to raise his children without help born out of protectiveness and his own insecurity rather than what he'd thought was plain common sense? Love for his son rushed through him and he reached out and gave him a hug, ignoring the water that stained his tie.

'Come on, you're starting to wrinkle. Let me dry you and then we can have a hot chocolate together while I read you a story.'

Chocolate of any kind was a treat as Alice didn't believe in sweets. Chris remained silent as Fenwick lifted him up but when he draped a towel around him and started to tickle him dry, the wriggles became giggles and he was back to his normal self by the time they went down to the kitchen.

Bess was sitting in her dressing gown at the large deal table in the middle of the family room. He noticed that her feet no longer swung above the tiled floor. When had her legs grown so long?

'I thought you were in bed, young lady.'

'Daddy!' She leapt up from the table and gave him a hug. 'Urgh, you're all wet.' She pulled herself away quickly and sat down again.

'Thanks to your brother. Do you want some hot chocolate? I'm making some.'

'With foamy milk?'

'Of course.'

He pulled the mugs from the cupboard and measured chocolate powder into them with only the tiniest sprinkling of sugar for Chris. Then he steamed and frothed the milk using the cappuccino machine.

'What's that you're doing?' he asked Bess.

'A project.'

Fenwick's heart sank.

'When was it due in?' he asked, dreading the answer.

'The day we get back.'

'But that's five weeks away – why the rush now?'

'Because I want it to be the best project ever in the whole school,' she said righteously, prompting Chris to mimic her until Fenwick told him to stop.

'Good for you,' he said, hoping that he didn't sound as relieved as he felt. He'd burnt the midnight oil on too many school projects to hear the word without wincing.

'But,' she sighed dramatically and leant back in her chair, 'I've only just started and I need to do at least ten sides to get a good mark. Mrs Parry said so.'

'Do you need help?'

She twisted her head and smiled up at him from under her fringe, looking exactly like her mother.

'Would you? I need some stuff off the Internet, and I've got to have at least a page in my own handwriting so that will take ages, and draw a picture, and trace a map...'

'What *is* this project? It sounds enormous.'

She turned to the front page and pointed to the beautifully designed graphics, which must have taken her hours to create. He read the colourful title:

HARLDEN MY HOME TOWN
WITH ITS FAMOUS HISTORY, HERITAGE AND HOSPITALITY

'Did you make that up?'

'Yes.' She glowed with pride. 'I invented the alliteration myself,' she said, trying unsuccessfully to make her choice of vocabulary sound casual.

'Good word.'

'Oh, I know lots more. Do you want to hear them?'

'Boring!' Chris gave an exaggerated yawn.

'Perhaps another time. Here's your chocolate.'

And despite the sugar rush they both remained calm and well behaved until bedtime, turning the evening into one of those that reminded Fenwick of why it was worth trying to be home at a reasonable time occasionally.

But after the children were tucked up in bed his mind returned to work. He couldn't get the faces of Malcolm, Paul and Sam out of his mind. He'd been forced to hand the investigation into Malcolm's death over to Harlden but he'd kept a copy of more than the poor boy's photograph. A duplicate of the whole file lay in his desk drawer; in his mind it was as current as the Choir Boy material that now swamped MCS. There was a link, his gut told him, and he felt certain that The Downs Golf Club, with its illustrious members, was involved somehow.

As he drained the glass of the wine he'd allowed himself with his solitary dinner, he made a silent promise to the boys' families that he was not going to give up on them, no matter what it meant, nor how many rules he would need to bend to live up to his commitment.

CHAPTER TWELVE

The congregation at Harlden parish church, St Magnus the Martyr, was considerably larger and noisier than usual despite the weather. Instead of quiet conversation or contemplative prayer, the nave was filled with sounds of righteous indignation. One of their most respected members had been accused of attempted murder and all for saving the life of a bungling policeman!

Sympathetic glances were cast surreptitiously, like loose change to a beggar, at Major Maidment's back as he sat three rows from the front in his customary pew. Margaret Pennysmith sat beside him like an overprotective poodle. From time to time someone would walk down and pat him on the shoulder or shake his hand. The gestures of support provoked a brief smile from lips that were drawn too tight but his eyes remained shadowed.

The atmosphere was similar but the outrage more explicit at the golf club, where expletives against the police were loud despite the assistant chief constable's presence at a corner table.

Maidment was served extra roast beef and two of the chef's excellent Yorkshire puddings. He was plied with drinks and wasn't allowed to buy a round. While he could manage the alcohol the food was an embarrassment. The foil-wrapped parcel of pink sliced beef that was thrust into his hands as he left the table wouldn't be used 'for a nice sandwich' at suppertime but rather to feed next-door's dog, a dachshund that was gaining weight almost as quickly as the major was losing it.

The whisky in the bar afterwards went down too easily and by five o'clock he wasn't in a fit state to drive. Lieutenant-Colonel Edwards, an old friend, offered him a lift.

'No thank you. I remember when you took me home in 1982 after we'd celebrated England's win over Australia. By golly, Broad was on good form; I can still remember his 162. I also recall that we almost ended up in the river because you were plastered. Just because you can walk and talk straight no matter what you drink doesn't mean you can still drive straight!'

'You and your bloody memory, Maidment. Don't you ever forget anything?'

'I can't remember.'

It was his first attempt at a joke in a long time.

The following day the major visited Stanley, driven by guilt and duty in equal measure. His old comrade was back in bed, a drip in his arm. Stanley's eyes flickered open when Maidment arrived but closed again almost at once. Remission, that fickle visitor, bringer of hope laced with fear, had departed without warning as suddenly as it had arrived.

An orderly brought tea in thick green cups on matching saucers. The major drank his while Stanley's cooled on the bedside locker. He finished his cup and waited another fifteen minutes before he stood to leave. Stanley woke with a start and stared at him in confusion. Then his eyes cleared and his lips twitched in a warm smile at odds with his pallor.

'All present and correct, sir.'

Maidment couldn't tell whether it was a joke or morphine-induced hallucination.

'Not a peep out of the bastards all night, Captain.'

Maidment rallied quickly.

'Very good, Sergeant. Keep those eyes open.'

'They won't sneak past me, sir!'

'I'm certain they won't; good man.'

Stanley's eyes closed as abruptly as they'd opened and Maidment eased his way around the bottom of the bed towards the door.

'She hasn't come, you know, my girl.'

Stanley was back in the present, speaking with none of his previous bravado.

'Hasn't she? I tried, old man, I really did.'

'Would you see her again for me, Major? Please?'

He could see the suspicion of tears on Stanley's lower lashes.

'She was my own special girl, my little rosebud.' Stanley's voice broke and he coughed in an attempt to cover the breach of etiquette. 'Do it for your old pal.'

Maidment thought of the dreary house with its miasma of decay and of the woman inside it with manic eyes. Most of all, he thought about her eyes. God could be cruel in his choice of punishment.

He'd expected to be able to serve his penance by doing good deeds for whatever remained of his life but it was obvious now that much more was required. He was being forced to confront a mother's agony born out of endless uncertainty for which he felt responsible.

'I'll go back and try again.' He patted the old soldier's dry hand and watched the blue lips whisper a thank you.

It was the last time he saw Stanley alive. Around lunchtime the next day, before he could revisit the daughter, news reached him that his old friend had died. He was surprised to learn from the relative who called him that the funeral had already been arranged for the coming Thursday. Apparently, a cousin worked in the funeral trade and had been planning ahead, with only the date to ink in.

On the day of the funeral he pulled his dark suit out of the cupboard, brushed it, pressed the trousers and tied the regimental tie over a laundered white shirt. He pinned a black armband around his sleeve. His medals stayed in the drawer. No doubt some would be worn today but he thought it a touch pompous for the occasion. There was an element of routine in his dressing, the gestures increasingly practised in recent years. He gave a last buff to his shoes and left the house, clasping his hat in his hand.

The chapel of the crematorium was full with the rustle of dry whispers as old friends shook hands too firmly and exchanged platitudes they'd used too many times before.

Maidment tried to ignore the hush as he moved forward. He'd been asked to speak. His addresses in memory of departed comrades had become something of a tradition at their funerals. A perfect memory meant that he was able to conjure up the ghost of the younger man as he recalled jokes, acts of bravery or compassion, and anecdotes that briefly brought the deceased back to life.

Despite the nerves he suffered beforehand and the effect they had on his digestion, he was usually grateful for the opportunity to pay a final compliment to an old friend. Today, the guilt and fear that had been eroding his spirits since he'd learnt that Stanley was Paul Hill's grandfather had robbed him of the gift of spontaneous, kind reminiscences. He tapped the pages of notes in his pocket and tried to convince himself that he wouldn't freeze when he rose to speak.

'Maidment! Over here.'

He turned to see Edwards beckon him to an empty seat at the front; he was wearing his medals.

'Bin saving it for you. Expect you're speaking? Me too, a few words as his senior officer, y'know.' He had reached the rank of lieutenant-colonel, a fact to which he drew the major's attention whenever the opportunity arose.

The major swallowed bile. He looked across at the family

mourners in the opposite seats, didn't recognise anyone and started to breathe easier.

Stanley's coffin was close by. Maidment concentrated on it and closed his eyes. His silent prayers for forgiveness were interrupted by a flutter of excitement. Faces turned towards the back of the chapel and swivelled forward again with expressions of disapproval. Sarah Hill had arrived. She was wearing an old camel-hair coat and worn boots. A plastic shopping bag was clutched to her chest protectively.

A woman stood up and helped her carefully into the front pew, easing aside other relatives reluctant to make room. Maidment snapped his eyes front and focused on the blue curtain that screened the hole that led to the fire. His bowels constricted and he had to concentrate hard to bring them back under control.

Throughout the service he could feel the woman's eyes on him. When he stood up his knees were shaking. He unfolded his notes and uncharacteristically read from them. His voice choked slightly and he noticed sympathetic glances. He started by reciting a poem that Stanley had written on his retirement from the regiment, an easy trick but it got them laughing. After that the words flowed more easily. Edwards stood up later, sounding suitably grand as he offered condolences to the family. Then there was a hymn and a prayer and it was all over. As the coffin slid along the rollers and the blue curtain parted the major closed his eyes.

Edwards gave him a lift to the White Harte where the wake was to be held.

'Can't believe this rain,' he remarked, as he sliced through standing water and turned into the car park. 'You were amusing once again, Maidment, though I was surprised to see you upset.'

'He was honest and decent, and no more inclined to swing the lead than any other man.'

'Yes, but he had a cruel sense of humour. D'you remember

when he switched Sergeant Cole's vitamin pills for senna tablets. Poor bugger thought he had dysentery.' Edwards' shoulders juddered as he laughed without sound.

'Now Cole *was* a bastard. I seem to recall that nobody bothered to tell him about the switch until the bottle had run out and he thought he was dying. Lucky for Stanley he'd moved on by then otherwise we'd have been attending his funeral a long time go.'

'Too true.' Edwards turned into the car park, narrowly missing a teenage girl who clearly hadn't dressed for the rain. 'Bloody hell! Your type, wouldn't you say?' Edwards leered at the major who averted his eyes.

Maidment scanned the room as he entered and exhaled in relief. There was no sign of Sarah's distinctive mane of unruly greying hair. There were a few muckers and mates from the regiment. Inevitably, they'd congregated around the stairs that led to the bar as Stanley's niece, the organiser of the wake, was a rigid teetotaller and had arranged soft drinks and tea only. Undeterred, a supply chain had been established and reinforcements flowed along it with comforting regularity.

The major drank freely; he wasn't driving and his appetite for alcohol had grown recently. The whisky dulled his reaction to Edwards' increasingly off-colour jokes. After an hour he decided that he'd had enough. There was a bus that he might catch if he left at once. He bade a solemn goodbye to the principal mourners.

She was waiting for him in the shelter of the porch outside.

'Major, wait; I need to talk to you.'

'Mrs Hill, my condolences but I'm in somewhat of a hurry.'

'I must talk to you; I think you can help me.'

'Madam, I am equally certain that I cannot.'

'That's so typical of your sort,' she almost spat at him. 'All fine words but I should've known you'd be as bad as the rest.'

Maidment felt the heat of embarrassment in his face.

'If I thought I could assist you in any way, I would – but really, I can't.'

'But I need you to find him. These are the papers about his disappearance: press cuttings, the book that bastard wrote – terrible things he said in there about my boy but I kept it anyway. Here.'

She thrust the carrier bag towards him but he ignored it.

'My dear woman…'

'Don't you "dear woman" me! You're rich and privileged. If I'd had your advantages I'd've found my Paul by now.'

'Mrs Hill, the police looked into Paul's disappearance very thoroughly. If they haven't found him in the last twenty-five years then there's nothing left for me to do.'

'The police? Oh sure, they were all over it at first but then…' Her eyes filled and she scrubbed at them with her sleeve before opening her handbag in a fruitless search.

Maidment offered her a square of laundered linen that made her white blouse look grey. His bus was long gone but he was still desperate to leave her, to return to the privacy of his house where he could pour himself a whisky in an attempt to silence his own demons.

'I'm sorry, it's difficult still but it's important you know everything if you're going to track him down.'

'I…'

She ignored him and carried on.

'They did look for him at first but then the stories started. I don't know where they came from; wicked lies but they kept repeating them. I blame the school, that headmistress never did like me and Gordon – that's Paul's dad as was. Useless man; he gave up searching after a year. It's as well he went away. If he'd stayed I don't know what I'd have done, seeing him sitting in that chair all day.'

Her eyes radiated hatred. He understood now the ripple of unease that had greeted her arrival at the funeral. Over the years she must have approached every member of the family, convinced that they would be able to succeed where she had failed in the quest to find her son. It was better after all not to become involved, to be strong now.

'I regret that I cannot help you, Mrs Hill.'

'But you must.' She clutched his hand, which he withdrew fastidiously.

'No.' The old firmness of command was back in his voice and she recognised that she'd lost. The light that had flared briefly in her eyes died and they went flat again.

'At least take the papers and read them. You'll agree the police failed me and my boy. Please?'

Her pleading was pathetic. It had more impact than her anger but he hardened his heart.

'They'll be better looked after if you keep them,' he said gently but she thrust the ageing carrier bag into his arms and let go.

He caught it reflexively then realised what he'd done. She was too defeated to acknowledge her small victory and he walked away without another word.

CHAPTER THIRTEEN

The last weeks of July went on record as the wettest since records began. Bookings for holidays abroad soared as parents faced the awful prospect of being caged with their little dears under canvas or in poorly heated holiday homes across the UK, their only escape steamed-up cars and yet another soggy picnic.

Fenwick had asked his mother to stay and Alice was taking a much-needed break to travel by coach to Germany for a trip down the Rhine with her sister. His mother had left a sunny Edinburgh on the train and woken up to floods north of London followed by a thirty-minute wait for a tube to take her to Victoria. Her mood improved a little on seeing her only grandchildren, whom she adored but would never let it show for fear of making them soft. When Fenwick cooked supper on her first night and opened a bottle of wine to go with it she almost softened.

He was her only child and the only male Fenwick of his generation but they had never been close, or 'lovey-dovey', as she would have called it with a sneer of disdain. Respect, good manners and no unsightly shows of affection were what mattered in raising children and she prided herself on her achievement. But one look at her grandchildren convinced her that Andrew wasn't being so successful. Bess dressed as if she was fourteen not ten and Chris sulked. Alice might be a decent housekeeper but she wasn't the children's mother and it was about time her son found himself a suitable new wife for their sake. She said as much as she accepted her second glass of Pommerol with a small sigh of delight that would have evaporated had she known its cost. Her son affected not to hear her comment as he cleared their plates.

'I said the children need a mother, Andrew.'

'I heard you but I can't magic one out of thin air.'

'And you're not seeing anyone?'

'No.'

'What about this Louise person that Bess talks about incessantly.'

'Does she?' He looked surprised.

'Yes. She told me that Louise comes over for lunch, dinner even. Is she special?'

'No, I barely know her.'

She recognised the defensiveness in his tone, which had always betrayed him as a child, but there was something else in her son's face that stopped her from pressing the advantage. There was sadness there and possibly regret. For the first time she realised that her handsome, highly eligible son might not be able to have the woman he wanted, and she knew him well enough to know that he would never settle for second best.

'This is terrible weather,' she said and smiled inwardly at his look of relief. 'What on earth shall I do with the children?'

They debated how to entertain Chris and Bess as they nibbled at cheese and biscuits and finally agreed that a visit to the Natural History Museum in London would suit them both.

'Keep an eye on them, won't you, Mum?'

She looked at him incredulously.

'Of course I shall, whatever next?' She was genuinely offended.

It was only when she was in bed later that it occurred to her that her son saw more horrors involving children than she could begin to imagine and she forgave him his fears.

* * *

'Have you been praying to your pagan gods again, Fenwick?'

Harper-Brown's clipped vowels were unmistakable, which was just as well as the voice at the end of the telephone rarely announced itself.

'Assistant Chief Constable, good morning.' Fenwick played for time as he tried to work out what on earth the man was talking about.

'Not only has this wretched rain wrecked the cricket pitch, flooded Mrs Harper-Brown's garden and done untold damage to our accident statistics, it's also brought you your wish.'

'I'm sorry, sir, I don't follow you. What wish?'

There was a chuckle from the other end of the line as the ACC enjoyed his moment.

'To excavate the terrace at The Downs, of course. Part of it's collapsed again; bloody architect should be shot. The surveyor's been in and thinks the whole west side needs to be demolished. If you still want to do some digging now's your chance. The secretary's agreed provided you get it over with while the weather's foul so the members won't be inconvenienced.'

'But the case has been passed to Harlden.'

'I know but both Quinlan and Blite are away on holiday and there's nobody else there that I'd trust so I've told Operations that the excavation is down to you. I think they're relieved.'

Fenwick begged, borrowed and stole crime scene technicians from across West Sussex Constabulary. Alison Reynolds located a small JCB with driver for hire and he arranged to meet everyone on site.

He put on his boots and Barbour, pulled an old hat down over his ears and stepped out of the car into the slime that had once been the second car park. His trousers were soaked by the time he reached the clubhouse where the secretary was waiting for him.

'Chief Inspector Fenwick? Daniel Ainscough; Alistair Harper-

Brown told me to expect you. At least you're prompt.' The portly red-cheeked man took in his visitor with a swift glance. 'If you don't mind waiting here I'll get my coat and umbrella and take you round.'

They didn't talk as they walked carefully along a gravel path that ran like a stream and then slopped across a quagmire that had once been a well-tended rose garden. When they reached the collapsing terrace Ainscough stopped and gestured to the remains of the stone wall.

'This is the fourth time it's fallen down in thirty years. The heat wave followed by this rain has wrecked it. Bloody mess. I think I'm going to propose that we move the whole thing to the other side of the club where we should be able to build on something other than this damned Sussex clay.'

'When was it last rebuilt?' Fenwick had to shout above the drumming of the rain.

'I had to re-lay a section further along three years ago but I don't think this part has been touched since the early Eighties when the then secretary added reinforcements to the outside as it was relaid within twelve months of the previous renovations. We all thought that his plan had worked but now...' He bent and picked up a stone to throw. He scored a direct hit and a piece of wall slipped sideways.

'What are you looking for anyway?'

'We won't know until we find it.'

The excavating equipment turned up at eleven. He showed the driver where to start work on the 1980s section of terrace, watched to make sure that he got it right and then went to share a pot of excellent coffee with Ainscough. When he put on his soaking coat and ventured outside again the digger had made little progress. He had insisted that every load should be tipped out onto a separate spoil heap for investigation by the team of five crime scene technicians he'd allocated to the challenge. The next load couldn't be added until they'd finished searching the previous one as he didn't want to risk them missing anything.

'This is going to take for ever,' the driver moaned. 'Why can't I start a second pile and you get some more coppers up here?'

'Good idea.'

He had to plead for the additional resources but they arrived by two o'clock and the whole process sped up. He left the team to their dispirited searching and returned to his office. At seven he called and agreed they could stop for the night as long as they were back by eight the next morning. A length of terrace a bare fourteen feet long had been removed.

He was at the club early, picking over the spoil in a brief respite between downpours. It looked depressingly ordinary but he refused to be despondent. The CSTs assigned to the search turned up at quarter to eight. They shared takeaway coffees until the digger driver arrived and the monotonous routine started again. The fact that Fenwick had bothered to turn up improved their mood and they promised to call him if they unearthed anything of interest. He sent Clive Kettering out in the afternoon with money to buy them all coffee and buns but it didn't change their luck.

There was no news on Tuesday or Wednesday when the ACC called and told him to speed things up. On Thursday the digger broke down. There was less than fifteen foot of terrace left and it was the most solidly built in an attempt to overcome particularly weak sub-soil. Fenwick was tempted to give up but instead he hired a replacement excavator and promised the whole team a night out on Friday at his expense provided they finished the job.

The call came at four o'clock on Friday just after he'd sent Alison Reynolds home because she'd been working seven days without a break. The team had erected makeshift shelters over the spoil heaps to keep out the rain. Fenwick stepped under the white plastic and walked over to where all eight technicians and

Clive Kettering were standing, a covered bundle at their feet. His heart rate quickened.

'What have you got?'

One of them, Cook, lifted a protective sheet away.

'Two waterproof sacks, one inside the other. The inner one is stuffed full of boy's clothing. I haven't disturbed them but we could see from the top that there's a blazer in there with a Downside School crest on the pocket. Is that where Malcolm Eagleton went?'

'No,' Fenwick said, disappointed; then he remembered, 'but Paul Hill did.'

Fenwick knelt down beside Cook and angled his head to one side to keep his shadow from obscuring their view. Although it was still afternoon the bad weather had reduced the light inside the tent to a gloom into which the arc lights threw pools of intense glare. Cook explained what they'd found.

'The outer plastic looks like wrapping from building material, probably bricks. This one inside,' he pointed without touching, 'is an old fertiliser sack, sort you'd find on any farm around here. It's tough, non-degradable. With luck it's kept the contents in pretty good shape.'

'Can I see them?' Fenwick knew it was a stupid question even as he asked it but the temptation was too great.

'Best if we transport it to the lab intact, don't you think? But you can tell it's a school blazer; look, there's part of the crest.'

'I see.' Fenwick fought the urge to reach out and pull the bag open and clasped his hands together between his thighs.

'We've done a KM test for blood on the bit of blazer that's showing,' Cook said almost as a reward for Fenwick's restraint. He held up a purple-stained cotton bud inside a tube. 'It's only presumptive but it's positive.'

'That's something. OK. Send it all over to the lab and tell them to give it priority.'

Behind his back the technicians exchanged pitying looks. The Sussex Forensic Service was down to a skeleton staff because of holidays and sickness.

'Have you found anything else?'

'Nothing, just this. We've about twelve inches of spoil left to go over but I'm not hopeful.'

'There must be more. I want the whole east end covered and searched. Clive, stay until it's finished.' Friday night drinks were forgotten.

By suppertime on the following Wednesday Fenwick had finally been forced to accept that there were no human remains under the terrace. He went back to the club again to thank the CSTs for their efforts and to tell them to go home and found himself confronted by Harper-Brown on his way out to the driving range.

'Just the person,' he said and steered Fenwick into the secretary's empty office.

He closed the door and started an immediate tirade about the costs of the fingertip search that Fenwick had authorised. It had consumed most of Major Crimes' third-quarter budget for crime scene work, even though it was only August, leaving him incensed at what he described as 'sheer profligacy'. Fenwick was saved from trying to defend himself by an embarrassed constable who'd been sent to find him.

'Yes, what is it?' Harper-Brown glowered at the poor unfortunate, whose face turned a deeper pink.

'Sorry, sir. I've an urgent message for the chief inspector.' He turned hopefully towards Fenwick. 'They've been trying to reach you for half an hour but your mobile's off.'

'Naturally, I'm with the assistant chief constable and I don't want to be disturbed. But as you've interrupted anyway you can at least tell me who "they" are.'

'Forensics, sir. They say it's urgent.'

'Then you did the right thing, Robin. You can go now.' He watched the beaky-nosed man depart.

'Shall I call from here?'

'You might as well.'

The ACC's face had returned to the carefully controlled expression of disdain that was customary whenever they were together but Fenwick could sense his excitement. He was put through to the head of the lab without delay.

'Andrew, at last. Tom Barnes here. I'm sorry it's taken us so long but we're very thin on the ground this month and with evidence as old as this we couldn't risk rushing the work. I think we have something for you.'

'Go on.'

'We've been able to lift three separate prints from the plastic on the inside of the bag and a partial palm print from the boy's shirt. The prints will be sent through to your fingerprint team first thing tomorrow marked as a top priority.'

'That's very good news...'

'There's more. We've also managed to separate out the clothes and will start work on them next. The blazer is in reasonable condition but the rest of the material is quite degraded so it'll be slow work but we'll do our best.'

'Tom, thank you. The ACC's here with me now and I know that he appreciates what you and your team are doing in challenging circumstances.'

'No problem. I'll keep you posted.'

Fenwick broke the connection and relaxed into a rare smile of satisfaction as he repeated the substance of the call to Harper-Brown.

'So, if the clothes aren't just so much rubbish we might have a lead to go on. Pity you don't think they belong to the Eagleton boy. Keep me posted.'

Fenwick escaped from the stuffy, pipe-smelling office and

stepped outside into the fresh air. After weeks of rain the weather had turned fine for a few hours and it was a beautiful summer evening. He listened to an owl greeting the dusk and watched as its ghostly white shape left the shelter of the trees and flew low over the water hazard by the second tee. Despite his disappointment at the lack of a body under the terrace, he felt curiously optimistic. His skin tingled and his thumbs itched as they did at the start of a big case. As he watched the owl's crepuscular feeding he knew with absolute certainty that Tom Barnes was going to provide him with a breakthrough. But he didn't know then of the magnitude of the discovery or of the scandal and outrage it would unleash in the community.

In his excitement about the discoveries at the golf club Fenwick forgot that he was due to give evidence on another case in court the following day. He only remembered when he arrived in his office at MCS early with the aim of clearing any work that wasn't related to Malcolm Eagleton or Paul Hill and saw 'COURT' writ large across his diary. He swore but offered a silent prayer of thanks that he'd prepared well in advance. There would probably be a wait before he was called so he filled his briefcase with emails and a copy of the only original papers on the Paul Hill investigation that he'd been able to track down.

On his way he rang Clive Kettering.

'Clive, Andrew Fenwick.'

'Morning, and isn't it a delight to see the sun again?' Clive sounded in remarkably good spirits.

'Lovely. Look, the lab is going to process the clothes today and I want us to be able to confirm whether or not they're Paul's or Malcolm's as soon as possible.'

'Good idea.'

Kettering had a reputation for being a charmer and never

losing his cool. It made him popular, particularly with the ladies. He was going for promotion to Inspector and worked hard to prove himself. So there was no logical reason why Fenwick should dislike him, but he did. There was something about him that smacked of the smart arse and Fenwick wasn't sure he could entirely trust him.

'We already have DNA samples for Malcolm but we need to pay a visit to Paul's mother, Sarah Hill. Interview her and follow up on anything you feel necessary. Cook should go with you.

'I'm going to be stuck in court so I'll leave you to it and we can talk later. Oh, and make sure I'm sent a message if anything comes from the fingerprints.'

Clive waited on the cracked doorstep for his knock to be answered. The doorbell looked past it.

'Mrs Hill,' he called through the letterbox, bending uncomfortably over his breakfast. 'It's the police. May we come in?'

The door was flung open without warning and he fell forward before recoiling from the musty odour of decay that assaulted him.

'You've found him!' A wild woman stared at him with fanatical eyes.

'No, Mrs Hill, not exactly.' The curtains at a neighbouring front window twitched. 'Look, can we come in? It would be better if we were inside.' Even as he said it his nose was protesting.

He introduced himself and Cook once the front door was shut behind them.

'And this is Julie Pride. She's a family liaison officer.'

'Oh my God.' Mrs Hill gave way at once to noisy tears.

It was undignified crying. Her nose ran and her face was covered in tears and slime long before she pulled a man's handkerchief from her sleeve and started to wipe her face carelessly. Clive was surprised to see that it was freshly laundered, in stark contrast to everything else.

Clive and Julie Pride held her gently under the elbows and eased her into a small sitting room. Between caring for Mrs Hill and trying not to gag on the smell, Clive failed to notice the shrine to Paul on the wall behind him.

'I'm here because we've discovered new evidence, Mrs Hill, not because we've found Paul or a body. Can we get you some water?'

'Yes. It's just that whenever family liaison officers are mentioned...well it's usually bad news.'

Clive stood up, desperate to get away from the woman who smelt worse than some vagrants he'd had cause to arrest.

'I'll go and get you that water,' he said, much to Julie's surprise.

His footsteps raised small puffs of dust from the carpet, glinting in the faint daylight that filtered through the filthy glass of the front door. The kitchen was at the end of the hall and reeked of rancid milk. An irregular line of part-empty bottles lined the window sill and more were clustered by the back door. The bowl in the sink held scummy water and streaked washing-up was stacked in a plastic draining rack, the corners of which were thick with slime. He found a reasonably clean glass and rinsed it under the tap before filling it.

'Here you are, Mrs Hill,' he said, holding the glass out at arm's length.

'Thank you.' She drank it noisily and calmed down. 'Where are my manners? Would you like a cup of tea?'

'No!' Clive responded so quickly that the others followed his lead and shook their heads vigorously. 'Don't trouble yourself.'

His gaze strayed at last to the wall and shelves of memorabilia. She noticed.

'My Paul.' Love and pride shone from her face. 'He was a wonderful little boy.'

'I'm sure he was.'

Clive sat down and tried to compose the words with which he would tell her that they thought her wonderful boy's bloodstained clothing had been found, having been buried for twenty-five years. Surprisingly, she helped him.

'So, you've found something serious enough for a liaison officer and for a crime scene technician but not a body. What is it?' Her mood had changed abruptly and she was now perfectly matter-of-fact.

'We've discovered some clothing, Mrs Hill: a uniform from Downside School; a blazer, shirt, vest and grey flannel trousers.'

'Is that all?'

'The clothes had been buried not simply discarded, which suggests that they'd been hidden deliberately.

'That might mean nothing.'

'Maybe but there are traces of human blood on the clothes,' he said gently.

'But no name tags?'

'No.'

'I never had time to sew them in,' she said, apparently not appreciating the significance of her words. 'So why do you think they're Paul's? They could belong to that poor Malcolm Eagleton boy.'

'He didn't go to school at Downside but we're looking into it anyway just in case.'

'They still might not belong to Paul.'

'That's what we have to determine. We need to take some samples from you so that we can try and match them to the hairs and blood we've found on the clothing.'

'DNA; I've read about that, though I can't say I understand it. You seem to use it all the time.'

'We do and we need some from you. It's only a swab from the inside of your mouth. My colleague will take it. After that I'd like to have a chat with you about Paul and what happened on the day he disappeared.'

Cook removed a buccal swab from its protective container and scraped the inside of Mrs Hill's cheek before returning it to the tube and snapping off the stick.

'Is that it?'

'Yes, it will be enough for us to retrieve your DNA,' Cook said confidently.

'And that will be the same as Paul's?'

'No, his is unique – he'll have received part from you and part from his father. I was going to ask you where we might find him.'

'No idea. He left me after Paul disappeared; hasn't been in touch since. Does this mean that you'll be able to tell for sure if it's Paul's blood?'

'Not one hundred per cent but we'll be able to tell whether the blood is from someone related to you and that should be enough to—'

'It's not right after all this time,' she muttered turning to touch one of the photos of Paul as an infant dressed in tiny dungarees. 'Where are you, baby?' she crooned to him. 'Whose blood is it? Is it yours? Why did you get your nice new blazer dirty?'

Clive coughed in embarrassment and she turned back to Cook.

'How can you get DNA from my mouth?' she asked.

'The little brush scrapes cells from inside your cheek; it's all we need.'

'A little brush…a little brush.' She looked at them in triumph and stood up. 'Like a toothbrush you mean?'

'We've been able to recover DNA from a used toothbrush in the past. A hairbrush can be good too, though sometimes it's only mitochondrial DNA and…'

But Mrs Hill was off, moving with more focus than Clive had believed she possessed.

'Come on.' She clambered up the stairs raising more dust as her feet pounded the threadbare carpet.

There was a small L-shaped landing onto which three doors opened with space for an airing cupboard that had lost its door at some point. Underwear in various shades of grey hung from its wooden slats. Clive averted his eyes.

Mrs Hill took a key from beneath her blouse. It was suspended on a long silver chain alongside a locket. She slotted it into the door at the top of the stairs and walked inside.

'I keep it locked in case I'm burgled. No one comes in here but me and Paul.'

Clive came to an abrupt halt as she stopped him on the threshold. The whole room was shrouded; ghostly shapes glimmered in the light that seeped through unlined curtains. As his eyes adjusted he could make out the design of fighter planes on them, faded to grey memories of their original glory. He watched in fascination as Mrs Hill threw back a dust sheet from what turned out to be a chest of drawers

'Here.'

She pushed a toilet bag into his hands. It still had a Woolworths price tag on the zip, 12p.

'It's his wash things. I've left everything else untouched but his favourite flannel was getting dusty and he liked the Action Man toothbrush so I put them in here to keep them safe and clean. You can take it but bring them back as quickly as you can. Oh,' she almost skipped back to the chest, 'his hairbrush.' Cook put the samples into bags and sealed and dated them. She watched, delighted. 'You're proper policemen, you are, not like the rest of them. I know you'll find him.'

Clive tried to step into the room but she moved to block his way.

'Apart from me only Paul can come in here. You might damage something and I couldn't have that.'

He did his best to persuade her otherwise but she remained adamant so he had no option but to precede her to the dowdy front room so that he could interview her. Even though they'd been in the house for fifteen minutes her smell still caught in his throat and he was desperate to leave.

Clive tried but failed to glean any real information from Mrs Hill. She was obsessed with the idea that Paul was still alive and became angry when his questions challenged that reality. The few facts she uttered were embedded in streams of endless diatribe against the police, her husband and various male relatives who she felt had let her down. Her opinions about Paul were biased to the point that Clive considered them almost worthless and her memories of his final days airbrushed to a rosy glow. When he considered that he'd done his best he left, followed gratefully by Cook and Julie. They sucked in fresh air as they walked to their cars, like smokers lighting up after a long-distance flight.

'That's about the creepiest experience I've ever had.' Clive wiped his face and looked at the dust on his fingers. Julie blew her nose vigorously on a handkerchief, sniffed for good measure and put it away.

'She reminded me a bit of Miss Havisham,' she said and Cook nodded agreement with a muttered 'bloody right'.

'I don't think I've met her,' Clive mused, missing the smiles that were directed at his retreating back.

CHAPTER FOURTEEN

At eleven-thirty Fenwick checked his mobile phone for messages; nothing. He still hadn't been called to give evidence and resented the sacrifice of his time to court procedure. A vending machine grudgingly gave up another cup of bitter, over-brewed coffee and he took it into a corner by himself where he could read his papers in private. The emails he'd been avoiding for days sat on top, accusing, but he ignored them. Underneath was a summary case file of Paul Hill's disappearance. It wasn't long and he knew it by heart but he opened it anyway in a search of fresh insight.

Paul Hill had disappeared on the first day of the school year. After the last lesson he had avoided his friends and cycled away from the town centre on his new racing bike. The alarm was raised by his mother at eight p.m., too early to be taken seriously; the police search started at ten when he failed to return home. Police spoke to some of his friends who said that Paul might have been going to Beecham's Wood. A search discovered cycle tracks and a patch of blood in a dirt car park but that was all.

More than one hundred police and volunteers combed the wood over the following days without success. The search area was extended while officers continued house-to-house inquiries and interviews with Paul's teachers and school mates. At its peak, eighty officers were involved in the hunt for Paul Hill and a chief superintendent was appointed SIO replacing the then Inspector Quinlan, who had originally been in charge.

Pictures of Paul, an angelic child who looked younger than his age, appeared all over Britain and the sightings started at once, as far apart as Brighton, Cornwall, Edinburgh, Birmingham and, inevitably, London. Each one had to be taken seriously and police resources across the country were diverted to find the fourteen-year-old. Some witnesses reported him in the company of a man. The official police statement was that they were 'seriously concerned for Paul's safety'. Unofficially, it was clear from the file that within days the police feared their hunt for a kidnapper would become a murder inquiry.

Three days after Paul disappeared, the police had the breakthrough they desperately needed. The mother of one of his friends, Victor Ackers, overheard her son talking in his bedroom. She distinctly heard him say *'all this fuss for that poncy fag. I bet he's gone off with Taylor'*. When challenged, Victor admitted that he thought Paul was 'a poof' and that the extra pocket money he boasted of wasn't from odd jobs as he claimed but because *'he was some old man's tart'*.

His suspicion had started over the summer when Paul bought a new bike and started paying for his friends' ice creams and sweets with crisp five pound notes. When he was seen in the company of Bryan Taylor in Beecham's Wood by a girl from school, curiosity turned to speculation, speculation to rumour and, like a spark igniting a blaze, rumour swiftly became accepted fact. With the unique cruelty of children, Paul was alternately ostracised and taunted, his summer turned into a hell of isolation punctuated by episodes of verbal abuse.

Victor's revelation turned the police investigation inside out. At first they continued to consider the boy a kidnap/murder victim, not wishing to fall in with the growing local opinion that he was a runaway, but as they reinterviewed his friends and followed up the emerging leads, independent facts began to corroborate Victor's story.

Taylor was a well-known handyman who sometimes did work

for the council. He lived on his own in a semi-detached house on the outskirts of town. When the police called, a neighbour told them he hadn't been around for a week. His car wasn't in the garage and his dog was being cared for by a neighbour who couldn't take its howling in the backyard any longer. Questions about his personal life prompted non-committal shrugs. No, there didn't appear to be a girlfriend on the scene, or boyfriend for that matter. But people in the street knew Paul Hill, who they said did odd jobs for Taylor. The police obtained a warrant to search the house for signs of Paul.

In a cupboard in the dining room, behind false panelling, they found a supply of hard-core child pornography: magazines, films, photographs. Some was home-made and in one bulging folder they discovered pictures of a young Paul Hill being abused by a man whose upper body was out of shot. There was photographic equipment in the loft and a bedroom had been converted into a darkroom.

The police search switched to Taylor. His bank card had been used to withdraw cash in Dorking on the evening of Paul's disappearance but there hadn't been a trace of him since. Suddenly the sightings of a man and boy resembling Paul became more relevant and the main investigation was refocused to a nationwide hunt. After twelve weeks the police search for Paul eased, despite protests from his parents, who denied any possibility of a relationship with Taylor. Their complaints were handled sensitively but they couldn't persuade the police away from their theory that Taylor had kidnapped Paul, with or without his consent, and had either then murdered him or was still on the run with the boy.

Police opinion about Paul polarised. Some officers saw him as an innocent corrupted by an evil man. Others considered him a male prostitute who'd become greedy and then grown fed up with life at home where he was dominated by a smothering mother, nagged by an ineffectual father and victimised by his school friends. As time passed with no new leads Paul's critics went unanswered. Sightings of Paul and/or Taylor continued to be followed up but a month would go by without a report being filed, then three and then nothing. The investigation stumbled to a halt.

Fenwick closed the cover of the report and stood up to stretch his muscles. His knee ached and he had the start of a headache. After another coffee and three paracetamol he looked back over the notes he'd made. All he had to go on was the summary file, one that had been kept at Harlden because the case was never officially closed. The rest of the material from the investigation had moved to secure storage years before. He called the team at MCS to ask how they were getting on with tracking it down. Almost a week had passed since he'd first asked for the reports and evidence to be retrieved and there'd been an ominous silence since.

A sergeant called Welsh had the misfortune to take his call.

'Thing is, sir, we haven't had much luck finding the stuff.'

'What do you mean? You've had almost a week to locate it.'

'Four days, sir,' Welsh objected.

'That's plenty of time. What have you lot been doing? Sitting on your backsides drinking coffee?'

'No, sir! It's not our fault. The files were transferred to civvie premises sixteen years ago. It turns out that there was this flood in 1999 that destroyed evidence from Harlden cases between 1976 and '83. The index for evidence stored from before 1990 is only partially computerised and finding the Hill boxes will be like searching for a needle in a giant haystack, assuming anything still exists.'

'So what's happened since you found all this out and decided not to tell me? How many have you got searching the premises?'

There was an ominous pause.

'Please, tell me that you *are* searching the premises.'

'Well, we don't think we're going to find anything, see. We did recover evidence for the Eagleton case because that came from Crawley and it was stored safe.'

'So you're telling me no one's looking for the Hill files?'

'Not right at this minute, no.'

Fenwick swore under his breath. They weren't a bad team at MCS but they resented work they considered beneath them and sulked when he made them do it. He should've known that no news was bad news. He told Welsh to organise a search for the Hill files personally, using as many officers as he thought it would take and not to go off duty until he'd found something.

It was at times like this that he missed Nightingale. She was good for him, sharing his obsession with cases that looked impossible. The way they worked couldn't have been more different. He relied on his instinct and inspiration to create theories that were then tested by detailed investigation he typically delegated. Nightingale was the opposite; she worked bottom up, rigorously going through every logical step, gathering evidence systematically as she went. It could have made her an uninspiring colleague but she had the uncanny knack of finding patterns in the detail that she then wove together until she had a picture. Together they were a formidable team and they had consistently produced results, unlike the original investigators into Paul's disappearance who had left him virtually nothing to work with.

He suspected that they'd become distracted by the rumours about Paul, with the consequence that their later work was less thorough; there were no references to interviews with Taylor's associates, the Hills' house hadn't been searched thoroughly and Taylor's car, a Volvo estate, had never been located. More worryingly, there was no trace of a follow-up by the vice squad into Taylor's activities making and potentially distributing child pornography. Worst of all, he couldn't find a list of the identities of the other boys in the material that had been recovered from Taylor's house and which was now missing. It was too late to fill in all the holes, but he'd made a list of Taylor's known acquaintances and employers from what he had so that they could be re-interviewed, and every one of Paul's one-time friends was going to receive a visit.

After the recess for lunch, Fenwick was summoned into the courtroom and delivered his evidence with practised competence. Two hours later he was driving back to Harlden listening to Radio Three in an attempt to ease away his frustration with the day. Unfortunately, as the hour changed they started broadcasting one of their 'educational' programmes. A twenty-first-century composer he'd never heard of was explaining why he found any structure in composition a constraint and consequently aimed to produce *'disharmony from the creativity of anarchy and thus reinvent the symphonic form for the new century'*. Fenwick gave the excerpt from his latest work less than fifteen seconds before judging it bollocks and switching to Classic FM. He'd heard the violin concerto they were broadcasting too many times for it to be pure pleasure but at least it had a tune he could follow. During an advertisement explaining how he could sell his unwanted endowment policy his phone rang and he switched the radio off with relief to take the call. It was Clive telling him about the time capsule he'd discovered in Sarah Hill's house.

'So what did Colin recover?'

'Paul's toothbrush and some of his hair, even after all this time,' Clive said with pride.

'Is that all, when you had the whole room to go for?' Fenwick was still in a bad mood despite his strong performance in court and didn't bother to disguise his disappointment. 'If you'd have asked, his mother would've given you the lot.'

'No chance. She treats his room like it's sacred. It's all she's got left and she has it ready for when he comes back. She's gone nuts with the waiting, I reckon.'

'And we're trying to end that waiting, aren't we? You'll need to go back if we identify the clothes as Paul's.'

'Sir! You're joking.'

'No I'm not. I'll get a warrant and you can take Colin with you to do a thorough search. You can promise her that we'll return anything we take in due course.'

'But—'

'Don't argue.'

He broke the connection, fuming, and his message service buzzed him at once. The forensic lab had rung while he was talking to Clive so he called them back and was put through to the scientist in charge.

'Tom, Andrew Fenwick.'

'Good. We're about to do the detailed processing of the clothes. I thought you might want to stop by.'

'I'll be there within the hour.'

When he arrived he put his jacket in a locker and donned coveralls. Even though it was a cold case and there was virtually no chance of him cross-contaminating the evidence he wasn't allowed past the receiving area until he was suitably covered. Tom Barnes was waiting for him in the Biology Unit with a scientist he introduced as Nicolette who'd already spread out the clothing inside the safety cabinet. Fenwick could hear the hum of the filter and instinctively followed the extractor pipe up to the ceiling above them. Music was playing loudly and Tom mistook his glance.

'Sorry about the choice of CD. It's Nicolette's turn and she's a classical music freak. Later on we'll be back to Duran Duran.'

Fenwick grimaced.

'I'm with Nicolette and Elgar.'

The accuracy of his observation brought an appraising look from her before she returned her eyes to the clothing in the cabinet. She'd laid them out in the shape in which they would have been worn: vest and shirt side by side with trousers and socks below. The blazer was placed separately.

'So far we've only managed to confirm the presence of human blood because we've been so busy with another incident.' Tom was apologetic. 'But we've taken samples successfully from the containers and each item of clothing and they're being worked on. I'm afraid the fertiliser sack was plastic so the hydrocarbons may have affected the traces on the clothing. We've done our best to reduce that by sampling from areas deep within the bundle and from creases where there will have been least contact with air.'

'How long before we know whether you've been able to extract DNA?'

Tom pointed to a young man at a bench near the corner. 'He's working on it now, together with the buccal and toothbrush you had brought in today. We'll know whether there's DNA in the samples in a few hours, then it'll take two to three days to extract it, match against the samples from Sarah Hill and run a check against the database.'

'What can you tell me from the bloodstain pattern?'

Tom nodded to Nicolette and she slipped her heavily protected hands into the airtight cabinet so that she could illustrate her remarks.

'There's heavy staining on the blazer front, little on the back. It's particularly thick at the end of the right sleeve, as if the wearer had his arm close to a major wound. The neck area of the clothes is relatively free of blood suggesting that if they were being worn when the injury occurred, the blood didn't come from the head or neck. But as the staining is generalised all over the front and sleeve I can't be more precise about the location or number of wounds.'

'What have you picked up there?' He pointed to the left arm of the shirt that had been turned inside out from the cuff to the elbow. It was almost free of blood except for a series of droplets that ran in parallel lines laterally across the sleeve.

'It's a different pattern of blood entirely, perhaps from a separate wound. The staining is heavier on the inside of the fabric, suggesting that this is blood that bled out but it's only light so the wounds wouldn't have been fatal.'

'Defensive cuts?'

'Possibly, yes. If the wearer threw an arm, across their face or body say, then the inner skin would be exposed. But again I can't be definite and that doesn't explain why the sleeve is intact, suggesting that however the wounds occurred, the shirt wasn't being worn at the time. Also, there's some microscopic spotting here on the collar, again a different pattern. It's possible that this was left by someone handling the materials afterwards, as the pattern suggests it fell directly onto the shirt from a distance away.'

'What about the trousers, shoes and socks?'

'Generalised stains, no discernible pattern. There's no heavy staining on the socks.'

'Suggesting?'

'Well, an injured person bleeding as heavily as this would be losing a lot of blood and eventually that would run down their legs and into the shoes, soaking into the socks from the ankles down and spreading from there to the heels and soles of the feet.'

'Whereas the socks here are clean except for some smudges.'

'Which look like the sort of marks made by bloody fingers as they were removed.'

'So, there's nothing very distinctive?'

He tried to keep kept the frustration from his voice. It wasn't their fault the evidence was so inconclusive.

'Not yet but it's early days. I've a lot more work to do and I'm as curious as you are about the story these clothes are trying to tell us. All I can say so far is that someone in close proximity to these clothes bled a lot and the blood source was in front of them. In addition, we have distinctive spots suggesting a different wound on the left sleeve and drops of blood on the outside and inner lip of the sacks into which the clothes had been placed. There are no stab or cut marks to the clothes so they weren't being worn when the injuries occurred.'

'So the boy could have been naked, bleeding and these clothes bundled on top of him.'

'That's certainly a possibility, yes and he might well have been wearing his shoes and socks but not standing upright.'

'Thank you. Can you keep me posted?'

'Of course.' Tom walked with him to the changing room where he retrieved his jacket. 'By the way, what do you think about this idea of a submission unit?'

Fenwick stopped abruptly and Tom almost cannoned into him.

'What submission unit?'

'Thought so.' Tom was enjoying winding Fenwick up. 'It's the ACC's latest brainwave. Apparently it will save money and help keep you lot within your forensic budget.'

'How?'

'There'll be a team that screens items you want to submit to the lab. The idea is that they'll stop stupid, wasteful requests reaching us, save money and reduce the backlog.'

'And how will this group know a wasteful request when they see it? If an SIO's made a judgement how will a bunch of bureaucrats know enough to overturn it?'

'Good question. Not that I'm against the idea in principle, mind, as we do get some extraordinary demands but usually we can sort those out ourselves. My worry is that we'll end up working with average people with too much power, making decisions beyond their skills and clogging up the system.'

'You've just described my definition of management. I just hope I never end up there; it'll be a sign that I've passed my sell-by date.'

Tom laughed and slapped him on the back in farewell.

Fenwick didn't go straight back to Harlden. Sight of the blood-soaked clothes had made the murder of Paul Hill very real and he couldn't get the idea of Paul at Chris's age out of his mind. He would have been innocent and trusting, unaware of his beauty and interested in the things small boys were always interested in: war games; tormenting girls in class with insects; and running from their threatened kisses in retaliation. Then that scum Taylor found him. How long it had taken the bastard to groom Paul was anybody's guess but he had eventually managed to corrupt him into accepting the worst sexual abuse a child could endure. Fenwick was almost glad the photographic evidence had been lost and the thought of what it contained made him feel sick.

My God, how had his parents borne the news? What if someone did that to Chris? Fenwick's stomach heaved and he had to pull into a lay-by. He needed air and stepped out of the car. Open fields surrounded him; he could hear sheep in the distance. There was a flutter of small birds in the hedge beside him then stillness. The ground beyond the tarmac was still soggy from the heavy rains so he was forced to walk along the narrow road as he thought.

He felt desperately sorry for Sarah and Gordon Hill and for Malcolm Eagleton's parents. Even after all this time their sorrow would run deep. Maybe they no longer thought about their sons every day but how often did they think 'my boy would have been this old...a father perhaps...successful and happy. And my grandchildren would look just like him.' Both sets of parents had split up after their sons disappeared, driven apart by grief and the never-ending uncertainty. They deserved better. Anger mixed with fear for Chris shot through him like a physical pain.

He drove back to Harlden in a chastened mood, slightly ashamed of his earlier irritation with the day.

Clive was waiting for him in his office with two cups of tea and matching slices of fruit cake. He was too used to Fenwick's brief spells of ill temper to have taken his earlier comments personally.

'Thought you might be peckish. Court always leaves me ravenous.'

Fenwick looked at his athletic build, without a trace of fat and concluded he must have a good metabolism.

'Thanks. Sorry about earlier. Sloppiness really gets to me and I took it out on you.'

'No worries. What did the lab have to say?'

Fenwick told him the bare facts and admitted that he'd left more confused than when he'd arrived.

'There's too much blood for it to be from a minor injury but the patterns are inconclusive.' Fenwick took a contemplative sip of tea. 'Have you heard of the SIO on the original case, Superintendent Charles Bacon? He ended up at Brighton; maybe he was still there when you joined.' Clive's father had been a local superintendent and hero and Fenwick was constantly amazed at what he knew.

'Smokey? My dad knew him; bit of a legend at one time. A sixty-a-day man with a foul temper. Took early retirement on health grounds and died soon after. Heart attack I think. Supposedly a good copper though.' Clive picked up the last crumbs of cake delicately with his index finger and popped them in his mouth.

'Have you read the file?'

'Yeah, had a flick through it.'

'What do you think?'

Clive sipped his tea while he considered his answer.

'I think Taylor killed Paul and panicked. He didn't plan the killing and scarpered afterwards. He used his cash either to leave the country or buy a new car and set up somewhere else. He was the sort who could blend in easily. All he'd need to do is shave off his beard, grow his hair, lose a bit of weight and he'd look completely different. What about you?'

'That's the most logical explanation I've heard so far but I still don't understand why the clothes were disposed of separately from the body.'

'People do daft stuff like that all the time when they've killed someone – that's why we catch them.'

Fenwick nodded but as Clive left he had an uneasy feeling he was missing something very obvious and could end up looking a fool.

CHAPTER FIFTEEN

Despite Maidment's release on bail, Nightingale's request to be assigned SIO for the Eagleton investigation was turned down by Quinlan. The case had gone to Blite with an inevitability that made her despair of ever crawling out of his shadow. It was small consolation that it had been passed back to Fenwick for the excavation while Blite had been on holiday because she knew he'd be lobbying for it now that he had returned.

Instead of having a murder to concentrate on, her desk was littered with obscure requests for information from CPS to support their prosecution of Maidment. It was obvious that somebody somewhere was taking a very close interest in the case and that that somebody was high up.

As Fenwick drove to the lab she was on yet another call with her CPS counterpart. The man's questions were driving her mad while at the same time feeding her well-hidden sense of inadequacy. When she stumbled in an answer to a particularly stupid remark he reminded her that the home secretary had vehement anti-vigilantism views, particularly when the perpetrator was a member of the middle class who might consider themselves above the law.

If only Fenwick had still been based in Harlden; it was at times like this that she really missed him. Ever since he'd made it clear to her that they could never have a relationship she had forced herself to banish the fantasies that she'd previously harboured. To fill the aching vacuum they'd left she had started dating again, finding it unfulfilling and insubstantial compared to the dream-life she'd woven about Fenwick, which she knew now was unobtainable. Then she'd met Clive at Bramshill where they had both been training and they had connected instantly. Starting an affair with him was easy and seeing him dulled the misery she continued to feel. It was even bearable to be friends with Fenwick now and she prided herself on the distance she was able to maintain whenever she saw him and his children.

But if her personal life had rebalanced itself somehow since his departure, in her working life at Harlden she still felt the void. Fenwick had been a true ally and it was only since he'd moved to MCS that she realised just how much she had grown to rely on his presence. It wasn't as if he'd sheltered her, she told herself, it was just that he believed in fair play and had zero tolerance for discrimination. Without him, Harlden was becoming inhospitable to anyone who wasn't one of Blite's cronies. Quinlan was a decent bloke but he was remote from the day to day and unaware of the bigotry that was flourishing in the detective room with Blite as a role model.

None of it helped Nightingale's shaky confidence. She'd taken to keeping a bottle of Pepto-Bismol in her desk and was gulping a surreptitious mouthful as her phone rang. It was Superintendent Quinlan.

'Louise? Good; I'm glad I found you straight away. I need you to execute an arrest warrant, urgently. It is already prepared, the application signed by the ACC himself.'

The agitation in his voice put her on immediate alert.

'Shall I come up to your office, sir, for a briefing?'

'That won't be necessary. My secretary is bringing the paperwork to you now. You must act quickly. I'm putting a lot of faith in you and, ah, well...'

'Sir?' She had no idea what could make him sound so nervous. 'If it's such a sensitive case should I come and see you?'

'No. Best keep a low profile on this one. And if anybody asks you later how you came to make this arrest instead of, say, er, more senior colleagues, I would be grateful if you could simply say it arrived on your desk for urgent attention when there were no other inspectors around. Got that?'

He rang off before Nightingale could answer but her time for speculation didn't last long as the file arrived seconds later. And when she saw what it contained she understood at once why Quinlan was uncomfortable. The warrant had come directly from HQ and it was clear from the file note that the ACC had expected the juicy bone of an arrest it contained to be thrown to his favourite lapdog, Blite, rather than to a girl some still considered a first-class bitch. With a silent prayer of thanks to Quinlan, Nightingale picked up her keys and literally ran to the operations room for an arrest team.

The drinks at the golf club were an impromptu affair. A hole-in-one meant that the lucky player had to stand a round, no matter if it was the result of a fluke. It had been Jeremy Maidment's stroke that produced the eagle at the sixteenth, which meant he'd had to buy a drink for all and sundry. It was a short par hole but his achievement was hailed as brilliant despite the curious stroke that delivered it.

The atmosphere in the oak-panelled room was cheerful and loud. The jokes grew saucier as they marinated in whisky and wine. The only person not enjoying themselves was Maidment. He acknowledged congratulations and accepted pats on the back with a half smile that left his eyes unchanged. Whenever Edwards delivered another joke from his well-worn repertoire he would force a laugh but an objective student of human nature might have wondered what had the major so worried.

At six o'clock he decided that it was time to leave while he could still drive. He was engaged in protracted goodbyes when he became aware of a hush settling across the crowd that made him stiffen his spine instinctively before he turned around.

'Major Jeremy Maidment?'

It was a quiet yet commanding voice. He looked towards it and saw the female detective, Nightingale, standing in the doorway to the bar. Behind her the hall was blue with uniforms.

'Can't you lot bloody well leave him alone?' Edwards' indignant protest sparked a murmur of support, across which the major said simply, 'Yes, I'm here.'

The inspector took two steps through the crowd, uniforms filing in behind her in an invading wedge.

'Jeremy Maidment,' she spoke without drama, in a steady voice that still carried to revellers outside on the remains of the terrace, 'I am arresting you on suspicion of the abduction and murder of Paul Hill on or around 7th September, 1982. You do not have to say anything but...'

The caution rolled on, falling into absolute silence as her words filled the room. One of the officers pulled Maidment's arms sharply behind his back and he felt the bite of cold metal on his wrists.

'There's no need for that,' he said mildly but the constable clicked them shut anyway.

Edwards stared at him, appalled. The major was pushed towards the door through a frowning crowd, none of whom muttered a squeak of support. Already some wouldn't meet his eye and looked elsewhere as he passed.

As the police were manoeuvring him none too gently into the back of a marked car, there was a shout from the club.

'Jeremy, your hat!' Edwards darted forward and bent down so that his lips were close to the major's ear. 'Stiff upper lip, old chap. Remember the regiment. We're still your comrades-in-arms. We've sworn oaths of friendship and absolute loyalty, don't forget those; we'll not forget you.' His words were low but emphatic and carried the unmistakable aura of a command.

The door slammed shut. At the station he was cautioned again and his wallet, watch, braces, tie and shoelaces removed before he was put in a cell in the custody suite. He was allowed to keep his jacket and handkerchief but the inability to measure passing time was disconcerting. He wondered why they weren't questioning him straight away before disciplining himself against pointless conjecture.

There was dust in the corners of the room and an unpleasant smell that he chose not to identify. The cell wasn't soundproofed and the commotion outside provided a welcome distraction as he didn't wish to think. There was no point in rehearsing what he should say as he planned to remain silent beyond a statement that he was innocent of the crimes of which he stood accused. He didn't even bother to ask for the one phone call to which he imagined he was entitled.

After an incalculable period he was escorted to an interview room containing a table, four chairs and a double tape recorder, but no clock or window. The constable stayed with him as he sat down.

Maidment told himself that he was used to waiting. Army service was made up of long spells of tedious inactivity interspersed with urgent aggressive moments that could bring with them injury or death. Nothing in his present condition could frighten him, not even the threat of trial for murder and subsequent imprisonment. He began to recite poetry in his mind. His prodigious memory had enabled him to consume and remember endless texts since boyhood. As he worked through Shakespeare's sonnets he estimated the time that was passing.

After roughly ten minutes the door opened and Inspector Nightingale walked in, accompanied by a nondescript, middle-aged officer in a polyester suit and poorly ironed shirt. The detectives sat down, unwrapped and inserted new cassettes into the machine before switching it on.

'Interview between Detective Inspector Nightingale and Jeremy Maidment, also present Detective Sergeant Watts, commences at,' she glanced at her watch and the major held his breath, 'nineteen hundred hours.'

Less than an hour in captivity; he would have staked a wager on closer to two.

'Am I entitled to a solicitor present?' Maidment asked because he liked things done properly, not because he particularly wanted one.

Nightingale nodded, looking pleased with the question.

'In my experience it is usually the guilty ones that ask for their solicitor at once.'

'In this country a man is innocent until proven guilty, Miss Nightingale.'

'Technically yes, but with the evidence we have against you I think you will find that is splitting hairs.'

Maidment's face remained calm but his insides writhed.

'Just the same, I should wish my solicitor to be present before we proceed.'

She nodded, quite composed, and switched off the tape recorder.

'Let him make his phone call,' she instructed, 'and find me as soon as his solicitor arrives.'

The door closed firmly on her retreating back.

Fenwick declined the seat that Quinlan offered and stood in front of the desk, his face set in an unreadable expression. He had driven to Harlden in record time since hearing the rumour he found impossible to believe.

'There was nothing I could do, Andrew. You were incommunicado and the ACC rang me.'

'It was my strategy that led to the recovery of evidence that has linked Maidment to Paul Hill. To give the power of arrest to another officer is despicable. There was no message on my mobile, no attempt to interrupt me.'

'I left a message with your office for you to call as soon as you were free, Andrew. Apparently this isn't to be an MCS case after all.'

'I'm going to fight to have it back.'

'Don't be foolish. You'll achieve nothing and alienate the ACC.'

'You knew I was working this. Couldn't you have declined to take the case? I've been completely undermined.'

Quinlan said nothing but his expression made it clear that it was a preposterous suggestion.

'Is the arrest happening now?'

'As we speak. We'll detain and charge Maidment here.'

'Nightingale's in charge, I understand. I'm amazed the ACC didn't insist on Blite.' Fenwick's sarcasm made the superintendent's lips twitch into a moue of irritation but his tone remained calm as he replied.

'I make the staff decisions in my station, thank you, Chief Inspector.

It was a dismissal and Fenwick stalked out. It was only when he was making his way downstairs that he realised he had discharged his anger at the wrong man. Quinlan was a staunch supporter of his, always had been. In retrospect, his quiet insistence spoke volumes. Handling the arrest here at Harlden had obviously been the ACC's decision and could not be argued with.

Fenwick opened the door to the custody suite and it swung back with a crash against the wall. It was empty apart from the custody sergeant who gave him a reproving look. He was a prickly individual and Fenwick wasn't one of his favourites. So it was perhaps understandable that he didn't volunteer to the chief inspector that Maidment had already been booked, charged and moved to an interrogation room. He watched with something approaching amusement as Fenwick stormed off.

At seven-thirty Maidment re-entered the interview room accompanied by Mitchell Stenning, a semi-retired family solicitor and old friend. He was seated beside Maidment in shock from the gravity of the charge facing his client. Stenning blinked a lot and let out great sighs of tension every few minutes. Nightingale was with the detective whose name he had forgotten – an extraordinary event that told him, even if his insides had been calmer, that he was more troubled than his demeanour would allow.

Nightingale repeated the formalities and looked at the major expectantly.

'Well, Major, have you thought any more about what you want to say?'

'I am not guilty. Beyond that I have no comment.'

'You've just been accused of a child's murder and you have nothing to say? Your lack of cooperation will tell against you at trial; you do realise that, don't you?'

Maidment remained silent. He noted a slight twitch in Nightingale's jaw and wondered whether she was irritated despite her apparent calm.

'Did you know Paul Hill?'

'No.'

'Are you sure that you never met him?'

'Positive.'

'He didn't come to the golf club?'

'I don't believe his father was ever a member so why would he?'

'Then how do you explain—'

Her question was interrupted as a uniformed officer entered the room and whispered in her ear. Nightingale nodded once and ended the interview with an instruction for them to await her return.

Maidment watched her disappear into the corridor with well-concealed concern. She was confident that she had incriminating evidence and during his long wait he'd worked out what it might be. Modern forensic science was marvellous, or so the *Daily Telegraph* informed him at regular intervals, so he could imagine the case they might construct. He became aware that he was squeezing and releasing the fingers of his right hand compulsively and forced himself to stop.

'This is all rot of course, Jeremy,' Mitchell said, not quite meeting his eye. 'I'll have you out of here in no time.'

'We'll see. Sometimes life is more complicated than we would either like or expect. But I can assure you, whatever they say, whatever "evidence" they produce, I did not murder that poor boy.'

Mitchell nodded without conviction and glanced at his watch.

'I'm sorry, Andrew, but the Hill case isn't within MCS's remit any more than the Eagleton one is. If you decide to pursue the Choir Boy investigation further – and heaven knows I'd support you if you decided that it was time to call it a day – then that's one thing, but to divert highly skilled resources into the investigation of two cold cases simply isn't appropriate.'

So that's what this was all about. Harper-Brown wanted the Choir Boy team closed down. Even though Fenwick had already concluded it would have to happen he'd hoped that the discovery of Malcolm Eagleton's body followed by the unearthing of another boy's clothes would have bought him more time.

'But we know from the fingerprint evidence that the clothing in the sack is Paul Hill's and I'd already identified the boy as fitting the profile for the paedophile ring.'

'Profile! Please, Andrew, we both know that you have arbitrarily defined a five-year age range for the victims and limited your search to Caucasian children because of a passing comment by the Yanks. That is hardly a profile.'

Fenwick took a deep breath and was glad that they were speaking by phone. It infuriated him that Harper-Brown was able to remain calm when he was eaten up with anger. He forced his voice steady. If he wanted to retain a link to the Hill investigation a little grovelling would be in a good cause.

'Of course you're right, sir,' he even managed to force a laugh, 'and I am reviewing Choir Boy...'

'Good man.'

'...If nothing happens in the next week then I'll be suspending active inquiries pending further developments.'

'That is absolutely the right call.' It was rare for Fenwick to hear approval in H-B's tone and it encouraged him to try his luck.

'During the next week I'd like to keep an eye on what unfolds here in Harlden.' He rushed on before the ACC could interrupt. 'You see, if there is a chance that Maidment was somehow involved in Choir Boy it wouldn't look good for us to miss it. He's already high profile and this is going to get carpet coverage in the papers. If it came out later that we'd missed a connection to a wider ring of abusers we'd look foolish.'

'Hmm.' Harper-Brown had a well-developed sense of self-preservation and a fine political nose. 'What role would you want to play?'

'I'd like to lead the interrogation of Maidment. I think my style will work well with him and it will give me a chance to test out any wider involvement without necessarily alerting him to what we already know.'

'And Choir Boy is to cease in a week?'

It was a trade.

'Yes, unless there are new developments.'

'Very well then but tread carefully in Harlden. You can take the lead in interviewing but in everything else it's Blite's call.'

Fenwick decided not to mention that it was Nightingale who had made the arrest. The ACC would find out soon enough.

'Er, understood. Harlden will lead the investigation into both Malcolm Eagleton and Paul Hill's murders.'

'It's irritating that we have the body of one boy but scant evidence, and ample evidence for the other boy but no body. Are you absolutely sure that Eagleton didn't go to Downside? It would be a lot neater for the two discoveries to be linked.'

'The first thing we did was check Malcolm's school records and he never went there; his parents are sure he never owned the clothes we found. But DNA tests are being run against both boys so we will – or rather Harlden will – be able to confirm our assumptions as soon as the results come through.'

'Hmm. Well, if we really can't make a connection...'

The ACC's voice trailed away and Fenwick decided for the second time to apply discretion; so he didn't insist that there could be some sort of connection between the two boys and that he was still determined to find it in the week of freedom on Choir Boy remaining to him. He had won his right to be involved in the Maidment interrogation and that was result enough for one phone call.

'Well, at least I didn't blow up at the ACC this time,' he muttered as he left the visitors' office in Harlden, startling a passing administrator. In the stairwell he paused and then climbed up a flight rather than down. Quinlan was about to leave when he caught him.

'I've come to say that I'm sorry, sir. I was out of order.'

'I'm glad you've realised. You've got to watch your righteous indignation, Andrew. It's an Achilles heel and you know it.'

'You're right but the ACC gets under my skin.'

'Get over it. He won't be there for ever; he's far too ambitious. Think of it as a temporary challenge not a permanent problem.'

'Is that what you do?' It was a cheeky remark and he expected Quinlan to treat it as a joke so he was taken aback by his response.

'Push the door to.' The superintendent waited until it was shut. 'Sit down. I'm going to give you two pieces of advice and I'm not going to elaborate on either, you understand?'

'Sure.'

Fenwick shrugged but didn't feel concerned. He'd received the lecture that he was sure was about to follow too many times before.

'Number one, your attitude will get in the way of your promotion if you don't manage it. I thought you'd improved since working with the Met – they even complimented your political skill, which is a first – but when you go off the deep end like you just did with me you undo all your good work.

'Off the record there are three other candidates from West Sussex up for promotion to superintendent, all of them strong contenders, but the ACC and the chief constable are going to advise the appointments board to make up only two.'

Fenwick's mouth went dry and the smirk he'd been trying hard to disguise vanished of its own accord.

'Why?'

'The local police authority has concerns about our ratios. Compared to the average for England and Wales we are "over-managed" to use their term. It's nonsense, of course, averages mean nothing but the authority doesn't want *anything* to attract attention to West Sussex given the mood the home secretary seems to be in these days.'

'How do I stack up, sir, if you can tell me?'

Quinlan paused then nodded as if answering his own question, not Fenwick's.

'I know I can rely on your discretion so I'll tell you, but if this ever leaks out...'

'It won't; I give you my word, sir.'

'You can't tell *anyone*, Andrew, understand, particularly someone else in the force.'

Fenwick nodded vigorously then stopped suddenly, confused by the emphasis.

'Of course.'

'On paper you come out as the leading candidate. Your arrest and conviction records are strong, your management experience is good and your recent work with MCS has really raised your profile. Also the Met gives you a good write-up, though that can be a double-edged sword at times.'

'You said "on paper".'

'Spoken words count for as much as written reports. As well as your record and the assessment programmes you've been on, the board will take verbal references. Given the quality of the competition it's my personal judgement that the verbals will count a lot.'

Fenwick tried to swallow but found he had no saliva.

'Who will they consult?' His voice sounded thin in his own ears.

'Me, MacIntyre, Cator I should imagine as he's written to them already, and of course the ACC.'

There was a silence loaded with significance. Both men had faces for poker so their expressions didn't change but inside Fenwick felt sick. When Quinlan remained silent he said the only thing he could think of to break the tension.

'You said you had two pieces of advice?'

'Ah yes.' To his surprise Quinlan flushed. 'This is hard for me to raise, Andrew, and it's all I'm ever going to say on the matter. For *both* your sakes, be very careful about how you act with regard to Inspector Nightingale. It does neither of you any good when you act as her advocate; in fact it does the opposite by creating and fuelling unhelpful conjecture. As to the reality of the situation, as you have moved to MCS, I have no interest whatsoever – that is your own...affair.'

'Sir?' Fenwick was completely baffled and let it show in his face. 'I don't understand.'

'I've said all I intend to on the matter. Think about it.'

'But...?'

'Enough. I'm already late and I'm told you have a suspect to interview. Let me know how it goes.'

Fenwick walked down the stairs slowly, pausing frequently as his thoughts went so deep as to stop his steps. The news about his promotion prospects was a shock but not a total surprise whereas the reference to Nightingale just confused him. But he wasn't a stupid man and he was used to solving puzzles, so by the time he'd reached the security door that opened onto the interview rooms he'd worked it out. There was nothing between them but an easy friendship, or so he told himself; they met up sometimes for a drink, and she came to supper with the children about once a month. But of course people were going to talk; of course there would be speculation about the nature of their relationship. It was ironic that it should be now.

No wonder he'd just been warned off, particularly with his promotion in the balance and hers the subject of jealous comments about preferment. He'd been an idiot to assume there wouldn't be rumours. Perhaps she had been naïve as well but he was the senior officer and he should've known better. It had been self-indulgent of him to continue to foster their friendship just because he enjoyed it so much. If he really cared about her, and to his surprise he realised that he did, very much, it was up to him to put a safe distance between them as quickly as possible. His emotions were in turmoil and his face grim as he punched in the code and made his way towards interview room three.

He found Nightingale waiting outside the interview room. Her body language radiated impatience.

'Is there somewhere you can brief me?' He ignored Nightingale's rapid blink at his tone.

'Here.' She signalled an empty interview room opposite.

'I've spoken to the ACC and it's agreed that I will be directing interview strategy personally.' Nightingale looked shaken but remained silent. 'What's happened so far?'

'Nothing. He insisted on a lawyer so I'd only just started. So far he's told us that he's not guilty and has nothing further to say.'

'Have you confronted him with the evidence?'

Nightingale tried to meet his eye, obviously confused by his abrupt manner and distance. Fenwick took a sheet of paper from a folder he was carrying and studied it instead. It was the fingerprint results that had prompted Maidment's arrest, a copy of which had found their way prematurely to the ACC while Fenwick had been in court.

'Not yet.'

'Good. We don't want to be premature, particularly if he chooses not to cooperate. What background have you gathered?'

'His service record is impeccable. He was decorated after action in Borneo and went on to become military liaison officer in France before a posting to Washington of some sort. There's not a lot about that on his file. He retired his commission twenty-three years ago and became secretary at The Downs Golf Club on the recommendation of his one-time commanding officer who was a member, a Lieutenant-Colonel Richard Edwards. He was also a non-executive director of three private companies until he retired three years ago when his wife became ill.

'He's an active member of the Baptist Church, has split a substantial proportion of his wealth between his only son and daughter-in-law and a number of cancer charities, and purchased a small house with the balance. He tithes one tenth of his income to the church, lives modestly and has no debts.'

'A perfect citizen,' Fenwick remarked. 'But I don't believe in perfection. Has he no vices?'

'There are rumblings that he had a mistress before his wife contracted cancer,' Nightingale said.

'Not all rumours are true, we need proof.' Fenwick avoided her eye and continued to look at the fingerprint evidence.

'There are three sets of prints on the outer sack, only Maidment's on the inner one,' he read out. 'But we haven't received the DNA analysis from the blood yet and may not be lucky enough to get a positive match. Apparently the blazer was soaked from several sources so it may be impossible to extract usable DNA. Were you running the interview before I arrived?'

'Yes.'

'Right, then you can join me but I'll take the lead and decide if and when to use the evidence against him. Send somebody to make sure the lab knows we need the DNA analysis urgently. And I want to see a copy of their report as soon as it's available. There's been one cock-up in keeping me informed and I won't tolerate another one, for any reason. Understood? Good.' He turned towards the interview room then paused.

'Oh, will you be involving Bob Cooper on this one now that he's been cleared by the internal inquiry?'

'Ah, yes, I could do. I see no reason why not.'

'That's good because you'll need someone of his experience on this one.'

Fenwick ignored her sharp intake of breath at the implied insult and put his papers in order, leaving Nightingale with flaming cheeks. If his back was burning as he walked away he gave no indication that he felt it.

CHAPTER SIXTEEN

Alison Reynolds sat in the middle of the conference room and stared at the photographs the surveillance team had taken over the previous months. It was the third time that she'd rearranged the boards looking for patterns. The first time the pictures had been set out in the order in which they'd been taken; then she had re-grouped them by location. Neither arrangement had produced any new insight. She had grown so familiar with the scenes that she was no longer seeing them so she told herself to take a break and went to buy a cup of tea in the canteen.

This was her fourth consecutive night of overtime. The money was welcome, particularly as that bastard husband of hers had stopped paying child support yet again and she was back to being the sole source of income for her little family. But her prolonged absences were causing pressure at home. She was lucky that her father and son got on as well as they did, but one was infirm and the other a typical twelve-year-old, which meant neither of them was very good in the kitchen or at keeping the house in order. They'd run out of her standby food from the freezer – good-quality home-made meals they enjoyed and that stopped James becoming so hyperactive – and were now relying on cheap ready meals. The additives weren't good for either of them and she felt guilty.

Alison forced herself back up the stairs at seven o'clock. There was no sign of Fenwick but then she was aware that he'd charged off to Harlden and wasn't expected back, whereas Clive had disappeared with no explanation and that annoyed her. They both knew they only had five days left to find something new or suspend the case and his apparent indifference had shifted the responsibility for handling Fenwick's expectations onto her shoulders. Clive was behaving as if he'd started another relationship, which was a bit quick seeing as his wife had only left him two months before and he'd supposedly been gutted by her infidelity.

'You're just jealous,' she told the empty room.

She hadn't had so much as a sniff of a steady boyfriend in the past twelve months and despaired of finding another partner. When would she ever have the time to begin looking?

'Right. Boards,' she said and turned to confront them yet again.

This time she arranged the pictures almost on a whim, without any logical sequence but based on photos she thought 'went together' rather like sorting a giant album. Looking at the hundreds of images it went through her mind that she must be mad to keep looking. There was nothing to help her eye through the deliberate chaos she'd created so her gaze skimmed the images, stopping briefly on aspects she hadn't noticed before.

In one picture Alec was selling an old Eurhythmics LP that she'd bought when it came out. It had been a favourite and seeing it again tugged a smile from the corners of her mouth. In another, she saw him pass over a single copy of the D–E part of the *Encyclopaedia Britannica* and wondered what on earth someone would want with that.

Alison walked along the boards grazing on the minutiae, indulging her curiosity. When she came to a picture of Alec selling the Eurhythmics LP again she was about to take it down as a duplicate when she paused in the act of pulling out the pin. He was wearing gloves and a scarf. She hurried back to the first board and found the image again. Here he was in a short-sleeved

T-shirt; it was summer. The photos had been taken at different times.

With a building sense of excitement Alison went through every board and pulled out those where products appeared to have been sold more than once. After an hour's solid work she had five piles. The same Eurhythmics LP had exchanged hands five times; she knew it was identical because there was a stain on the cover. A battered hardback of the *Wind in the Willows* had been sold ten times; *Lord of the Flies* six times; an obscure punk band LP – Vomit Psycho II – had been bought by the same person on three occasions; and a Stevie Wonder special edition single appeared a grand total of twenty times.

For every item she confirmed with the aid of a magnifying glass that it was the same piece being resold. She put each set in date order and then concentrated on the purchasers. After five minutes she needed pen and paper to keep track. At nine she called Fenwick at home, ducked his nagging about working late and told him she had some news.

'Alec Ball's using his market stall as a front for something. Some of his sales aren't legit.'

'But that's too obvious. It was the first thing the previous team checked out. And we've browsed his stuff time and again since as "customers" – it's all cheap books and old LPs. He's never taken the bait when we've trawled for porn or paedophilia.'

'So how do you explain him selling the same copy of some records repeatedly in the period we've had him under surveillance?'

She talked Fenwick through what she'd found; her excitement was contagious.

'But this is incredible – how did I miss it?' he asked, unconscious of his arrogance.

'Wasn't just you. We all overlooked it. It's your point about wood for the trees. And to be fair, there was always a gap before the item was resold so it wouldn't have been in recent memory, even assuming we'd spotted it.'

'So what's inside those covers?'

'Exactly. And who's buying them?'

'Are there any repeat purchasers?'

'A few. Again, they don't come very often but there are enough to follow up.'

'This is excellent work, Alison. Tell the rest of the team I owe them a beer.'

'Er...right.'

'First thing in the morning I'll be in Harlden interviewing Maidment...'

'I thought we'd had to pass that on.'

'I'm directing the interviewing while Choir Boy's still live and thanks to your breakthrough that could be for longer than anyone's expecting.' He chuckled, sounding remarkably relaxed. 'As soon as I'm done there I'll come back for a team briefing. Can you set it up for one o'clock?'

'Sure, no problem.'

'And Alison, you don't need to be in much before then, OK? This could be a long haul and you need to pace yourself.'

You're a fine one to talk, she thought but didn't say as she finished the call.

Despite his explicit instructions to go home Alison went back to the conference room and finished making notes to use in the morning briefing. Then she placed the photos in groups on the boards and annotated them so that she wouldn't forget anything. It was gone eleven when she'd finished and she felt exhausted. She'd have to be up at six to do some ironing and see to her father before preparing breakfast and lunches for the day. Even so she hesitated before she left.

There were some boards that she hadn't yet studied with fresh eyes; the ones with all the recent missing boys from West Sussex.

It broke her heart to look at them. So many; such a waste of life. Of course most would be runaways, nothing more sinister, but even so she thought of them as victims – maybe of their families, society, or their own characters. Her son was twelve, same age as the youngest on the board. If he ever ran away...her heart skipped a beat.

Maybe she *would* come in late tomorrow. She'd walk him to school, making sure not to do any embarrassing 'mum stuff', as he called it, and then she'd go shopping for their favourite foods. They'd have a bang-up supper tomorrow and she'd make sure she was home in time to cook it.

Sam didn't have to work again for a week. He was allowed to stay in bed as long as he liked. William visited regularly, bringing little treats that had Sam more confused than grateful.

On the day after Nathan's visit he'd brought him a giant bar of chocolate but Sam felt too ill to eat it. His body ached and he could barely swallow the sips of water that he craved. Most of the time he slept, deep, dark draughts of sleep that plunged him into nightmares from which he couldn't wake.

Somebody came to see him on the second day, a man he didn't recognise who carried a black bag and examined him. He was barely conscious. Despite his thirst his throat was too swollen to drink the water William tried to force on him. Sam was moved to a room of his own and the man stuck a drip in his arm. He could see him talking to William and once he thought he shouted but he couldn't understand the words and had no interest in them anyway.

Sometime later that day William changed the bag above the drip. Sam was awake enough to notice and starting to feel hungry. He still couldn't swallow properly but William brought him a cold yoghurt drink and he managed it all. In the evening he had mashed potato with gravy and some ice cream.

When he woke up the next day he had a headache but the pain in his body had eased. He was very hungry and although he still couldn't eat properly he sucked down scrambled eggs and chopped up the bacon so that he could swallow without too much discomfort. William came to see him again. This time he brought comics and a radio as well as sweets. He sat on the edge of Sam's bed and ruffled his hair gently. Not a lot was said but Sam got the impression that William was pleased with him. He managed sausages and chips for lunch and a burger for tea. There were no more drugs and Sam wondered whether the man with the bag had insisted they be stopped.

Next day he started to worry about when he'd have to work again. The bruises round his throat were greeny-yellow but other than that he looked OK. When William stopped by for one of what had become his regular visits, Sam waited with trepidation to be told that he was due in the room that evening. It didn't happen. Instead William started a long monologue about life; how sometimes things happened that weren't meant to but could turn out for the best; about how it was important to recognise these events as opportunities and make the most of them.

The lecture went over Sam's head. Once he knew he wasn't expected to work he concentrated on eating his way through the jumbo pack of sweets that William had brought, saving the liquorice wheels till last because they were his favourite. But when William mentioned Nathan's name he stopped chewing and concentrated.

'...Not a bad man really. In fact he's been very good to us. He's got connections, you see.'

Something in Sam's face must have betrayed his feelings because William put his hands on his shoulders, not threateningly like normal but in a soft kind of way.

'I know he hurt you a bit, Sam...'

'A bit!'

The words were out before Sam could stop them and he flinched instinctively at the anger in William's eyes. He tensed, ready for the blow but it never came. With obvious effort William kept his cool. Sam was amazed.

'He didn't mean it, Sam. It's never happened before, not even with Jack when he went mental on him. It's just that...well...it's you. You're his type. The word's out, you see. If any of us end up with someone with your looks we're to let him know. And he really liked you.'

'But I've been here weeks, William,' Sam said, emboldened by the apparent unwillingness to hurt him.

To his surprise William flushed and looked guilty.

'He had Jack.' He paused uncomfortably. 'Anyway, best not mention that to him when you next see him.'

'He's coming back?' Sam's voice held a note of pure terror. 'He can't be. He nearly killed me! You don't let people do that to us. I've heard you, kicking men out that go too far, telling them to fuck off and never come back.'

'Nathan's different.'

'He's a killer, that's what he is!' Sam shouted, 'He...' but his voice cracked and his throat hurt too much for him to continue.

'Enough.' William hit the back of his head hard with his fist so that Sam saw stars. 'Just because I've been decent to you doesn't mean you can take liberties. Got that?'

Sam felt tears on his cheeks and looked down at the bedding that covered his legs.

'I said, got that?' William hit him again.

'Yes, William,' he whispered.

'What? Can't hear you?'

'I said, "Yes, William".'

'Good boy.' William ruffled his hair and patted his arm, his temper disappearing as quickly as it had come. Sam continued to cry quietly.

'Come on,' William put an arm around his shoulders, 'it's not that bad.'

'He scares me.'

'He won't hurt you again, he's promised me. He got a little bit carried away, that's all and he's assured me it'll never happen again.'

'But why, William?' he asked timidly. 'Why are you letting him back after what he's done?'

'Because he's a very important man, Sam. You don't know how lucky you are that he's taken a fancy to you.' Sam flinched at his words but William continued, unaware. 'One word from him and a house is either made or it fails. Him liking you is going to be very good for us.'

'Did he like Jack as well?'

Sam remembered Jack in the days before he disappeared, hunched against the wall, sometimes muttering to himself, avoided by the other customers. There'd been something not right about Jack that made everybody keep their distance and Sam now thought he understood why. William shrugged but answered his question.

'For a while he liked Jack, though not as much as he likes you. He called you perfect when he rang me yesterday. He wanted to know how you were.'

'What did you say?'

'That you were almost your old self, of course.' William glanced at Sam's neck and then looked away again quickly.

Silence filled the small room, punctuated by an occasional sniff from Sam.

'I'm giving you the rest of the week off,' William said eventually.

Sam wasn't fooled.

'When's he coming back?'

But William didn't answer. Instead he stood up and patted him on the head.

'You just relax and enjoy your rest, young man. Don't worry, we're going to take extra special care of you.'

When he went out of the room Sam heard a key turn in the lock on the other side of the door. He jumped out of bed and tried the handle. It wouldn't budge. He shook it anyway and then hammered on the door, kicking it with his bare feet when his fists started to ache. It was no good. He was locked in tight and there was nobody out there who would risk letting him out.

He slumped back on his bed, crying. When the tears ran out he put his head under the bedclothes and sulked, but that became boring after a while and eventually he started to read the comics that William had brought him. By seven o'clock, when his supper was brought to him, he was fast asleep, the remains of a liquorice wheel stuck tight to his hand.

PART THREE

SEPTEMBER, 1982

Paul huddled in the corner of the toilet trying to keep his feet up off the floor while holding the door closed with his back at the same time. It was a useless hiding place but the only one that he'd been able to find after running away from the men outside. He had assumed there would be a back door that he could slip out of and away into the woods. Instead he was trapped in a dead end, terrified and alone. He pressed himself harder into the corner against the hinge and wedged his feet against the back wall but they kept slipping.

When they'd pulled his clothes off and thrown him into the pool he'd panicked but he was a good swimmer, particularly under water, and he had managed to slip through their legs and reach the steps at the other side while they were still laughing at their sick joke. As he'd leapt away from the pool he'd heard Alec swear and shout out his name. The man's tone had sent a shot of fear through him that added speed to his feet and he'd made it to the pool house in seconds. Only when he was inside did he realise that there was no way out but back to the pool.

So he huddled against the door, shivering with fear and cold. His ears were straining to hear the slightest sound and when the whisper of a man's soft breathing filled the room, he went rigid with fear. His wet feet slipped down the wall again and he strained his legs to try and hold them. His toes splayed, grasping desperately for purchase.

The breathing came closer. He could sense bare feet padding on the white tiles and screwed his eyes shut tight. He started to cry ever so softly so that no one should hear.

'Paul?'

It was Bryan's voice, gentle not angry but that was no comfort. He knew that Bryan couldn't protect him from the men outside, had never intended to. It was all about money; Bryan had only pretended to care for him. If only he had his knife with him he'd leap out and stick him through and through until he was dead. But the knife was with the rest of his things by the side of the pool, far away and of no use.

'Paul, I know where you are, don't mess about. Don't you realise that wet feet leave tracks?'

Paul looked down with horror at the splashes that had puddled on the floor beneath him and failed to stifle a sob.

'There, there, don't cry; there's no need to. No harm will come to you if you're a good boy. Come on back with me.' Bryan's voice grew louder and his face appeared over the door.

Paul let out a wail of dismay and slid to the floor in a heap, sobbing helplessly.

'Come on, my dear. Crying spoils your pretty face and they won't like that.'

Bryan bent down to lift him up. Paul brought his head up suddenly and connected so hard with Bryan's chin that both sets of teeth crunched together loud enough to hear. Bryan stumbled backwards and Paul scuttled around his legs, bolting for the outside without looking back.

'You little bastard!' Bryan cried. 'Get him, Alec. Catch the little prick, he's coming your way.' He lumbered after Paul but the boy had already left the building and was haring towards the woods at the edge of the property as if the hounds of hell were after him.

Behind him he could hear shouts, swearing and the thump of running feet but he didn't care. He was only little; if he could make the fence he'd be able to squeeze over it and hide. He'd almost made it when a massive hand clamped his shoulder fast, making him miss his step. He lashed out and had the satisfaction of feeling his fingernails slash flesh, but the movement made him lose his balance and he fell to the ground. A fist descended and hit him in the side of his head so hard that he saw stars. The hand rose again but before it could fall someone else grabbed it from behind.

'What the fuck do you think you're doing, Alec?' It was Nathan's voice, angrier than Paul had ever heard it. 'No bruises, remember?'

'If you think this little bugger's going back home after what he's just done to me, you've got another think coming!' Alec hit Paul again to prove he meant it, earning a clout round the face himself from Nathan with something hard enough to raise a long red weal.

'I said enough. Now get off him, I mean it.'

Something in Nathan's tone sobered Alec and he lifted his knees off Paul's chest. He gulped air gratefully. Out of the corner of his eye Paul saw something silver in Nathan's hand and with a shock of pure terror realised it was a revolver. He rolled on his side, his stomach heaving, his head on fire.

'Bring him,' Nathan instructed and he felt hands lift him as easily as if he were a side of meat. His head swung low over someone's back and he recognised Bryan. He moaned.

'Please, please, Bryan, let me go.' He pleaded. 'I want to go home. I won't say anything, I promise.'

Bryan ignored him.

'Bryan!' he cried, desperate now, 'don't take me back, they'll hurt me, I know it. Please!' He was sobbing, his tears splattering the small of Bryan's naked back.

'You should never have run away, kid. I can't help you now.'

'But you're my friend. Help me please.'

Bryan swung him upright and stood him on his feet. Paul swayed a little as the blood rushed from his head but he kept his balance and threw his arms about Bryan's waist, begging him to protect him from the others. His cries were so pathetic that Bryan pulled him close to his body so that their skins touched, his warm from exertion, Paul's icy cold.

'Listen, love,' he whispered, 'be a good boy now and I'll get you out of here. You've got to do what they say – and make as if you enjoy it so that they start to like you again. When it's all over I'll make sure you reach home.'

Paul pulled away from him again, his eyes full of hope and fear.

'You promise?' he asked tentatively.

Bryan took a deep breath and held Paul's hands tight.

'Yes,' he said, 'I promise.'

'Really?'

'Have I ever lied to you?' he replied with a smile.

Paul shook his head automatically and followed his friend back to the pool. It wasn't until much, much later that he realised his whole friendship with Bryan had been a lie.

CHAPTER SEVENTEEN

Something had changed. Maidment sensed it as soon as the new detective entered the room. He radiated authority. Attractive blighter, probably had women falling all over him. Fenwick he called himself, a good North Country name. He looked as if he came from strong stock and in other circumstances he would have appreciated the straightforward intelligence he thought he saw in him. But if Fenwick was now in charge of his interrogation it would become more difficult to hold the line.

No further mention was made of the evidence they had against him. Apart from during his caution, which was repeated yet again for the benefit of the tapes, Paul Hill wasn't mentioned. Instead Fenwick appeared to be curious about his life history from childhood through his service days.

He was courteous, interested and above all patient but the major knew that he was merely trying to establish rapport. A bond of trust was meant to be woven from the threads of his shared life story. Had he not been trained to withstand hostile interrogation while in the army Maidment thought that he might have been fooled.

As it was, he preserved his detachment behind a polite façade but that didn't stop him studying the pair of detectives – his interrogators – exactly as he had been taught to do. Maidment picked up tension between them as if they were husband and wife and had just had a row. The thought made him smile.

'Was that a happy memory?'

Maidment frowned at Fenwick's enquiry.

'You smiled.'

'Oh…just thinking of arguments between husbands and wives.'

'Ah,' it was Fenwick's turn to smile, 'did you have many with Hilary?'

At the mention of his wife's name Maidment felt the familiar blade twist in his gut.

'No more than the average couple…and probably no less.'

'You were married for thirty-five years – a long time.'

'Thirty-six. I suppose it seems long but a happy marriage can't be measured in years. It becomes a form of joint existence. You wait, you'll find out, particularly when the children leave home.'

'I'm a widower.'

Fenwick coughed and looked down at his notes, turning pages as if searching for something but Maidment wasn't deceived. He recognised grief from personal experience and felt a rush of sympathy for the man.

'I'm sorry, I had no idea. You're too young.'

Fenwick laughed without humour.

'You should know better than anybody, Jeremy, that death is no respecter of age. Even young boys die before their appointed time.'

Maidment felt as if he'd been struck by a friend. The implied accusation hung in the air between them. Stenning looked distressed, Nightingale as lean and hungry as Cassius. Only Fenwick's expression was unchanged as he looked up.

'I was referring, of course, to your experience in the army. You must have seen men die in combat.'

Maidment could only nod in reply, unable to trust his voice.

'What's death like close up? I've rarely seen it happen, only the bodies afterwards. What's it like to see the eyes glaze and hear the last breath?'

Maidment couldn't answer. The question sounded sinister despite its context and he was concerned that however he replied he might incriminate himself.

'It's not something I talk about, Miss Nightingale.'

'But you have killed, have you not?'

'In the line of duty, yes; in Borneo, defending a gun emplacement and...later.'

The woman leant forward.

'How did it make you feel?' she asked.

'Feel?' He scratched his head. 'It's...hard to describe...'

'You don't need to answer this, Jeremy.' His solicitor glared at Nightingale.

'It's all right, Stenning, I have nothing to hide.'

He was feeling tired suddenly and glanced at Fenwick's watch. Stenning had explained his rights to him. They would have to apply to a magistrate for remand or release him. So far they'd gained nothing from the interviews. If he could keep them diverted he might yet be allowed home. At least so he rationalised but deep down he didn't trust this sudden desire to talk, which he suspected might be motivated by the need for them to see him as the man he had once been and to realise that such a person was incapable of killing a boy of fourteen.

It was inevitable that he should feel this way but any desire, even one as self-serving as this, was dangerous in an interrogation. He would just have to be careful. Perhaps he could turn the whole thing into a history lesson; that would serve her right.

'I don't mind telling you of my army experiences. My years of active service fell in the late Fifties and Sixties, a strange time for Britain. Your generation is too young to remember the impact of the break-up of what remained of the British Empire. We were determined not to abandon our colonies despite what is said today.

'Oh don't shake your head like that,' he said to Nightingale. 'Colony isn't a dirty word, it's a statement of fact. I accept that sometimes our attempts at handover fell short of what was required but that wasn't a matter of policy, it was usually due to human failure.

'Great Britain had been a global super-power. At one time our empire was the envy of the developed world. Oh good grief, grow up, Inspector Nightingale!' he burst out suddenly. 'That wince reminds me of my son.'

Nightingale could no longer contain herself.

'You mean Britain grew rich on the systematic exploitation and rape of weaker nations.'

'Socialist propaganda!'

'Nonsense. In the nineteenth century Britain sent gunboats to China to defend our right to pay the labourers their pathetic wages in opium! We created a generation of addicts and used our might to defend the practice. I call that disgusting.'

For the first time the major faltered, then he nodded slowly.

'I accept that power corrupts and I cannot excuse some of the excesses of the Victorians but most of what we did was good. We built a valuable legacy and that's what soldiers such as I strove hard to preserve as Britain withdrew control. We had an enduring sense of responsibility towards our Commonwealth.'

'Rubbish...'

'Enough, Nightingale.' Fenwick leant forward with the first trace of impatience. 'You were going to tell us about your experience in Borneo, Major. We don't have time for a history lesson.'

He glared at Nightingale in an open instruction to keep her mouth shut.

'Very well. The British had been a power in South-East Asia for centuries. We were committed to the introduction of self-governance by the terms we agreed with the League of Nations but our goal was to go beyond that to full independence. Now in

Malaya and Burma, independence happened quickly as a result of the war...'

'Because the Japanese threw us out and set up sympathetic nationalist regimes!' Nightingale muttered under her breath but Maidment didn't catch it and Fenwick kicked her foot under the table hard enough for her to shut up.

'...but afterwards there was a lot of manoeuvring. Indonesia started to get ideas that it should control all Malay-speaking areas. I say, you do know the area I'm talking about, don't you, my dear?' he asked Nightingale. 'It's a large group of islands that lies south of Vietnam and China. The vast southern part of the island of Borneo was under Indonesian control; the strip along the north was made up of three separate states: Sarawak, Brunei and—'

'Sabatan, yes thank you so much.' Nightingale almost spat out the words.

'Well, well.' He looked at her in surprise and then nodded. 'The head of Indonesia, a chap called Sukarno, started to get ideas. He tried to assume control of the whole area and create a pan-Indonesian confederation of states. We couldn't stand for that so troops were sent in. What followed was one of the most successful British campaigns ever.

'Sukarno never declared war so technically we never went to war. He used what today would be called terrorism: stirring up trouble in Brunei, backing armed rebels who attacked the oilfields, taking hostages and beheading some of the poor blighters.'

'I had no idea. The parallels with Iraq...'

'Exactly, Mr Fenwick, and if only the British Army now had been allowed to use the tactics we did back then, things would be very different. Anyway, the trouble in Brunei spread to Sarawak.' He saw Fenwick's confused look. 'Remember it was part of the northern coast of Borneo; General Waller was made Commander of British Forces, Borneo.

'He was an inspiring leader; he decided to run everything from a joint headquarters – army, navy, air force and the local police. It was a brilliant decision.

'Problem was we couldn't attack Sukarno's insurgents, even though they were free to raid the north whenever they wanted.'

'That sounds an impossible situation; very demoralising I would have thought.'

Maidment detected real interest in Fenwick's comment and warmed to his theme.

'Not with Waller in charge. He had previously established and commanded the Jungle Warfare School in Malaya and was a better tactician in that terrain than the natives. He negotiated with the British Government – Healy it was then – that we could cross the border provided we were in hot pursuit of the rebels for a distance of up to three thousand yards.'

'About two miles, not far.'

'Far enough at first. He also set about winning the confidence of the natives. British servicemen and medics befriended the Dyak villagers whose lands straddled the border with Indonesian Borneo. They received food and medical aid and quickly saw us Brits as friendly and their Indonesian neighbours as dangerous aggressors. As a result we received excellent information and the rebels were denied assistance by the villagers.

'Then Sukarno was stupid enough to attempt an invasion of Malaya and Waller was allowed to undertake proper cross-border operations. Eventually, in retaliation for raids we were allowed to go in twenty thousand yards.'

'Did you use guerrilla tactics?' Nightingale asked.

'A pretty accurate assumption,' Maidment conceded. 'At first it was only the SAS that penetrated enemy territory but when Waller started what he called his "Claret" operations he needed more men. These were top-secret missions, personally authorised by him and very risky.

'He only used tried and tested troops; civilian lives were not to be put at risk – very important that. We went in without air support and the planning was immaculate; knowledge of any attack was restricted to a few people; and...' he paused to wipe his forehead, hoping they hadn't picked up his distress, 'on absolutely no account could any soldier involved be captured by the enemy, dead or alive.'

'Pretty dodgy; you could have been accused of spying.' Fenwick seemed impressed by their daring.

'Only if they caught us and they never did.'

His throat closed up preventing further speech. Emotions he'd thought buried for years surfaced without warning and he was taken aback by their strength.

'I'm rather tired; can we call it a day, do you think?'

Stenning nodded vigorously.

'We've only interviewed you for two and a half hours including a break for coffee. There's plenty of time for you to conclude your story.'

Maidment took a deep breath. Really, he told himself, there's nothing to worry about. It was all dead history.

'Very well. My battalion had benefited from General Waller's jungle training so when we arrived we were moved to the front line. Once there we received guidance from the members of twenty-two SAS who'd been sending out four-man patrols for months. I participated in many incursions during my tour there.'

He stopped abruptly.

'Go on.'

'I've already said that these missions were top secret. I'm not sure that it's right to say more.'

'Come, Major, the Borneo conflict was resolved forty years ago and has been written and talked about widely since. I appreciate that some memories are difficult...'

'Especially guilty ones,' Nightingale interjected, ignoring

Fenwick's glare. 'I thought you said you had nothing to be ashamed of. Prove it.'

Maidment was irritated by her aggression but took care that it shouldn't show.

'A man doesn't need to prove his innocence in Britain. It is one of the things that keeps our country Great.'

'I'm sensitive to that,' Fenwick's tone was relaxed, almost friendly, 'but you've captured my imagination and General Waller sounds like a man under whom I would have been proud to serve. Please, complete the picture for me. What was it like in the jungle, at night, undertaking an operation that wasn't even supposed to be happening but upon which the stability of the region depended?'

Maidment warmed to Fenwick's obvious respect. He angled his body towards him and tried to blot out Nightingale's presence.

'One is terrified beforehand, naturally. Any man who says he isn't is either a liar or a fool. It's not necessarily fear for one's own survival, although that's there of course. For me it was more fear of failure, that it would be the patrol I commanded that was captured.'

'But that never happened.'

'My patrols didn't fail but we were almost captured…once.' He paused but their silence spurred him on.

'All raids were undertaken by small parties, typically four men like an SAS patrol. We'd picked up news that the enemy was establishing a new base near the border and were moving in heavy armament. Our job was to infiltrate the base and set explosives to destroy the weapons before they could be used.

'It was a very hot night as always. Our hands slipped on our rifles and the mosquitoes found any bare skin. We didn't use repellent because the smell could give one away but we plastered on mud and that slowed the blighters down a bit. It was cloudy, which was good for us, with a quarter moon. We set out as soon as it was dark because it would take up to six hours to find the camp. One of the Dyaks we were working with met us at the edge of his land about a mile behind the Indonesian line. He said he'd take us the rest of the way, which was brave of him as he didn't need to do more than give us directions.

'About one in the morning we heard the sound of someone spitting. It was a guard on their camp. He was less than fifty feet in front of us but he hadn't heard a thing. Jimmy went forward and dealt with him, then we all moved on. I sent the Dyak back. He was a decent fellow but unarmed and not in uniform and there was a danger that he might get hurt by accident. We circled around to the south side of their installation where there was a pile of munitions. Jimmy kept watch while the rest of us, Stan, Archie and I, set the charges. It took us less than twenty minutes and we were about to leave when Jim ran back to say that a dozen men were coming up the track into camp.

'They were bound to notice the absence of the guard. The charges were primed, timers set. I sent the others back to a rendezvous point while I reduced the time delay on one charge to a minute. That way we could take out some of the new arrivals and create a diversion, allowing us to escape.'

He paused and closed his eyes. The smell and noise of the jungle came back to him. He could recall the sweat on his hands, making his fingers clumsy as he fiddled with the final timer.

'I don't know how it happened but as I was leaving the munitions pile I heard a gunshot. It wasn't one of ours but that didn't make any difference. Another one followed and I heard my lads returning fire. I was down on my belly and crawling so fast you wouldn't believe it. It didn't matter about noise as all hell was breaking loose. One of the bastards switched on a searchlight, another lit a flare. It threw the jungle into relief like a lightning bolt and caught Jimmy in the open. I think he was coming back to find me, against my explicit orders. Whatever, he was shot instantly. The round caught him in the right shoulder and spun him flat less than fifty yards from me.

'He was conscious when I got to him but bleeding badly. Together we managed to reach the others and we set off along our original track. One of us would stay and give covering fire while the other two would help Jim. Then the coverer would peel away to the side and we'd take over firing till he joined us; a classic retreat, except that poor old Jim slowed us down. He must have been in agony but he didn't cry out once.

'When the first of the charges went up we managed to give our pursuers the slip. It took us an hour to cover the distance we'd done originally in half that and I knew we wouldn't make the border before daylight, but we had no choice but to keep going or Jimmy would die.

'I blame myself for what happened next,' he said and stared at Nightingale as if daring her censure. 'Some time around four in the morning we paused to rest and apply new dressings to Jimmy's shoulder. He could barely stand because of loss of blood. We'd been moving fast so I thought we had a good chance to stay ahead of them and keep going in daylight if we could only find some way of carrying Jim. We found a thick patch of undergrowth and I sent Archie off to find wood that we could use to make a sling. Meanwhile Stanley and I changed the dressing on his shoulder. We couldn't risk any light but I could tell from the feel of the wound that the bullet had gone straight through and that it was still bleeding. Between us we did the best we could for him and gave him a shot of morphine.

'Archie came back and I made them eat and drink as I tied Jim to the poles, using webbing to strap him so as to avoid pressure on his shoulder as much as we could. Still it must have been agony for him despite the drugs. Then we set off again. I estimated that we had at least three hours' travel left before the border and more like five to one of our camps. We went in single file, the two carriers leading. Dawn came about six and I had to make a decision – hole up and wait out the day or keep going. I took one look at Jim, who was semi-conscious, and we kept going. We stopped again briefly after two hours to rest from carrying Jim. He was unconscious by this time and had started groaning. I'm afraid we gagged him to stop the noise. It sounds repulsive, I know, but we couldn't risk him betraying our location.'

Again he closed his eyes. There was silence in the room but for the faint whirr of the double tape recorder.

'The border was less than an hour away when one of their search patrols found us. We were bent down adjusting some of the webbing on Jimmy when an Indonesian soldier almost fell over us. Archie slit his throat but he let off a round as he died and half a dozen of them emerged from the trees less than twenty yards away. There was no real cover. We let fly at them and they fired back at us. Archie was by far the best shot; he took out two immediately; Stanley and I downed three between us but we missed the sixth man and he fired straight at us.

'The bastard caught Archie in the face before I could kill him. Archie was still alive when he hit the ground.'

There was a stunned silence. The three men swallowed audibly but Nightingale simply asked, 'And how old were the boys in your patrol, Major?' She sounded cool and dispassionate in the silence of the room.

It was impossible to tell which of them gasped at her callousness, perhaps they all did. Nightingale merely raised her eyebrows to emphasise her enquiry. Maidment swallowed hard and answered her without bothering to disguise his contempt.

'Jim was the youngest; twenty from south London. He was the wild one, always a step ahead of the MPs, but he wrote to his girlfriend every chance he had. Let me tell you what happened to Jim. He was lying on the ground when the fire fight started. A stray bullet hit him, entering his groin and travelling up and out of his back. The exit wound was so big I could have put a golf ball in it. It killed him instantly.

'The next oldest was Archie; he was twenty-two. He was skinny as a rake, with crazy red hair and freckles so he suffered miserably in the sun. Archie was a quiet man, thoughtful but as tough as old boots. The bullet took half his face off, jawbone, ear and the side of his mouth. Do you know what it's like to stare at the inside of a man's mouth, to see the tongue desperately trying to talk with cheeks and lips that no longer exist?' He stared pointedly at Nightingale who for once didn't have a ready answer. 'No, I didn't think you would.

'Stanley and I were older. He escaped with a head wound, a graze really.'

'And you?' Fenwick's tone was gentle.

'Relatively minor wounds; Archie took the bullet that was meant for me.' Maidment had to look away but then he turned back, his face betraying his anger. 'So to answer your earlier question, miss, about what it's like to see the eyes of the men I killed and to hear their last breath, I can't tell you. But I saw my men as the sun broke through the clouds, so red I thought it was gorged with their blood. I saw them slashed open, mutilated, eviscerated and still breathing. And I see them still in my dreams, or on bad days even when I'm awake. Don't you dare imply that I enjoyed that slaughter. The men I've killed all died in a fair fight and I would kill again if called upon to do so by my country because that is my *duty*, Chief Inspector, and not my crime.'

Fenwick was stunned into silence by the passion of Maidment's words but they had no impact on Nightingale.

'You're not under arrest for those deaths, Major Maidment,' she said, 'but for the abduction and murder of a young boy.' She actually managed a smile.

Maidment was speechless, his solicitor furious and ready to complain.

'I think we've all had enough for now,' Fenwick intervened quickly. 'I'll have you escorted back to your cell and we'll start again tomorrow. Yes, our twenty-four hours isn't up, Major, and you'll be enjoying our hospitality tonight.'

He and Nightingale watched as the two men left. When the door closed he turned on her.

'What the bloody hell are you playing at?'

She shrugged, indifferent.

'Good cop, bad cop. You've obviously decided to become best mates with our prime suspect so I need to play the hard bitch.'

'Play? It seemed to come quite naturally. The old guy was clearly shaken and you just put the boot in – with relish!'

'I can assure you I remained dispassionate throughout the interview, which is more than you did. Falling for the old soldier's sob story. He's a kiddie killer! May I speak frankly?'

'Please do.' Fenwick's voice was like ice but she appeared not to notice.

'I think your attitude was more dangerous to the interrogation than my detachment.'

'That was not detachment, Nightingale, that was cruelty. You were close to the line and with his solicitor present.'

'Going close to the line is part of our job, remember?' Suddenly she was angry. 'And as for cruelty, don't you dare lecture me. I can assure you I learnt it from a master.'

They glared at each other under the harsh fluorescent light, her look daring him to read everything into her words that she'd intended.

'I'll ignore that last remark,' he said eventually and angled his face away from her as he made a show of gathering his notes.

She grabbed her bag and flounced out, slamming the door behind her and leaving Fenwick alone with his doubts. Had he gone soft on the major because of his war record? He was an easy man for another man to like but he was old-fashioned, arrogant and – yes, she was right – a bit too good to be true. But, no, he wasn't fooled. The major had shown himself to be a robust professional. Whatever demons haunted him he'd learnt to cope with them, which meant that he could as easily conceal his involvement in a crime, even one as hideous as the abuse and murder of a child. If he had been involved in Paul Hill's murder it was going to be difficult to squeeze any information out of him. He had few hopes for the interrogation the following morning and, in the event, was proved right.

CHAPTER EIGHTEEN

The police interview tactics changed as Maidment entered his second day in custody. Overnight Fenwick had decided to be blunt and confront him with the evidence rather than try and coax a confession out of him. Although he wouldn't admit it to Nightingale, he'd concluded that his previous approach would get them nowhere. Maidment was too practised in handling interrogations and had almost perfect self-control so he couldn't afford to waste precious custody hours in the hope of softening him up.

He ignored the look of disapproval on Nightingale's face when he told her that he'd asked Sergeant Bob Cooper to join him in the interview room at eight o'clock. Strictly speaking it was her case and she should have been there but as he had been given the lead on the interviews he reasoned to himself that it was his call who participated. And anyway, he thought, it would give Nightingale more time to concentrate on the inquiry.

By nine o'clock neither Fenwick nor Cooper had succeeded in squeezing another word from their suspect. At nine-thirty the DNA results arrived and Fenwick stopped the interview. Nightingale was waiting for them in the detectives' room and the look of triumph on her face told him all he needed to know before he opened the file.

The lab report confirmed that the blood on the sack was Maidment's, as were microscopic spots on the collar of Paul's shirt. Traces of Paul's own blood had been found on the inside of his shirt sleeve but the blood on the blazer came from more than one person and there was no way of telling whose it was, or whether Paul's blood had been on the blazer and then contaminated by another's. The findings were a bitter blow to Fenwick as the blood from the shirt alone wouldn't be enough to support a charge of murder as it wasn't sufficient to indicate that Paul bled to death.

Blood removed from the trousers was neither Maidment's nor Paul's and there was no match in the system. Hairs taken from the blazer were visually identical to those taken from Paul's hairbrush but Fenwick asked Nightingale to have the lab extract DNA from the root for confirmation as without it they might not be able to prove at trial that the blazer was his.

As SIO it was up to Nightingale to decide on strategy and Fenwick left her to it, knowing that if he sat in he would be unable to keep quiet. They had a lot of work ahead of them and he hoped that she wouldn't be arrogant enough to be over-confident. Although the forensic evidence was strong it wasn't conclusive. The prosecution wouldn't be able to rely on it alone given the suspect's character and impeccable past. Building the case was also going to be complicated by the fact that in 1982 the police had another suspect, Bryan Taylor, a man they never found and a perfect gift to the defence. Fenwick was frustrated that he couldn't be more involved but he consoled himself with the thought that he would soon be busy enough with Choir Boy now that there were fresh leads to follow up. The only thing left for him to do in Harlden was to try to connect Maidment to the Choir Boy ring. He rejoined the interview and watched with interest as Cooper interrogated the major with all the subtlety of a JCB building a sandcastle.

'Where were you on the afternoon of 7th September, 1982?'

'How is my client supposed to remember that?' Stenning looked exhausted despite his night's rest but his voice was spirited enough.

'It's all right, Stenning. In 1982 I was retired from the army after more than thirty years and started working at The Downs Golf Club as secretary. In September 1982 I would have been engaged in overhauling the membership records, which I found to be in a poor state, approving plans for an extension and new terrace, and dismissing one of the groundsmen for moonlighting, petty theft and inappropriate behaviour.'

'Who was it you dismissed?'

'A man called Bryan Taylor.'

Fenwick ignored Cooper's meaningful glance.

'And on the 7th?'

'What day of the week was it?'

'A Tuesday.'

'In the afternoon, you say. Well, that's easy. The membership committee met on the first Tuesday of every other month and I acted as secretary.'

'At what time?'

'Five o'clock, finishing at six-thirty unless we had a particularly tricky matter to address.'

'And you would have been at this meeting?' Cooper tried to hide his scepticism.

'It will be simple enough to check. The diaries from that time are in my loft at home.'

'And after the committee meeting?'

'Typically I would have written up the minutes, had a drink in the bar and a late supper in the club restaurant.'

'At what time?'

'I left for home at twenty-one hundred hours.'

'Did this routine ever vary?'

The major paused, his face a picture of careful consideration.

'When my wife became ill it was different. Her appointment with the specialist was on a Tuesday afternoon. If it coincided with the membership committee then someone else stood in as secretary. I think that happened three or four times but that started in 2001.'

The questioning reached a dead end, and Fenwick took over.

'How do you explain your fingerprints on the sack containing Paul Hill's blazer and shirt?'

Stenning blanched but the major's expression remained calm. 'I can't.'

'Are you surprised that they are there?'

'Yes.'

'Fingerprints are unique, Jeremy. If yours are on the sack containing his clothes you must have touched it.'

'Maybe someone took a sack belonging to me and used it.'

Stenning nodded vigorously, some of the colour returning to his face.

'Then how do you explain your blood on the inside of the sack?'

For a brief moment the major looked surprised, then there was a fleeting look of calculation and an almost imperceptible nod before his face folded into its customary neutrality.

'Surely that is consistent with someone taking the sack.'

'But spots of it were on Paul's clothing as well.'

'Perhaps they were transferred from the sack to the clothing.' The major shrugged and shook his head as if mystified. 'Check my diaries; I'm certain that you will find I have an alibi.'

His sustained self-confidence was infuriating but it encouraged his solicitor into a rare intervention as if he suddenly realised that he had an active role to play in the process.

'The major is renowned for his prodigious recall. He is also a most honourable man, as any number of character witnesses will testify.'

Maidment smiled at him briefly in thanks and Fenwick decided it was time to test that prodigious memory further.

'Do you know anyone by the name of Joseph Watkins?'

Maidment was startled by the abrupt change in questioning and wrinkled his brow in concentration.

'Member of the club since 1987; I don't really know him; we never socialise.'

'Really, are you sure? Because we'll be checking up. Better you tell us than we find out from someone else.'

'If you must know, I was against Watkins' membership but as secretary I didn't have a vote on the committee and others were supportive.'

'Why weren't you keen?'

'Wrong type. Johnny-come-lately with more money than taste. Not even a particularly good golfer; didn't play often enough.'

'Who nominated him?'

Maidment hesitated. It was only brief but it was enough for Fenwick to be on the alert.

'Richard Edwards. He was chair of the membership committee for a number of years and had a lot of influence.'

Fenwick made a note of the name.

'And is he still a member?'

'Very much so, president year before last.'

'Do you know somebody called Alec Ball?'

'No.'

'Are you a member of Burgess Hill Gentlemen's Club?'

'That place? Good Lord no. Used to be all right but very run down now. What is this all about?'

Fenwick ignored the question. For the next hour he tried every tactic he knew to press Maidment into revealing anything that might connect him to Choir Boy. Eventually he had to admit defeat and the major was returned to his cell.

Fenwick and Cooper went to the canteen to buy an early lunch.

'He's an arrogant so-and-so isn't he?' Cooper remarked as he asked for extra poppadoms with his chicken curry.

'Yes. It's no wonder Nightingale can't stand him but I bet he gets on well with his cronies.'

'Too right. She called me last night to ask me to dig into his background and talk to his mates. I was meant to be starting on that this morning.'

Both men looked a little guilty as they acknowledged that Fenwick had arbitrarily overridden the wishes of Nightingale as SIO on the case but it didn't affect their appetites.

'She's made the right choice. Are you going to add this man Edwards to the list?'

'He's already on it. They were in the army together; it was Edwards got him the job at the golf club when he came out.'

'What's he like?'

'Too early to say, really. I'll give you a call when I've seen him if you like.'

'Thanks. I'm going to leave you to it and get back to MCS. I'll probably have another go at Maidment later this week.'

'No problem. You busy?'

'There's lots on as always.'

'Anything special? Only I wondered why you were so interested in the Maidment case, that's all.' Cooper took a large forkful of rice and curry as if to emphasise that his question was only casual.

Fenwick wondered whether rumour of Choir Boy had reached Harlden but decided to keep quiet.

'The possibility of a connection, that's all. Nothing really special. Don't suppose you've heard the latest cricket score, have you?'

Nightingale found them drinking coffee in the canteen when she returned from a search of Maidment's house. They looked relaxed and friendly.

'I rushed back,' she said, slightly breathless from her run down the stairs. 'We found a long knife that looks foreign and a whole pile of press cuttings about Paul Hill.'

'Have you brought his diaries back with you?' Fenwick asked before draining his coffee.

'Diaries? Oh you mean the journals we found in his attic. There were about fifty of them; they'll be processed in the normal way.'

'Even the ones for the years covering Eagleton and Hill's disappearances?'

Nightingale flushed but kept her temper in check.

'Let me speak more clearly, perhaps words of few syllables will help. Yes, we found them. They are coming here with the other items we recovered.'

'Good. Well, I need to be heading back.' Fenwick stood up, not quite looking at either of them. 'I'll leave you to it.'

Nightingale sat down as Cooper went, unasked, to fetch her a coffee and a bun as a peace offering. She stared for a moment at Fenwick's retreating back but then decided that life was too short to allow him to get under her skin. It was a good resolution but one she found hard to hold on to as she sipped her coffee and discussed with Cooper her plans for the investigation.

Fenwick was late for the briefing but Alison had made use of the time by distributing a copy of her notes from the night before. The Choir Boy team was clustered around the boards in animated conversation which died when he walked in.

'This is good work,' he said without preamble. 'Well done all of you involved.'

There was a moment's sheepish silence, then Clive said, 'Actually, this is all down to Alison, sir. She's the one who did the hard slog.'

There was muttered agreement and Alison shrugged.

'Everyone was involved somehow.'

'Whatever,' Fenwick had little time for false modesty, 'it's given us something concrete to work on. Who are the regular buyers of the dodgy goods?'

Clive answered, automatically taking the lead as he did given any opportunity but Alison didn't appear to mind.

'There are three main repeat purchasers: these two blokes that we haven't identified yet and, guess who?' He paused dramatically but Fenwick waved him on impatiently. 'Joseph Watkins!'

'At last.' Fenwick grinned, as if he could already taste Watkins' conviction. But instead of offering congratulations he asked critically, 'Why didn't we pick this up during surveillance?'

Clive looked uncomfortable. A significant part of tailing Watkins had been his responsibility but he had his answer ready.

'We had a look at that this morning, sir. When Watkins went to the stall he typically spent less than a minute there. A little bit of casual browsing and then one purchase. He always stopped by in the middle of his visit to the market and by the time he reached Ball's stall he had other packages and bags so it wasn't even obvious sometimes that he'd bought something. Honestly, there was nothing in the least remarkable about his behaviour.'

'Obviously. Go on. Tell me more about Alec Ball.'

'Alec Ball keeps his stuff in a storage depot north of Brighton, goes there about once a week. We've never gone for a warrant to check his store because we didn't want to alert him to our surveillance. Maybe it's time to go in there. If we find stuff we could bring him in and he might give us something under interrogation.'

'It's a big decision,' he said, not as dismissively as he felt because he owed them respect. 'Once we do that there's no way back. No, I think we'll keep that up our sleeve. What I'd like to do is set up a watch on the depot itself. If Ball goes there who knows who else uses it.'

'That's a third surveillance team,' Clive said mildly. There was a rustled murmur of support.

'I know, and we've already blown our overtime budget for the month, but it's now or never with this investigation and we're going to give it every effort.'

Work was divided up, a conference time agreed for the following day so that they could compare results and the team dispersed. As the others left Alison hung back by one of the boards.

'Is there something else?' Fenwick asked.

'It's these missing children, sir. Are we just going to ignore them?'

He joined her, his back to the photos.

'Unless we can find substance to support the Choir Boy allegations we have no basis for continuing.'

'Yes, but—'

'I know, it's hard to walk away but they wouldn't be ours to find anyway, unless there was some sort of conspiracy behind their disappearances. But you know that's highly unlikely. These are runaways, missing persons; sad social statistics not police cases.'

'Until one of them is yours,' Alison said, 'and you just can't believe your son would walk away from you.'

Fenwick had nothing to say. If Chris vanished he knew what he'd expect, and Alison had a son too. He could understand her reluctance to turn her back on the boys whose faces smiled out at them.

'Best get on,' he said eventually.

But after she left he turned and stared at the board. There were perhaps thirty boys pictured on it, aged between twelve and sixteen. Without meaning to he started to rearrange the photos: fair-haired boys on the left; redheads in the middle; brown next to them and then dark on the far right. Two of the dark-haired boys reminded him of Malcolm and Paul. He pulled their pictures off the board and took them over to a desk where he compared them. The similarity was striking, particularly between the younger lad and Paul.

He flipped the picture over and read the sketchy details on the reverse; of course it was Sam Bowyer. He winced as he recalled his last meeting with his father. The other photograph was new to him. He turned it over and read the details on the reverse: *'Jack Trainer, 15. Missing since November last year.'* In black ink beneath had been written: *'Died London, July 16th; coroner's verdict pending, likely suicide; thought to have jumped off Blackfriars Bridge. Signs of massive drug-taking and sustained sexual abuse.'*

Fenwick looked at the smiling photograph of Jack on a beach somewhere with his family and bundled his picture with Sam's into his briefcase. A 'sad social statistic'; had he really said that? He was ashamed of himself.

Sarah Hill didn't know about Maidment's arrest until she opened her door the following morning to pick up her regular milk order: two pints, one silver and one gold, Paul's favourite. She threw most of the milk away but it meant the fridge was always stocked for when he came home.

When she opened the door she saw a young man waiting in the shelter of the eaves and her heart leapt. When he turned to face her and she saw his eyes, her hope died as it did uncounted times every day.

'Mrs Hill? I'm Jason MacDonald, from the *Enquirer*,' he stuck out his hand and she took it automatically. 'Might I come in?'

'Why?' Sarah hadn't started life with abundant social graces and the ones she'd worked to acquire vanished the day Paul disappeared. MacDonald modulated his tone to solicitous and tilted his head on one side in what he imagined was a kindly manner.

'Perhaps you haven't heard.' The hidden sadist in him enjoyed her blanched face and he pushed his advantage. 'I think it's best that I do come in – more private.'

She backed into the musty hall, clutching her two pints of milk to her chest. He followed quickly and was almost sick at the smell, but then the scent of an exclusive blotted it out.

'Paul?'

He barely heard her but he nodded and lifted the cool bottles from her hands. Over his shoulder he saw a new Rover turn into the road; the competition was starting to arrive. He closed the front door firmly and made sure it was locked.

'Is this your sitting room?' He gave her back a gentle nudge and she led the way obediently.

'Paul?' she said again. He could hear hysteria creeping into her voice.

'They haven't found a body...yet.' MacDonald placed the bottles on the dusty coffee table, unmindful of the condensation that started to drip onto the cracked mahogany veneer.

His eyes were everywhere, noting the racks of files and the shrine to Paul. He'd need to return with a photographer, assuming he gained his exclusive, but he was feeling good about that.

'But they have arrested someone for his murder.'

'Murder?'

'Yes, the police seem pretty certain that Paul is dead, Mrs Hill.'

'They only found some clothing.'

'Soaked in blood.'

'But not necessarily Paul's; the family liaison officer, Julie, she told me. She's a nice girl. She explained to me that there were traces of Paul's blood on a shirt but it wasn't much.'

'Whatever,' Jason felt the advantage of surprise slipping, 'the police have enough evidence to arrest a man for murder and he's in prison already.'

'The police think Paul's dead?'

He nodded.

'But Julie said...' Her voice trailed away and he pressed on.

'Thing is, given the arrest, your life will become very difficult and I want to try and help you through that.'

'Dead?' She hadn't heard a word he'd just said. He swallowed his impatience and repeated his line.

'So the police think. That's why I want to offer you help, not just practical but financial as well.'

'Dead!'

Her legs folded and she collapsed into a chair, her skin the colour of putty. It would be inconvenient for her to faint so Jason thrust her head between her knees and darted out to the kitchen for a glass of water. When he came back she was sitting exactly as he'd left her.

'Here, drink this, you've had a bit of a shock,' he said as kindly as he could, though her behaviour was a touch indulgent given that the boy had disappeared over twenty-five years before. He watched her impatiently as she took sips from the greasy glass. Colour started to return to her face.

'How did he die?' She was hugging herself, trying to withdraw her extremities to protect them from the pain of contact with the outside world.

Jason suppressed another sigh.

'I don't know, Mrs Hill. They haven't released that detail yet. Once they've finished interrogating the suspect I'm sure they will.'

'Detail!' The word was like a rifle shot.

'Pardon?'

He couldn't understand where this woman was coming from. A right nutter in his opinion. It'd be best to move fast, get her signature on the exclusivity contract he had in his pocket and come back with a photographer sharpish.

'Now, if you could just sign this, it will stop all those bastards out there bothering you and give you some peace and quiet to get over the shock. I did mention that there'd be a financial consideration, didn't I? No one would wish to profit from Paul's death, you least of all, but it's only right that you should have something to help you recover – pay for a holiday perhaps so that you can get away for a bit. We'd be paying you,' his mind did some rapid calculations, 'five thousand pounds. I know it sounds a lot but holidays don't come cheap these days and you might want to take a friend.'

'Detail,' she repeated, 'you called how Paul died a detail.'

Jason didn't like the rising cadence in her voice.

'Get out! You're a scavenger. You don't care about Paul or me.'

'Now, Mrs Hill, don't get worked up; you're upset and of course that's understandable...'

'GET OUT!'

She uncurled her body and grabbed the water glass. Jason rose rapidly but hesitated enough to place the contract on the table.

'I'll give you a moment to think about it then, Mrs Hill,' he said as he retreated towards the sitting room doorway.

'OUT!'

The glass missed his head by an inch and bounced off the wall onto his shoulder, spraying him with water.

'I'll call you later,' he shouted over his shoulder as he ran to the front door, cursing the deadlock that moments before he'd checked was set.

As he bent to undo it a bottle sailed over his head and crashed into the door jamb, soaking him with milk, but he managed the lock and yanked the door open in a state bordering on panic. He ran down the path and vaulted over the low wooden gate as the last of the day's delivery smashed into the paving behind him.

The screams from the house blended with mocking laughter and he looked up to discover that he was the centre of attention in a circle of jeering faces, some of which he recognised as belonging to rivals from other nationals. Worst of all there was the lens of a news camera less than ten feet from him that must have captured the whole embarrassing incident on film.

'Shit!' he said before remembering that he could end up on TV and forced a smile and a laugh that would sound false even to his own ears when he watched his dismal performance later in the day.

'The lady's a little upset,' he said amid guffaws and jibes that he did his best to ignore. 'I suggest that we all give her a little space and time to recover.'

'Just like you did, you mean.'

He recognised the voice as belonging to a youngster who'd just joined the *Sun*. He saw something of his old raw energy in the lad and hated him for it. With what he falsely imagined was great dignity he shook his jacket and trousers free of splinters of glass and walked away.

Inside the house, Sarah managed to lock the front door before crumpling to the floor. She crawled back into the lounge, closed the curtains and hugged a cushion to her chest. Throughout the morning she wept into it, paralysed by the grief that devoured her. Each year without Paul had only added to her pain. Hope, fuelled by the continued mystery of his disappearance and lack of a body, had blossomed, pushing back the devastation that acceptance of his loss would bring to every aspect of her life.

In the space of ten minutes a crass journalist's ego had demolished decades of hope, deflating it as easily as a jealous child bursts a balloon. Into the vacuum of its destruction rushed agony that had accumulated for more than twenty-five years. For every day that she'd woken and defined Paul's absence as temporary, for every night that Sarah had gone to bed still expecting him to make contact the following morning, there was an equal and opposite shard of bereavement that fell now onto her unprotected soul, lacerating it beyond recognition. It was a poor enough thing to start with, her soul, unsupported as it was by love or belief, but it had been resilient. Its endurance had become the foundation for the remains of her sanity and in its near destruction the tendrils of latent madness unfurled and entered her mind.

Her bladder returned her briefly to reality and she cursed it, just as she had the weakness of her body in the days immediately following Paul's disappearance when it dropped her into snatches of sleep despite her determination to stay awake until he came home. It had seemed a betrayal then to escape into an oblivion from which she would wake with a momentary absence of pain because she'd forgotten that he was gone.

As she sat on the loo, her head bowed, she pinched and scratched herself as she had then. When she flushed she was overcome with thirst and sucked water noisily from her palm as she bent over the sink. She became aware of noises around her. The baby was crying next door; a dog yapped somewhere and another barked in reply; there was banging and an incessant ringing that drilled into her brain, adding to a headache she realised she must have had for a while because her bones ached from her spine through her jaw and into the pits of her eyes.

The ringing was from her phone, the banging was at her front door. The curtains were still drawn from the morning but she could see shadows beyond them. At the sight memory rushed back to engulf her and she moaned.

Paul…Paul…

The man said he was dead. No, that wasn't it, not exactly. He said that the police had arrested somebody for his murder. The thought made her physically sick. Water and bile swilled around the basin as she gripped the porcelain for strength.

She managed to crawl into the sitting room and turn on the television. On the hour, every hour, Paul's murder was headline news. She watched as his school picture appeared on the screen, then there was an interview with a handsome man in police uniform. '*We never gave up on Paul, we never give up on anybody,*' she heard him say, then stared in astonishment as Major Maidment's photograph filled the screen.

They'd arrested the major! He was Paul's killer. She'd trusted him, begged him to find her boy, and all the time he'd known he was dead. The thought made her ill again but when she'd finished retching her head felt better.

In the kitchen, she drank the remainder of yesterday's silver top, leaving the gold for Paul as always...except that there was no point now, was there? A man was in prison, charged with his murder. The police were so sure of themselves that it had to be true. Why hope any more? She went upstairs, still in her housecoat, and lay down on top of her unmade bed. The noises from outside her house drifted away and she slept.

It was a remarkable dream. Paul walked into her bedroom and stood beside the bed. But he wasn't the Paul of fourteen, this was a grown man with a scar on his face, though still handsome. He laid a hand on her forehead and it felt cool, reassuring. '*You're not to worry anymore, Mum, I'm fine,*' he said

'*What's the matter with your face, Paul? That's a nasty scar. Did the major do it to you when he killed you?*'

The grown-up Paul shook his head slowly. She could see tears on his cheeks and she raised a hand to wipe them away. His face was cold, as if he'd just stepped inside from a winter's day, but then he was dead so what did she expect?

'*Let it go, Mum. You deserve some peace. It's been too long – you must bury your grief now.*'

Sarah shook her head angrily and brushed his hand away. Who was he to lecture her about grief? He was dead, beyond caring. What she did with her life was her business. But he was right about one thing, she did deserve peace. Hope had made that impossible. Now that it too had died she had room for other emotions and perhaps peace would take root and grow. In her dream she imagined gossamer-light seeds of peace floating through the air to drop onto her but when she tried to catch at them they blew away. She became angry, swiping at them, punching out with such force that her body twitched in its sleep. She began to feel stronger. Emotions other than grief and hopelessness bloomed inside her: hate, fury, terrible jealousy against anyone who had children, and a desire for revenge.

When she woke up she found the bedding and pillows on the floor. Her bedside light lay smashed beside them. Outside it had grown dark. In the glow from the street lamps she could see three reporters and a photographer waiting, the rest had gone. Without switching on a light she made her way to the kitchen at the back of the house, where she risked turning on the lamp in the extractor fan. She was ravenous and cooked last month's eggs, some dried-out bacon, tomatoes and toast from the previous day's bread and washed it down with strong tea into which she poured more than a splash of ancient whisky that she found at the back of a cupboard.

Feeling better, she tidied the house, not caring now whether the journalists reacted to signs that she was awake as she felt strong enough to deal with them. As she cleaned, a plan developed and became more concrete. The germ of it had been there when she woke up and she realised that it was the source of her new energy. Step one was to appear respectable and calm. There could be no trace of madness about her. Of course she wasn't mad, she knew that, but sometimes people looked at her as though she might be and that would be unhelpful.

It took all night and most of the following morning to clean the house. Then she had a bath and washed her hair. It was unkempt and grey but she could remember how to put it up and experimented with several styles until she was satisfied. By now it was almost midday but she didn't feel tired. Instead she inspected her wardrobe, uttering small tuts of annoyance at her dowdy clothes. Her best suit was ten years old and looked it but at least it was clean; her shoes were worn and she had no stockings as she'd given up wearing them in favour of knee-length nylon socks. This wouldn't do. Perhaps she could sneak out of the back door and into Harlden to buy a new pair that would look good in front of the cameras.

As she crept out of the back garden and caught a bus into town she worked over the pieces of her plan in her mind, fitting them into a more coherent whole. By the time she returned she had all the details in place. She heated a ready-made shepherd's pie from Tesco and changed into her clothes. Then she picked up the phone.

Jason MacDonald was surprised to receive a call from Mrs Hill the day after she'd thrown him out of the house, closely followed by her daily milk delivery. He considered her invitation to return with serious misgivings until she mentioned the contract he'd left behind on her smeared coffee table. In his experience the thought of money worked like magic on the most unlikely subjects and he believed that it had done so again.

They agreed that he would join her immediately with a photographer and that she would speak to no other journalist until he arrived. On the way he warned Kirsty, the latest female photographer to fall for him, that Mrs Hill was a wreck and that she would need a serious makeover to take a sympathetic picture. The house was as bad. It stank and showed signs of years of neglect and poor housekeeping.

Most of the press pack had left when he arrived, just a few diehards remained, drinking strong coffee and eating bacon sandwiches. They shouted catcalls at his leather-clad back as he pressed the doorbell. A woman answered at once, medium height, neat, wearing a black and grey suit. He took her to be a neighbour.

'Is Mrs Hill at home?'

'I'm Mrs Hill.' She stepped forward and he saw her face more clearly.

There was no mistaking the sunken eyes and worry lines but if it hadn't been for these he would have called her an impostor. Kirsty shook her head at him as they followed Mrs Hill inside.

The sitting room smelt of polish and cleaning fluid. There were fresh yellow and white daisies by Paul's shrine and a matching vase full on the gleaming coffee table. The worn patches in the carpet and lack of paint on the skirting board were unchanged but otherwise it was a different room.

'Would you like something to drink?'

'Tea, please.' Jason decided to forget his own advice and risk a cup. 'Can I help you?'

'No, that's fine. I won't be long.'

As soon as she'd gone Kirsty turned on him.

'They told me you exaggerated, Jason but this is ridiculous. She's the perfect picture of a grief-stricken mother.'

'I'm telling you, this was a tip yesterday. When I sat down I was covered with dust!'

'Right.' Kirsty concentrated on setting up her equipment.

'Honestly, something's changed her.'

'Either that or your overactive imagination has got the better of you again.'

He decided that to reply would be demeaning so he ignored her and went to study the photographs of Paul that covered the walls.

'You won't need those.' Mrs Hill spoke from behind him. 'I've looked out some others that aren't faded. They're in that box; help yourself – I'd like them back of course.'

He pawed through them like a dog at a butcher's rubbish and identified ten brilliant pictures.

'Fair enough,' she said when he showed them to her, 'but I'm surprised you haven't chosen this one.'

She picked up the greying black and white photo of Paul in a Scout uniform in front of a grand but anonymous building.

'What's so special about this?'

'It was taken at the golf club where Maidment worked, less than three weeks before Paul...before... The Scouts were doing odd jobs there to raise money for camping equipment. I believe that must have been when the major first saw him.'

Jason's jaw dropped.

'Why didn't the police take it as evidence?' he asked, automatically inserting a cassette into a mini recorder.

'Good question. It was another part of their bungling, I suppose. At first all their attention went on this man Bryan Taylor, then on the theory that Paul had run away with him.' She poured some tea. 'But before I go on, we need to sign the contract. There's so much more I can tell you then.'

'Yes indeed!' He passed her a fresh copy and a pen.

'But it will cost more than £5,000 for exclusivity. I need £20,000.'

'What?'

He was shocked by her mendacity. He had her categorised as an unsophisticated loony – a walkover.

'I've been thinking about what you said, about needing to take a complete break. That's what it's going to cost.'

'For a holiday?' he asked incredulously.

'Yes, and for this and that.' She smiled at him, an unpractised gesture that didn't change her eyes.

'I'll need permission from my editor.'

'By all means, call him.'

'Her,' he corrected and pressed the speed-dial on his mobile phone. 'Are you prepared to negotiate?'

'Oh no.'

The photographer started clicking preparatory Polaroids to check the lighting. Sarah Hill took a sip of tea and wondered again how much it would cost to have a man killed. Kirsty had to ask her to stop smiling.

CHAPTER NINETEEN

Prison was uncomfortable but not as bad as he had anticipated. He put up with it without complaint though he noticed that he'd not been segregated despite his alleged crime. It was better this way, he decided. It was easier to protest innocence when not surrounded by sex offenders. '*A person is known by the company he keeps,*' his father had always said and Maidment was inclined to agree with him.

Initially he was left alone, he imagined because of his age and bearing, though his accent irritated some. Then word of his alleged crime circulated and the mood became overtly hostile. When he was confronted for the first time he looked his accuser directly in the eye and said simply, '*I did not do it. I swear on my wife's grave and on my regiment's honour that I am innocent of the charges.*' Then he had turned in a slow circle, looking each of his would-be attackers squarely in the face, exposing his back to the most aggressive as he did so.

For some reason they believed him; whether it was his unflinching gaze or military demeanour, it was hard to say. Even the doubters eventually fell silent when the toughest prisoner chose to speak a word in his defence.

On his second evening the television broke and the mood became ugly. There was a brief fight and one man ended up in the infirmary. He recognised the signs of bored aggression. It was deleterious to discipline, far worse than fear. The disinterest of the guards piqued him. They were supposed to be in command, to create a stable environment, not to patrol with a swagger of superiority and leave trouble to boil over. He confronted one of them on their next round and told him so, demanding that some form of entertainment be provided for 'the men' as he called his new mess mates.

The guard he challenged laughed in his face and attempted to trip him up as he passed. But Maidment's reflexes were quicker than his age might suggest and he kept his balance.

'Nice one, Major.' Kelly was a squat bruiser on remand for GBH, with old prison tattoos on his knuckles.

'It's irresponsible,' Maidment commented. 'I wouldn't have had any of them under my command.'

This tickled Kelly and a few of the others joined in his laughter. Frank, a wife-beater who'd gone too far the last time and was up for attempted murder (though mention of his wife's name brought tears to his eyes) swirled around in his chair, ignoring the blank screen for the first time.

'Did you see any action, Major?' he asked and a few other faces turned towards him, mildly curious.

'Yes, I did.'

'Kill anyone?' Kelly challenged.

Maidment saw no reason to prevaricate. Coy didn't work with hard men. Simple truth was best.

'Yes.'

'Hand to hand?' Bill was charged with murder, an unpredictable man regarded as the hardest nut on remand – he'd bitten off part of a policewoman's ear during his arrest, chewed and then swallowed it.

'Yes. Hand to hand, knife to knife, with rifle and explosive.' He said it without bravado, a simple statement of fact.

They were all staring at him now.

'Where were you on active service?' Bill automatically took the lead as he did with anything that captured his attention.

'In Borneo, under the command of General Sir Walter Waller.'

'Walter Waller – what a wanker!' Frank laughed at his own joke but no one else did. It was more interesting to hear what the major had to say about killing and death.

'He was the most remarkable man I've ever known,' he said, ignoring Frank, 'served in Burma in the Second World War, then Malaya. He set up and commanded the Jungle Warfare School – some of the finest military training available anywhere in the world. Jungle Warfare is the most demanding there is. Grand manoeuvres don't work in confined areas. Your enemy knows the terrain better than you do and can appear, attack and vanish back into it without sound.'

'Like the Elephant and Castle on a bad Saturday night,' Frank interrupted.

'Shut the fuck up,' Bill said in his normal speaking voice. Frank went pale. 'Go on, Major.'

So he told them his story about the Brunei revolt and the Borneo operation that was meant to last for three months and went on for over three years. He didn't tell them about the near loss of his own patrol. It still shocked him that he'd revealed so much to Fenwick and he had no desire to repeat the spectacle. But he did describe Lieutenant-Colonel John Woodhouse's brilliant strategy for twenty-two SAS. How the four-man patrols had befriended local tribes with medicine and food, thus denying the rebels support while gaining valuable information. He quickly disabused them of their belief that he'd been in the SAS, explaining that he was in the Guards Independent Parachute Company. Yes, he'd been trained by the SAS; yes, he'd led his own patrols into the jungle well behind enemy lines; and yes, he could still recall the methods he'd been taught forty years later.

With the aid of his remarkable memory he shared some of this learning, how to move without noise in a jungle; his preferred weapons; and the best way to kill a man silently.

When the guards announced lockdown, there was muttering from the thirty men gathered around him in a wide semicircle but the mood was calm again.

'Major.'

'Yes, Bill.'

'Anyone give you grief, you let me know, awright?'

Bill stuck out his callused hand and grabbed Maidment's manicured fingers in a crushing grip.

'I will but I trust that will not be necessary.' He nodded his head in acknowledgement without saying thank you. That would have suggested weakness.

As he'd thought, prison wasn't so bad.

The interrogation next day was the most intensive yet. Instead of being taken back to Harlden he was driven to an anonymous police station close to the prison and into yet another sour-smelling interview room. He declined his right to have his solicitor present. Poor old Stenning wasn't reacting well to the pressure of constant questioning and had developed a nervous tic that Maidment found distracting.

He watched as Fenwick broke the cellophane wrappers from two cassettes and put them into the machine. The second simultaneous recording would be sealed and dated after the interview as a secure record, should the police be tempted to 'doctor' evidence. He considered it an unnecessary precaution with Fenwick in charge. Integrity was a characteristic he recognised.

Fenwick started by explaining that his questions were related to another enquiry and not to Paul Hill's murder, about which they could no longer question him.

'Where were you on 16th December, 1994?' This was one of the dates the FBI had squeezed out of their witness, on which he claimed there had been an orgy involving young boys at a large house in Sussex. Though the witness said that he didn't know the address.

Maidment closed his eyes briefly and thought back.

'In Harlden, at work.'

'Can you prove that?'

'You have my journals for the period.'

'We've checked those, they're blank.'

'Hmm, curious. It must have been a quiet day.'

'I find it remarkable that you can recall precisely where you were on that day.'

'It's a quirk. I have very good recall for facts and figures, including dates. You may check me on others if you wish.'

'We might well do that. 9th April, 1987.' Another of the volunteered dates.

'April is a busy month at the club. I was probably very involved in organising our tournament. It started on the first weekend of May, you see. Still does.'

'Have you ever visited Crawley, Jeremy?' Fenwick's use of his first name amused Maidment; a classic ploy to build familiarity and to establish the interview hierarchy.

'Crawley, well yes. It's not my favourite town but I've visited it. Hilary used to be a hospital visitor there and I drove her many times.'

'Is the hospital close to the swimming pool?'

'I have no idea, Andrew.'

'Rank or Mister, please, Jeremy,' the chief inspector said mildly.

'Likewise.' Maidment allowed himself an inner smile at Fenwick's expense. 'I've never visited a public baths in my life. It's one of those places to which I have an abiding aversion.'

'Talk to me about August 1981.'

'That was my first month as secretary at the club, I remember it very clearly. There was meant to be a proper handover but my predecessor announced that he was going away on holiday three days after I arrived. I was really thrown in the deep end.'

'Was one of your responsibilities to dispense locker keys for the changing rooms?' Fenwick continued.

'Of course. It was important that they were looked after securely; I kept duplicates in my safe.'

'Did people lose them?'

'All the time; we had a number of repeat offenders. In the end I introduced a forfeitable £10 deposit. Not terribly popular, I can tell you. The first time I asked for a second £10 from a member all hell broke loose but I stuck to my guns and fortunately the president backed me up.'

'But you could have helped yourself to a new key at any time without paying, couldn't you?'

'Why on earth should I?' He stared at Fenwick blankly. 'I had no need of a locker as I had an office, and even if I had I should have applied the same rules to myself.'

'You're sure you didn't have a locker?'

'No, Chief Inspector, of course not. I was secretary. Although I played when time allowed, I had the luxury of an office in which to change and leave my things.'

He watched as Fenwick wrote down a careful note on a piece of paper then tucked it in his pocket. While he didn't object to their line of questioning as it was preferable to a continued interrogation on Paul Hill's disappearance, he was confused by it.

'How about parking permits, did you give out those?' Fenwick continued.

'Yes, in fact they were renewable annually from September each year so one of the things I had to do that August would have been to issue the new ones. I introduced colour coding and permit numbers, again far better from a security point of view. We chose blue for the first year, I recall.'

'And did they too get misplaced by members?' Fenwick asked the question innocently but Maidment knew that it had to be significant so he was very careful in his answer.

'Rarely.'

'So, with your memory you'd remember if you'd had to issue a replacement. It might even be mentioned in your meticulous journals.' Fenwick flicked through the pages for August 1981 casually.

Maidment found that he was staring at the book and dragged his eyes away.

'I doubt there's mention of such a trivial matter in there. My office records were kept separately and I believe most were destroyed by my successor.'

'And the name of anyone to whom you issued a duplicate in 1981?'

'I don't believe I had cause to do so.'

'Indeed.' Fenwick looked up from the books and stared him in the face. 'I'm afraid I don't believe you, Major.'

For the first time, Maidment realised that he might well end up in prison for a long time.

That night, as he tried to coax himself to sleep in his cell, Maidment went over the dates mentioned by the police again and again but failed to find a connection. He had deliberately not asked about their significance and now regretted not doing so, partly out of curiosity but more importantly because he was afraid that the police would interpret it as the action of a guilty man who already knew. The thought brought sweat to his forehead and chest and he turned over on his damp pillow, searching for comfort in its lumpy stuffing.

Maidment was finally drifting towards sleep when the relevance of their questions about keys and permits clicked into place. He'd been so diverted by the puzzle over dates that he hadn't really thought about them, but as he relaxed his sub-conscious threw their significance into the front of his mind.

He recalled the argument about a second £10 key deposit, out of all proportion to the money involved but driven by principle for both protagonists. Only one man had taken it to the president for resolution, and only that man had had occasion to remark sarcastically, as he demanded a replacement parking permit, whether he would be required to pay for that too. The thought propelled him upright on his bunk and he banged his head on the underside of the springs above.

One man, the same man, had needed both a new permit and a new key in late August 1981, and it was because of that man that he was in this cell now, charged with Paul Hill's abduction and murder. The realisation made him feel sick. He needed to find out why August 1981 was significant; he needed to work out how he was going to defend himself in the face of the physical evidence they had against him that linked him to Paul Hill; but most importantly he needed to find a way of speaking to that man. Only then would he be able to face the police, and more importantly his conscience, with equanimity.

Fenwick and Nightingale sat in the beer garden of the Broken Drum overlooking an idyllic village green with cricket field beyond. On this muggy August working day the only people taking advantage of the village amenities were dog walkers and mothers with children home for the school holidays. The wooden bench was damp and they had placed a plastic boot liner on top to protect their clothes. In front of them a plate of cheese and ham salad sandwiches sat untouched; two glasses of tomato juice were growing warm.

He had just told her about his conversation with Quinlan, watching her go pale as she had realised the significance of what he was saying, and unconsciously angle her body away from him.

'I'm sorry, Nightingale. I should have had more sense than to behave in a way that's left you vulnerable to rumour.' He was genuinely contrite, miserable that she should be suffering because of their friendship.

'It's OK. I'm as much to blame as you are. I'm a grown-up after all, though I appreciate I haven't exactly been behaving like one in the last week. My mood has been unprofessional and I apologise.'

'Don't, for heaven's sake. You've had reason enough to be upset and my reaction to what Quinlan said didn't help.'

'Even so...'

'No, stop it. Now we're trying to outdo each other in contrition!' She laughed but it sounded sad. 'What?' he asked.

'I was just thinking that it's ironic. Last year you decided that an affair would be too risky for both our careers and now...now, well, we're the victims of rumour anyway. It wouldn't be so bad if there were some substance behind the speculation.'

'Wouldn't it?'

'No,' she replied softly.

There was silence. A fly decided that their sandwiches looked appetising and settled on a crust. Neither of them flicked it away. Eventually Fenwick reached out and took a sip of his drink, pulling a face at the taste.

'Yuck! That's disgusting. Can I get you something else?'

'Why not,' she said with a one-sided smile. 'A glass of white wine and a water; st—'

'Still, no ice or lemon, I know.' He swung his legs over the bench and stood up. As he walked behind her he squeezed her shoulder, letting his hand stay there long enough that she put her own on top of it. Then he was gone and she was on her own.

Her mobile rang a minute later. It was Blite.

'Just thought you'd want to know that Quinlan is looking for you. I said I'd track you down. He wants to see us in half an hour to discuss whether he should combine the Eagleton and Hill investigations under one SIO. I told him I thought it was a good idea but for some reason he wants your opinion before he makes up his mind.'

Nightingale's heart sank. She'd made a lot of progress on the Hill/Maidment investigation in a short space of time and she didn't want to see all her effort subsumed into an inquiry with Blite as SIO. But her tone gave nothing away.

'I'm on my way back from interviewing Maidment again.'

'So when will you be here? I suppose you've stopped for lunch.'

Nightingale realised the full implication of his words and made an instinctive decision.

'A quick sandwich. Look, Rodney,' she said and carried on quickly before she could change her mind, 'I know there are rumours going round about me and Andrew Fenwick.'

She heard his intake of breath.

'Well, I want you to know that they're not true. If they were, I'd tell you but there's nothing between us other than a casual friendship.' She knew she sounded sincere and hoped he would realise the truth when he heard it.

'Right, course,' was all he said. 'So when are you likely to be back?'

'In time for the meeting. I'll see you in Quinlan's office, shall I?'

'Yeah, see you then.'

She broke the connection as Fenwick returned with a tray bearing wine, water and fresh food.

'That was the station,' she explained. 'I need to get back.'

She wrapped the sandwich and put it in her handbag.

'Developments?' he asked hopefully.

'No, just Quinlan, he needs an update.' Nightingale drank the glass of water but left the wine untouched. 'I must go. If anything interesting happens, do you want me to call you?'

'Of course.'

She was gone before he had a chance to find the right words of goodbye. The memory of their previous conversation hung about the table as he sipped his fresh tomato juice and finished his sandwich. There was a sense of an opportunity missed, of his life taking a tiny, fraction of a degree shift that would take him in a direction that he didn't want it to go. But the shift had happened and he had done nothing to prevent it. After a few minutes' introspection he gathered their empty plates, her untouched glass of wine and took the debris of their meal back into the pub.

Back at the station, Blite called Dave McPherson and changed his bet. He put £20 on against the affair but declined to say why. He reckoned he was on to a winner.

CHAPTER TWENTY

'I'm buggered!' Cooper leant back against the hot vinyl of his car seat and addressed the empty air. 'Bloody background. This poor sod's got more background than a sodding Turner.'

He was quite pleased with himself for the artistic analogy. On his way back to the station he stopped for lunch at the Saucy Sailor, a fish and chip restaurant that, in his opinion, did the best batter in Harlden. He ordered a large piece of hake but compromised with only a small portion of chips because Doris was becoming very insistent about this low-fat diet idea of hers.

Writing up his reports took hours. Cooper belonged to a police generation that had mastered a clumsy two-fingered typing technique. It was accurate but rarely exceeded fifteen words a minute. He was relieved to receive a call from Nightingale explaining that the team meeting she'd originally scheduled for five had been brought forward to three-fifteen because Superintendent Quinlan wanted to sit in on it. Oh, and Andrew Fenwick might be there as well, she added, with nonchalance Cooper was certain was studied.

Cooper cast his eye around the meeting room and calculated that his presence had just lowered the average rank of attendees by at least one level. As well as Nightingale there was Fenwick, looking bemused and Quinlan. Nightingale hadn't asked for a large team to investigate Paul Hill's murder but she had hand-picked them. In addition to himself, there was another detective sergeant and two young detective constables, one a fast-track graduate who reminded Cooper of Nightingale when he'd first met her.

His task of digging into Maidment's background was demanding, solitary grunt-work of the sort that was often given short shrift. That's why it had been dumped on him, he knew. Nightingale already had a reputation as a stickler for detail...rather like her old boss, Cooper realised and the thought made him smile.

The DS – Ken – and graduate trainee, whose name Cooper was always forgetting, were searching for Bryan Taylor. Nightingale and the other constable had been reviewing the original Paul Hill case and re-interviewing the witnesses they could find. As he looked at Quinlan and Fenwick, Cooper tried to work out why the case was attracting so much attention from the higher-ups.

'Bob, good. Now we can start.' Nightingale sounded in remarkably good humour. 'Chief Inspector Fenwick is here because of a potential link to a case MCS are working on and the superintendent has asked to participate in the meeting because this case has the particular attention of the ACC.

'The chief inspector's investigation is a highly sensitive investigation and his interest in our activities must remain confidential.' Her tone made it clear that no details of this case were about to be shared and he saw a slight relaxation in Fenwick's shoulders.

'So, Bob, could you tell us where you've got to, please?'

Cooper paused, trying to collect his thoughts. He'd spent the past week trudging around Maidment's friends and acquaintances, past and present. The major's worst crime so far, in the words of one churchgoer, was that he was 'too good to be true'. Only one person had voiced real suspicions; a neighbour who lived close to Castleview Terrace whose son had sometimes been given a lift by the major. Cooper had spoken to the son about it, a strapping lad of ten, who'd told him not to be daft. Still, Cooper would have to organise a follow-up with a specially trained police interviewer. He relayed all this quickly, playing down its significance, and to Nightingale's credit she didn't try to make it sound more relevant than it was.

'What do they say about him at the golf club?'

'More of the same: decent bloke; efficient secretary; not a bad golfer; good reputation in the army. One curious thing maybe.' He paused and scratched his paunch without being aware he was doing so. 'He was popular and a good mixer but no one I've spoken to claims to be a really good friend. Mind you, I've a couple of his army mates to talk to yet and I'm told that they were closer to him than anybody. I suppose combat does that.'

Fenwick and Nightingale glanced at each other then quickly looked away.

'OK, keep digging. Ken, what progress have you and Teresa made?'

Teresa, that's her name, Cooper thought. *Typical of Nightingale to refer to them both rather than just the DS.*

'We've spent most of our time looking for the original case files and evidence as well as reconstructing as much background on Bryan Taylor as we can. There's still no trace of the files and it's looking more and more likely that they're lost or destroyed. Teresa is going through every piece we have from the period anyway in case something was misplaced.

'So far, what we know about Taylor is that he drifted into Harlden around 1977 from Essex. People recall an unmarried, shaven-headed man with a goatee and earring; back in those days he was automatically considered gay. He had a snake tattoo and no interest in women or football, but nobody remembers seeing him with other men.

'No surprise when his name was linked to the disappearance

of Paul Hill; he's the sort of loner the public prefers for its villains. This is all we have on him.'

Ken circulated a copy of Taylor's driving licence (an old one without a photograph), and a rough e-fit based on people's recollections of what he'd looked like, for what it was worth. He'd also tracked down the registration number of Taylor's red estate car though there was no trace of its whereabouts; the vehicle had never been sold, nor been involved in any traffic offence.

Cooper watched Nightingale digest the scant information and the implications for their investigation, which were not good. Taylor looked like a man for whom it was second nature to disappear. He could be living anywhere in the UK under an assumed name, earning his living without throwing up a whisper of a national insurance record. They didn't even know the colour of his eyes. It was enough to make anyone want to abandon the search, but not Nightingale. She squared her shoulders.

'You've made more progress than I thought was possible in the absence of the original evidence but you'll have to go further. It's obviously key that we find Taylor and either eliminate him from the case or link him to Maidment. If we don't, no matter how strong our forensic evidence against Maidment is, we will have a gaping hole in our case. Taylor was the prime suspect in Paul's abduction.'

Ken nodded.

'There's still more we can do. We're still tracing anyone who might have known him, starting at the golf club, where we've discovered he did some casual work.' *Not helpful,* Cooper thought, *he could have dumped the clothes.* 'Taylor was universally disliked but he was a cheap worker so people kept using him. He did odd jobs for local schools and social clubs – in retrospect it looks like he gave heavily discounted terms whenever he could work around children.'

'It's disgusting that he was allowed to get near them.' Cooper was outraged.

'He wasn't on a register and it was all casual work; he didn't even bother with a contract most of the time. Taylor could turn his hand to most things: carpentry, tree clearance, decorating, maintenance, even helping out at harvest time. His dealings were usually in cash and only a small portion of it found its way into his bank account.'

'When his house was searched did they find any money? If he'd planned to abduct or kill Paul it stands to reason he'd have taken it.' Fenwick had kept silent far longer than Cooper had expected.

Nightingale answered.

'All we have to go on is a summary record of the case that was kept in a master file here in Harlden. As you heard from Ken the original files and evidence are still missing. But based on the record we have there was no cash recovered from his house.'

Quinlan shifted at her words and Cooper looked at him, expecting him to speak, but he remained silent.

'I know this isn't a popular question to raise but what if we don't find Taylor?' Cooper asked, not wishing to undermine Nightingale but anxious that they didn't build their hopes on completing what he thought could be an impossible task.

Nightingale didn't answer straight away but looked at Superintendent Quinlan. After an increasingly pregnant pause he took a deep breath and said, 'It's absolutely vital that we find Taylor. You see, there's been a new development. Since Maidment's arrest a week ago we've received a number of letters from people claiming that he's innocent.'

'Well, that's standard enough.' Cooper didn't see the significance.

'Two of these letters turn out to be important. They arrived on consecutive days and the first must have been posted immediately after the news broke.'

Nightingale handed out copies of a word-processed letter.

Dear Superintendent Quinlan,

You are responsible for the arrest of Major Maidment. I am writing to tell you that you have remanded the wrong man. The major did not kill Paul Hill. I know that for a certain fact.

You must release him without charge and concentrate your efforts elsewhere. The school blazer and the bloodstains are a distraction – don't be fooled by the obvious no matter how tempting.

Yours,

A Well-Wisher

'The letter was posted in London and sent first class. Unfortunately it took six days to arrive. Here's the second one.'

Cooper was still only part-way through reading it when he heard Teresa gasp. He read on quickly and even forewarned couldn't suppress his own '*Bloody hell!*'

Dear Superintendent Quinlan,

You have not released the major and I must insist that you do. He is a God-fearing man whose transgressions are minor when weighed in the grand scale and are already forgiven by God.

It seems that you will not take my word for his innocence. Very well, I enclose with this letter some items that Paul Hill was carrying on the day he disappeared. If you have fingerprint technology you will note two sets of prints. One is Paul's own. The other set belongs to Bryan Taylor, a man who seduced and sodomised Paul for years before his disappearance. Why don't you concentrate your search on finding the guilty, Superintendent, and let the major go?

Yours truly,

A Well-Wisher

Attached to the letter were photographs of a paperback – Salinger's *Catcher in the Rye* – complete with school library stamp of ownership. On the reverse was a copy of the title page with the usual list of student borrowers. The last name belonged to Paul Hill, the date stamp alongside it 7th September, 1982.

'Paul borrowed the book from the school library on the day he disappeared.' Quinlan stood up and started to pace. 'It's already been sent for analysis and, as the Well-Wisher claims, Paul's fingerprints are on it.'

'So who sent it?' Cooper raised the obvious question. 'Bryan Taylor?'

'Why would he implicate himself?' Fenwick was dismissive. 'Isn't it more likely to be from an ex-lover of Taylor's, perhaps even another boy seeking revenge for their own abuse? Maybe Taylor bragged to them about Paul. Sending us an anonymous letter is an easy way for someone to get their own back without becoming involved, particularly if they don't know where Taylor is.'

'So, what are we going to do? Should I stop the background work on Maidment?' Cooper asked hopefully. 'Because there's no way he could have sent the book.'

'No,' Nightingale was insistent, 'the investigation continues unchanged except that we now have another line of inquiry. I'm going to follow up on this letter to try and trace the writer.'

'To have the book, someone must have seen Paul *after* he'd been to school on the day he disappeared. Can we be sure it was Taylor? Does the other set of prints match any on our records?' Fenwick looked at Nightingale expectantly.

'No, though we haven't finished checking. The letter had no prints on it at all and the envelope and stamp are self-adhesive so there's no chance of DNA.'

There was silence in the room. Cooper's thoughts were going in circles and he imagined everyone else's were too. Still, he had his reports to finish and time was passing.

'Well, that's all for now,' Nightingale said as if reading his mind. 'I know I don't have to remind you how sensitive this new information is so please keep it to yourselves.'

Everybody started to gather their papers but as they did so Superintendent Quinlan cleared his throat and stood up. Despite his unassuming demeanour such was the respect in which he was held that the room fell quiet almost instantly.

'There is one further announcement I would like to make,' he said and looked briefly at Nightingale. 'I've decided that it makes sense to combine the investigations into the murders of Malcolm Eagleton and Paul Hill. So, with effect from today, Inspector Nightingale will assume SIO responsibility for both. I have significant expectations, Inspector, as you know.'

'Yes, sir.' The inspector gave him a brief smile, which was reciprocated before he left.

There was a hush of significance in the room. Everybody recognised what had just happened; Quinlan had taken a case away from an experienced inspector and given it to the upstart. The action suggested that Nightingale's career really was in the ascendant and Cooper wasn't the only one grinning as he left the conference room.

Fenwick handed out freshly brewed takeaway coffee and pastries to the members of the MCS surveillance team. They were installed in a warehouse opposite the main entrance to the storage depot where Alec Ball was known to keep his legitimate goods for sale. It was the end of the afternoon on the sixth day since he'd authorised the operation and this was the first time they had called him with anything remotely interesting.

On the wall behind them were photographs of people they were watching out for with a brief résumé of their involvement. Fenwick studied the list as he waited for the team to sort out sugars and debate who would have which doughnut.

Name	Involvement
Joseph Watkins	Named by FBI source; arrested but released
Alec Ball	Stall owner; acquaintance of Watkins; trip to London relevant?
ANO 1	Regular visitor to Ball's stall still to be ID'd (not seen since June)
ANO 2	Regular at Ball's stall still to be ID'd
Richard Edwards	Sup'ted Watkins' club mem'ship; knows Maidment; no other info

'So, what have you got for me?'

'There's a bloke in there now we're pretty certain we've seen at the stall. We couldn't see his face properly when he went in but it could be Watkins. Ball was here earlier.'

After a non-eventful week Clive was delighted that things looked to be moving on his watch.

'Did he carry anything with him?'

'A carrier bag and a laptop bag.'

They drank their coffees in silence. After ten minutes the man came out.

'It is Watkins,' Fenwick said. 'Can I have those?' He took the binoculars from Clive. 'One of you follow him, see where he goes. Keep in radio contact via Harlden Operations as we're on their turf.'

Clive was out of the room before Fenwick finished and was in time to see Watkins turn a corner and step into his car, which he'd parked away from the depot. He radioed the registration number to Operations and gave them the direction in which it was driven away. He made his way back to the warehouse, deflated.

Ten minutes later Watkins' car was spotted by a motorcycle patrolman entering the multi-storey car park in the centre of Harlden. Fenwick made his way to Harlden Police Station while Watkins was followed from a discreet distance, and went straight to Operations so that he could direct what happened next.

Fenwick decided that he needed more foot power, preferably the sort he could trust. As Bob Cooper already knew something was going on thanks to Nightingale's briefing, he called him, dragging his extension number from memory. The sergeant had just finished yet another report and had been contemplating sneaking off early as he'd been working all hours.

'Bob, can you do me a favour?'

'Course.' Fenwick was the one person Cooper would never say no to.

'Take a stroll into the town centre; it's only five minutes away. There's a man there in the newsagent's next to the main car park. He's aged fifty-five but looks younger; thinning red hair, wearing a red sweatshirt over his shoulders and a green checked shirt. He'll be carrying a Hackett carrier and a PC bag. Follow him. Operations should be able to give you directions to find him as there's a patrolman hanging around. He has no idea he's being followed so keep it casual and your radio low once you've got him in your sights.'

'I'm on my way.'

That was one of the things Fenwick liked about Bob; he never stopped to ask dumb questions. He passed a difficult ten minutes waiting for something to happen and it was almost five o'clock when MCS Ops called to say that Bob had found Watkins and was now following him into the post office. Half an hour later Cooper was back at Harlden Division standing in Fenwick's old office, having refused the offer to sit because the chairs always started his sciatica.

'He had packages in the carrier bag,' he told Fenwick and Clive, who'd also joined them. 'Four of them were already sealed in envelopes with sticky tape all round them. He sent them special delivery and from the price I would say they were going to addresses in the UK.'

'Could you read any details?'

'Afraid not. He was three people ahead of me in the queue and it would've looked odd for me to get any closer.'

'So, had he picked those up from the depot or did he have them already when he went in?' Clive voiced the question Fenwick was thinking. Cooper did his best to look disinterested as MCS discussed their case in front of him.

'There's one way to find out,' Fenwick said, nodding to himself as if he'd just made a decision. 'We can get a warrant for the CCTV tapes at the storage depot; they're bound to have cameras inside for security reasons. I think I should have enough based on Alison's work with the photos and the information from the US.'

'Isn't there a risk that Ball or Watkins will find out?'

'A remote one but now's the time to chance it. I'm going to try and persuade the magistrate that I can ask for all tapes and rental records so that suspicion doesn't fall on anyone in particular. If I can convince them that this isn't a fishing expedition I might get away with it.'

He did. At eight the following morning Clive and Alison were going over tapes covering the location of the depot units rented by Ball. They had discovered that Watkins had a unit there as well, though as he wasn't named in the warrant anything they found from the tapes would not be allowed as evidence if it related to him alone. Ball rented three units, Watkins one. The CCTV tapes were reused every week so they had seven days' worth to check. They'd started with the previous twenty-four hours.

At two-twenty Ball had come in and deposited a bundle of packages in one of his storage units before locking the door behind him. Two hours later Watkins entered and withdrew the packages and placed them in his carrier bag. He was seen taking something out of his bag before refilling it with the material from inside.

'Delivery and payment,' Alison commented, noting the times of the frames so that they could get stills run off for future use. 'And as he's accessed Ball's unit we can use everything we've just seen.'

Watkins had then walked to his own unit and gone inside. He was in there for an hour. They made notes of the frames and called Fenwick, who joined them in the projection room.

He watched the selected footage in silence, replaying key scenes.

'Tell me what you conclude,' he said eventually. Typically, Clive leapt in.

'Ball gives Watkins a key and security code hidden inside whatever they buy at the market. They take it to the storage depot where what they're actually buying is inside one of Ball's units. They pick up the goods and leave money in exchange plus, probably, the key.'

'What's to stop them raiding Ball's store and not paying?' Alison asked. Clive answered.

'Two things. Firstly it takes a key and a combination code to open the lock. Ball can limit what's inside and reset the combinations whenever he wants. Secondly, if they did that they'd lose their supplier. Don't you agree, sir?'

'Yes; it's a clever arrangement. Had it not been for Ball's laziness in reusing the same LP covers we'd never have spotted it. How do they pay for the storage?'

Clive shrugged but Alison was ready with the answer.

'Cash. That way we'd never be able to trace them from their bank accounts in a routine check.'

'Does Ball strike you as someone with the brains to organise this supply line, because he doesn't me?' Fenwick started to pace. 'I think someone else set this up but we have no way of proving it unless Ball makes a mistake.'

'It is clever.' Clive was rewinding and fast-forwarding a section of tape again and again as if searching for something. 'They never once reveal what they've got in their bags to the cameras.'

'It's even more devious than that. What do you think Watkins was doing in his unit for an hour?'

'No idea.'

'Think, Clive.' Fenwick took the remote out of his hand as if removing a toy from an irritating child. 'He goes in with a laptop bag and the contents he's just bought from Ball and stays inside for an hour. What's he doing?'

Clive's forehead creased with thought then he said, with an appalled look on his face, 'You mean he's in there...enjoying the stuff? That's disgusting!'

'I agree, but it also means that if we raided Watkins' house we would find only a laptop recharging with nothing on its hard disk to reveal his perversion. Nor would we find any materials in his home because he's smart enough to keep them in his lock up. All he has to do is have two PCs, charge one at home, then swap them over and keep everything else stored in the unit on USB sticks or CDs.'

'Is he the brains behind Ball's operation, do you think?'

'I don't think so. It wasn't very smart to take child pornography into the town centre in a carrier bag before mailing it through the normal service. Why would he be mailing it anyway? I wonder whether Ball knows that what Watkins is buying may not be for personal consumption alone.'

'You mean he's trading it on.'

'Could be and that might make him the weak link. But

arresting him won't automatically bring us closer to the people behind this.'

'If Ball is linked to wider activity,' Alison said as she re-entered the room with fresh coffees, 'he must obtain his supplies from somewhere.'

'We've got more than enough for a warrant to search their storage,' Clive said confidently.

'Maybe,' Fenwick didn't sound so sure, 'but supposing we do, where does that take us? I want the man at the top of the chain, the one with enough brains and money to create a set-up this intricate. So far we only have two men – Ball and Watkins – we don't even know the names of the other regulars at Ball's stall. There must be dozens more to make this worth his while. Would Ball give all the names to us, and the supplier behind it? I'm not sure.' He stood up and rubbed his knee. 'This is one to think about. Keep up the surveillance on Ball and Watkins as well as the storage depot for the weekend. We'll meet back here early Monday morning and I'll make a decision then on what to do next.'

'If anything happens in the meantime, where shall we find you?' Clive asked but his tone said clearly: *so what are you going to be doing?*

'My mobile – use that,' Fenwick replied and left them to it.

'That's if he remembers to keep it charged up.' Clive shook his head.

Fenwick, usually so punctilious and correct, could be hard to reach when he wanted. He had the ability to drop out of sight for hours and no amount of calling his mobile would raise him if he didn't want to be found.

Clive and Alison would have been mystified if they had been able to follow Fenwick for the rest of the afternoon. Instead of going back to his office and completing more of the endless paperwork that clogged up the smooth running of the twenty-first century British police force, Fenwick paid visits to a handful of families across West Sussex, spending no more than half an hour with each of them. But for every one, his donation of time brought with it some relief that a missing boy wasn't just a sad social statistic after all.

CHAPTER TWENTY-ONE

A male pheasant barked from across the long lawn and Cooper looked up instinctively to catch sight of the strutting bird.

'Cocky bastard. Another month and I'll roast him.'

'Do you shoot here?' Cooper hadn't much time for the sport but respected the interests of others – as long as they were law-abiding.

'Rough, that's all. Better at Napp Farm. Simpson's got a bloody good gamekeeper, poached him – no pun intended – from the Langley Estate. D'you shoot? I could get you in.'

'Occasionally, but I'm more danger to the dogs than I am the birds.'

He leant forward, determined to resume his careful questioning of the lieutenant-colonel but he was pre-empted.

'Another, Sergeant?' Edwards gestured towards the ridiculously fine bone china cup in Cooper's paw. He'd declined something stronger, to his regret.

'No, thank you.' Earl Grey wasn't to his taste and anyway, it irritated him that these military types insisted on using his rank, as if it put them at an advantage. 'I don't wish to take up too much of your time. As I explained, I'm only doing routine background checks on Major Maidment.'

'I don't know what you think I'm going to tell you.' Edwards bristled. 'The man was an excellent officer, loyal and absolutely trustworthy.'

'Good under fire?'

'I should imagine so. We never saw action together.'

'He was awarded the DSO during his time in Borneo. Do you know why?'

Edwards' face took on the appearance of a baboon's bottom. His cheeks flushed fuchsia pink and his lips contracted into a wrinkled sphincter surrounded by the yellow-grey bristle of his moustache. Cooper doubted that any uncontrolled utterance would escape such perfect muscle control. The question was, if and when the lieutenant-colonel chose to speak, would it be a load of shit?

'The usual reason: bravery in the field.'

It was a less fulsome comment than Cooper had expected. He sipped the dregs of his cold tea and waited for more. Instead, Edwards drained his drink and rose to mix another.

'When did you first make the major's acquaintance?'

'1965 or 6, I think. Can't be sure. You should ask him, he has a perfect memory for facts and figures.'

'And you served together for how long?'

'Ten years or so.'

'I thought it was longer.'

'We were in the same regiment but I was moved about a fair bit. I was an expert, you see – in a field I'm not at liberty to disclose – and that meant I was called upon regularly as an adviser. Maidment was more of a sedentary type by the time he returned to the UK.'

'In the time that you knew Major Maidment, were there any suspicious deaths in the regiment?'

'Certainly not.'

'And the major's behaviour was normal?'

'Define normal, Sergeant.'

'He showed no interest in young boys?'

'I thought the police were supposed to have shed their homophobia.'

'By boys I mean children not men. That's not normal in anyone's definition.'

Edwards glanced at him and added more ice to his glass.

'No, Maidment was – and is so far as I am aware – strictly heterosexual.'

'Did he ever do anything that he might have felt guilty about later?'

Nightingale had insisted on adding the question so Cooper had dutifully repeated it in every interview. Edwards had his back to him and appeared to be fussing with the ice bucket.

'I said—'

'I heard you, Sergeant. Not that I am aware of.'

Edwards turned to face him and Cooper thought that he caught a hint of prevarication in his face. He wrote *avoided the question* in his notebook.

'Were there any complaints against him, either when he was in the army or later at the golf club?'

'Again, none that I'm aware of. As I said to you at the beginning, Maidment and I are more acquaintances than friends, so my knowledge is somewhat limited.'

This wasn't what Cooper had been told by others. He made another note and considered his last question. He wasn't a subtle man and was aware that he would be unable to dress it up.

'You're aware of the charges against the major, sir. Could I ask for your reaction to them?'

'Preposterous, of course.' Edwards sat down and took a drink.

'And why is that?'

'How can you possibly ask such an asinine question, Sergeant?'

'Because I haven't known Major Maidment for more than forty years, or had the opportunity to serve with him. You have and, as a man of your rank, I respect your assessment of his nature.'

Edwards raised his eyebrows at the crude flattery but nonetheless paused to consider his answer.

'Until the allegations made against Maidment, I would have said that he was the most decent and upright of men.'

'I see, well, thank—'

'Wait, I said *until*. Since he was arrested, in front of us all and on such terrible charges, well…let's just say that I have had some deeply uncomfortable hours.'

'Really?' Cooper sat forward, unable to believe that he might be about to hear a criticism from within Maidment's clique.

'Yes. You see, Sergeant,' Edwards too leant his body at an angle towards Cooper so that there was less than three foot separating them. Someone walking in would have seen co-conspirators hatching a plot, 'Maidment was – is, I should say – a tricky man. Not straightforward, not straightforward at all. It held back his career. You've already alluded to his active service and his promotion at a young age. He should have been destined for great things – yet he retired a major.'

'A decent rank, surely.'

'Of course, a highly creditable one, but below expectations for Maidment. You need to ask around about why he didn't progress further and I'm afraid I can't enlighten you.'

Cooper dutifully made a note in his book.

'Is that all, sir?'

'All that I feel I can say,' he glanced at Cooper, 'so don't press me, I've gone far enough.'

Cooper went on to his final appointment in a confused frame of mind. This wasn't unusual. He lacked Nightingale's decisive insight or Fenwick's leaps of inspiration. He was a diligent, thorough copper but he wasn't a fool and he drove away from Edwards' estate feeling that he had been played for one. Nothing the lieutenant-colonel had said necessarily rung false but even so something felt amiss. Maybe it was the disappointment he'd felt watching one regimental colleague shaft another, because that was precisely what Edwards had done. 'Damning with faint praise', his mother would have said.

He pulled up in front of the Hare and Hounds in a grey mood. Jacob Isaacs, the publican, was a retired quartermaster and had served with Maidment for nine years. If he too stood back from supporting his one-time colleague then Cooper would have to accept that his own assessment of Maidment's character was unduly influenced by his current standing in the community.

Jacob was at the bar nursing a pint of beer. A second pint, untouched and with a creamy head, stood before the empty stool to his left. His handshake was firm and businesslike.

'Shall we find some seats elsewhere?'

'Nope.' Isaacs shook his head. 'Here'll do. Anything I have to say can be said openly. Cheers.'

Cooper took a quick sip, paused as the perfect brew exploded on his taste buds and then took a second with a deep sigh. Isaacs watched every movement.

'Local and perfectly kept. You won't find better bitter in Sussex.' He drank fully from his own glass. 'You want to talk about Jeremy Maidment. I'm sure you have plenty of questions in that little black book but you can forget them and listen to me.

'I'll tell you what sort of man you've put under lock and key in Her Majesty's name and with my bloody tax money! I've half a mind to write to my MP. You lot have got it so wrong. Let me tell you…'

And he did. Cooper's only frustration was that he was prevented from drinking a most excellent pint of beer because he was taking copious notes.

Isaacs had served with Maidment in Borneo and in the UK. He told Cooper *exactly* why the major was awarded the DSO, delighted at the fact that he accumulated a wider audience as he did so. Then he explained why internal politics (in his opinion) robbed the major of deserved promotion and how the man's curious lack of ambition had kept him in his place to retirement. When Cooper attempted to challenge the rosy view Isaacs painted, his questions were flicked to one side as irrelevant. As he sipped his pint, Jacob drained and refilled his own glass and said in a clear voice for the benefit of those in the penny seats.

'I've learnt a lot about life in my time, Mr Cooper, and I've learnt even more about men. There are those that sail true and those who move with the wind and tide of the times. Jeremy Maidment was, is, a man with his own internal compass. It points true and gives direction to his thoughts and deeds. He's remained solid while others devoted their lives to spin and expediency. It cost him dear at times but that compass – call it a sense of duty if you will – is still with him and it would *never* let him fall into the actions that he's accused of. I'd stake my honour on that.'

'So you'll be volunteering as a character witness, will you?' Cooper said with half a smile.

'Try and stop me.'

Cooper enjoyed the rest of his pint and paused to sample the Hare's famous ploughman's lunch, smiling gratefully when extra cheddar cheese and pickled onions appeared on his plate with a second individually baked cottage loaf. He thought he deserved the small rewards that arrived unexpectedly and too rarely during the hard slog of routine police work.

Although he wasn't a man to become despondent easily he did feel that he'd drawn the short straw on the Hill investigation and he wasn't about to rush on to the next of his interviews and spoil this treat. He had two interviews left and, so far, with the exception of Edwards' slightly off comments, he'd found no hint of anything interesting about the major. Nothing connected him to either Malcolm Eagleton or the Paul Hill boy. Still, he would stick at it and report fully because that was his way and he was a man who didn't cut corners.

The last names on his list were Zach Smart and Ben Thompson. Smart lived nearby in Slaugham so he decided to call on him first. He eased himself into his car and wound the windows down to let it cool off.

A shout from a toddler playing on a slide in the pub grounds woke him and he glanced at his watch guiltily. Three o'clock. Ah well, the Spanish swore by their siestas so he doubted his forty winks would have done any harm.

Slaugham is one of the prettiest villages in West Sussex, boasting a charming church and a very decent pub of its own. People waited for years for the opportunity to buy a cottage there and even then they would have to pass the undisclosed scrutiny of the villagers beforehand. Cooper drove through twice before he realised that Smart lived outside the village itself down a gravel drive that led through pastures of sheep. The house was set on the far side of what would once have been a working farmyard but had been converted with taste into additional accommodation and garages. A vintage Bentley was parked outside one and as he clambered out of his car he heard swearing emanating from under the open bonnet.

'Mr Zach Smart?' he called out.

'Who wants him?' The mechanic's voice was muffled by the depth of the engine.

'Detective Sergeant Cooper, Harlden CID.'

That brought his head up quick enough.

'I'm Smart, what do you want?'

Cooper took in the oil-stained overalls and scruffy shirt and tried to reconcile the speaker with the owner of the property around him.

'Do you live here?'

'You found me, didn't you? Now get to your business, I'm busy.'

'This is your car?'

'One of them. I use it for weddings and I've got one tomorrow. The bugger refuses to start and all the others are booked out. What do you want?'

'I'm here because you knew Jeremy Maidment.'

'No I didn't.'

'You were in the same regiment.'

'Doesn't mean I knew the man, though maybe I saw him about. He was a lot older than me. I quit when my cousin died and left me this place on condition that I continued to farm it.'

'I thought officers got to know each other in the mess.'

'I was an oik, a mechanic as it happens; didn't exactly mix with the Maidments of this world. Is that it?'

He bent down to pick up a spanner and peered down at the car engine impatiently.

'No, it's not. Did you know a man called Bryan Taylor?'

'That crook!' Smart lowered the spanner reluctantly and dragged his attention back to Cooper. 'He was as bent as they come and I mean that in every sense of the word. I wouldn't have anything to do with him, couldn't stand the bastard. What's this all about anyway?'

'The murder of Malcolm Eagleton in 1981 and disappearance of Paul Hill in 1982.'

Smart put down the spanner and wiped his hands on a rag.

'The name Eagleton means nothing but I remember the Hill boy going off. I knew Gordon Hill. He bought a neighbouring farm in the late Seventies; decent bloke, didn't deserve what happened to Paul. It wrecked his marriage, you know.'

'I know; we've met Mrs Hill.'

Smart shuddered.

'What a witch. She came round here soon after Paul disappeared and virtually accused me of hiding him from her.'

'Why?'

'When Paul was younger he'd be over playing with my

youngest, Wendy, all the time. They were quite close for a while before she went off to live with her mother.'

'You knew Paul?'

'A little. They played by themselves mostly.'

'When did you last see him, sir?'

'Blimey, now you're asking. Probably at a school sports day or something like that. That's when I usually bumped into poor old Gordon after he'd moved the family back into Harlden.' He picked up the spanner again. 'Look, I've got to get on with this. If I can't fix it I'll have to call in the garage and they're devils to get out past four o'clock.'

'I really do need a statement from you.'

'And it's urgent after all this time? Give over. It won't spoil for a day or so will it?'

Smart had already bent into the engine again and it made Cooper's blood boil. This cocky bastard was dismissing him.

'I think a boy's murder is a darn sight more important than your car,' he said, with annoyance that he knew at once would rile the man. 'What I meant was—'

'I heard what you bloody meant, officer,' Smart face was flushed, 'and you heard what I said. Now, unless you're going to arrest me I suggest you leave and let me get on. I'll come into Harlden after the weekend and make a statement if you insist but that's as good as it gets.'

Cooper knew when he was defeated. He retreated to his car and pulled away without a flurry of gravel but with enormous frustration. He'd met somebody who admitted to knowing Maidment, Taylor and Paul yet the bastard wouldn't speak to him. One thing was for certain, he was going to look into Mr Zachary Smart's background in great detail before he spoke to him again.

The interview with Ben Thompson didn't happen. His wife was at their home in Harlden when Cooper knocked but she explained that her husband was away on a golfing break with some friends from the club until Monday. She'd never heard of Maidment or Taylor so he left her to her gardening and decided to call it a day. It was Friday after all. Doris would be pleased to see him and he'd be able to catch up on some odd jobs that had needed doing outside for a while. The reports could wait for Monday; after all, Maidment wasn't going anywhere. He was almost home when his mobile rang and he cursed the fact that he hadn't followed Fenwick's example and switched the bloody thing off.

It was Nightingale, full of excitement. All the original witness statements and reports for the Hill case had been found, filed with another case from 1992. He was needed at the station at once to help her and the rest of the team go through them. *Bloody typical*, he thought as he swung the car around and headed back into town. That woman lived by different rules to everybody else. Fancy starting a massive job like that when most normal people would have decided a beautiful summer Friday afternoon meant that it should wait until Monday.

CHAPTER TWENTY-TWO

On Friday evening Nathan returned to William's establishment. He was welcomed as an honoured guest. Sam was still segregated from the other boys so there was a wait while William sent for him during which Nathan amused himself by inspecting the boys who were not with clients. There were five of them: one Eurasian, another Afro-Caribbean and three Caucasian. All of them were attractive, clean and well fed. None looked older than fourteen. As he called them forward in turn their chests filled with the held breath of expectancy.

News of what had happened to Sam had spread. Unlike Jack he was popular, not just with the boys but with the staff as well. The staff's disgust at the injuries he'd sustained had been enough to set them gossiping among themselves and some of it had inevitably reached the boys. As Smith ordered them into the light at the centre of the room, they struggled to maintain their composure, even the oldest and most experienced.

Smith repeated the same ritual with each one. He would have them stand upright then prod and poke them with a single finger, uttering a brief commentary: 'overweight'; 'flabby'; 'legs too short'; 'poor colouring'; 'never could stand red hair on a boy'. So it went on. With each criticism the boy under examination would breathe slightly easier. He was asking the Eurasian boy to bend his head so that he could examine his neck when Sam was pushed into the room. Everyone turned to stare at him and for a moment there was an eerie silence, like the pause that follows the command to a firing squad before the fusillade begins.

'Sam, go on, don't be shy.' William sounded like everyone's favourite uncle as he nudged the child closer to Smith.

'What have you got the boy dressed up in, William? He looks ridiculous. Take it off, Sam. He had no right to truss you up like that.'

Sam was frozen to the spot. Rough hands pulled the short satin dressing gown off his shoulders, leaving him standing there in only his underpants, his feet bare. He started to shiver and his upper lip turned down.

'It's all right, my dear,' Nathan said and stepped towards him.

Sam tried to back away but William blocked his way.

'There's no need to act coy. Come here.'

But Sam couldn't move. William sensed trouble and lifted him bodily off the ground. Sam whimpered.

'Careful, you oaf. If you damage him...' Smith's tone was harsh but he saw Sam flinch and stopped at once. 'Take him upstairs. I'll have my usual room.'

Sam was bundled away, his eyes magnified by unshed tears. After he'd gone, his friends eased back into the shadows and waited for the door to open on what their night would bring. Whatever it might be it wouldn't be as bad as the fate that had just moved on. No one mentioned Sam; it didn't do to talk of the fallen.

The man William knew as Nathan was in an excellent mood when he returned home the following day having spent the whole night in London. The boy William had found for him was superb, exactly his type and very biddable. He knew he'd have to ration his visits or risk breaking him but that only added anticipation to his excitement. He was ravenous and was delighted to find a curry with all the trimmings in the fridge, waiting to be reheated for his lunch. The phone rang when he was halfway through his meal and he ignored it, half listening to the voice leave a message.

'Hell!' His fork clattered to the ground as he stood up and ran to the phone.

'William, I'm here. What did you just say? Speak up, man. I can't hear your bloody whisper.'

'I said he's come. I told him in no uncertain terms last time that he should stay away but you know Alec…'

'Unfortunately, yes. He requires firm handling, very firm. You must have been too weak, William. That's part of your problem, you're too lily-livered. Did you kick him out?'

'No, you don't understand, he's *still* here! I can't shift him. Says he needs more material because he's dry now Joe's out of the picture and he won't go until I put him in touch with a supplier.'

'You will do no such thing!' Nathan said, sounding exactly like a headmaster scolding an errant schoolboy. 'Put Ball on the line, now.'

While he waited Nathan worked through the options he had for dealing with Alec Ball. He was a tricky man; violent, erratic, not the brightest penny in the jar. It was a combination that made him difficult to manage and Nathan regretted ever becoming entangled with him. But they shared secrets, some of the darkest secrets it's possible for men to share, and that made Ball a problem that needed careful management. Despite his comments to William, Nathan knew that toughness wouldn't work with Ball. He needed coaxing, gentling like a half-tamed bull.

'Alec,' he said, warm and friendly as soon as the receiver was picked up. 'What are you doing all the way up there in London when we could much more easily have solved your little problem locally?'

There was a pause as Ball adjusted to Nathan's tone; he'd clearly been expecting a bollocking. Some of his anticipatory bolshieness lingered in his reply.

'It's not a little problem, Nathan; it's a fucking big one. I've got customers to satisfy and if I let them down my reputation will be ruined. And anyway,' he said as an afterthought, 'you said I was never to contact you directly, it always had to be via Joe.'

Yes, Nathan thought, *because I could trust Joe to be discreet and keep his mouth shut; and even he never saw me in person – just as well as it turned out.*

'Well, Joe's not involved any more, is he? And you should have known I'd never abandon an old mate. But you were right not to see me directly. There's a little too much interest from the Old Bill around here right now. We can still get together though and I'll bring something useful with me. I know some people—'

'That's the thing, isn't it, Nathan?' Ball's tone had turned threatening. 'You've done very well for yourself over the years and it was on the backs of blokes like me and Joe that you feathered your nest. But at least Joe benefited from you in the end; funny how he suddenly has all the money he needs to live a "respectable" life now, isn't it? Though it's weird him being a customer instead of supplier now.'

'A customer?' Nathan sat up straight and an unpleasant smile transformed his face so that he resembled a hungry stoat. 'Well, well. Fancy that. I thought he'd left his old life behind for good now that he's found God. Hah! The old hypocrite.'

It pleased Nathan to know that Joe Watkins had been unable to rid himself of the obsession that had filled his life for so many years; in fact, it made him feel even more superior in his ability to manage his own life so well. He could imagine the demons that were eating into Joe's soul and the thought brought with it the enjoyment of a rush of power. But he had Alec to manage and was irritated that he could no longer rely on Joe to do it for him. Ball was still ranting about how unfairly he'd been treated and how he needed more supplies. Nathan interrupted him.

'Haven't I always made sure that you have access to buy

whatever you need, Alec? Frankly, I'm surprised you've got through all the material you had last time. I understood you to have bought out one of the best collections in the country.'

'Access! You gave me a name and money that you made clear was a fucking loan, Nathan; hardly generosity itself, are you?'

'Have I ever pressed you for repayment?' He had intended to but it had become apparent that money ran through Ball's fingers as fast as he made it.

'No, well...'

Nathan could sense that Ball's bubble of anger, fuelled by injured pride and defensiveness, had burst. His greatest strength was his ability to read people, not that he bothered to unless it was necessary.

'So, when are you free to meet? Shall we say tomorrow, six o'clock, at the site of the bonfire?'

'Why d'you want to go back there of all places?' He could hear the shudder in Ball's voice.

'It's as private a place as any and I don't believe in being afraid of ghosts.' There, Ball would have to say yes now or look a coward.

It was agreed. Nathan went back to his congealing vindaloo and scraped the food into the waste bin with distaste. He was still hungry and found cheese and biscuits in the cupboard. As he poured himself a large glass of a particularly good Barbaresco he pondered what to do about Ball. The man was becoming a real liability. For years he'd been manageable – though to be fair that had been Joe's job and he'd been well rewarded for it – but now with Joe out of the loop the burden looked like falling on his own shoulders. That wasn't a situation that was going to work at all.

He savoured the cleanliness of the wine on his tongue, deep, subtle, very fine, it demanded his full attention; he thought it a wine that mirrored his tastes in life. Only when he had finished the bottle did he return his attention to what he should do with Ball.

PART FOUR

It was very dark in the cellar, so dark that Paul couldn't see his hand in front of his face. He didn't know what time it was, and wondered whether it was past his normal teatime. If so, it would mean that Bryan had no intention of returning him home in time to pretend that nothing out of the ordinary had happened. As if that would be possible given the state of his body. He shivered.

Despite the warmth of the evening outside it was cold here. He just needed to stay warm until Bryan came. Paul tried jumping and running on the spot. It worked for a while but the pain in the lower half of his body stopped him long before his legs started to ache or the skin on his feet grew tender from the stones.

Where was he? They'd put a sack on his head and a gag in his mouth, and then carried him from the pool. It hadn't taken more than five minutes so he must still be somewhere in the grounds of the house, but where? He tried again to explore his prison, remembering to count his paces this time: fifteen from where he'd been standing next to the rough wood of the door. He pounded on it, shouting to be let out until he was hoarse. Nothing. When he leant his ear against it he couldn't hear anything from the other side so perhaps it was too thick. No, wait, maybe there were two doors. Yes.

He dragged out the memory of the sounds that had accompanied his imprisonment. Alec had been carrying him, he was sure, because of his smell and the roughness of stubble against his skin. Joe and Bryan must have stayed at the pool, at least he thought they had as there had only been one other set of footsteps as he'd been rushed through the woods. They had taken him along a stream, walking on rough stones that skidded beneath Alec's feet. Soon after they'd set off he had lost the feel of the sun so they'd either walked behind a hill or under thicker trees. Alec had nearly fallen at one point and he'd cursed the wet stones beneath his feet. Nathan told him to shut up; they were the only words spoken the whole journey.

When they'd reached the entrance to the cellar he had heard the jingle of keys, a creak and then silence but instead of moving forward immediately Alec had waited, for what? Paul remembered another noise like the faint squeak of rusty hinges. It could have been the sound of another door opening at the bottom of the long flight of steps they'd climbed down. The idea of being shut up behind a double barrier made him feel worse.

Fifteen paces. He put his right hand out as far as it would go along the wall to the side of the door, facing in towards the room he paced after it. Ten paces then he reached a wooden shelf of some sort. His fingers explored. After a few inches there was an upright, then another one. He counted twenty before he touched the chill stones of the wall again. With his other hand he skimmed the surface of the shelving. The rows were close together and every one of them was divided into boxes too small for books. Where on earth was he?

Instead of panicking he turned ninety degrees and found the next wall. This too was covered in wooden shelving. His fingers groped on and recoiled suddenly as they touched something slimy. It was even colder than the wood and stones and he thought it must be some sort of lurking reptile. His breath came fast as he waited for the sound of the thing moving but the silence was unbroken. Eventually he found the courage to reach out again; it was still there. The cold didn't seem so intense this time and it wasn't slimy, it was smooth, like glass. It was glass; it was a bottle. He pulled it from the shelf and felt along its length to where the neck narrowed and metal capped the end. Wine; he was in a wine cellar.

The thought made him feel better. He wasn't in some derelict building or abandoned mine shaft. The wine had to belong to Nathan. He had the keys; he would come for it at some stage, there's no way they'd just leave him here. But supposing it was only the one bottle, that Nathan had abandoned the cellar. It was suddenly very important to know how many bottles were stored with him. Paul counted, then counted again and, when the number was different, did so for a third time.

Three hundred and twenty-seven! The result made him laugh. Not abandoned! No way, he was only locked up while they decided what to do with him. The thought coincided with a terrible stomach cramp that left Paul doubled over and gasping for breath. It came again and he was sick. His first thought on recovering was that Nathan would be furious because the smell of vomit was so strong. His second was that he was even colder than before. His body was shaking uncontrollably, his teeth chattering so loudly he could hear them. They had to come soon, surely, they must. Bryan was his friend.

How long before he'd come for him? It wouldn't take Bryan long to get rid of Alec and Joe so that it was safe for him to go outside again. That's what he'd be doing. Bryan was his friend; he'd promised to look after him. But the thought of what he'd just endured sent Paul into a spasm that hurt his injured body and made him sick again. This time he didn't have the energy to lift his head fully off the floor and some of the vomit clotted his hair and neck. He huddled into a ball, hugging his knees for warmth and comfort, tucking his head down into his chest.

That was how Bryan found him later when he eventually came for him.

CHAPTER TWENTY-THREE

Fenwick received Clive's call as he watched his housekeeper put the finishing touches to Chris's birthday cake. It was in the shape of a cowboy, complete with hat and sheriff's star, decorated with nine candles. He walked into the study to have the conversation.

'When did he arrive in London?'

'An hour ago. He's just gone into a house south of King's Cross, off Farringdon Road. I'm outside now.'

'Have you let the locals know?'

'Not yet; thought you might want to do that.'

'OK, leave it with me. What about back-up?'

'Operations are sending Walsh and someone else.'

'That'll take at least an hour. You're exposed meanwhile if he leaves by another exit or he spots you. I'll see what the Met can do for us and check out whether the house has a history. You'd better give me the full address.'

Half an hour later he was back on the phone to Clive.

'The house is clean as far as they know; I've asked them to dig out the ownership records anyway. You should be on the receiving end of some help any moment.'

'They've just arrived, complete with unmarked car and camera. He's still in there; all's quiet.'

'What else has been happening in the meantime?'

'It's still early – not yet eleven. There was one visitor half an hour ago, respectable-looking bloke; other than that, *nada*.'

'Well, keep me posted. I'll be at home all day; it's Chris's birthday party,' he added and was surprised when Clive said, 'Say Happy Birthday to him from his Uncle Clive, would you? And tell him I hope he has loads of presents.'

'There are no worries there,' Fenwick laughed. 'He's having a party this afternoon and no doubt he'll be spoilt rotten.'

Four hours later Fenwick watched with a deep feeling of contentment as Chris and his friends went mad among the makeshift tepees and tents he'd created the night before so that they'd be a surprise. The invitations had specified cowboy and Indian fancy dress and he was astonished at the inventiveness of the mothers of these boys, and the few girls who were honorary boys as far as Chris was concerned and so invited. Fenwick had decided there should be no sign of Raymond 'the best magician in Sussex (as seen on TV)' Clark, Desmond the clown (and his charming assistant Zoë), nor hint of a bouncy castle.

Instead there were rubber tyre stockades, tree houses conveniently close to the ground, old blankets strung up on branches and a wooden picnic table groaning with Wild West food (bacon, sausages, cherry tomatoes, bread, crisps and Coke or lemonade).

The idea that a widowed father could organise a children's party unaided broke unwritten rules of male dependency. Consequently, several mums had volunteered to help. He'd accepted offers from those he thought wouldn't have a fit of the vapours at the idea of their little dears running around in make-believe battles to the death all afternoon. While he told himself that he could have coped unaided, he was silently amazed at the way they kept the smaller children out of harm's way, cleared the debris and praised their offspring's exploits all at once. The afternoon was turning into a great success.

Clive called him to say that Ball had left the house in London and then caught the train straight back to Harlden. He'd followed him and was on the same train. The Met agreed to keep an undercover team on the house and cover it for twenty-four hours, photographing visitors and trying to make sense of the activity. Fenwick had mixed feelings about the news. On the one hand he'd wanted a breakthrough but on the other he was relieved that he would be able to enjoy the duration of Chris's party.

When it was time for their guests to leave, his son was unusually well behaved. Only after the other children had gone did he notice that Bess was missing. A panicked search found her reading in one of the abandoned stockades.

'Come on, Bess, the garden's yours again.'

His daughter refused to meet his eye.

'What is it, love? Don't be jealous of Chris on his birthday; that's not like you.'

Two tissues and a hug later he managed to coax her back to the house but she refused his offer of ice cream. While Alice cleared the remaining paper plates he took her inside, not sure why she was miserable nor what he could do about it.

'Please talk to me,' he begged. 'What did I do wrong?'

'You forgot to invite Nightingale,' she said, barely audible. 'She promised me ages ago she'd be here to keep me company and she would've kept her promise so it must be that you forgot to invite her.'

Guilt opened inside him, making his stomach twist and his face harden. Bess was right; he had forgotten to invite her. A few weeks previously it would have been automatic but not now. Because of the rumours they'd drifted apart and he simply hadn't made the effort to see her recently.

'Perhaps she was busy.'

'Not so busy that she couldn't bring Chris a present.' His daughter glared at him.

'Are you sure?' This was news to Fenwick. Bess nodded.

'She brought it while you were ogling Justin's mum. Alice took it from her but I saw her. I said hello.' Bess turned from him again. 'She bought me an un-birthday present like she did for Chris on my birthday. It was cruel not to invite her in.'

'I didn't know she'd come, honestly.' Whatever guilt he'd felt was nothing compared to the confusion that wormed through him at his daughter's revelations. Bess shrugged and waved him away imperiously.

'I'm going to bed early and I don't want a story, thank you.'

He was dismissed. Fenwick retreated downstairs. Chris was building a kit dinosaur in front of the television.

'Who bought you that?'

'Nightingale. It's wicked. She even brought the batteries. When it's finished its eyes flash and it roars.'

Fenwick went to find Alice.

'You could've told me that Louise Nightingale called.' He was too annoyed to be diplomatic.

'She only stopped by. She looked too busy to stay.'

'Any message?'

'No. Pass me that bowl, will you? I think I can just fit it on the top shelf.'

He did so, then waited in protracted silence for Alice to finish loading the dishwasher and to say more. Instead she set the controls, closed the door and went to talk to Chris, leaving Fenwick thoroughly defeated and depressed despite the success of the day.

It was nine o'clock when Alice found him collecting tyres from the garden.

'Assistant Chief Constable Harper-Brown is on the telephone. He says it's urgent.'

Fenwick ran indoors.

'Good evening, sir.'

'Fenwick? Good, switch on your television and watch *BBC News*.'

He did as he was told, choosing the small screen in the kitchen rather than risk a fight for the control with Chris. The news item was nearing its close, he could tell by the announcer's tone of voice.

'Got it?'

'Yes.'

'...*the question raised by the* Sunday Times *tomorrow is why the West Sussex Constabulary continue to hold decorated war hero Major Jeremy Maidment in connection with the killings of Paul Hill and Malcolm Eagleton when they have received explicit information, with corroborative evidence, which implicates another man. They have apparently not named him because of the hearsay nature of the information but the* Sunday Times *has been told by their source that the police have been given substantive evidence, yet continue to fail to act upon it.*'

'Damn!'

'Precisely. My house, fifteen minutes.'

When he arrived the ACC met him on the doorstep and didn't invite him in. Harper-Brown held out a videotape of the news coverage like a weapon.

'What's going on? You've been shadowing this thing; how has this media disaster happened?'

'I think they must be referring to the letters Harlden received enclosing the school book with Paul Hill's fingerprints on it.'

'I recall. Was there a threat from the Well-Wisher to go public?'

'Not so far as I'm aware. If you remember, the theory is that the letters were sent by one of Taylor's victims or someone trying to get back at him.'

'But the BBC report stated categorically that the *Sunday Times* alleges we are not taking this information seriously.'

'It's being treated very seriously, sir. Inspector Nightingale sent the book, letter and envelope to the lab for full analysis and is leading the investigation to trace the sender – this Well-Wisher – personally.'

'And the major remains in custody?'

'Yes. Two letters don't counter-balance the weight of physical evidence. Do you think Harlden should release him?'

'Anything from the interrogation?' The ACC ignored his trap.

'He knows more than he's saying. I'm convinced that he's hiding something. By the way, are Superintendent Quinlan and Inspector Nightingale joining us?'

'Can't seem to track him down.' H-B ignored the reference to Nightingale. 'How would you propose to respond to the *Sunday Times*' allegations?'

'Me?' Fenwick was confused; the case had been prised away from him at H-B's insistence and now he was being asked how to handle the mess it had turned into, through nobody's fault.

'I'd follow the guidelines set out, of course.' There was a well-established procedure that had been introduced nationally following previous unfortunate experiences. 'The *Sunday Times* are taking a big risk running the piece but their lawyers must have cleared it, which means they have more to go on than we do. I'd make an immediate request for the material that led to their report and its source but they might reject it. If they do, I'd seek a warrant for the information, which will eventually be handed over. But even if the *Sunday Times* knows the identity of the source they'll claim journalistic privilege and won't tell us who it is.'

The ACC had stepped outside and was pacing up and down his gravel drive.

'Precisely. Very well, in Quinlan's absence you're to do exactly what you propose. I want you to step in to manage this debacle.'

'What about Inspector Nightingale? She's the SIO after all.'

'That's as maybe but I doubted her ability to handle a case of this magnitude from the beginning and this cock-up simply proves me right. The matter has become far too hot for her to handle, particularly with her lack of experience. And as Quinlan is inexplicably incommunicado, with Rodney Blite halfway through a personal development course that cannot be interrupted, I have no option but to intercede here.' The ACC spoke with determination, obviously relishing the opportunity to tell Quinlan that Nightingale had somehow screwed up.

Fenwick opened his mouth to argue but closed it again, knowing there was no point.

'Just make sure you keep me informed at all times, Andrew. Obviously we will need to make a press statement; I'll give it but you must have it drafted for me tonight.'

'Of course.'

'And, Fenwick.'

'Yes, sir?'

'Nothing dramatic and no surprises. I expect to be involved before any strategic decisions are made. It's already embarrassing enough. Got that?'

'Of course.'

Fenwick concealed a smile in the turn of his head. One man's strategic decision was another man's tactical solution and he had an awful lot of those.

CHAPTER TWENTY-FOUR

Her summary dismissal from Chris's birthday party propelled Nightingale back to the station despite the fact that it was a Saturday. When she was truly furious she did some of her best work. In fact, work was the only remedy for her most extreme moods. She drove into the town centre with scant regard for gear shift or brake.

For weeks she'd been telling herself that Fenwick's disregard was due to his preoccupation with the Choir Boy investigation and its implications for his promotion prospects. Being barred from his son's party, when barely a month before she would have been an automatic guest, had forced her to confront reality. Their friendship was over. His recent behaviour towards her should have been clue enough but she'd been deliberately blind. With acceptance of the truth came a deep hurt at his callousness.

At the age of sixteen she'd made a pledge to herself that she would preserve her emotional independence so that she could never be wounded again by the sort of abandonment she'd suffered from her parents. She called herself a fool for relaxing her guard and blinked hard to clear her sight.

The station was quiet, the CID room unusually deserted. She walked into the Hill incident room to find the research officer Shelly hurriedly extracting herself from the close attentions of DC Robin. Robin was married and Nightingale did not approve. She let her feelings show, unaware that her own emotional turmoil magnified her censure.

'I want the original Hill files in date order set out on that table, ASAP.'

'Would that be all of them, ma'am?' Shelly was stunned into a title that Nightingale rarely asked for or received.

'Yes. I'll be back in fifteen minutes.' She glared at them both and when she heard Robin's muttered oath told him to shut it. His look of shocked contrition had no effect on her whatsoever.

In the canteen she forced down a cup of tea and a slice of cake then bought a large bottle of water to take back to the incident room. When she returned, the centre table was covered with boxes and files, some of them still dusty, which raised a question as to the thoroughness of the work she'd delegated to others in the past twenty-four hours. It made her even more determined to see through the plan that had formed as she drove away from Fenwick's house. She was dressed for a boy's birthday party in an oversized rugby shirt, jeans and trainers, perfect for the hours of hard labour she'd assigned herself as penance for being dumb enough to get hurt yet again.

While Shelly entered information into a computer with more than her customary diligence, Nightingale opened the first box and retrieved a pile of files so large she could only just lift them. She put them to her left, a fresh A4 pad and pen to her right, and rolled up her sleeves, aware that this was hardly the work an SIO should be doing. She didn't care; she was good at rigorous research, finding patterns in data that could overwhelm others; and anyway, she reflected, she hadn't exactly had the best role model for delegation in Fenwick. Thought of her old boss merely fuelled her anger and she focused her eyes resolutely on the piles of paper in front of her.

As she opened the first report she was plunged back into the world of Harlden in 1982. Her speed-reading had always been impressive and she quickly developed a routine of identifying relevant extracts to copy from reports and taped interviews.

Shelly, eager to re-enter the good books of a female officer she admired, volunteered to help with any photocopying and transcription, which made the work easier.

At the end of an hour Nightingale stopped and studied her notes. She was already saddened by the depressing tale that was emerging from the dusty files. Mistaking the source of her expression, a nervous Shelly continued to work well past her normal departure time.

Nightingale took a long drink of water and started to read from the extracts she had made:

7th September, 1982

8:15 p.m. **Duty Officer: Sergeant JJ Atkins:** *Call received from Mrs Sarah Hill, 26 Penton Cross, Woodhampstead, Harlden, telephone # Harlden 632390. Reports that her son, Paul Christopher Hill, has not returned home from school and is not at any of his friends' homes. Atkins advises caller to wait until 10 p.m. and to call again if son still missing.*

9:58 p.m. **Report by Constable NC Davis:** *Sarah Hill arrives at station to report her son missing. Father, Gordon Hill, remains at home. Mrs Hill very distressed, taken to interview room by WPC Alison Major.*

10:15 p.m. **WPC Alison Major and DS Stephen Ingles interview Mrs Hill.**

10:25 p.m. **Search authorised by Inspector Quinlan.** *Team of officers despatched to Penton Cross and Downside Comprehensive School. 11 p.m. Search team increased to twenty and Chief Constable Windlass advised of possible missing child.*

Thorough search initiated of Paul's home and surrounding vicinity. Separate search underway of school and grounds. The headmistress, Mrs Emily Spinning, and caretaker, Mr Alex Jones, on site until 0100 hours when the search is extended to playing fields and other school grounds. Neither Mrs Spinning nor Mr Jones saw Paul Hill leave the school grounds.

Interviews conducted between 10:30 p.m. and 11:45 p.m. on 7th September with friends of Paul identified by Mrs Hill. Interviews reveal nothing. None of the friends recalls seeing Paul leave school.

Case number: 0816-23 7:30 a.m. 8th September, 1982: *Volunteers join search team of forty-five officers covering two areas: Wasteland stretching from the allotments behind the Penton Cross estate as far as the bypass, the A623. Second search continues in and around the school and into Harlden Park at 8 a.m. Additional officers deployed to question pupils and staff and conduct door-to-door inquiries in Paul's neighbourhood.*

9 a.m. News conference attended by Chief Constable Windlass, the boy's parents, Sarah and Gordon Hill, and Quinlan. News of the boy's disappearance was first released to the press at 10:30 p.m. on 7th September and mentioned on local radio as a news bulletin shortly afterwards.

The matter-of-fact style of the first reports was ironic with hindsight. How easy to say to the overanxious mother of a fourteen-year-old 'give it another hour or two'. Eight-thirty in the evening was hardly late for a teenager. She could understand why Sergeant Atkins had been relaxed and no one could have blamed him, but in reality the investigation had lost precious hours of daylight at a crucial time.

She was certain that the initial police response had been all it should have been. Under Quinlan's command the energy and determination of the searching officers would have been relentless. Paul had only been missing a few hours and their hopes of finding him alive would have been high. She pitied them and read on quickly, finishing the first box and moving on to the next. Shelly asked apologetically whether it would be OK to leave as she had a date. Nightingale waved her away with a brief word of thanks. Beside her, a fresh sheet of paper steadily filled with more notes as she extracted what she judged to be the most relevant and reliable witness statements from the hundreds bundled into files around her.

Case number: 0816-23 8th September, 1982 WS 52

Extraction from witness statement taken by Constable Justin Daley from Miss Julie Ackers, 20, of flat 26 Midland Court, Harlden.

'*On Tuesday, 7th September, I was working in Stan's Corner Shop, West Street, Harlden from 8:30 a.m. to 4:30 p.m. Around 4:10 p.m. Paul Hill came in and bought some sweets – a packet of Polos and some crisps.*

'*I am certain that it was Paul because he is friends with my brother Victor and he has been round to our house. He was riding his new bike, the red one with flashy handles. I know because he leant it against the shop window. He's not meant to do that, it makes Stan upset. I spoke to him briefly but he did not say where he was going. I did not see in which direction he went when he left the shop as I was serving someone else, whose name I do not know.*

'*Paul came into the shop on his own and I did not see anyone else outside. He was wearing his blazer, full school uniform with long trousers and carrying a bag on his back.*'

Case number: 0816-23 8th September, 1982 WS 166

Taken by WPC Alison Major from Mrs Angela Rush, housewife, 63 Whitemoss Drive, Harlden, W. Sussex.

Mrs Rush telephoned the station at 6:35 p.m. after hearing of Paul Hill's disappearance on the evening news. In her statement she said: 'I saw a boy that I am sure was

Paul Hill in the lay-by at the end of Whitemoss Drive at about half past four yesterday. I am certain it was Paul because I had occasion to tell him off only last week. He and his friend Victor Ackers, plus some other boys I did not recognise, were fighting in the lay-by and one of them knocked the rubbish bin over...

'I did not see anyone other than Paul. I know the time I saw Paul. It was just after 4:30. I checked my watch to make certain of it in case there was any more trouble and my watch is accurate to the radio. I went to do the potatoes for supper and when I looked again at about a quarter to five he was gone.'

10th September, 1982 Ref 0816-23: WS 251

Taken by Constable Dorian Smith from Mr Daniel Anchor, farmer of Upper Downs Farm, Lower Beeding at 6 p.m.: 'I was driving my tractor through Wyndham Wood some time after five on 7th September. I had just taken some fresh hay into East Paddock two miles away and I needed to get back for a second load and take it to Three Mile Field before six because I was due at a darts championship at seven-thirty. I am certain that the time was well after five because I was running late for the darts match.

'The road through Wyndham Wood is narrow, single track in places, and Taylor's red car came round a bend fast. I had to brake hard but he barely slowed down. There's a drop at the side of the road, so I was looking over to make sure I didn't go down it.

'I did not see Taylor's face but it was definitely his car. I recognised the make and the number plate. I know the car because he's done work for me and at the Red Lion public house, my local. He drives to work in his car so I know it. I can't say whether anyone was with him in it because I was too busy staying on the road.'

The mention of Bryan Taylor confused her. There was no explanation as to why Wyndham Wood was relevant to police inquiries and yet by day three a sighting of Taylor driving through it had warranted a full witness statement. According to her own research, Taylor hadn't been considered a suspect for almost a week – three days after this report. Nightingale checked her watch – ten past seven. It was too late to call Superintendent Quinlan at home but there was a chance he might have popped into the station to catch up on the day's activity; a regular habit.

She was in luck. Quinlan was just leaving as she reached his door.

'Excuse me, sir; can I walk with you to your car?'

'Something the matter, Louise?'

'Just some questions about the Paul Hill case.'

'I've already spoken at length to one of your team, you know.'

'I realise that but you were SIO—'

'Briefly. I was an inspector then and the powers that be soon bumped me off when we didn't get a result.'

He seemed quite matter-of-fact about the implied slur on his leadership. Nightingale was surprised. If it had been her she would have fought to stay as SIO and then resented the demotion intensely. Something of her feelings must have shown on her face as Quinlan laughed.

'I didn't take it to heart. There was no point fighting the politics. And as it turned out, I was glad that it passed to Superintendent Bacon. The way Paul's name and reputation was dragged in the dirt left a very bad taste, I can tell you.'

'You mean because of his alleged association with Bryan Taylor?'

Quinlan's face lost its smile and he paused before heading down the stairs to his car.

'Oh, it was more than alleged, I'm afraid. There was considerable evidence that Bryan was a pimp and Paul one of his boys. It's all in the files.'

'Yes, but unfortunately the photographic evidence that supports the witness statements is still missing. What I'm confused about is why Bryan became a suspect so early on. I can't find his name being mentioned yet we're taking statements about him from people on day three of the inquiry.'

'Really?' He screwed up his face in an effort of memory. 'Well, he became a suspect when I was still SIO, I'm certain; and that only lasted five days. Then later on it looked like Bryan and Paul might have run off together. There were sightings of them all over, though we never found Taylor's car, which was strange.'

'But how did Taylor's name first come up?'

They were still standing on the stairs and Nightingale noticed Quinlan glance at his watch.

'Please, sir, it's important.'

'I realise that but I was due to meet my wife at the Arts Centre five minutes ago; she has tickets for some concert or other.'

He sounded as if he'd like an excuse to miss the whole evening but didn't dare. Nightingale wondered briefly what Mrs Quinlan was like and smiled at him encouragingly; she didn't want to lose her chance. He gave in and continued.

'I seem to recall that one of Paul's friends mentioned Taylor quite early in the investigation and we checked with the school. Taylor had done some maintenance work for them so it was possible he could have met Paul there.' A grimace crossed his face.

'What is it?'

'I've just remembered. It's funny how one can blot out unpleasantness so easily. I had to interview his parents about it. At first they were eager to confirm that Paul did work for Taylor occasionally but then, when I started to describe the stories that were circulating…well, it became most unpleasant. They ordered me out of their house.'

'So Bryan Taylor became your prime suspect?'

'Yes. We obtained a warrant for his house and found the...material that confirmed he was a very active paedophile.'

'But people later thought they'd gone off together?'

'They did. Paul had threatened to run away before and did so once, although he only went to stay with family. According to Mrs Hill he'd had an argument with his father before he left for school on the 7th and said he never wanted to see him again, that sort of thing. My superiors started to think there could be some truth in the rumour that was being circulated by his so-called friends, that Paul had "done a bunk", as they put it. Sympathy for the lad had been wavering – he'd become unpopular at school and was known as a bit of an oddball. Once the press picked up on the gossip I'm afraid it was hard to keep an open mind.'

'But you did.'

Nightingale could tell from the sadness on the superintendent's face that he bitterly regretted the course the investigation had taken.

'Paul was a victim, I am absolutely sure about that. He had a besotted, depressive, overprotective mother and an ineffectual father who resorted to bullying in an effort to control his son. Paul was headstrong, difficult, I'm sure. Probably quite confused about his sexuality as well and ashamed of the fact that he was small and had a delicate feminine beauty – he looked more like twelve than fourteen at the time he disappeared. I have no doubt that he was the victim, no doubt that his friends and family drove him further into Taylor's embrace, and sadly no doubt at all that Taylor killed him.'

Quinlan finally turned and walked down the stairs.

Nightingale noted the stoop in his shoulders and then watched his back straighten as he walked out of the door.

She returned to the incident room and continued her painstaking research. Quinlan had thought Taylor a murderer but it was clear from the later case files that he'd been in a minority. Within a month police attention had turned to a nationwide search for the runaways. They were kept busy with reports of sightings as far apart as Edinburgh and St Ives.

It was past eight-thirty when she finally found the tape of the interview Quinlan had referred to, given by Paul's friend Victor Ackers and misfiled with some papers at the bottom of an archive box. Nightingale heard it through, unaware of the sneer of distaste on her face.

Initial interview 9th September, 1982 by DI William Black, WPC Alison Major with Victor Ackers, age 14, in the presence of his mother, Mrs Janice Ackers, both reside at Flat 2b, Midland Court, Harlden, West Sussex. Time 7:30 p.m.

VA: *'My name is Victor Ackers and I'm a friend of Paul Hill, sort of. We used to be mates but I didn't see as much of him, like, this summer.'*

DIWB: *'Why not, Victor?'*

VA: *'He sort of started getting airs, like he was better than we was. He had all this money and he'd show off with it. Like with his bike.'*

DIWB: *'Do you know where the money came from? [Long pause.] Come on, Victor, you might as well tell me. We're going to find out anyway.'*

Mrs Ackers: *'Go on, Victor, tell him what I heard you saying to Neil this evening.'*

VA: *'Well, he said he got it from doing odd jobs. "I work hard, not like you lot," he used to say, but, like, we didn't believe him. He'd have to work every hour to get money for that bike, and he had some to spare, like a roll of notes he kept hidden somewhere in a tin in his bedroom that he showed me last time I was there. I don't know where he kept it – it was a big secret. He said it was impossible to find and I never had the chance.'*

DIWB: *'And how did he earn that money?'*

VA: *'He had…sort of…he was… [Long pause.] There was something going on between him and that bloke Bryan Taylor, you know, the odd job man. He, like, gives us all the creeps and we stay well away from him but Paul was always hanging out with him.'*

DIWB: *'Go on.'*

VA: *'Well, he'd…they'd…been seen together, y'know, doing…like stuff.'*

DIWB: *'Did you see them yourself? [There was a long pause then Black's neutral voice.] Victor has just shaken his head. So if you didn't see them, who did?'*

VA: *'Wobbly Wendy. Ow, Mum, that hurt! I mean Wendy Smart; she's in year one and follows Paul everywhere. Like she hasn't got friends of her own. She said she saw him and Bryan in the woods.'*

DIWB: *'Which woods, Victor?'*

VA: *'Wyndham Wood, I think. That's where Paul always went, usually. Anyway she said she saw them…' [Another silence]*

DIWB: *'Go on, this is very important… Look, your mum won't be embarrassed, will you, Mrs Ackers?'*

MRSA: *'Course not. Get on with it, Victor. We haven't got all day!' [Victor Ackers leans over and whispers something to his mother. They appear to have an argument but eventually Mrs Ackers leaves at Victor's request.]*

VA: *'Sorry but I couldn't, like, not with her here.'*

DIWB: *'Would you like your father instead? It is your right.'*

VA: *'No way! You'd have to find him first and it's past opening time – he could be in any one of a dozen pubs by now.'*

DIWB: *'Tell me what Wendy told you she saw.'*

VA: 'She saw them, y'know, sort of touching each other like, y'know?'

DIWB: 'Did she see them in a sexual act?'

VA: 'What's that mean?'

DIWB: 'Were they kissing, or touching each other in intimate areas?'

VA: 'I dunno. What she said was that they, y'know, had their clothes off and were doing stuff.'

DIWB: 'And she never described the "stuff" to you?'

VA: 'No. You'll have to ask her.'

Nightingale had to stop. She felt somehow dirty just touching the tape. After some more water she listened to the rest but it contained little. No doubt Wendy had been called in to make a statement but that too wasn't filed in order and probably lay in one of the other boxes.

Her neck was stiff and her fingers grey with dust. It was time to go home but she hated the idea of returning to her empty flat and was too aware of the scale of hurt that her anger-fuelled industry was keeping at bay. She searched through the other boxes and found the catalogue of missing evidence that had been taken from Taylor's and Hill's homes when the warrants were executed. The list noted that the search of Taylor's house had taken place on 10th September. A large quantity of pornography, photographic equipment and pictures, many of Paul, had been seized, together with some clothes, bedding and samples of all the fabric in his house. There was no reference to an address book or diary, or to the hoard of cash Taylor was rumoured to have kept at home out of sight of the Inland Revenue.

Material hadn't been taken from Paul's house, other than for samples to help the tracker dogs, until more than a week later. Superintendent Bacon, then SIO, had requested and received a warrant for a full search on the basis that Paul was in possession of the proceeds of crime – his rumoured roll of notes kept in an Ovaltine tin and flaunted in front of his friends.

She scanned the list quickly but there was no reference to Paul's money either, only to an empty tin. It supported the theory that Paul had run away but Quinlan hadn't been convinced and neither was Nightingale.

'Suppose,' she said out loud to the empty room, 'that Taylor did kill Paul then did a disappearing act. His neighbours say that he didn't return to his house on the 7th or subsequently, so if he had the money with him the murder would have been premeditated. That's unlikely though because he would have packed and taken the pornography from the house rather than leave it to be found by the police. Far more likely is that the death was an accident. If it was, then why did he have the money on him? That doesn't make sense. What happened to Bryan's money?'

She drained the last drops of water from the bottle and then sat upright as another thought hit her.

'What happened to *Paul's* money?' she asked the empty room, frowning at its lack of answer. 'He wouldn't have taken it to school because he'd have to leave his bag in the changing room during class and it would be too risky.'

She tore off a clean sheet of paper and wrote on it:

Reasons no money at Paul's/Bryan's house:
1. *Paul/Bryan took it with them – liked to carry it around but Victor says he kept it in his bedroom and Taylor would be too smart...*
2. *Paul took it with him – told to by Taylor.*
3. *Paul's parents confiscated money before police arrived, having searched bedroom and found it – but they had no reason to know it existed.*

4. A friend stole it after he disappeared but unlikely as Mr
& Mrs Hill wouldn't have let them in and Taylor didn't
have friends/would have it well hidden.

She paused then added, reluctantly:

5. Money stolen by officer(s) conducting search.

It happened, she knew it did, and looking at the options it was a plausible explanation. Had one of the officers on the case been bent? She had no idea. Even current gossip rarely reached her ears but she knew a man who'd know.

'643726.'

'Doris? I'm sorry to disturb you. It's Louise Nightingale. Can I have a quick word with Bob, please? I won't keep him long.'

She could hear Cooper's wife calling for him, then the noise from a television grew louder as a door was opened before being cut off completely as it was shut.

'Cooper.'

'Bob, it's me. I need your help but don't worry, it's only a quick question.' She heard his sigh of relief then an intake of breath as she said. 'In 1982, who in Harlden Division was bent? I know someone was but who was it?'

'Bloody hell, Nightingale, you can't expect me...'

'I do, and if it's not Louise it's ma'am, remember that.'

'Sorry...ma'am...' Cooper sounded shocked. 'I'm serious, though. I don't go blabbing, never have.'

'So he's still alive then and it wasn't Bacon.'

'No, Bacon was straight as a die.'

'Atkins...Quinlan...'

'For heaven's sake, you can't say that!'

'So if it wasn't them, it must have been Inspector Black then; that figures.'

She waited for a denial that didn't come.

'It was Black, wasn't it? Anyone else?'

'Why is this relevant after all these years? Let sleeping dogs lie for God's sake.'

'No, I can't do that, and not because I'm a vindictive, narrow-minded bitch either.'

'I'd never say that about you.'

'No, but others might.' Again she paused for a comment and moved on quickly when he remained silent so that he wouldn't think she'd expected one. 'This matters because if Black took the cash from Paul Hill's and/or Taylor's homes and pocketed it, it means that Paul wasn't planning to run away, was he?'

She could hear Cooper's steady breathing as he worked through her logic.

'No, I guess not.'

'Only the empty tin was entered into evidence. To me that doesn't make sense. Why would Paul remove the cash rather than leave it at home?'

'To put in his pocket?'

'There was too much according to witnesses. And he'd be stupid to take it to school where it might get stolen. According to his friends he showed it off only once during the holidays and was very secretive about it.'

'If you're right...I suppose this has got to come out, has it?'

'It's only my theory, Bob, and there's no way of proving it after all this time but Quinlan will need to be told. We can try and keep the information tight. I'd like nothing better than to arrest Black but even I have to admit that that's unlikely. Where is he by the way?'

'He retired early and went to live in Spain.'

'Naturally. Do you deny my theory?'

'No, Louise, I don't.' Cooper sounded shamefaced.

'Well, we'll keep this conversation to ourselves for now. I'll let you get back to your evening. See you Monday.'

He barely muttered a goodnight.

Nightingale replaced the receiver and prepared a handwritten memo for Quinlan. As an afterthought she took a copy for Fenwick as well. There was no way she was going to record her misgivings electronically given what she knew about information recovery from computers. She found envelopes that she addressed and marked 'strictly private and confidential, addressee only', before signing over the seal and putting Sellotape on top. Then she hand-delivered them, enjoying the stretch in her leg muscles and the easing of tension in her back as she climbed up and down the stairs.

When she returned to the incident room she stared blankly at the remaining unopened files before shaking herself into action. She re-filed a note of Victor's interview in correct chronological order, put the files she'd read away neatly and then forced herself to open the next box. Most of its contents covered the interviewing of people who claimed to have seen Paul or Bryan or sometimes both. A few concerned break-ins that might have been perpetrated by the runaways. She skimmed them quickly as they were of little interest but one held her attention and she noted the name and address of the witness alongside a summary of their statement.

Work on the second batch of files went much faster and she was over halfway through when the door to the incident room was flung open. She glanced up, expecting someone from the night shift curious about the light and activity. Instead, in walked Fenwick. Had she not been so hurt, the look of dismayed surprise on his face would have been comical. As it was, it simply confirmed her mood.

'What do you want?'

'I'm trying to find Quinlan. He's not answering his mobile and neither he nor his wife is at home.'

'They're at a concert. What's happened?' She was instantly alert and watched with growing disquiet as Fenwick's face flushed with a rare show of discomfort.

'The ACC's blown up about something and roped me in when he couldn't find the superintendent.'

It wasn't a lie but she could tell it wasn't exactly the truth either. He wasn't telling her something important and the realisation added to her sense of aggrievement. She turned back to the files though in truth she could barely see them. Fenwick took a step towards her. She angled her head away so that he couldn't see her face.

'Nightingale...Louise. Look, I'm sorry about today. I had no idea that you'd turned up at Chris's party.'

'Yeah, right.' She bit her tongue, cross with herself for speaking when she'd been determined to keep quiet.

'Honestly. I was so busy in the garden with the boys that it wasn't until afterwards I realised you hadn't been there.'

His words cut deep. He must have realised the implication of what he'd just said because he stumbled around an apology.

'It's not that we didn't miss you, or anything like that, it's just that...well, like I said, I was so busy...and look, are you free for lunch tomorrow, or perhaps a quick drink might be better? I've been meaning to ask you for some time.'

'For heaven's sake, Andrew,' she said, her voice flat and hard, the words painful, 'forget it.'

Nightingale picked up the files she'd been working on and threw them into a box, then slammed its lid on, missing the first time. She tossed her empty water bottle at the waste bin and missed again.

'And why, when he couldn't find Quinlan this evening, did the ACC call you and not me?'

It was a good question and he owed it to her not to prevaricate.

'Because the brown stuff has hit the fan big time and he wants more than you working on it. We're dealing with a major problem, Nightingale.'

The seriousness of his expression drove the sense of hurt she was struggling to cope with out of her mind.

'On one of my cases?' she asked, her stomach twisting with tension.

'Yes, I'm afraid so.'

He went on quickly, telling her about the news coverage and what the papers would be saying the following day. It was enough to knock any lingering anger from her system and her natural professionalism took over.

'I can see why he didn't turn to me,' she admitted reluctantly, 'though I could have coped, you know.'

'I know but it wasn't my call.'

'Understood; now, what can I do to help?'

He looked relieved that she was an ally again.

'We've a long night ahead of us,' he said, taking off his sports jacket. 'I need to work on the ACC's press statement so if you can track down the press officer from HQ and get them on the line that would be a big help. Then we must pull together everything we know about the Well-Wisher. Have you made any progress towards tracing him?'

'None. The lab has nothing on the materials he sent us and the sorting office the letters went through services such a large area it gives no clue as to his whereabouts.'

'OK, then we have to work with what we've got – which isn't much.' He pulled out a chair at the end of the table and opened a fresh pad of paper. 'You may not believe this but I'm pleased that we're working together again, despite the circumstances.'

She bit her lip to stop herself from adding '*Me too*,' and went in search of the press officer.

CHAPTER TWENTY-FIVE

Superintendent Quinlan received a message to call the ACC during the interval and left the concert at once, much to his wife's annoyance, it being their wedding anniversary and one of the few evenings to which he had committed. He found Fenwick and Nightingale working together in the incident room, the press officer from HQ in the process of approving the draft statement and everything under control. If he was upset to find that the ACC had intervened and imposed Fenwick above his chosen SIO he didn't let it show, leaving both individuals to speculate privately as to what would happen the following day.

Fenwick found out when the ACC called him after returning from church on Sunday morning.

'You're to remain SIO; Quinlan has agreed.'

'And Louise Nightingale's role?'

'You heard my opinion of her last night. Of course I'm glad she was promoted, although personally I was surprised that she made it so fast, but it was good for us...'

Helps your diversity statistics you mean, Fenwick thought but said instead. 'Don't get me wrong, I'm glad to have the Hill case back but Quinlan has combined it with the investigation into Malcolm Eagleton's death, which makes it a double murder. And with Choir Boy likely to come to a head this week...'

'Choir Boy? You really think so?'

Fenwick brought him up to date quickly on the discoveries they had made, conscious that perhaps he should have done so sooner. Fortunately the ACC was too preoccupied with the publicity over the Hill case to be concerned.

'I've been considering what to do next on Choir Boy all weekend, sir, and I think it's time to take action. What I really want is the man at the top with the intelligence and money to have organised it all. For that I need to break one of the men we have under surveillance. There's a case conference tomorrow morning at eight-thirty and I'm going to tell the team to pick up Joseph Watkins and secure a warrant for his house and lock-up. I think Watkins is the weak link. He's married with grandchildren and goes to the Methodist church so he's got a reputation and family life at stake.

'Ball's a loner with a history of ABH and while that might mean that he's a bully at heart and they can be relatively easy to break, he could just as easily turn out to be a hard nut. I don't want to risk alerting him before I have to while surveillance remains interesting.'

'Interesting how?'

Fenwick told him about Ball's visit to London and the house that remained under watch by the Met. For once, Harper-Brown seemed satisfied.

'The thing with the Hill case,' Fenwick continued, 'is that there are now two separate lines of inquiry to follow up. We need to find the Well-Wisher but we also need to conclude the case against Maidment. The two investigations may lead in different directions and while I'd normally be happy to direct both, with Choir Boy so active I think I'll need back-up if I'm to become SIO.'

He could almost hear the cogs in the ACC's brain turning.

'Very well, Nightingale can be your number two on the Eagleton/Hill investigation, though I'd like you to handle the Well-Wisher and support me personally with the media side of things.'

'That should work well,' he said, thinking that it still gave Nightingale a significant operational role as long as he left her room to prove herself.

Sunday was a hectic day for Fenwick, re-immersing himself in the evidence for the Hill case while at the same time preparing for the Choir Boy team meeting the following day. When he had a large workload he instinctively changed to a different mental gear and became almost frighteningly efficient to those around him. He would consume detail rapidly and forget none of it, develop and discard ideas so quickly that others lost track of where he was going; and then he would decide on the eventual strategy suddenly, with absolute conviction. Fortunately for the Eagleton/Hill team at Harlden, he did most of this on the Sunday with only Nightingale for company, who was used to his methods. He called the rest of the team in late in the afternoon so that they would have a head start on the week.

Nightingale was pleased with the way he divided the responsibilities and lived up to her role by preparing meticulously and leading her part of the briefing with a confidence and clarity that even had a few of the old lags taking notes. Only after the others had gone and they were on their own in the incident room did she alert Fenwick to the memo she'd written to him and Quinlan on Saturday.

'Are you certain Taylor's and/or Paul's money was taken?'

'No, but Black was bent – Bob virtually confirmed it – he worked on the case and signed the inventory from the search of Taylor's property. Look, I'm not interested in starting a witch hunt. My sole purpose in pointing it out is to emphasise that, if it did happen, then it would increase the probability that Paul was murdered. It also explains why some of the detectives on the original case were so keen to push the theory that Paul was a runaway. Maybe, and I hate saying this, it's also a reason we can't find the photographic evidence. Perhaps Black sold it on.

I'm more than happy to leave it with you to take forward with Quinlan as you see fit.'

Fenwick said that he would and quickly forgot about it as he returned his focus to his options for tracking down the Well-Wisher as quickly as possible. By the time he reached home the children were already in bed, though not asleep. He read them both a story until he felt his eyelids drooping, then fixed himself a pizza and salad rather than attempt to reheat the Sunday lunch Alice had left for him.

At seven o'clock on Monday morning Fenwick stopped at Harlden to see Quinlan, knowing he was an early riser. He wanted to be sure that the ACC had talked to him and that Quinlan approved the arrangements. He did, particularly pleased that a decent role had been preserved for Nightingale.

Fenwick was in a rush to drive on to MCS for his eight-thirty meeting and kept the conversation with Quinlan short, which meant that he forgot to mention Nightingale's note. He was on the Harlden bypass when his mobile phone rang, caller-ID throwing up Quinlan's name.

'This da...letter from Nightingale; have you read it?' The superintendent's tone was clipped. Fenwick recalled that he had been the first SIO on the original investigation.

'Yes, I spoke to her about it. Sorry, it had slipped my mind. Could it be true?'

There was a pause.

'She's speculating but...I think, sadly, there's a remote chance it might be. I had a few suspicions years ago but there was never any concrete proof and then Black retired early. Thank goodness Bacon's dead otherwise we might have had to tell IPCC.'

'So you propose that we don't?' Fenwick had expected that he wouldn't want the Independent Police Complaints Commission sniffing around the edges of a live inquiry but he wasn't entirely happy about it. As far as he was concerned, the statute of limitations didn't apply to police corruption.

'What good would it serve? The Hill inquiry is already a mess.' Quinlan, as always, sounded eminently sensible.

'If Black were corrupt it could mean that he was willing to bend the rules on other cases. He might have been responsible for miscarriages of justice. Innocent people could be in prison because of him.'

There was a deep sigh.

'I think he was greedy, that's all.'

'It's your decision but—'

'I haven't finished. I don't think you're right about the likelihood of him putting innocent people away. In fact, I recall that his arrest rate was barely average. Trouble is, as you say, if he was bent in one respect, it might have been the same in others.'

'So?'

'This is pure speculation on Nightingale's part. She hasn't one shred of concrete proof...Tell you what I'll do; I'll have a look personally at the old Hill files and at a sample of Black's other cases. If anything seems in the least...suspect, let's say, I'll reconsider my decision. In the meantime, you concentrate on finding the Well-Wisher and keep the ACC off our backs.

'By the way, what was Nightingale doing going through the original paperwork herself? That's not the sort of activity I expect from an inspector. Keep an eye on her, will you? It's time she stepped up to the plate, showed more leadership, rather than bury herself in minutiae.'

Fenwick bristled protectively but none of his feelings sounded in his voice as he said a mild goodbye. His trust in Nightingale's judgement might have been shaken though had he known what she was doing at that moment.

She was sitting down to a large mug of tea with a Mrs Anchor in the kitchen of the farmhouse she shared with her husband and youngest son, Oliver.

From the road outside the house looked idyllic. It was thatched with exposed beams and a sprawling cottage garden. Closer inspection revealed patches of bare paint, weeds and a broken-down tractor. This was a working farm that had been badly affected by the foot and mouth crisis and had never fully recovered.

'They'll be back for coffee well before eleven because we're due out for lunch. It means a wait for you but they're in Three Mile Field and it'll take me as long to reach them and to come back.'

'That's fine, Mrs Anchor. You could probably help me anyway.'

Wariness entered the farmer's wife's face. It wasn't, thought Nightingale, the law breaker's caution, just a natural country aversion to getting involved with 'they Police'.

'I don't know what I could tell you, I'm sure.'

Mrs Anchor stood up and started to dry the breakfast plates stacked on the wooden draining board. The kitchen was old but clean, except for the flagstone floor, which had already accumulated an early morning's worth of muddy boots and paw prints.

'I'm working on an old case, a boy that disappeared from Harlden over twenty-five years ago.'

'Paul Hill?' Mrs Anchor half turned towards her and Nightingale's spirits lifted.

'You remember.'

'Only because it was on the telly again. Apparently you've got some army bloke locked up despite letters and proof telling you he's innocent.'

'That's not why I'm here,' said Nightingale, determined to avoid becoming sidetracked, although the television coverage was a blow, not least because people's memories would now be less reliable. She cleared her throat. 'When Paul first disappeared your husband reported seeing a car driven by a man we needed to question in relation to our inquiries.'

'You'd have to ask him about that.'

'I will. But shortly afterwards he called the station again, this time to report a theft. Does that ring a bell?'

'Theft of what?'

Nightingale thought that she saw a flicker of memory in the woman's eyes but it was quickly masked by caution.

'Some money, food and a bag of some sort. You used to keep housekeeping in a blue jar on the mantelpiece.'

Both women's eyes went to the Aga and travelled upwards. There was a willow-patterned jug on the blackened oak beam above.

'Still do,' Mrs Anchor put down the dishcloth with which she had been wiping the draining board, 'though now it's just some ready cash in case I need it before I can get to the bank.'

'And you have a large pantry with marble shelves where you keep fresh produce?'

'Used to; it's gone now that we've got the chest freezer. But maybe you're right, I think I do recall as some food went missing, with a shooting bag of Danny's – that's Mr Anchor. I didn't know he'd reported it. It wasn't much: at most five quid, some bread, cheese – oh, and a roast leg of pork I'd done the day before for lunches. I wonder why he bothered you lot with that, even though it was his favourite bag.'

'He thought that it might be connected with Paul's disappearance. He told us that Bryan Taylor knew this house and could have helped himself as he was getting away.'

At the mention of Taylor's name an expression of pure hatred filled Mrs Anchor's face which she struggled but failed to control.

'I will not have that man's name mentioned in this house. I hope he's dead and rotting with the devil.' Immediately the woman realised she'd revealed too much. Her face closed up again with effort.

'Why do you feel so strongly? Did you know him well?'

But Mrs Anchor just shook her head and would say no more. Nightingale decided that she needed to watch a video of the TV coverage to see how much, if anything, it had said about Taylor. It might explain Mrs Anchor's hatred, but if it didn't...Her speculation was interrupted by the sound of a car pulling up outside.

'That'll be them. Now look, miss,' Mrs Anchor leant forward so that her whisper wouldn't carry, 'my Oliver's a delicate lad. A bit simple maybe but sensitive and he was friends with Paul before he disappeared. I don't want him upset all over again. We had the dickens of a job getting him straight last time. You just wait until he goes to feed the dogs then ask away all you want.'

Nightingale had finished reading all the witness reports the previous day, including those from the school, and Oliver's name wasn't among them. However, she decided to do as she was asked – at least initially.

Oliver was over six feet tall and weighed about seventeen stone. He walked in, picked up a sack of dry dog food and went straight out again without saying a word. The conversation that followed with Mr Anchor was over in minutes and added nothing to his original statements. His reaction to questions about Taylor was to clam up and she left feeling frustrated, certain that there was something the Anchors weren't telling her. She could feel their eyes on her as she climbed into her car and eased away from the house. On her way down the drive she passed Oliver standing by the side of the road, the bag of dog food spilt at his feet. She pulled over and walked back to him, keeping her distance as if he were a large scared animal.

'Oliver?' She said it gently but he started and took a step backwards. There were marks of tears on his face. 'Oliver, my name's Louise. I'm a police officer. Can I talk to you?'

He turned his back to her and she heard him sniff. Nightingale tried to remember her early training for handling child witnesses.

'It's my job to catch bad people and lock them away so that they won't hurt anybody. I think you might be able to help me, Oliver.' Another loud sniff. 'I'm looking for the man who hurt one of your friends: Paul Hill. You remember Paul, don't you, Oliver?'

She had a flash of insight.

'Of course you do. You saw the television programme, that's why you're upset.'

Was that a nod, so imperceptible she almost missed it?

'I should think you'd want the man who hurt Paul caught as much as I do, don't you?'

'Course.'

Nightingale took a deep breath to keep her voice steady.

'When the police went to the school to talk to people I don't think they saw you, did they?'

A shake of the head.

'Why not? Were you away from school?'

A nod.

'Would you mind talking to me now instead?'

Nothing. She waited, counting to sixty, but the hulking great man in front of her stood stock still.

'Look, maybe you can't remember anything; it was a long time ago.'

'Course I can remember,' Oliver swung round, his face flushed, and it was Nightingale's turn to take a step back. 'I'm not stupid y'know, even if you talk to me like I am. I'm not.'

'Of course you're not, I didn't think you were,' she lied.

'Most people do. They ignore me and talk about me as if I'm not there. And I've got a good memory.'

'Good, I'm pleased. So, can you help me by telling me about Paul and the time he disappeared?'

'You're pretty.'

'Thank you. I'm also trustworthy.'

'Mum said I should never say.'

'Say what?'

But Oliver shook his head and bent down to gather up the dog food that was lying on the road.

'So you're good at keeping secrets?'

A nod.

'So am I, you know, and there shouldn't be any reason for your mum to know that you talked to me. I won't tell her, not unless you let me.'

'I dunno.' He finished gathering what pellets he could and lifted the bag up one-handed as if it weighed nothing.

'You're strong, aren't you?' she said admiringly.

A blush crept up from the grubby collar of his shirt and a sly grin transformed his face.

'Always have been.'

'You know, as an adult you can decide what secrets to keep and which to share. It's not up to your mum anymore.'

That got him. A look of defiance crossed his face.

'That's right.' He stepped closer and dropped his voice to a whisper so that she had to bend to catch it. 'There was a fire, you know, a big fire. I went and looked and it was a car.'

'Can you remember anything about the car, Oliver?'

He shook his head and shut his eyes, as if blotting out a bad memory.

'I think you can. I think you're clever enough to know more.'

Her use of the word clever had an extraordinary effect. His face cleared and lost its redness. He opened his eyes and then almost stumbled as he took a step towards her. She thought she recognised the look in his eyes and for the first time she realised what an enormous man he was when he lost his slouch and pushed out his chest. He must be at least six foot four and nearer twenty stone; it wasn't all fat.

'No girl's called me clever before,' he said with a smile.

It could have been sweet in other circumstances but Nightingale barely noticed as she backed slowly towards her car.

'Have you got a boyfriend?' He didn't wait for an answer. 'Can I be your boyfriend?'

'I've...I've got one already, I'm afraid, Oliver. But thank you for asking.'

'Can we be friends then – special friends like I was with Wendy until she moved away?'

'That's a bit difficult. You see, I'm a police officer and we're not allowed special friends. It's against the rules.' She had almost reached her car door when Oliver took a long stride to block her way.

'They do on telly. On *The Bill* they're always doing stuff to each other. You don't like me.' He scowled.

'Yes, I do. I also think you're clever but I really do have a boyfriend and telly isn't the same as real life.'

He leant a hand the size of a joint of pork against the side of the car, blocking her access.

'I must go but if you remember anything about the burning car you can call me at the station. Look, see, here's a card with the number on it.'

'And you'd see me again?'

'If you remember anything of course I'll see you but it would be police business, not because we're special friends, OK?' She was surprised at the firmness that had returned to her voice. 'Now, stand away from the car and let me go back to work.'

He paused for a moment then nodded, docile again.

She opened the car door and sat down, ready to turn the key in the ignition. Oliver tapped on the window and she opened it a crack.

'I can show you where I saw the fire if you like but you'd need to take me there.'

After a moment's pause she agreed and unlocked the doors though her heart was racing. She told herself he was slow not dangerous and that his earlier interest was because she'd flattered him, but his bulk beside her made her feel tiny. He directed her back to the road for a mile then left down an unmade track. Her heart rate was too fast for her to pretend that she wasn't worried but she concentrated on sustaining an air of confident authority.

'Pull off just here.'

He indicated a lay-by almost overgrown with blackberry bushes on one side. Oliver stepped out into them heedless of their thorns. Nightingale opened her door and followed him down a footpath that was barely discernable as it cut through hedgerows already thick with bright green brambles. The can of pepper spray that she carried in her handbag was concealed in the palm of her hand. Oliver stopped suddenly and she almost walked into him.

'Over there.' They were standing a hundred yards from a barbed-wire fence bordering a pasture and small wood. Oliver seemed nervous and wouldn't venture nearer.

She edged past him and walked to the margin of the field. There was nothing to distinguish it from any other and certainly no sign of a burnt-out car.

'There's nothing here,' she called out. 'Are you sure?'

But Oliver had stopped talking. Even when she went back to him he remained silent and averted his eyes.

'It was over twenty-five years ago, Oliver. Are you certain? Please, I need your help and I'm sure you have a good memory.'

'Certain. Certain positive.' He was becoming distressed. Sweat beaded his forehead and his eyes were going crazy, looking everywhere but at the area of nondescript land to which he'd forced himself to point.

'Just a couple more questions. Is this your father's land?'

A shake of denial.

'So whose is it?'

It was an innocent enough question but Oliver turned and ran. As he lumbered away up the footpath, spilling dog food as he went, she could feel the shock from his steps through the soles of her feet. She was used to seeing fear and something about this place terrified Oliver. Whatever it was she decided that she had to find out. Oliver had been Paul's friend, the only one who seemed to have liked him at the time of his disappearance. He'd seen a burning car on the night Paul vanished so he'd been well enough to be outside then, yet the next day he didn't go to school and for some reason was never interviewed. There was something not quite right about him and his mother hated Taylor. Had Oliver been abused by Taylor? It was pure conjecture as Oliver wouldn't have been an attractive child. But if he had been abused, and if she persuaded him to talk, she might be able to learn more about the man and his methods.

Nightingale was so disturbed by her new theory that she paused by the field. To give herself chance to think she squeezed under the barbed wire and walked over the lumpy meadow. Oliver had pointed towards a copse and she ambled towards it. There would be nothing there of course, after all this time, but she was curious. Some of Fenwick's almost superstitious need to immerse himself in the places associated with a crime had rubbed off on her.

There was little to distinguish this patch of countryside from any other. Halfway through the tiny wood, sycamores, hazel and thick banks of nettles blocked her way. She retraced her steps and noticed that the nettles on one side had been trampled down recently in a path that led to the centre of the copse.

She followed the path. Three fresh cigarette butts lay on the ground. A lovers' meeting place, she thought, and turned away.

As she did so she saw several splashes of red on the nettles and bent to look, sniffing carefully. There was the distinctive aroma of dried blood. Some animal caught here by a fox probably, but it was an odd coincidence, this sign of recent violence at a place Oliver associated with Paul's death. On the day after it was all over the news.

'What would Andrew do?' she asked herself out loud then laughed. 'Probably waste half his crime scene budget digging up the woodland in search of the fire and heaven knows what else!'

But the thought stopped her anyway. She took a latex glove from inside her jacket and an evidence bag from her pocket. Carefully, she lifted the cigarette butts and sealed them inside, then opened a sterile q-tip and rubbed it over a bloody patch before snapping the lid shut. Then she cut off one of the leaves and put it in another bag. It was daft, and she'd feel a fool when the lab came back and told her she'd investigated the death of a pheasant, but she had learnt at Fenwick's knee and one thing he swore by was paying attention to detail. He would have been proud of her; the idea made her smile and ignore her doubts.

By noon Joseph Watkins was in custody – shell-shocked, his face sickly beneath his ruddy complexion. Fenwick decided to let him stew. He had twelve hours before he needed to go before a magistrate again and was confident that what he'd find at the storage depot would give him enough ammunition to keep Watkins in custody. Clive had gone into the warehouse as Watkins was being arrested and within thirty minutes was able to confirm what they thought. The room he rented was full of child pornography: photos, magazines, films, DVDs and computer discs.

'It's disgusting, sir, bloody disgusting. I've never seen anything like it. Just let me interview Watkins, please, I'll have that bastard talking in no time.'

'I need you there, Clive, someone I can trust. We don't want anything to go wrong with evidence recovery. And remember, if Ball turns up you're to keep out of their sight and make sure no one at the depot does anything to scare him off. What you're doing is vital. Leave Watkins to me; I think he's ready to crumble.'

Fenwick didn't want Clive's nervous energy and emotion in the MCS building. He was gradually starting to respect him, and liked his light-hearted humour, but he didn't yet trust him to keep his head in a crisis. He asked him to send a PC with sample material back to MCS at once.

At one o'clock Fenwick entered interview room one where Watkins was waiting for him together with a Legal Aid solicitor the police had found for him. Alison Reynolds went in with him; a woman in the interview would increase the man's shame. Watkins had been adamant that he did not want to call his solicitor, who happened to be a close family friend.

'Good afternoon, Mr Watkins,' Fenwick said, placing an evidence bag on the table between them. 'Lawrence.' He used the lawyer's first name deliberately, which annoyed the solicitor and did nothing to help Watkins' frame of mind.

'Have you both had an opportunity to read the warrant thoroughly?'

Lawrence Parks nodded, Watkins looked blank.

'If you haven't, Mr Watkins, it may have eluded your attention that our powers of search extend to Unit 345 at Storewell & Co, London Road, Harlden. This item...'

But he had to stop. At his words Watkins stumbled up from the table, his hand over his mouth.

'I think my client's about to be...oh, too late. Perhaps he's unwell.'

'Not unwell, Mr Parks, merely in a state of shock. Constable, see if one of the other interview rooms is free, could you, and have this one cleaned up?'

They moved into room two. Watkins was accompanied to the bathroom to clean himself up and returned looking green, barely able to support himself.

'We'll start again shall we, Mr Watkins?'

'What have you got there?' Watkins managed to ask, though his voice was barely audible.

'It's a USB stick, one of many we've recovered from your storage unit. I'm about to send it to our technical support unit so that they can download the material from it as evidence. Mr Watkins, if you're going to be ill every time I say something we're going to be here a very long time.'

Fenwick's tone was cold; he was indifferent to the distress of the man opposite. Alison was looking at Watkins with open disgust.

'At least behave with a shred of dignity,' she said. 'I have a twelve-year-old son; is he the age you prefer?'

The venom in her words would have killed if it could have found a way into Watkins' bloodstream. Even Lawrence Parks hesitated before he came to his client's defence.

'A man's innocent until proven guilty, remember that.'

'Does your client look innocent to you?' Fenwick pointed to Watkins's slumped shoulders; his head was now in his hands and he was sobbing uncontrollably.

'Here's just one picture from the hoard he has stored safely away from his home and family.' He passed a black and white image over to Parks who tried, unsuccessfully, to keep his face neutral. 'Now, that's enough to make a normal man sick but it's the sort of material your client masturbates over on a regular basis, unperturbed that the children being abused in those pictures are real kids, in agony.'

Lawrence Parks was a Legal Aid solicitor still motivated by the ashes of an ideal that was based on the belief that there should be equal justice for all. He spent most of his time trying to secure hearings for asylum seekers, or preventing recidivist kids from being given custodial sentences that would seal their fate before they reached the age to vote. He studied the photograph again carefully, glanced at his lachrymose client and asked Fenwick whether they might have a word in private.

'Chief Inspector,' he said in a half-whisper once they were outside, 'I'm not sure I can represent this man. You see, I have a family, three small boys, I... Could you find someone else?'

Fenwick was sympathetic but he didn't want to waste time with a false start and risk Watkins regaining his composure.

'I have children too, Lawrence, a boy and a girl both of an age to be interesting to the Watkinses of this world. Looking at that stuff turns my stomach. Do you know what it is that helps me keep focused and not beat that bastard into a pulp?'

'You'd be fired?' It was a half-joke, sarcastic. Parks had seen what he thought was police brutality going unpunished too often.

'No, it's the desire to see men like Watkins taken off the streets and locked up where they can never cause a child to be hurt again. The only way to do that in my book is to make sure they're dealt with fairly. I need you to represent him. That man has a right to a solicitor, to ensure he's processed properly within the law. And his victims have a right to his incarceration.'

Lawrence Parks looked away.

'Please, Lawrence. Don't make me start all over. Between us,' Fenwick looked up and down the corridor to enforce the intimacy of what he was saying, 'I think he's going to crack, make a confession. If he does, your job will be straightforward; no more confrontations with evidence; no need for you to take his side when your gut's churning.'

Parks was a shrewd solicitor who'd been around the system.

'Is there a deal on the table if he's cooperative?'

'We need the men higher up. There's a well-organised, well-funded supply chain and we think their activities extend beyond the supply of pornography.'

'Prostitution? Serial abuse?'

Fenwick shrugged, he was dealing with the opposition after all.

'There would have to be a custodial sentence and treatment. We can't allow him back on the streets. But, depending on what he gives us, we'd talk to the judge, tell him that Watkins has been helpful. It would still be the judge's decision but information could help him.'

'So, no promises?'

'I wouldn't give you them if I could.'

Lawrence Parks walked the length of the corridor and back. By the time he returned, he'd made his decision.

'Very well. At least you're straight. If you can do it, so can I. Let's go back inside.'

CHAPTER TWENTY-SIX

'Nathan Smith', as William and many others in London and elsewhere in the UK would have called him, tossed the newspaper to one side with a loud curse. It was only ten o'clock but he stalked over to the bar and poured himself a stiff whisky over plenty of ice.

'Bloody rag!' he said and sat down heavily in one of the wing chairs beside an Adams fireplace, bright with an arrangement of late summer flowers. He'd forced himself to read the *Sunday Times* the previous day and it had stiffened his resolve before his meeting. Ball had been predictably volatile and there'd been some tricky moments before he'd finally calmed him down and sent him happily on his way. Nathan rubbed his wrist ruefully, careful not to disturb the plasters he'd applied over the scratches he'd suffered as a result of a stumble into the brambles as he'd side-stepped a punch from Ball.

Afterwards, back in the comfort of his study, with a reassuring glass of malt in his hand, he had managed to persuade himself that the Hill story would blow over, just like the coverage of Matthew Eagleton. The continuing speculation in the article on page three of *The Times* that morning had therefore upset him badly. When Maidment was first arrested for the murder of Paul Hill he'd had a few nights' disturbed sleep but then, when the police didn't arrive to bundle him into custody, he had started to relax again. Now the defence of Maidment's innocence was daily news and he wondered what was going to happen next. There was no way that Maidment had blabbed, not after all this time and with what he had against him, but if the police were forced to dig deeper to prove their case there was no knowing what they would turn up. They might, and he drained his glass at the thought, even stumble on the truth despite the fact that it was so well buried.

No, he told himself, not after all this time. They'd have to be geniuses to work out what had really happened a quarter of a century before and he knew the police; they didn't recruit high IQs. He was still safe.

Without warning his mind switched to last Friday night and his visit to William's profitable but otherwise very average establishment. There were better places in London but they were rather more punctilious about the quality of their returned goods and inclined to become uppity if things got a little out of hand, even with him, whereas William could hardly evict the owner of the establishment. No, he saved the rougher nights for his own houses. It amazed him the way William was able to find delightful boys – there seemed to be no shortage of fresh flesh in the capital these days.

His memory conjured up a picture of Sam. What a lovely creature he was, almost perfect; almost a Paul. Could he think that? Paul had been exceptional; was Sam really that good or was his mind playing tricks? No matter. All he needed to know was that Sam was there, waiting for him, whenever he needed him.

William had better bloody well stick by his promise to keep the boy exclusive, but come to think of it, it was unlikely that the boy would be up to much for the next few days anyway. Things had got a little out of hand again. He'd have to remember to go easy on the booze beforehand. It wasn't as if he was a violent man, far from it, it was the whisky that made him angry and Sam was too good for the usual rough stuff.

An unbidden memory of the boy as he'd left him the last time engulfed his mind and he thrust it away in denial. Despite his obsession with young teenage boys of a certain look, and his addiction to violent sex, Nathan didn't think of himself as either a paedophile or a sadist. If forced to describe his sexual predilections he would have done so in artistic, even loving, language. His self-deception was complete. It made him a very, very dangerous man.

CHAPTER TWENTY-SEVEN

The major was treating prison as an endurance test and on the surface appeared to be coping well but inside he was prey to his troubled conscience. It was wearing him down in a way that physical challenge and fear never had.

His demeanour in front of the other inmates remained the same; cordial, firm and detached, and they still respected him. Nobody thought him guilty except the guards, and when word of the coverage on BBC News and in the *Sunday Times* circulated through the prison, despite the governor's attempts to suppress it, even the guards' attitude softened towards him. Bill tracked him down in the library, where he was trying to distract himself by reading a teach-yourself book on Spanish.

'Got a minute, Major?'

'Yes, Bill, what is it?'

'Me 'n' the boys have bin having a natter, about your predicament so's to speak. If we was to find the geezer who really killed that lad, you'd be out of here in a flash, see? We've got mates outside who could put the word about – do a bit of sniffing for you if y' like. No bother and nothing owed – our pleasure.'

Maidment was horrified. It was bad enough that the police and media were raking over old ground but to have men from what he thought of as the underworld pushing their noses in would lead to disaster. Yet, if he declined, it might create doubt about his innocence, despite what was being reported. He decided to use his reputation as a law-abiding citizen as cover.

'That's very good of you, Bill, but I need to think about your offer very carefully. You see, it has always been my custom to trust our police.'

'Look where that's got you.'

'Indeed, but no system of justice is foolproof and I still expect to be released in due course.'

Bill stood up and patted him on the shoulder, rather like a priest who is fond, but despairs, of a persistent sinner in his flock.

'The offer's open. You just say the word.'

Maidment watched him strut off and wished life were that simple.

Miss Pennysmith was ready ten minutes early and waiting for the volunteer transport that would take her to the day centre. Normally, she'd be looking forward to some company but the gossip was bound to cover that piece in the *Sunday Times* and she would be asked her opinion. Of course, she would have to tell the truth.

When she entered the lounge she was confronted by Abigail Jones with an armful of photograph albums.

'My great-niece Michelle's wedding photos!' Abigail said joyfully. Miss Pennysmith suppressed a sigh.

When Abigail finished it was the turn of Jeff and Pam Seabright to show off their holiday snaps. Miss Pennysmith composed her face into an expression of polite interest. She learnt quickly that any comment would be interpreted as a request for more information and kept silent until the bell rang for lunch. Her joints had stiffened and it took her some moments to rise so there was no choice of where to sit by the time she moved through to the dining room towards the vacant place next to Jasper.

Jasper was eighty-three and boasted that he was six foot tall, though Miss Pennysmith could almost look him in the eye. He considered himself a ladies' man and enjoyed the advantage of a male/female ratio that, from his perspective, improved with age. When he saw her coming he stood up, pulled out the empty chair with an elaborate flourish and gave what was meant to be, and in his mind still was, a gallant bow.

'Ah, the delightful Margaret Pennysmith is going to grace us with her presence. And you're looking particularly charming today, if I may say so, my dear.'

The delightful Margaret glanced down at her grey and white striped dress and summoned a smile as soup was served. It was French onion, a favourite of many if eaten in the privacy of one's own home but a significant challenge for good manners and dentures when in public. Only after she had negotiated her way around the cheese topping did she pause to take in her table companions.

A sprightly-looking woman called Bettie sat on her right. On her left was Jasper. To Jasper's left sat Judy, a pleasant retired teacher with whom one could talk sensibly about books and films. Then there was Trudy, who hardly ever spoke except about her grandchildren. George Stevens sat next to her and was at that moment engaged in conversation across the table with Jasper about England's cricket performance. And, making full circle, next to Bettie sat a very elderly woman whom she'd never seen before. As if she could sense eyes on her the woman abandoned her soup and looked up. She smiled at Miss Pennysmith, creating a network of lines across her face.

As the plates were cleared the conversational groupings changed. She had almost finished her roast beef and she was starting to relax, when the conversation veered off in the direction she had feared. Judith was defending the role of public broadcasting and the need for an 'independent voice', when

Jasper retorted, with some vehemence, 'Nonsense! You mean we should pay them to broadcast news like that rubbish on Saturday night. A waste of licence payers' money that was.'

It was as if the whole table had been waiting for the subject to be raised. Everyone chimed in with a comment, everyone that is except the old woman next to Bettie and Margaret herself.

Opinion quickly polarised along the lines of those who believed in the major's guilt and those who did not. Miss Pennysmith kept quiet and concentrated on cutting the remaining slice of beef on her plate into tiny pieces to eat slowly. She hoped fervently that the conversation would pass her by but of course it was inevitable that her opinion would be sought.

'So, what do you think, Margaret – you knew him quite well, didn't you?' It was Jasper who directed attention towards her.

Miss Pennysmith picked up her glass of water and took a sip, then another, despite the growing silence about her. She put the glass down and looked up at nobody in particular.

'I think him innocent,' she said simply and heard at least one intake of breath.

'How can you say that?' Jasper was astonished.

'It was a crime against a child,' said Trudy, disgust resonating in her tone.

'I think you've got some nerve saying that in front of Hannah.' Bettie put her hand lightly on the old woman's arm.

'Hannah?' Miss Pennysmith asked, turning towards the old lady.

'I'm Hannah Hill,' the old lady extended a brown hand. 'How do you do?'

Miss Pennysmith took it automatically, noting that it felt like a worn leather bag of dried sticks, before her brain had a chance to process the significance of the woman's name. When it did, she felt her cheeks flood with shame.

'Oh, Mrs Hill, I had no idea who you were. We shouldn't be

having this conversation in front of you; it's quite thoughtless.'

'That's quite all right, my dear. I'm ninety-seven and I've had to live with speculation about Paul's disappearance for more than twenty-five years. I can assure you that I've heard all that can be said on the matter. And anyway, I agree with you. I don't think Major Maidment's guilty either. In fact, I'm certain of it.' With that she returned her attention to the last of her Yorkshire pudding.

The conversation died abruptly; the tasty cheesecake was eaten in virtual silence but by the time tea was served a sense of normality had returned. When they rose Miss Pennysmith sought out Mrs Hill.

'Forgive me for raising the subject again but I should like to know why you said what you did.'

'About the major?'

Hannah Hill had astonishing blue eyes that still sparkled when she smiled. She put her scrawny brown hand on Miss Pennysmith's arm and gestured to the terrace where smoking was still tolerated.

'Let's find a quiet corner, shall we? Then I'll tell you all about it.'

They chose two padded chairs where sunlight filtered through a rose trellis. Hannah Hill lit up gratefully.

'As I said, I'm ninety-seven. My Clem was ninety when he passed away and we'd been married for sixty-nine years and two months. Clem started out as a boot boy at the Savoy, doing the shoes overnight. "My word," he used to say, "the state of some of those shoes – and no excuse neither."'

Miss Pennysmith didn't mind the chatter. She recognised in Mrs Hill a mind that was still sharp so she would get to her point in time.

'We married and had two boys, then Clem went and joined up and got himself caught – daft bugger. For almost two years I didn't know whether he was dead or alive. Anyway, when he got home and was demobbed he'd changed; he had something more about him. One of his mates in the camp gave him a loan to set up in business. Guess what it was?'

'I don't know.'

Hannah Hill started laughing.

'A cobbler's of course. He'd still got friends at the hotel and they sent him the overnight repairs. From that he started to get the odd commission and then, before we knew it, he was shoemaker to half the gentry in west London! My, those were exciting times.' Her eyes misted over. 'I helped out where I could, though raising six boys – yes six, we made up for lost time when he came home! – was hard work in itself.

'Gordon, Paul's father, was the youngest, a bit of an afterthought really. He was a lovely lad, a real gentle man. By then, we were doing very well. Gordon went to the local public school, then university. That's where he met her.' Hannah scowled.

'Paul's mother?'

'Sarah Jane Anderson. She was older than Gordon, studying drama. We didn't like her from day one. Oh, there was *something* about her. Gordon thought it was dramatic potential but we weren't so sure, felt more like histrionics to us. Whenever she visited the whole household walked on eggshells. Still, they went ahead and married and they got the same gift from us as all my other boys, £5,000.'

'My word, that was a lot of money in those days, still is.'

'So you and I would say but Miss Sarah didn't think so. We could've offered more but Clem thought, and he was probably right, that too much easy money would spoil Gordon.

'Anyway, I can see they're setting out the card tables so I'd better hurry up.' She took a long drag on her cigarette and held the smoke deep in her lungs before exhaling with relish. 'All the other boys put down a deposit on a house and did nicely over the years but not Gordon. He went into partnership with a so-called friend from school and lost the whole lot when the business went bankrupt.

'He and Sarah were living in a flat in London that was well beyond their means. They had such grand ways it annoyed Clem. He refused to give them more capital and it got so that Sarah wouldn't speak to him.

'Then she had her miscarriage, the first of several as it turned out. Now, I wouldn't wish that misery on any woman. I'd had my own share of that sadness and I felt for the lass. I'd go round and look after her because she really was poorly, and against all the odds, we became quite close.' Hannah heaved a sigh. 'But as soon as she was well she was off out again partying, auditioning, back to her old ways.

'Gordon got some sort of job with Lloyds of London through another friend. It paid well but I could tell he hated the work. They moved to a small house – a tiny place in a good location but with a huge mortgage. It terrified Clem and me how much they owed the bank.

'Sarah had two more miscarriages in a year and they almost destroyed her, not just physically either. She'd always been highly strung but I could see it was becoming more than that. She shut herself away and refused to see anyone but me and Gordon. Then she started saying she was being poisoned and that's why she'd lost the babies.

'She wouldn't drink water from the tap, it had to be boiled first; then she'd only eat from new packets and tins that she'd opened herself. Eventually we persuaded her to see a doctor and he gave her some pills. They calmed her down but she was never the same.

'Gordon decided country air would be good for her so he sold up and borrowed money from another friend to buy a farm.

'To our surprise it went quite well at first. Sarah became pregnant and Paul was born. I was so pleased for her. He was a beautiful baby. I'm not just saying that because he's my grandson; complete strangers would stop us in the street to say so.

'I'd go and help out for weeks at a time because Sarah tired easily. Paul grew up on the farm until he was seven then something went wrong. Gordon's friend needed his money because of problems of his own and the bank wouldn't back him. Of course Gordon went to Clem for the financing but it was too much. Clem told me it was into seven figures and we didn't have that sort of capital as we'd passed the business on to our second and third sons to run and they were halfway through a big expansion. Well, when Clem said no that was it. Sarah came round and the things she said! It still makes me flush to think of it; it ended with her refusing to allow us to see Paul ever again.' Hannah paused and wiped her eyes.

'I have other grandchildren and I love them all dearly but he was my little lad. We'd seen such a lot of each other since he was a tiny baby and were very close.

'Anyway, enough of that...Yes, yes, Bettie, we'll be with you in two shakes.

'So, where were we? They had to move to some awful house in Harlden. I never saw it but I felt for Paul, going from the farm to that. If we hadn't fallen out I'm sure Clem would've helped them for Paul's sake but they never asked again and he never offered.

'Gordon would call me occasionally. That's how I found out he was studying to be a teacher. When Paul was ten Gordon started supply teaching. It was obvious that he'd found his niche and I was happy for him.

'Then the most extraordinary thing happened. About a year before he disappeared Paul turned up on my front doorstep in

London. It was the 27th July, 1981. I opened the door and I knew at once that it was him. He was still such a beautiful child. We both burst into tears and I hugged him until I thought he'd break.

'He'd had a terrible row at home and run away. He'd found out where we lived and taken the train. Of course I had to let his parents know even though he begged me not to. Gordon answered the phone, thank goodness, not her, and he agreed that Paul could stay for a couple of days until things calmed down.

'It turned into a wonderful week. Paul was cheerful enough but I could tell that something wasn't quite right. I knew him too well to be fooled and I knew he was keeping something from me. Try as I might though I couldn't get it out of him before he went home.

'After that we saw him every school holiday for a week and there wasn't a cross word between us the whole time. Never saw Sarah, not until the memorial service she insisted on organising for Paul.'

Miss Pennysmith felt that she had earned the right to interrupt.

'So, why do you say that the major isn't guilty?'

'Oh, because Paul's still alive. I thought you knew that.'

Margaret tried to keep the disappointment from her face. Her hope that Hannah might somehow know the identity of Paul's real killer deserted her. Instead she was faced with an old woman's illusions. She was so upset that she missed part of the continuing conversation.

'...I was knocked down and they hit me over the head. Mugging, the police called it, but Clem said it was more like attempted murder. It made the headlines in the *Evening Standard* and I was in a coma for a day before I came round. It was then that I saw him.'

'Saw whom?'

'Paul of course.'

'When was this?'

'Like I said, almost twenty years ago. When I came to, there he was by the side of the bed holding my hand.'

'But he'd have been what, eighteen?'

'Nineteen, but I knew it was him. There was no mistaking his eyes. He said something I couldn't hear – I was deaf for a while – but I think it was "you'll be all right, Nana". Then he bent down and kissed me. I blacked out again and he was gone when I woke up. So you see, your major can't have murdered the lad if he's still alive, now can he?'

CHAPTER TWENTY-EIGHT

Watkins collapsed before he'd finished his first breakfast in custody and a doctor had to be called. He diagnosed an anxiety attack, prescribed mild sedatives and insisted that the interrogation cease. Any evidence Fenwick could have extracted would have been wasted anyway so he decided he'd have to be patient. But as soon as the doctor left, Watkins insisted on seeing Fenwick, brushing aside the advice of his solicitor that he should say nothing until he had recovered. His reason soon became clear. He wanted to make a deal; he would tell them everything he knew about the supply of child pornography but in return he begged for something Fenwick simply couldn't give him: anonymity. He wanted his crimes to remain secret so that his family and friends would never know.

'It's very unlikely, Joe,' Fenwick explained, as Alison looked on with contempt. 'There'll be a trial even if you plead guilty. There's no way that I can promise to keep that out of the press; it's beyond my powers.'

'But there are such things as witness protection programmes, aren't there?'

'For people who give evidence against major crime syndicates where there's a genuine risk that their life would be in danger, yes. Are you saying that's the situation here?'

Watkins' face was alive with nervous tics. One eyelid fluttered almost constantly and the corner of his mouth spasmed into bizarre grins without warning. When Fenwick said the words 'major crime syndicate' Watkins jerked back in his chair, his hands waving as if he had palsy.

'I think that's enough, Chief Inspector,' Lawrence Parks said, regarding his client with growing concern. 'Mr Watkins is really not well enough for this to continue.'

'I agree.' Fenwick was too conscious of the tape to push the interview further but the way Watkins was reacting had begun to make him think that maybe he did have knowledge beyond the activities of Alec Ball. For the first time he wondered whether, by pure chance, they had arrested someone who knew about the paedophile ring the FBI insisted was operating in Sussex. But looking at Watkins it could be days before any evidence he gave them could be treated as legitimate. The last thing Fenwick wanted to do, now that he had come this close, was question the man before he was considered fit enough to be a credible witness. He found he was chewing his lip in frustration and forced himself to stop.

Parks, an experienced and canny solicitor, was watching him with a half-smile on his face that suggested he knew exactly what Fenwick's dilemma might be. *Sod him,* Fenwick thought uncharacteristically and returned his expression to one of studied neutrality.

'We'll be going before a magistrate in a couple of hours, Joe,' Fenwick explained. 'After that you'll be remanded to prison. Don't worry, you'll be segregated from the main population. As soon as the doctor and your solicitor consider you fit enough we will continue questioning you.

'If at that time, you still wish to become Queen's evidence, and if at that time we consider that what you have to say is valuable, there might be a deal on the table.'

'And anonymity? I don't care about prison time – I could say I was going in for some other crime; tax evasion, fraud...I really don't care as long as it's not p...ah, it's not...Oh God, forgive me!'

Watkins dropped his head into his hands and wept.

'Why can't I just go straight to prison, in a closed van and serve out my sentence?' he moaned, almost incoherent.

Lawrence Parks intervened.

'Enough is really enough now, Chief Inspector. But be sure, I will remember this conversation when the time comes.'

Fenwick couldn't work out whether Parks' words were a threat or a promise; maybe both. His gaze followed Watkins' shaking figure as he left the interview room to be taken back to his cell.

'Tell the custody sergeant to have him watched closely. I'm not happy with his mental state. And make sure he's assessed by a psychiatrist when he reaches prison. I don't want him killing himself before we can use him as a witness.'

Alison nodded, not caring about the callousness of Fenwick's remark.

'You off back to Harlden again, sir?'

'Yes. I want you to push ahead with arrest and search warrants for Ball while I'm gone. Think you can handle it?'

'Of course.' Alison nodded, then hesitated before leaving.

'What is it?'

'Did you hear that the team lost Ball yesterday?' she asked, not wanting to drop anybody in it but aware it was the sort of detail Fenwick would expect to know.

'No, I did not! Why didn't somebody tell me at once?'

'I think they left a message on your mobile.'

'But I was between home and Harlden station all day; why not call me there? I expect to be tracked down with news like that, not for some random message to be left in the ether on the off chance I might pick it up!'

'He turned up again at home three hours later so there was no harm done.'

'That's not the point.'

She didn't bother to argue.

By four o'clock Alison was on her way to the storage depot with a warrant to search Ball's lock-up while Clive joined the surveillance team outside Ball's flat. Their actions were going to be coordinated to the second. A team of MCS detectives and scene of crime technicians was ready and waiting her arrival in the warehouse opposite the depot, their impatience almost palpable. For these men and women who had maintained surveillance on Ball for so many long, unproductive weeks, this was their moment of vindication. Whatever doubts they'd had about Fenwick, and his stubborn determination to keep on with what most of them had thought was useless, mind-numbing work, had vanished. Some were even prepared to admit to being impressed with the chief inspector; rare praise from a hardened bunch drawn from the most experienced but sceptical detectives in Sussex.

Someone who'd known for as long as he could remember that Fenwick was exceptional was, at that moment, consumed with gloom because he felt he was letting his old boss down. Cooper had criss-crossed West Sussex in a vain attempt to discover something incriminating on Maidment and was dreading making his next report. He was unaware of the Choir Boy breakthrough, as news of it was being kept within MCS with the one exception of Nightingale, whom Fenwick had entrusted with the secret. So Bob felt the weight of the cold investigations on his shoulders as he trudged back to his car with a notebook that might as well have been empty.

His stomach rumbled as he eased himself into the driver's seat and he cursed Doris's muesli breakfasts. How was a man supposed to keep going on bird food all morning? He looked at his watch; almost twelve. Time for a spot of lunch maybe? As he often did when he was feeling low, Cooper decided that food would be his consolation. He was less than ten minutes drive from the Hare and Hounds and he could still recall the excellent ploughman's lunch they'd served him – and the second helpings that had arrived as if by magic.

The pub was almost empty when he walked in apart from some hikers drinking cider outside. Jacob Isaacs was behind the bar taking a sneaky swallow from what looked suspiciously like a glass of whisky. His wife was nowhere to be seen.

'Sergeant Cooper! You're a sight for sore eyes. The missus has buggered off to her mother's for a few days leaving me with moping Maureen.' He gestured aggressively towards the door that led to the kitchen and store room behind which Cooper could see a bulky silhouette through the glass. 'It's enough to drive a man to drink. What're you having? On the house!'

Cooper had entered the bar with good intentions to stick to an orange juice, or at most a shandy, but the smell of the ale drove the words from his lips as he ordered a pint of best to go with his ploughman's lunch. Both arrived promptly and, as he tucked in, his mood started to lighten.

Isaacs was distracted by a steady flow of customers as Cooper ate but the sergeant could see him looking at him from the corner of his eye whenever he thought he was unobserved. Maybe he was feeling guilty about the whisky but maybe not. Cooper decided it would do no harm to take his time over his lunch.

'Slice of apple pie, Mr Cooper?'

Maureen's offer broke into his thoughts and he'd said yes before his brain had even thought about it, some reactions being purely instinctive. It came warm, with vanilla ice cream melting into the buttery pastry. Cooper was, briefly, in heaven.

But all good things have to end and by a quarter to two he thought it was time for him to leave. His wallet was waved away unopened by a blurry Isaacs who had given up any pretence of serving and had retreated to his favourite spot at the end of the bar away from Maureen's disapproval. Cooper wandered over, meaning only to offer his thanks for another excellent lunch but as he reached the man he was struck by the deep melancholy that surrounded him. His natural reaction was to ask 'what's up?' but he was experienced enough to hold his tongue.

'Mr Cooper...'

'Bob,' he said, emphasising the informality of the moment.

'Bob, look, about what I said last time you were here.'

Isaacs took another mouthful of whisky and grimaced. Maureen glanced over at him and shook her head. Cooper sat down on a stool nearby endeavouring to look relaxed.

'Well, maybe I shouldn't say anything...'

'Go on, Jacob, you've got something on your mind and it's not doing you any good. Now's as good a time as any to deal with it.'

Isaacs sighed deeply and nodded. He was clearly struggling with a decision. Cooper gave him time and waited in silence, judging that he was a man to make up his own mind and would react against any attempt to influence.

'Thing is,' he said eventually, 'there's no way Jeremy would be interested in young boys.'

Cooper thought he picked up the faintest emphasis.

'Young *boys*,' he said.

'Yes. The major was – is – a full-blooded heterosexual with normal desires.'

'Tough then, being on active service, away from home comforts, for months on end.'

Isaacs flushed a deeper crimson and drained his glass. He gestured for another but was ignored, forcing him to get up off his stool and serve himself. Cooper cursed silently, afraid that the moment would pass, but he needn't have worried. The publican was back at his side within a minute, his face determined.

'You have to understand what active service does to a man.

When you're living with the knowledge that you might die life becomes very precious.'

'Oh, aye, I understand that,' Cooper said with feeling. 'I know exactly what the relief afterwards does to you.'

'It's pure instinct,' Isaacs agreed, keeping his voice low. 'And when you're young, in your twenties, thirties, there's a hell of a lot of testosterone circulating and that's got to be dealt with.'

'Course it does; only natural. The more threat to life the stronger the urge to procreate. It's Nature's way of forcing us to keep the species going.'

'Exactly! Couldn't have put it better. Well, we were in the thick of it for the best part of three years with hardly any leave. So it was inevitable we made the most of R&R.'

'I'd have been the same,' Cooper said, silently asking Dot's forgiveness. 'What else is a man to do, other than go nuts?'

'Precisely; a decent sex life keeps you sane. Of course some men don't need it as much as others; we all have different appetites.'

'And Jeremy?' Cooper interjected, feeling it was about time for Isaacs to become specific.

'Appetite of an elephant and equipped to match!' He laughed and Cooper forced a smile.

'How the hell did he cope?'

It was the key question and Isaacs knew it. He was in a corner and the only way out was to come clean or look a fool.

'Not with boys,' he said emphatically, 'though some did. There was everything on offer when we went on leave, and openly too. We had some money and entertainment was cheap. As long as we kept the peace and didn't offend the natives the MPs would turn a blind eye.'

'So what were Jeremy's tastes?'

Isaacs nodded to himself and exhaled slowly, making his decision.

'Well, he was engaged back home and he took his promise seriously, he was that sort of man. But eventually he was tempted.' He took a fortifying mouthful. 'There was this native family that befriended us. They had three girls, absolute beauties all of them; youngest was about ten. The major – except that he wasn't a major then of course, though he did get promoted to captain incredibly early – well, he was a bit of a hero to the Dyaks. They spoilt him rotten. This particular family decided he'd make a good husband for one of the girls and set about getting their man.

'The rest of us could see what was happening; we thought it was a great laugh. But Jeremy was always a bit naïve, so he was slow on the uptake and too bloody polite. Anyway, as I say, eventually he and the eldest girl got together; then they go through some local ceremony and he ends up hitched to her in their eyes. It was a secret, of course; if the brass had known they'd have had a fit. But he wasn't the only one and at least he didn't play around.'

'But he was already engaged. Why not just buy some relief when he had his R&R?'

'You don't know Maidment. He probably thought it was a bit more honourable going through a local ceremony.'

Cooper held his tongue. It was still bigamy when he married later. If anything, he thought Maidment had made the deception worse by dressing it up with local acceptability just to ease his damned conscience.

'What happened?'

'The inevitable. The girl got pregnant; he became a father. It all remained quiet; nobody wanted to drop a man like Jeremy in it with the brass. Then he got posted home. The family expected him to take his "wife" and child with him. Instead he bought them off. Paid them a lot of money, more than he needed to but enough for them to save face and provide a dowry for the girl big enough to persuade a local to ignore the fact she was already married with a kid – though if she chose to marry again I don't know.'

'I bet she was broken-hearted,' Cooper said before he could stop himself.

'Yes, but her family were satisfied that her honour had been protected and she was young enough to start again.'

'How old was she when he left her?'

'Oh, couldn't have been more than sixteen. They mature early there and marry young.'

So Maidment had engaged in sex with a minor and fathered a child by her, then bought his way out of trouble. Cooper felt the sick betrayal we all do when a hero turns out to be a weak human after all.

'Did his English wife ever find out?'

'No! Never. What happens on a posting remains out there, trust me. You've got to understand, he was very popular and most of us had some sort of secret or other we were only too happy to leave behind. I'm only telling you now so that you realise just how unlikely it is that he was involved in the Hill boy's death.'

Maybe, Cooper thought, but a weakness for sex and a secret like that, and perhaps others accumulated over the years, would make him an easy man to blackmail. He took his leave of Jacob, assuring the man that his revelations would only need to come out in extreme circumstances and would remain confidential in the meantime.

There was a lot for him to digest, and it wasn't just the apple pie. Nightingale was going to be delighted. She'd known there was something fishy about Maidment, had done from the moment she met him. Woman's instinct? Maybe she had sensed his sexual appetite and been put off by it. Whatever, she'd been right and he was looking forward to telling her so. As he drove away it occurred to him that he was still thinking of Nightingale as in charge of the Maidment case, not Fenwick.

When Fenwick had taken over, Cooper had been relieved – not that he resented Nightingale being given more responsibility, of course not, more that it felt *right* for the SIO to be a man the team would respect. But Fenwick had been clever; he'd given her the room to assume responsibility while making it clear that anyone who objected would have to deal with him and, to be fair to the lass, she'd done a bloody good job. He smiled as he put his foot down so that he could make good time and share the news.

Instead of enjoying the moment of arrests as the Choir Boy investigation came to a head, Fenwick was trying to persuade the Forensic Laboratory that there was something they could identify from the Well-Wisher's letters that would help to trace him or her. Tom, the head of the lab, was sympathetic but resistant to the idea of performing yet more tests.

'They've told us all they're going to, Andrew. The letters are virtually sterile – not even the most painstaking analysis has given us anything beyond confirmation that they were written on mass-produced stationery using an HP printer and ink that are sold in thousands of outlets across the UK; the envelopes have been sent to the fingerprint unit but quite honestly I think they're wasting their time because the sender is too smart to leave a trace. And the book has nothing hidden inside it – no secret messages that we could detect in the margin – and you already know from the fingerprint team that Paul held it at some time.'

'I know; I just hoped there might be something more.' He sounded despondent.

To cheer him up Tom said, 'I tell you what, we'll give priority to the samples we've just received from Louise Nightingale if that helps.'

Fenwick was too experienced to let his surprise show but as

soon as he broke the connection he speed-dialled her number, was put straight through and asked her what she'd found. Nightingale explained about her interview with the Anchors and being taken to the field where Oliver had seen the car burning on the night Paul disappeared.

'I'm thinking that it could have been Taylor's car; it would explain why there was no trace of it after Anchor saw it.'

'So you decided to collect soil samples after all this time?' Fenwick was torn between disbelief and admiration.

'Well, no, not exactly.'

She told him about the cigarettes and blood, sounding nervous, as if waiting for him to scoff. He remained silent.

'It's probably nothing, of course, and if it hadn't been for the fact that there'd been recent news coverage about Paul I probably wouldn't have done it but—'

'You don't need to make excuses. You thought maybe the killer had returned to the scene just to make sure all traces had vanished. It is totally illogical but we've known murderers do more stupid things.'

'Exactly.' He could hear her relief. 'There's something else too.'

He could hear a note of triumph in her voice.

'Bob Cooper's just been in to see me. He thinks he's discovered Maidment's guilty secret.'

Nightingale gave him the story about the major's first family.

'Plenty of grounds for blackmail there,' Fenwick observed. 'What are you going to do with the info?'

'Nothing immediately. Maidment's where we want him; we already suspected that he was hiding something and now we know that he might have been forced to do so or risk being exposed as a bigamist. His wife might be dead but I doubt his son would welcome being called a bastard. Frankly I've never bought the idea that his silence was all to do with honour and protecting the regiment; protecting his reputation more like. If I confront him I'm not sure what reaction I'll get. I sense that his silence has become habit after all these years. He's convinced himself that he's done nothing seriously wrong and until we can give him hard facts to show he's involved in a murder we'll get nothing from him.'

'You could be right. Why not give Cooper another crack at finding out who he's covering for?'

'That's what I've got him doing now. He's cross-checking the list of Maidment's friends and acquaintances against the people who were interviewed when Malcolm and Paul disappeared.'

'What about trying to find other potential victims of abuse?'

'Already in hand. Robin is re-interviewing school friends but has nothing so far. I've had an idea though.'

'Go on.'

'How about a press conference, appealing for abuse victims to come forward?'

'That's a big step.'

It was one he'd already considered and dismissed until they had firmer information against which to judge what the people claiming to have been abused would say. Inevitably, among the potentially genuine victims would be the delusional, the mentally ill and the hoaxers. It would consume enormous resources to screen each one carefully, particularly as not all his detectives were trained to handle the work. It required great skill to gain the confidence of an abuse victim, extract and then evaluate their statements, and he would need to borrow trained interviewers from outside Sussex to handle the workload.

Fenwick told Nightingale he'd consider the idea. The other reason for delaying a public appeal was that it might be the only possibility to flush out more information about the Well-Wisher. He was sketching out what a press statement might contain and the best way to handle the briefing when his desk and mobile phones rang simultaneously.

'Fenwick,' he said holding one to either ear.

'We're in! Everything we could need is here.'

'He's dead!'

'What? Alison, hold on, Clive's on the other line. Who's dead, Clive?'

'Ball.'

Fenwick closed his eyes in dismay but forced his voice to be calm.

'Alison, call me back in ten minutes.' He replaced the receiver on his desk phone.

'Go on, Clive. How did he die?'

'It's not obvious from the body. There's an almost full bottle of whisky and a glass beside him but no pills so it doesn't look like suicide.'

'What type of whisky was he drinking?'

'What? Er...I...Hang on, I'll find out.' Fenwick could hear him calling out what he obviously thought a bizarre question, then his reply, 'Oban twelve-year-old single malt.'

'Very nice but not his normal tipple. We know from weeks of surveillance that he bought Bells – and plenty of it.'

'How the heck did you remember that?' Clive asked, before realising that if Fenwick knew such detail then he would certainly expect the officers actually involved in watching Ball to remember it. He went on quickly. 'The doc's on his way, so are SOCO. I called them straight away.'

'And the scene is sealed?'

'Yes.'

'I'm coming over as soon as I've spoken to the ACC. In the meantime you can find out from the team on duty yesterday where and how they lost him. I want chapter and verse.'

His call with the ACC was brief; he couldn't hide his

disappointment but Harper-Brown was surprisingly supportive.

'God knows, Andrew, you've achieved more than anyone else could have done. Don't beat yourself up that Ball chose to die on you.'

'Unless it was murder.' Fenwick told him how the dead man had given them the slip the previous afternoon.

'But he was seen fit and well returning to his flat and was there until the body was discovered.'

'Even so, I'll only be satisfied that there's no connection to his disappearance when the autopsy confirms natural causes.'

Alison called him on his mobile as he was leaving and he told her about Ball.

'How did he die? Is it murder?'

'I'm on my way to find out.'

Clive was grim-faced when he met Fenwick outside Ball's flat.

'You are going to be seriously pissed off,' he warned, before telling Fenwick how sergeant Welsh had let Ball slip away from him just after lunch on Sunday. He had been tailing him in his car, completely routine, when Ball had suddenly done an illegal U-turn before heading down a one-way street the wrong way.

'Had he clocked the tail, do you think?'

'Welsh swears not, says he was several cars back and until that point the surveillance had been routine.'

'Hmm, unlikely but supposing for a moment he's right, why would Ball suddenly take off like that?'

'A precaution, just in case?' Clive volunteered.

'Exactly, which means he was going to meet someone or do something very important. I wonder if that led to his death.'

'The doc's inside now. Maybe he can tell us something.'

Fenwick had recognised Pendlebury's car double parked in front of the flats. He was one of the best pathologists in Sussex, the very best in Fenwick's opinion, and he stepped up to the crime tape hopefully.

'My lucky day!' he called over it. 'How did they drag you away from your lab, Doc?'

'You make me sound like Frankenstein.'

'I wouldn't use that brain if I were you. Any thoughts on time of death?'

'You know me better than that. The skin's cold and clammy, there's no rigor in the neck and it's resolving in the body. All that suggests he died eighteen to twenty-four hours ago but the room is warm and closed so I could be out by up to four hours. Lividity is fixed and the pattern suggests he died where he's sat. I've finished with him – you can move him now.' Pendlebury raised himself from his knees and took off his gloves.

Fenwick followed him to his car, a beaten-up estate that looked as if it should be put out of its misery.

'Can you tell me anything at all?'

'I'm not being difficult but honestly, no. I doubt it's alcohol poisoning – unless he'd been drinking heavily before – because there's too much of the whisky left in the bottle for that. It could be a natural death – heart attack, cerebral haemorrhage, embolism, or it could be suicide – alcohol plus some sort of drugs. Were any found by the body?'

'No. Might it be murder?'

'No obvious wounds. Poison's a possibility. Is he a likely victim?'

'We think he knows some very nasty criminals and we were about to arrest him.'

'Then I'll ask for the tox screens to be run urgently.'

'Thanks. I appreciate it. Call me anytime.'

'You won't be attending the autopsy? I can do it straight away if it's urgent.'

'It is, and thanks again but Clive Kettering can join you; it'll be good for him and I've got other things to do.'

* * *

Nightingale was relieved to hear from Clive that he was going to be late; could they postpone dinner? She was busy reading Cooper's interview notes, trying to find in them something that would tell them whom Maidment was protecting. She knew from Fenwick that he was no closer to finding the Well-Wisher and she wanted to escape any more media embarrassment.

Cooper had made good progress cross-checking the people interviewed in 1982 after Paul disappeared with the list of the major's army acquaintances. She put her head into the CID room and asked him to join her so that they could discuss what he'd found out.

'There was more overlap than I'd expected,' he told her. 'A few of them also knew Taylor so they'll get top priority tomorrow. There are nine men in Sussex who were in the army at the same time, knew Maidment and Taylor. All of them were interviewed when Taylor became a suspect and I saw some of them only last week so they'll not exactly be overjoyed to see me.'

Nightingale scanned the list of names he gave her:

> Adrian Bush
> Alex Cotton
> Richard Edwards*
> Vernon Jones
> Ernest Knight
> Patrick Murray
> Ben Thompson
> Zach Smart*
> *interviewed already

None of them rang a bell.

'So what's next?' she asked him.

'See them again. I'm particularly keen to visit Smart because he promised to come in and make statement and hasn't, and he knew Paul. Thompson has been elusive as well. How about you? Enjoying yourself?'

'Yes. It feels good to be in charge. What are they saying about it out there?'

Cooper shrugged and looked a little uncomfortable.

'Go on.'

'Most of them are OK – jury's out until you've finished; they'll work for you, do a decent job.'

'And the others?'

'The usual bigoted pigs you've been used to handling for years. Don't worry about them.'

'Funnily enough, I'm not,' she said, meaning it. 'As long as they do their job and obey orders they can think what they like. And if they don't.' She paused and smiled. It was a wicked smile. 'If they don't I'm going to quite enjoy putting them straight.'

'Good for you. Just make sure I'm around to see it; I wouldn't want to miss the show. Best get back to it then.' He made to leave.

'Oh, Bob,' she said, just before he reached the door, 'if you've got a bet on with Dave McPherson, you'd better make sure it's placed the right way. I wouldn't want you to lose any money.'

Cooper's mouth fell open; he couldn't even think of a denial.

'And if you want to know which way's the right way, just ask Dave about Blite's bet; I gave him some inside information.'

She was still laughing when Fenwick rang her.

'You sound cheerful.'

'Just enjoying a joke at poor old Bob's expense.' She hesitated, then thought *blow it, why not?* and proceeded to tell Fenwick of her conversation.

'You what!' He sounded appalled.

'Why not? If you don't confront the demons they only eat you. I just hope McPherson loses a lot of money. He's carrying the book and if I know Bob, he'll make sure he's the last to know the truth. It'll be a sweet moment.'

Fenwick was silent.

'Andrew? Are you OK; you're not angry, are you?'

'Not with you. I was just thinking. We're both going to be very late; I'll miss the children's bedtime anyway so how about my stopping by the station on my way home – say sometime after nine o'clock – and we can have a quick bite to eat?'

'Perfect!' she said, laughing again. 'I'll just make sure that McPherson knows what's happening.'

'My idea exactly.'

CHAPTER TWENTY-NINE

Jason MacDonald stood at the bar and waited for the landlord to notice his outstretched £20 note. From time to time he glanced back over his shoulder to check that Sarah Hill was still there, tucked in an alcove away from the main lounge. He would have preferred to interview her at her home but for a reason still beyond him she'd insisted on coming out. When he had argued against the idea she'd threatened to cancel their agreement and he'd backed down rather than risk losing her.

Over the past painful week he had extracted her version of Paul's last days word by excruciating word. She broke down frequently and once she had kicked him out of the house. Yet the next day she was almost normal and greeted him as if nothing had happened.

'Two gin and tonics, please, and a packet of peanuts.'

They had reached the final day of Paul's life and he was close to completing the best story he'd ever written. He had started to play with the idea of writing a book about Paul and the major. That wasn't in the contract of course but let her try and stop him. It was the least he deserved for spending hours cooped up with a complete nutter. He picked up their drinks, fixed a smile to his face and manoeuvred back to their table, ready to press record for the last time.

Another package arrived from the Well-Wisher; this time it was sent to ACC Harper-Brown. Inside was a letter, a photograph taken at an angle as if it had been snapped in a hurry and a pair of boy's underpants, grey with age. Harper-Brown summoned Fenwick to his office where he stared at the latest delivery in astonishment.

'The laboratory is on standby to process everything urgently; a bike is waiting to take them as soon as you've had a chance to see them.'

Fenwick put on protective gloves and opened the bag carefully.

The photograph was out of focus and badly taken. It showed part of a wall, surrounded by trees with a section of ornate ironwork to one side.

'Could be a fence or even a gate. I've had enhanced copies made and distributed to traffic across the county already in case they recognise it.' The ACC's normally self-satisfied tone was absent; he was all business.

'Good, you never know.' Fenwick turned the picture over. There was writing on the back, badly faded with age. 'Are these names?'

'Yes, don't bother straining your eyes because he mentions them in his letter, here.'

Dear Assistant Chief Constable,

  I am writing to you because you made a statement in response to my last letter which missed the point entirely. Your investigating officers seem determined to ignore my correspondence and waste further police time in futile attempts to find me. Your reputation for efficiency and astute judgement is well known and therefore I am directing my efforts to secure justice now solely to you.

  Major Maidment did not kill Paul Hill, nor was he involved in the abduction. I know this for a certain fact. Paul Hill never met Maidment, though he was unfortunate enough to meet others from the army, thanks to Bryan Taylor's pimping. The major was not among them and I can only imagine that he has in some way been implicated in Paul's disappearance by design or a quirk of fate. Whatever evidence you have was planted somehow and I confess that I do not know how.

There was great evil in Harlden at the time of Paul Hill's disappearance. You should seek out the man who lived, and maybe still does live, at this house. I apologise for the quality of the image; I understand that it was taken under somewhat trying circumstances.

Ask the man that lives/lived here about Paul Hill and Bryan Taylor and about what really happened on 7th September 1982. He will not tell you the truth but you will recognise a liar when you meet him. The very fact that you ask the question will fill him with fear and, with God's help, you will achieve the rest.

I mentioned that Hill introduced Paul to other army men. The names I have been told may be false but I give them to you anyway: the man who lived in this house called himself Nathan (though I heard him once called 'The Purse'). In addition, Paul met an Alec and a Joe. Alec had a tattoo of an octopus.

'Alec Ball has a tattoo,' Fenwick interrupted. 'Could the "Joe" be Watkins?'

As further proof of my sincerity I enclose an item of Paul's clothing; no doubt the stains of his sins and those of the others involved will have degraded by now but one hears of such extraordinary advances in DNA science that I am placing my faith in you to find something. It is painful to part with even one item of Paul's. I have kept some of his things in memory of the boy he once was. Please do not force me to part with more.

One final word. I do not wish to cause innocents pain but you must realise that Taylor's dirty hands will have left their mark on other boys. They too will vouch the major blameless should you find them.

Justice now lies in your hands, Mr Harper-Brown, and I pray that you pursue it urgently and wisely for it is the Lord's work that you do.

I know that extracting DNA and searching your databases for a match takes time so I am giving you five days before I send a copy of this letter and photographs of its contents to the press. Use your time well.

Yours truly,

A Well-Wisher

Fenwick reread the letter and studied the picture. As he did so there was a knock on the ACC's door and Nightingale walked in.

'Sorry to be late, sir, but I was out following up a lead and only learnt of the meeting a short time ago.'

The ACC stared at her with disdain.

'I was not aware that you were invited.'

'I left a message for her, sir,' Fenwick interrupted. 'The ACC has received another letter,' he told her.

She read a copy quickly, her forehead lined with concentration, nodding as if the contents confirmed her own thoughts, then studied the picture.

'Observations, Inspector?' Harper-Brown had decided to make her earn her right to stay.

'I imagine it was postmarked London again, same paper and envelope, no prints or saliva.'

'Probably, the lab hasn't processed it yet.'

'The names are interesting. If they relate to Ball and Watkins it means firstly, they were confident Paul would never identify them again, and secondly that they knew this Nathan character as well as Taylor. Maybe Nathan's the man behind the paedophile ring you're investigating.'

The ACC raised an elegant eyebrow at Fenwick at this mention of Choir Boy but directed his remarks to Nightingale.

'All rather obvious comments, hardly worth your interruption.'

For once, Nightingale didn't blush at his words. If anything she seemed to agree with him.

'Quite, but it's always best to get the straightforward out of the way first. What really interests me is the language of the letter. There are some odd, almost archaic, phrases: *"I confess...there was great evil in Harlden...seek out the man"* and so on. It's almost biblical.'

'I thought the same,' Fenwick leant forward eagerly, 'and that might explain a lot.'

'I fail to see how.' The ACC leant back in his rather grand chair, his calm demeanour the antithesis to Fenwick's enthusiasm.

'We've been struggling with the motivation behind the letters. Why tell us snippets of information but not give us Taylor's current address, or the location of Paul's grave? It doesn't make sense. We speculated that the writer might be an ex-lover of Taylor's, or one of his clients with a grudge, even a boy he'd abused, but if that were the case they would have told us more.

'But supposing the sender is a priest. He might have come by his knowledge in the confessional, or in a conversation he considers bound by the same rules. So he tells us only what falls outside those conversations!'

Fenwick's tone had grown increasingly animated as the attraction of his theory grew. The ACC conceded that it was an idea worth pursuing.

'What else does this letter tell us?'

Nightingale interrupted, eager to demonstrate her thinking.

'This is about more than Taylor. Our Well-Wisher wants us to find this house. Taylor left the area years ago. He's directing us towards the man who owned it – Nathan or The Purse as he was called.'

'It's a terrible picture.' Fenwick's mood sobered as he looked at it. 'My son could do better.'

His words hung in a sudden stillness as everyone realised the significance of what he'd said. He spelt it out for them.

'Paul took it, didn't he? He risked a shot at the house. It explains why it's blurred and at an angle.'

'So the picture was with Paul's things that the Well-Wisher has kept.'

'But how did he come by them?' Despite his determination not to get carried away, the ACC was as eager now as the others.

'That,' said Fenwick, 'is the key question, a very good point.' The ACC's lips twitched upwards. 'What do you think, sir?'

'Well, the obvious answer is that Taylor took Paul's duffel bag with him rather than bury it with the body or the clothes. He was overcome with remorse, found a priest, confessed and handed the bag to him. The priest was unable to share his knowledge with anyone but kept the bag and its contents as, what does he say, a "memory of the boy Paul once was."'

The ACC sat back with a satisfied smile on is face.

'That would explain a lot,' Fenwick agreed, 'but not the underpants. There doesn't appear to be any blood on them and why weren't they buried with the other clothes?'

'A detail I am sure you will iron out.'

Harper-Brown pressed a button on his phone and called his secretary into the meeting.

'These are the items I mentioned earlier. The lab is expecting them and they are to have top priority. I know some of the evidence is old and degraded but they have exactly four days to deliver results. They're to come to me personally as soon as they are available. Tell them to find me wherever I am and have DCI Fenwick join me.' There was a discreet cough. 'Oh, and Inspector Nightingale as well, I suppose.'

'Only four days, he gave us five,' Fenwick commented as the secretary left.

'We'll need a day to make our decision and plan a response. If we release the major and this letter remains secret all hell will break loose. If we don't, our so-called "Well-Wisher" will go to the media, Maidment's lawyer will challenge the grounds for our arrest or at the very least our insistence on remand. We'll need to be extremely well prepared for either eventuality. It is now Wednesday, 31st August. I suggest that you keep all of Sunday afternoon and Monday morning clear.'

He turned his attention back to the few items on his scarily ordered desk and Fenwick and Nightingale assumed, correctly, that they were dismissed.

CHAPTER THIRTY

The initial post-mortem examination of Ball was inconclusive. The body showed signs of liver damage consistent with heavy drinking and some arteriosclerosis but neither was enough to be the cause of death. On Wednesday afternoon Pendlebury rang.

'The toxicology results are back from the lab,' he told Fenwick. 'Thought you'd want to know at once. He had a lethal level of Seconal and amylobarbitone in his system. With the condition of his liver he would have been dead within half an hour of ingestion. Source is the malt whisky found beside his body. On its own the Seconal would have induced coma but mixed with alcohol and the amylobarbitone, death was inevitable.'

'You say it was mixed in with the whisky?'

'So the lab says; the bottle was the source and there were traces in the glass.'

'We didn't find anything to explain the presence of barbiturates in his flat – no prescriptions or empty pill bottles in the rubbish, nothing.'

'I'm sure the coroner will be fascinated. My job is to tell you the cause of death and it was the ingestion of an overdose of barbiturates the effect of which was accelerated and amplified by moderate liver disease and alcohol.'

'Thanks, Doc. I'll have Clive prepare for the inquest.'

He was about to call Tom Barnes at the Forensic Laboratory when he was saved the trouble.

'Andrew, we're working flat out on the ACC's bumper bundle but I thought you'd want to know we managed to finish processing some of the material Louise Nightingale sent us first. I was going to call her direct but there's something I thought you should hear. The DNA from saliva on the cigarette butts belongs to Alec Ball.'

Fenwick sat up straighter in his chair.

'It was Ball's? So when he gave our surveillance the slip he was heading out to the copse where the Anchor boy says he saw a car burning on the night Paul disappeared. That's too much to be a mere coincidence. What about the blood?'

'Definitely human but we haven't had a chance to extract DNA so it will have to wait until we've finished the ACC's work. I'm sorry but we're at full stretch.'

'Tom, as ever, you've been incredibly helpful and I know you'll do your best. I'll let Nightingale know about Ball being at the site.'

He rang her, explained what had happened and called an immediate case meeting of both the Choir Boy and Hill/Eagleton teams for five that evening, in Harlden.

The incident room was packed with around ten officers of all ranks, Superintendent Quinlan among them. Fenwick and Nightingale stood at the front, three large whiteboards behind them, crammed with photographs from the cases. On the centre board there was a blank silhouette with a question mark inked across it.

'This afternoon we received news from the lab that suggests a strong link between the murders of Malcolm Eagleton and Paul Hill, and a current MCS investigation into a paedophile ring in Sussex, codenamed Choir Boy. Choir Boy is a sensitive operation and for those of you from Harlden I must emphasise that what I am about to tell you *cannot* leave this room.'

He walked to the board on his left and pointed to one of three photos.

'Joseph Watkins. Identified during an FBI investigation as the purchaser of paedophile material over the Internet; arrested last week in possession of such material and now remanded in custody. This morning we received information from an unknown but credible source that a man called Joe – possibly Watkins – might have been involved in Paul Hill's murder.'

There was a soft rumble in the room like the growl in the throat of a dog as it picks up the first scent of prey. The hackles of the Harlden team rose in unison.

'Problem: Watkins suffered a nervous breakdown on arrest and we cannot interview him until the prison doctor clears him as fit. Second problem: his condition has deteriorated since he's been in prison and the psychiatrist has prescribed drugs that mean any statements we extracted from him now would be inadmissible. Which is a bugger,' Fenwick shook his head in frustration, 'because we really need his evidence. Still, there's plenty more we can do in the meantime.

'MCS watched Watkins for months and identified Alec Ball,' he patted the picture next to Watkins, 'as an acquaintance. Ball lived in Brighton and was found dead yesterday of barbiturate poisoning.'

'Murder or suicide, Andrew?' Quinlan interrupted and Fenwick nodded to Clive to answer.

'Too early to say, sir. The drugs had been mixed with whisky Ball was drinking at the time of his death. The only fingerprints on the bottle are his but so far we haven't been able to find the source of barbiturates in his home, which is suspicious but not conclusive.

'We were about to arrest Ball on evidence we'd secured as the result of weeks of surveillance. What's more, the same source that gave us the name "Joe" as one of Paul's murderers also told us that a man with an octopus tattoo called Alec was party to it. Ball has such a tattoo.'

Cries of 'Bring the source in', 'Who is he?', 'When can we interview them?' filled the room. Fenwick waited for them to die down.

'Our next problem,' he said with a wry grin that suggested that his confidence was in no measure damaged by a further setback, 'is that we don't know the identity of the source. They communicate by letter, call themselves the Well-Wisher and remain elusive. But they have sent us physical proof to support their assertions, which has been validated.'

Nightingale took up the briefing, standing by the board on the opposite side.

'Paul Hill and Malcolm Eagleton. Two local schoolboys who vanished in the early Eighties. As you know, Malcolm's remains were found in July with traces in the grave that led to an excavation at The Downs Golf Club in Harlden and the discovery of Paul Hill's bloody school uniform. Despite a considerable amount of work we've been unable to confirm that Paul and Malcolm were abducted by the same man or men but circumstantially there's enough for us to continue to treat the crimes as connected. At the time, suspicion for Paul's disappearance fell on Bryan Taylor but he hasn't been seen since the day of Paul's abduction and we still don't know what he looks like beyond this artist's impression.

'Major Jeremy Maidment was arrested for Paul's murder earlier this month because his blood and fingerprints were found on the sack containing Paul's clothes. We have no suspect for Malcolm's death and Maidment has a confirmed alibi for the day he disappeared. Based on the interrogation of Maidment and a lot of background work by Bob Cooper and his team we've concluded that the major might be covering up for the real killer,' she walked to the centre board and tapped a blank silhouette, 'for reasons we don't as yet know. Progress towards a trial for Maidment was continuing well until the intervention of the Well-Wisher two weeks ago.'

The presentation slipped seamlessly between Fenwick and Nightingale, reinforcing an impression of professional, close cooperation that subtly worked its influence on their teams.

'The Well-Wisher has given us credible information about Paul's abduction,' Fenwick explained. 'He insists that Maidment isn't guilty, that Bryan Taylor was a pimp who introduced the boy to a number of army men, including someone called Joe,' he tapped Joseph Watkins picture, 'a man called Alec with an octopus tattoo,' Ball's tattoo was obvious in the photo pinned to the board, 'and a man named Nathan or possibly, "The Purse".' Fenwick went and stood by the central blank silhouette.

'The missing link. According to the FBI, we have a significant paedophile ring here in Sussex that's been running for years. It's just possible that Paul and potentially Malcolm were sucked into that ring and became some of its early victims. None of the men we've identified so far has the ability or resources to organise crime on the scale the FBI has suggested. Unfortunately, neither Ball nor Watkins is in a state to give us the name of the man in the middle. And while we are close to arresting two other men seen buying suspicious goods from Alec Ball,' he pointed to two surveillance photographs pinned beneath Ball's picture, 'from the information we've gathered they look like punters, not our missing link.'

'This missing link? Andrew, are you suggesting that the man the Well-Wisher calls Nathan is also behind the paedophile ring?' Quinlan asked.

'I can't say that,' Fenwick shrugged, 'but he could be. Maidment is protecting someone who's either blackmailing him or towards whom he feels extraordinary loyalty. Such a person could be influential and organised enough to be behind Choir Boy but it's by no means certain it's the same person.

'What is already clear is that the two investigations are

connected by Joseph Watkins and Alec Ball; and that was before a further development, thanks to Inspector Nightingale.' He turned towards her. 'You tell them.'

'Last week we were able to trace a friend of Paul's who wasn't interviewed at the time of his disappearance. Oliver Anchor told us that on the evening Paul vanished he saw a car similar to Taylor's red estate burning on farmland close to where he lives. This week, following coverage of Paul's disappearance, Ball visited the exact location of the burning car, on the Sunday afternoon before he died. He left behind cigarette stubs that bear his DNA. At the site we also found a trace of human blood that isn't his.'

Her news caused a stir in both teams and a rush of questions. Fenwick again let the noise subside before he spoke.

'We need to find answers – and quickly. From now on the two investigations will be run together but with distinct lines of inquiry: we need to find other victims of abuse. They may have been seduced by Taylor, or be part of the Choir Boy ring, or the two things may be linked. We'll be going public about Choir Boy within the next few days and I want Sergeant Alison Reynolds to take the lead.

'The site where the car was allegedly burnt needs to be processed properly and we need to keep close to Watkins in case he recovers. Clive Kettering will take the lead for this.

'Most importantly we need to identify Nathan/The Purse who may be the person Maidment is covering for. Bob Cooper is already handling that for Nightingale and will continue to do so as a high priority.

'And we need to cross-check the results from the Forensic Lab, including those that will be delivered later this week as a result of more material from the Well-Wisher. Nightingale will oversee that, working with both the Harlden team and MCS.

'Meanwhile, I'm going to continue to try and trace the Well-

Wisher and follow up with the Met on the surveillance they've been doing on a house in London visited by Ball last week. I'll need daily reports on all these lines of inquiry and there will be regular coordination meetings. This is a critical week and whatever aspect of the work you're involved in, don't treat it as routine, no matter how trivial it seems. Whatever you find out could be absolutely critical.'

By working around the clock and prioritising the ACC's case above everything else, the Forensic Laboratory extracted and matched DNA from Paul's underpants by midnight on Friday. A copy of the report was taken by police bike to the ACC's home and another to Fenwick.

Fenwick read the contents carefully and rang Nightingale even though it was nearly two in the morning. She sounded remarkably alert.

'The report's come in and the ACC has called a meeting for first thing tomorrow. Ahead of that I want us to get together in Harlden, say six-thirty?'

'No problem. I'll see you there.'

Just before the receiver was replaced he was certain that he heard a man's voice in the background say 'Who was that?' It was vaguely familiar. He set the alarm for five-thirty but couldn't get back to sleep. Even though he told himself it was because he was puzzling over the implications of the lab findings, it was the sound of that voice that echoed in his mind and eventually drove him from his bed as the birds started singing.

The aroma of bacon sandwiches greeted him when he walked into the incident room. Cooper was there as well as Nightingale so he imagined she'd called him.

'Toasted sandwich?' Nightingale threw him a warm greaseproof bag. 'They're from the all-night café. There are sachets of brown sauce behind you, and mustard.'

She was tucking into her own with gusto and it was soon gone. A trickle of grease and HP Sauce lingered at the corner of her mouth after she finished and Bob Cooper leant forward to wipe it off. Fenwick concentrated on tackling his own breakfast and tried not to speculate on the reason for Nightingale's appetite and bright eyes.

'You look a bit rough, guv, if you don't mind me saying.' Cooper looked at his former boss with concern.

'Didn't get much sleep. Here's the report, read it while I make us some proper coffee.'

When he returned with three steaming mugs – milk and two sugars for Cooper, the others black – the mood in the room had changed.

'Both Ball and Watkins abused Paul before he died,' Cooper said, outrage in his voice. 'Plus two other bastards.'

'Probably Nathan and Taylor,' Fenwick said, passing the coffees around, 'but nothing to tie the abuse to Maidment.'

'The Well-Wisher's bona fide. Maidment didn't kill Paul.' Fenwick could hear disappointment in Nightingale's voice. 'He's given us names, the tattoo and DNA in a neat package.'

'Not just any DNA,' Fenwick reminded her, 'semen on Paul Hill's underwear. The report confirms that his DNA is on them too, see – here.' He pointed to the paragraph; she read it and looked sick.

'This means Paul was gang-raped before he was killed.'

'Looks like it but today the most important finding is that there was no trace whatsoever of Maidment's DNA on the items the Well-Wisher sent us.'

'The ACC is going to want to release him on bail, isn't he – perhaps even drop the charges?' Nightingale chewed her lip in frustration.

'That's my guess, except that it's not entirely his call. CPS will make the final decision and, given the profile and seriousness of the charge, I expect this will go all the way to the top.'

'To the DPP?' It was rare for Nightingale to be in awe of anyone but the idea that the Director of Public Prosecutions might be involved in one of her cases had clearly shaken her. Fenwick noted her anxious glance towards the ranks of files around the walls and smiled inwardly. He sympathised.

'I've asked Quinlan to join us in ten minutes given the profile of this decision. He and I will go over to Harper-Brown.' He pre-empted Nightingale's protest. 'There's no point either of you coming. The decision will be between the ACC and CPS. All I can do is try and exert some influence.'

'In which direction?' Nightingale accepted the logic of her exclusion begrudgingly.

'That's why we're here now. I want your views. Do either of you think Maidment killed Paul or Malcolm?'

'No.' Bob Cooper spoke immediately. 'He's just not a paedophile.'

'How about helping to cover up on someone else's behalf?'

'Hmm.' Cooper scratched his ample stomach, a sure sign that he was thinking deeply. 'He's bloody loyal to the regiment and if someone had threatened to tell his wife about his little secret... But he's a devout Christian and I can't seem him protecting the killer of an innocent boy under any circumstances.'

'Are you saying Christians don't commit crimes? They're no better or worse than anybody else and Paul wasn't exactly an innocent, was he? Perhaps Maidment was told he was a prostitute, maybe even a blackmailer who had set out to entrap one of Maidment's mates,' Nightingale suggested.

'That's too harsh a judgement on Paul. We don't know when Taylor started abusing him but by the time he was fourteen he'd have been totally conditioned.'

'Maidment needn't have known that,' Nightingale continued, knocking Cooper's words aside.

'But—'

'Enough.' Fenwick ran his fingers through his hair and suppressed a yawn. He'd never felt less prepared for a difficult day. 'Our job is to consider the evidence we have and present it fairly, not to sit in judgement on Paul or the major. And we need to do it quickly; the superintendent will be here any moment.

'Let's go back to the hypothesis that Maidment was set up, blackmailed even; his fingerprints and blood end up on the sack but he wasn't involved in the abduction or killing. We know he had a guilty secret, one that would probably have wrecked his marriage and destroyed his reputation if it ever came out. What evidence is there that contradicts that theory?'

'Nothing. It explains why he's said nothing to defend himself. Despite all our work we can find no evidence that he knew Paul Hill or Malcolm and his only interaction with Taylor was to fire him.' Nightingale agreed reluctantly.

'But did he know what the sack contained?' Cooper challenged. 'I don't see him covering up a murder for any reason.'

'His fingerprints are all over both sacks and his blood's not just on the outside. If he didn't know about the contents why go to the trouble of dumping them at the site and then, presumably, covering the sack up sufficiently to prevent it being seen by the workmen? No, I think he knew what he was doing.' Fenwick was inclined to agree with Nightingale's obvious conclusion that Maidment was in some way complicit.

'So what's your recommendation going to be?' she asked, testing him.

'That we drop the charges for murder and rearrest him as an accessory. We have enough for that, don't we, Nightingale?'

'Yes; and I agree with you. I think Maidment took the bag as a favour to someone, never mind how he was persuaded, puts it somewhere – say in the boot of his car – but when he takes it out it rips. Maybe he catches his hand on whatever tore the bag and leaves blood as well as prints. So he decides to find another bag.'

'But did he notice the contents? Maybe he didn't.'

'Cooper, you're going to have to keep your soft spot for the major under control. Our working assumption is that he *did* know.'

'Right,' Nightingale continued, 'and that makes it even more damning that he went ahead with the disposal. It also means that he trusted the person who gave him the sack enough to hide it for them anyway.'

'And when the news of Paul's disappearance broke?' Fenwick pressed her.

'He was trapped, wasn't he? The builders would have carried on with the terrace. You can bet that he chose a place to dump the bag where it would have been cemented in the next day, too much risk otherwise. So to retrieve the sack he'd have had to ask for the terrace to be dug up. There'd be no way to do it discreetly.'

'I'd have put money on him being the sort to go straight to the police, whatever the consequences,' Cooper insisted.

'But he didn't.' Fenwick drained the last of his coffee and tried to force his brain to think clearly. 'Maybe he was convinced that Paul wasn't murdered – that he died accidentally say or even ran away – the body never was found. Whatever,' Fenwick stood up and stretched elaborately, 'I think we've got enough. Nightingale, you prepare the paperwork to support an arrest on the lesser charge.

'We have to assume that Maidment will be released on bail as no magistrate will want to back a call for remand from us now. But I want to keep the pressure on him. I can't believe that Maidment knew Paul was raped and murdered. I want him in here this afternoon. It's time to be tough. Nightingale, you can take the lead in his interrogation and you're free to be as aggressive as you like short of physical assault. I expect you to break him; understood?'

The unexpected responsibility made her smile with pleasure.

'I'll need to destroy his trust in whoever persuaded him to cover up so I'll share the facts about Paul as we know them...and about the possibility of other boys. But I'll keep back our knowledge about his bigamy and family in Asia until right at the end.' She stood up, eager to get to work.

'And it's shoe-leather time again for me, I suppose,' Cooper said but he didn't sound despondent. 'I'm not sure he'll break that easily so you'll still need me to find the man he's covering for; it has to be someone he knew well and I'm not convinced he's going to give us the name, no matter how hard you interview him, ma'am.'

Fenwick blinked at Cooper's show of respect but noticed Nightingale took it for granted. He felt an unexpected rush of pride and decided to share the rest of his plans despite his usual caution.

'By the way, I've persuaded the ACC that we need do more than make a simple press announcement. We've been given a slot on *CrimeNight*.' He ignored their surprise. 'I've had MCS handle the preparation and filming and it will be aired Tuesday night, which is another reason to have news of the major's release out of the way today.'

'Morning, all. My word, you are early birds.' Superintendent Quinlan looked newly minted in the bright sunshine that flooded into the room when he opened the door.

'Ready, Andrew? The traffic's terrible. You can tell me what you've all concluded on the way.'

Early on Saturday afternoon Major Maidment was released from prison as the charges against him for murder were dropped. He was immediately rearrested and charged with being an accessory to Paul Hill's murder. The police request that he be remanded in custody, on the grounds that he might impede an ongoing investigation, was denied by a magistrate already furious about the previous erroneous charge. Maidment was given police bail on condition that he report to Harlden Police Station daily, starting that afternoon.

Inevitably, there was immediate news coverage of his release but the police statement made it very clear that he was still helping them with their inquiries. Maidment declined the offer of police protection, against their advice, just as he'd refused segregation whilst on remand. It was as if he felt that his innocence was protection enough.

The lads were delighted at his release but Bill made a point of repeating his offer to help if things went 'tits up' again. He'd been suitably grateful but non-committal. It wouldn't do to alienate Bill when he knew that he would probably end up in prison again and might need his help inside.

Maidment was required to go straight to Harlden Police Station, even though the smell of prison lingered in his hair and clothes. He travelled south by train, his mind a blank. At some stage he would have to make decisions but at that moment all he could do was breathe in freedom. The noise and space were intimidating yet he felt exhilarated. He chose to travel first class, in part to try and avoid public scrutiny but also because he had a *choice* for the first time in weeks and he wanted to take full advantage of it.

The smell from the takeaway coffee bar in Victoria made his mouth water. He wasn't a man who believed in eating or drinking in public but he couldn't resist the idea of real food. When he asked the waiter-chap for a coffee and a *pain au raisin* the man had looked at him quizzically but said nothing, though he thought the food and drink were slammed down on the counter rather hard. His mouth was watering as he walked to his train and he was embarrassed to find that his eyes were too. This wouldn't do; he had to be in control of himself when he saw the police, not snivelling like an emotional idiot. He stiffened his spine.

Despite his attempted bravado, his sense of paranoia increased the closer he travelled to Harlden. On the train he felt people stare at him but he was left alone to his great relief. He picked up a paper that had been left behind by a previous passenger but felt like a criminal when he came across his photograph on page five, alongside an article that rehashed the circumstances of his arrest. It was a good likeness and he felt even more conspicuous.

When the train reached Harlden his dread increased. Here he would surely be recognised. He pulled his hat a little lower than normal but refused to slouch and squared his shoulders. Nevertheless, the route he took to the police station was a circuitous one along quieter streets and through the park.

When a stone hit him between the shoulders blades he thought that something had fallen from a tree, but the sky above was empty.

'Fucking pervert!' The shout came from behind him.

He turned to see three boys about twenty yards away. They'd expected him to duck and run in response to their assault but instead he took a step towards them and raised his walking stick. One of them actually flinched before he turned and ran away. He'd only waved his stick, as he did when shooing Mrs Nichol's dog off his lawn, but they'd thought he meant them harm. The look of fear on the young boys' faces hurt him more than he would have imagined possible.

The major picked up his pace. As he walked through the gates to leave the park he stood back to let two women with baby strollers past. One spat on the ground by his feet.

Ahead was a stretch of open pavement then a wide public thoroughfare. He saw Mrs Perkins from church on the far side but she turned and went into a shop at the sight of him. The fact that it was Ladbrokes would normally have made him smile. In

West Street a middle-aged man muttered 'sick bastard' as he passed but he left him behind as he turned down Neal Yard to cut up to the police station. He could see its red bricks at the end of the road a hundred yards away and started to relax. The only obstacle that remained was a group of teenage girls waiting at a bus stop on the other side of the road.

As he strode past he was spotted. The whole gang swivelled in his direction. Their leader walked towards him and the others followed like a pack of hunting animals waiting for the signal. The major continued with an unbroken stride, his head high. They crossed the road to confront him.

'Fucking perv,' the lead girl shouted, spitting her words past the stud in her bottom lip. 'People like you should have their fucking balls cut off.'

Another girl bumped into him and his hand brushed her bare midriff as he tried to fend her off. He recoiled immediately but it was enough.

'He fuckin' touched me up, bastard ponce!'

By now all the girls had surrounded him, their elbows sharp against his ribs as he tried to back away. They started knocking their forearms into him, casually at first then with force. One spat in his face, smearing his glasses so that he could no longer see clearly. He felt a punch to his back, then another and his hat went flying. As he bent to retrieve it he was kicked hard on the thigh. A blow to the side of his face knocked his spectacles askew and out of the corner of an unprotected eye he saw long painted fingernails heading towards his face. He ducked to avoid the talons and was thumped on his kidneys. He winced at the pain and struggled against the instinct to fight back. No matter the provocation he could never strike a woman.

His fingers touched the brim of his hat as he stretched out to pick it up. One of them stamped on his hand. Spots of blood splattered the pavement. For the first time he realised they meant to do him serious harm. He tried to straighten up but a girl launched herself onto his back and he almost fell under her weight. If she forced him to the ground they'd be able to hold him there while their nails ripped him apart and their feet pummelled his body.

He tried to throw the girl off but she'd wrapped her arms about his neck, choking him so that he could barely breathe. The blows to his body became too numerous to note and his knees started to buckle. He fell forward and a booted foot caught him in the side of his chest forcing the air from his lungs.

'Oi! What's going on here?'

The voice was authoritative but the girls ignored it.

'Police! Let that man go right now.'

He felt the crush of bodies around him ease and took a deep breath. Pain shot across his chest and back. Looking up from the ground he saw two policemen pounding toward him. The girls ran off but one tripped and the leading officer grabbed her unceremoniously around the waist, lifting her off the ground.

'Oh no you don't! As long as we've got you we'll find your mates. Geoff, call this in.'

The creature he'd caught screamed and swore. She kicked out and tried to scratch but the officer held her tight while his colleague cuffed her hands behind her back.

'Less than a minute from the station and the dozy buggers haven't even noticed.' Geoff shook his head and bent down to help the major.

'Are you all right, sir? Why did they attack you?'

''Cos he's a fucking pervert, that's why. Fucking queer bastard should be locked up!'

Geoff helped him stand and passed him his hat.

'You're Major Maidment, aren't you?'

He nodded, not yet trusting his voice. The pain in his left side was agonising every time he tried to breathe.

'You'd better come with us. We can call an ambulance from the station if you need one. Will you be pressing charges?'

'No,' he whispered, shaking his head for emphasis, 'and no need for an ambulance, I shall be fine.'

'Even so, we need to get a doctor to look at you.' Geoff encouraged him along gently while his assailant was dragged, still screaming abuse, ahead of him and around to the main entrance to Harlden Police Station.

He waited patiently while a police doctor completed a none too gentle check of his cuts and bruises, inspected his pupils and tested his blood pressure.

'As far as I can make out you're lucky; minor contusions only. No blow to the head? Good. Well unless you start passing blood I should say you're fine. Take painkillers for any discomfort and you'll do.'

Of all the events that had beset him since he'd left the relative safety of prison, the contempt in the doctor's voice wounded him most.

From being early for his police interview he was now late. He was escorted to a room and given a cup of machine tea while somebody went in search of the inspector. While he was waiting, he closed his eyes and experimented with his breathing. As long as he took shallow breaths the pain was bearable. His spirits, already bludgeoned by his journey home, sank lower when Nightingale walked in followed by a young man he didn't know. She dispensed with the formalities quickly, confirming for the benefit of the tapes that he'd waived his right to have a solicitor present. Then she said nothing. After the business of the introductions he found the silence unnerving.

He didn't try to meet her eyes, knowing that he'd be likely to look away first and give her the advantage. Even so her gaze was disconcerting and eventually he glanced up without meaning to. As soon as their eyes met she shook her head. The look of pity on her face had an extraordinary effect on him. He felt his throat harden and his eyes grow moist. His gaze flicked away.

'Would you like another cup of tea? That one's gone cold.'

'Thank you.' Her concern confused him.

'Robin, could you arrange for the major to have a cuppa with milk and sugar, and I'll have a black coffee, please.'

When the door closed they were left alone, with only a uniformed officer standing like a statue out of sight behind him. A sense of intimacy grew in the continuing silence, adding to his feeling of displacement. He was annoyed with himself for letting her have this effect on him and spoke despite his resolve not to.

'I'm sure you're a busy woman, Miss Nightingale, and I too am anxious to return home. How may I assist you?'

'That's just it, Major, I don't know.' He stared at her in amazement. 'You see, I *know* that you're not guilty of harming Paul Hill.'

'I'm glad you've finally recognised my innocence.'

'I didn't say that now, did I?' She smiled, and although it was gentle he sensed that he'd allowed her to turn the conversation in the direction she wanted.

'Now look, Inspector, let's not descend to the level of semantics. You said that I didn't harm Paul Hill and in that you're quite right.'

'But that doesn't make you innocent. You disposed of his bloody clothes, you've wasted police time by impeding our inquiries and,' she paused to make sure that he was listening, 'you know the identity of Paul's killer yet refuse to tell us. That makes you an accessory to murder. That alone is enough to earn you a prison sentence.'

'I was *not* an accessory to Paul's death; I could never behave in such a manner!'

'There is such a thing as being an accessory *after* the fact, Major, and that is exactly what you are. The guilt is the same.'

'Rubbish! There's no way I would have assisted in that boy's death.' His uncontrolled indignation cost him a hot rush of pain as he forgot to control his breathing.

'And yet you have. By your silence at the time and your refusal to cooperate now, you're assisting the murderer.'

'Nothing I could have done would have saved Paul,' he said, furious that she'd goaded him into defending himself.

'Oh, I'm quite sure of that,' she said with that small, sad smile on her face again, 'but how do you know that the people you covered up for haven't harmed other boys?'

'People?'

'Didn't you know? We have evidence now that confirms that Paul was raped by four men before he was killed.'

'Raped?'

'Without question. You're protecting the identity of a child abuser as well as a murderer. I've met one of the victims, one who survived. There will be others.'

He was appalled but then realised they had another witness; he felt a wash of relief.

'So you don't need my testimony after all,' he whispered, trying to draw air into his lungs despite the pain in his chest.

'How dare you!' All trace of understanding vanished. 'You'd rather we put a damaged man through the trauma of recalling his childhood abuse than give up the sick bastard you're protecting?'

Maidment could hardly hear her. Blood drummed in his ears and the pain in his lungs was like fire. He could barely see as black flecks crowded his vision. She was shouting at him again but he couldn't hear her, let alone answer. His mouth opened and closed like a landed fish as his body screamed for oxygen and his arms and legs turned to jelly.

'I...' He tried to ask for help.

'Yes, go on, spit it out.' She was leaning over him, her breath warm on the chill of his face.

'I...' The words died in a groan as the band of pain about his chest tightened and choked him into silence. He slid off the chair and onto the cold of the floor, his legs unable to save him, his arms useless.

'Major? Major, are you all right?'

Her words were insubstantial as she loosened his tie. Somewhere an alarm was ringing faintly, then it faded to silence and all he was aware of was her face floating above him before that too vanished into the greyness that swallowed him up.

CHAPTER THIRTY-ONE

'Good grief, Nightingale, you didn't need to give the man a heart attack!'

Fenwick tried and failed to stop laughing. He'd left a message for her to join him in his Harlden office as soon as she came in on Sunday morning.

'It wasn't a heart attack. I thought it was as the time but the hospital says his ECG is fine. He's got fractured ribs and a collapsed lung. That, plus the anxiety of the interview, made him black out. He'll be in hospital for up to a week and then allowed home.'

'Assuming he wants to go. He was daft to refuse our protection. Have you been to his house?'

'Yes.' Nightingale shook her head. 'I don't like him but even I think it's gross what people will do just on suspicion. I thought a man was supposed to be innocent until proven guilty in this country.'

'But we both know that he's not innocent.'

'That doesn't matter. The people who desecrated his home should be locked up.'

'I agree, assuming he files a complaint but he may not. He's going to let the girls who attacked him get away with it.'

'I know.'

'It was looking like a good interrogation, by the way.'

'Thanks. I was pleased with it and I thought I was going to break him until he blacked out.'

'What do you propose to do now?'

'Visit him in hospital, continue the same line. I'm hoping that he sees the collapse as a close brush with death… I might even take a Bible with me.' She laughed but then grew serious. 'Can I ask you a question, off the record?'

'Go on.'

'Do you think we have any chance of finding Malcolm Eagleton's killer?'

'I wish you'd asked me another one. It's ironic; we have his body but no suspect or leads, yet with Paul we have no body and an abundance of evidence. If I'm honest I'm pinning my hopes on finding Paul's killer and then being able to link him to Malcolm's death.'

'It's a long shot. The Well-Wisher hasn't mentioned him at all.'

'I know but what else can we do? Maybe if we find the Well-Wisher he'll be able to tell us more. But why do you ask?'

Nightingale hesitated, opened her mouth, then shook her head imperceptibly; all signs Fenwick recognised so that he knew, when she spoke, he was only going to get a version of the truth.

'The last letter – "There was great evil in Harlden" – that phrase gives me the creeps.'

It was a lame explanation but he didn't press her.

'I know; I keep telling myself that we're much more sensitive to child crime these days but then you read the stories that keep emerging of long-term abuse and it's enough to test your faith in the system. We might have improved our techniques but the paedophiles have just become smarter. Look at us here in Sussex; if it hadn't been for the FBI tip-off we still wouldn't be aware of what was happening.'

'At least we're not dealing with a serial child killer. That we would have noticed!'

'You're right. In some ways the deaths don't fit at all. My theory is that they might have been accidental or part of a cover up, not sexually motivated.'

Nightingale just looked at him, scepticism etched on her face.
'You hope. Not that it makes things any easier for the parents.'

She glanced down at his desk and saw the missing persons'
photographs stacked to one side. He'd said nothing to the team
about following up on any of the current cases but she could tell
they preyed on his mind. Every time they talked about Paul or
Malcolm his eyes would stray to the pictures as if they pained
him. But the police could only become involved if there was
suspicion of a crime.

'Have you heard anything from the Met on the house Ball
visited in London?'

'They called yesterday; it's looking promising. The case has
been passed over to their specialist child protection squad and
they're keeping up surveillance. So far, all they have to go on is a
suspicious pattern of visits by single males but it's enough to keep
them interested.'

Fenwick picked up the school photograph of Paul and then
another that lay on top of the pile of what he thought of as his
lost boys.

'Who's that?' Nightingale asked gently.

'Sam Bowyer; don't you remember him? He ran away from
home earlier in the summer; hasn't been seen since.'

'He's very like Paul.'

'That's what struck me, but apart from his parents' conviction
that he's been abducted there's nothing for Brighton to go on.
And it may even be that he's simply run away. He packed a
rucksack, took all the money from his mum's purse and
deliberately played truant from school.'

'But?' He looked up at her quizzically. 'There's a but in your
face.'

Fenwick raised his eyebrows in rueful acceptance.

'But boys like Sam have to end up somewhere. They don't just
vanish. Here's another one, another Sussex lad who ran off to

London.' He passed her the picture. 'Jack, his name was. He killed himself in June; jumped into the Thames. They look so young, so innocent. But when the picture of Paul was taken he'd been a child prostitute for two years.'

Fenwick took the pictures back and studied Paul's eyes for a sign of what had been happening to him but found only a trace of mockery, as if Paul were enjoying a secret joke. Perhaps that's how he'd coped with the bitter reality of his life. If so, his self-esteem must have been rock bottom to allow him to treat his exploitation so lightly.

'Penny for them.'

'I was thinking about Paul, why his life ended up as it did, what he would have done had he lived.'

Nightingale had never told Fenwick that she'd been a runaway at one stage in her life; it was a secret of which she remained ashamed. But it had shaped her view of the world; toughened her skin and wiped out any tendency towards sentimentality.

'Paul would eventually have run away for good is my guess, and died young like Jack, an anonymous statistic in some urban nightmare. Which is probably where our abuser satisfies himself now. I don't think I could work Vice.' Nightingale shuddered.

'It wouldn't be my first choice either, particularly now that my children are getting older. I find it very hard not to think of them when I look at these files.'

Fenwick stopped himself. They'd drifted into the sort of half-personal conversation that had once been normal between them. He fussed with the papers on his desk, unaware that it was a certain sign of discomfort and that the smarter members of his team recognised it.

'Look, Nightingale, there's something I've been meaning to say for a while.' He kept his eyes on a memo on recycling rubbish that happened to be on the top of the paperwork he was suddenly so interested in.

'Go on.'

'It's, ah, well, you see, it's about...'

'Your erratic behaviour towards me?'

He looked up with something approaching relief.

'Yes, exactly.'

'Forget about it.'

'But I need to...that is, I'm sorry if I behaved...ah, badly at all.'

'Apology accepted.'

'Just like that?'

'Yes, why not? Andrew, let's just move on.'

Fenwick re-sorted his papers without seeing them. Eventually he said, 'That's it?'

'Isn't that enough?'

'Well, you haven't commented on our...friendship...outside work.'

'And I don't intend to. If you've taught me one lesson in the past few months it's not to mix business and pleasure. You can rest assured your message has been received and understood.'

Her words were all business, keeping him in his place. He reflected that she wasn't the only one who'd been taught a lesson the hard way.

Nightingale and Fenwick stood up at the same time and almost collided at the side of his desk. Their mutual embarrassment was interrupted by a brief knock on the door a fraction of a second before Cooper walked in.

'Oh, excuse me.'

'It's OK, we're just finishing. What is it?'

'Thought you'd better see this sharpish.' Cooper handed him a copy of the *Sunday Enquirer*.

Under an 'EXCLUSIVE' banner the headline read THE DAY MY PAUL DIED. The sub-head continued: '*An exclusive interview with Sarah, Paul Hill's grieving mother, the day after the police release*

his alleged killer from custody, continues pages 5, 7 and 8.
Suspect in hospital after police interrogation, page 3.'

'Oh great! Just what we need and they're suggesting the major had a heart attack during his interrogation in police custody. I need to brief Harper-Brown at once. Can you call the press officer at HQ, Nightingale; this will best be handled from there. Bloody Jason MacDonald.'

'You have to admit he's good though,' Nightingale said ruefully, memories of her own treatment at his hands still painful. 'I would've laid odds against Sarah Hill ever giving an interview about Paul, particularly one that accepts he's dead.'

'I'm not exactly in the mood to be impressed by that weasel's journalistic prowess when he's just wrecked the way I want to handle my case. This will be a massive distraction.'

Nightingale and Cooper backed out of his office and closed the door on a stream of muttered expletives.

'Shit's hit the fan now,' said Cooper, 'excuse my French.'

'No problem, I believe that's technically the accurate expression. We're going to be knee deep in the stuff before the day's over.'

They were. Everywhere the team went the people they tried to interview had an opinion about the police handling of Paul's disappearance and the subsequent arrest and release of Maidment. Fenwick called a meeting for five-thirty, more in an attempt to boost morale than in the expectation of any progress. It was a grim affair.

By six-thirty the whole team was in the Dog and Duck and he was buying. Over pints of best bitter he and Cooper commiserated with each other over their day. Aspects of the *Enquirer's* article were on the midday and six o'clock news and the ACC had been forced to hold a brief press conference in an attempt to deflect criticism by explaining that his SIO had made significant progress. As a result, Fenwick had been overwhelmed with calls, most of which he passed straight back to the press office. He'd decided to deal with only one directly, an interview with a BBC reporter for Radio Four, which baffled Cooper.

'Why did you go on air, guv? You said you were going to leave it to the PO.'

'I've been thinking about Maidment and Taylor.'

'Haven't we all.'

'Maidment's covering up for someone and we know it simply couldn't be a man like Taylor. So I went on the radio to say that we were pursuing additional promising lines of inquiry in the hope that it might rattle the murderer(s) badly enough to make them do something stupid.'

'Bit of a long shot, if you don't mind me saying.'

'I know, but you and the team are redoing all the interviews at the same time. That's why I said in the meeting just now, *don't* make it feel routine, make it feel special, as if there might be a reason we're interested in them.'

He could tell by Cooper's expression that he still wasn't convinced.

'It's all we've got, Bob, unless you can think of anything else?'

There was a long pause, which Fenwick interpreted as a struggle to find the words to disagree with him. He waited patiently, enjoying his beer, trying not to be amused.

'Thing is,' Cooper said at last, 'I've been wondering about the boy's family. They were barely considered suspects whereas these days we'd be all over them until we were sure.'

It was a good point and Fenwick was annoyed that he'd failed to consider it.

'That's fair.'

'And with Nightingale going to visit Malcolm's parents yesterday,' Cooper continued, missing Fenwick's expression of surprise, 'well, it put the thought into my mind, that's all.'

'And does she suspect the Eagletons of Malcolm's death?'

'Nope – she's convinced they're innocent. I think she just went along to reassure them that we were still treating his death seriously, that with all the hype over Paul we hadn't forgotten their son.'

'That was good of her,' Fenwick murmured, reassured that perhaps she hadn't become as hard as he'd feared.

'Well, she had to really – they were threatening to complain.' Cooper chuckled and Fenwick sighed.

'But about Paul's family, Bob,' he said, changing the subject, 'perhaps it's my turn to pay them a visit. I should meet Mr and Mrs Hill myself.'

It was well into Monday morning when Fenwick pressed the button to the right of the wooden front door for a second time. It looked as if Paul's father had done all right for himself, at least compared with the run-down semi where his ex-wife lived. He'd just come from there, and from one of the most disturbing interviews he'd ever conducted in his career.

He thought Mrs Hill was extremely unstable; that she might even need sectioning for her own good. The woman could hardly string a sentence together one minute and the next she was quoting Shakespeare or lines from obscure plays by Brecht. Fenwick knew they were from Brecht because Mrs Hill had told him so. He'd been worried enough to call social services immediately afterwards. They said that they would look into it when they could and he'd had to be satisfied with that. But he had left her house with his skin crawling and was trying to reach an itch between his shoulder blades when the front door swung open, apparently of its own accord.

'Can I help you?'

His eyes tracked down to the source of the voice. From one witch to another, he thought, but this one was as wide as she was tall, with a face that resembled an old leather glove left too long in the sun, surrounded by soft white curls that didn't quite cover the pink scalp.

'I'm looking for Mr Gordon Hill. I'm DCI Fenwick, I'm with the—'

'Police, it's written all over you. I'm his mother, Hannah Hill. You'd best come in.'

The old woman led Fenwick into a sitting room that was tastefully furnished in tan and burgundy leather, except for a faded paisley chair next to the fireplace.

'That isn't real, that fire. One of those gas things. More convenient, I grant you, but hasn't got the soul of a real fire if you know what I mean.'

'I do.' Fenwick liked Hannah Hill immediately despite his customary desire to remain neutral. 'Is your son at home?'

'No, the whole family are out today: that's Gordon, Michelle, his second wife – lovely girl, she is – and the two kiddies. Gone to the beach and good luck to them. I'm sure they'll enjoy it but it's not for me. The days of wanting to feel sand between my toes have been replaced by a simple urge to have any feeling in the damn things. And anyway, the racing's on this afternoon and I've got twenty quid on Paul's Delight to win. Coffee?'

Fenwick hesitated. His body was crying out for caffeine but in his experience an old person's idea of coffee was to show a kettle to the Nescafé jar and then drown any flavour that struggled to survive with too much skimmed milk.

'I make it properly, trust me,' Hannah laughed, 'though I don't blame you for being careful. Some of the stuff as gets served up at the centre is enough to turn you to drink. Talking of which it's...' she glanced at the clock on the mantelpiece which read ten twenty-three, '...almost eleven o'clock and I'm not due my medicine yet. Fancy a snifter? Good stuff, five star.'

'I'm driving, thanks all the same.'

'Suit yourself but you won't mind if I do, will you?'

They went to sit in the sunny dining area that ran from the kitchen to sip strong black coffee, one with and one without a shot of brandy. Sunlight angled across the tiled floor onto the back of a black and white cat that was purring in the heat.

'I realise that this might seem strange after all this time but—'

'You're here to ask about Paul. I saw on the news how you had to let the major go. I'm glad. He didn't look like a killer to me.'

He was taken aback by the woman's attitude. Where he had expected anger he had found relief instead.

'But you want us to find your grandson's killer, don't you, Mrs Hill?'

'It's Hannah and no, I don't. See, I've got something to tell you...'

And she did, at length. Hannah Hill repeated her story, word for word, enjoying his undivided attention. Fenwick tried to look respectful, even interested, but after the first few sentences he tuned out, realising that he had committed himself to wasting fifteen minutes of his time because of his urge for a decent coffee.

The listening stretched on; the cat went to sleep. Fenwick finished his coffee, made his excuses and left. Mrs Hill watched him go, smiling a little sadly, and then went to take her medicine.

Cooper and Nightingale were waiting for him in his temporary Harlden office to help him prepare a progress report for the ACC. Alison and Clive joined by phone. Fenwick told them of his fears for Sarah Hill's sanity but didn't bother to mention his frustrating meeting with her ex-mother-in-law. He was more certain than ever that the family hadn't been involved in Paul's disappearance. His father apparently had a solid alibi, the grandparents had been busy in London and the mother was genuinely deranged with grief, not guilt.

Cooper was making slow progress cross-checking those interviewed in 1982 with the major's list of army acquaintances and Nightingale's day hadn't been much better.

'Oliver Anchor wasn't at home when I called and his mother virtually threw me out of the house. There's definitely something going on there. I'll need a warrant to get Oliver's medical records because his doctor isn't going to release them without one and as yet I haven't enough to persuade a magistrate. But I've traced and spoken to some of Oliver's friends from school. I got their names from Paul's file. They told me Oliver was slow but otherwise fine until Paul disappeared then he had some sort of breakdown and was taken out of school completely. Oh, and I tried to interview the major again but was refused by his doctor. Said he was too poorly and to phone back before I visit again so as not to waste time.'

'Not your day with the medical profession.'

'Damn right.'

'Clive, how about you?' Fenwick directed his voice to the conference phone.

'We've found a piece of old tyre at the copse that I've sent to the lab. Nothing else.'

'Alison?'

'We're working through all the images taken from Watkins and Ball's storage units. There are over ten thousand of them and we're at the stage of simply sorting them into categories – those where the child is potentially recognisable, those where there are distinguishing features on the adult that might lead us to identify them and those where the background might tell us where the photo or video was taken. We've found one picture of what might be Ball's tattoo but that was the highlight of the day. It's going to be painstaking work and it's frankly disgusting. I've had to excuse two of the team, they simply couldn't cope.'

'Have you spoken to the Child Internet Protection Unit? They have lots of experience and they might even be willing to loan us an expert.'

'They called me,' Alison replied. 'Our technical support team is meant to log any Internet-related paedophile material so I've made sure they're following procedure.'

Fenwick finished the call, glad that Alison had done the right thing, but his face was grim as he looked up at the familiar faces of his old teammates.

'The long and the short of it is we're one day on and no further forward.' Fenwick took a long swallow of cold coffee. 'Oh joy. The ACC's going to love this. We just have to hope that *CrimeNight* on Tuesday will give us the leads we need.'

PART FIVE

The three men watched as the car burnt. A smell of gasoline mingled with the throat-catching stench of melting rubber, almost masking the sickly sweet smell of roasting flesh.

No one spoke. The time for recriminations and the apportionment of blame would come. For now they were united by the need to cover up a crime and destroy the evidence.

'Twenty-four hours and it should be cool enough to break up. We can use the old silage pit on the farm; it's abandoned and I can fill it in later.'

The older man, Nathan, spoke in a manner that suggested he was used to giving orders and being obeyed.

'We'll need transport.' Of the three the tall man who called himself Joe was least comfortable. His eyes looked everywhere except at the corpse.

'No problem. I have a trailer and jeep but I'm concerned about clearing up where it happened. Alec, I want you to go over there. Bryan's given us directions and it's better that a new face shows up; someone not known around here.'

Alec pulled his eyes reluctantly from the body in the car. The raised clenched fists, black against the flames in the interior, fascinated him.

'It looks like he's fighting it,' he said, almost in awe of the power of the body in death.

'Read your textbooks.' Nathan was dismissive. 'It's called the pugilistic pose. The tendons tighten in the heat. Have you never seen a man baked in a tin?' His casual reference to death in the oven of a tank on fire made Joe turn away.

'Now get going. Bryan was hardly in a state to give us comfort that he didn't leave something behind. We'll meet at the house in three hours.'

He turned abruptly and walked away, leaving the two men to stare at each other. They waited until he'd disappeared from view until they spoke.

'Arrogant prick! He doesn't change, does he? Sometimes I think about putting him in his place, just once.'

'Forget it, Alec. He's the boss, like it or not. Anyway, this isn't the time to argue. We need each other.'

'Maybe,' Alec didn't sound convinced, 'but if he'd chosen a better boy we wouldn't be here now. He landed us with a little piss ant fighter. Prissy bastard; he deserved everything he—'

'Shut up! Can't you leave it alone? You've done nothing but complain since we arrived. If you hadn't been so rough with the boy maybe we wouldn't be here now with this...' he gestured helplessly towards the car, '...cock-up,' he finished, his words a whisper.

'So now it's all my fault, is it? Bloody typical. You don't blame Bryan for failing to get rid of him when he had the chance; or Nathan for scaring him near to death in the pool. Oh no, it's me again; always fucking me. It pisses me off.'

His fists clenched and took a step towards Joe.

'Calm down, Alec. We've all had a hand in this. I just meant that...' He paused, lost for words. 'Never mind, forget I said it. You're right, it was a cock-up from start to finish.'

'Bloody right. What say you we just clear off right now, leave him to clear up his own mess?'

The same idea had occurred to Joe but he'd rejected it. Their best chance of getting away with what they'd done would be if the car and the body were never discovered. They were burning it miles from where Bryan had told them...it had happened. Even now, he couldn't quite believe the mess they were in and he certainly couldn't bring himself to name their crime.

'No. Our best chance is to stick together, like in the old days. None of us will talk and there's a real possibility they'll never *find the boy. Even if they do there won't be anything left to link him to us.'*

'His parents will miss him. How do we know that they won't tell the police that Paul was friends with Bryan?'

'Ssh!' Even in the solitude of the woods Joe looked over his shoulder at the mention of Paul and Bryan's names.

'He told us never to mention him again, not even among ourselves. Look,' he glanced at his watch, 'you'd best get over to Wyndham Wood like he said and make sure it's all clear while it's still light.'

'Don't you try to give the fucking orders now!' Alec moved in, closing the gap between their chests. Joe raised his hands, palms out – 'peace'.

'OK, OK but you'll do a better check than I will.'

Alec shrugged and lit a cigarette. When he'd smoked enough to demonstrate his independence he left without a word. His companion stayed behind and waited for the flames to die down. Only then did he turn his eyes to the front passenger seat. To his relief the silhouette was crumbling. Ashes to ashes.

CHAPTER THIRTY-TWO

He listened to the two messages a second time as he swirled the ice around his glass, chilling the whisky. They'd been waiting for him on his return from a three-day golfing break.

'Maidment here. I must see you. They've just let me out. The old charges against me have been dropped but they've rearrested me as an accomplice. Look, you promised me it was an accident but...' There was a long pause and the listener could imagine Maidment 'getting to grips', as he'd have put it. The pips went and there was the sound of movement. *'...There's more but I don't want to leave it on that damn machine. Call me at home when you get this.'*

The man had no intention of calling. He knew the police could requisition phone records. They might even have a tap at Maidment's house if they suspected him of being an accomplice. He deleted the message and drank deeply, enjoying the feel of the spirit as it burnt its way down his throat. That was one of the many joys of living a single life. When his wife had finally had enough and left him he'd felt nothing but relief. Even though they'd barely seen each other towards the end of their sham of a marriage the fact that she was around somewhere had always depressed his spirits. Now he was alone and enjoyed every hour of his freedom.

He took another drink, draining the glass except for the clinking ice, and rose to pour another measure. The bottles of spirit were arranged on a trolley to the side of French windows that looked out on his magnificent garden. After leaving the army he'd invested his savings wisely in both legal and illegal ventures. The illegal investments in particular had done well and he could afford the large house and the services of the married couple who saw to his needs while remaining virtually invisible. Just the way he liked it.

He refreshed his glass and added another ice cube from the insulated bucket that was filled daily at five-thirty by the housekeeper before she left, his supper already cooking slowly in the kitchen. His drinks had to be ice cold, a habit he'd fallen into while in the tropics. As he waited for the liquor to chill he stared out at the swimming pool, covered now for the evening.

Maidment's message echoed in his mind. He'd sounded most unlike himself and that had worried him even before he'd listened to the second call. Perhaps he should have moved years ago, put some distance between himself and the past. That he hadn't done so he realised was partly due to pride. He had a name in the local community and he was damned if he was going to let some scruffy tart of a boy drive him away because of an accident.

It was an accident, he told himself. The kid had been feisty and rebellious from the moment he'd arrived. Trust Bryan Taylor to screw up so badly. There was nothing to link them, he'd made very sure of that, and no physical evidence remained. He'd watched it burn, and then Joe and Alec had helped him to pulverise and bury the ash. Ball was now safely beyond the reach of the police and Joe – or Joseph as he now insisted on calling himself, as if a return to his biblical name could somehow expunge his guilt – well, Joe's arrest had been a huge shock. He'd been preparing his finances, ready to leave the country, when a chance remark at the golf club had reassured him. 'Poor old Joseph' had had a complete, and probably irreversible, breakdown and was under sedation in a prison hospital, barely conscious. How he'd laughed about that when he'd returned to the privacy of his home! Now, there was only Maidment left to worry about.

He should remain safe provided Maidment kept his head. Even the second message need not be a cause for concern. He turned around and walked back to his machine. The disembodied voice that filled his drawing room had the unmistakable lilt of a local Sussex accent.

'Ah, this is Sergeant Cooper here. I wonder if I might come and see you, sir. It's in connection with the disappearance of Paul Hill. You were interviewed at the time and I know we've re-interviewed you since but there are some additional questions we now need to ask.'

Cooper had signed off by leaving his telephone number and a request that his call be returned as soon as possible. The question was, should he do so or stall for more time? It would be useful to know what Maidment had to say before he spoke to the police again but on the other hand to delay might look suspicious. He sipped his drink ruminatively then reached out towards the receiver. The phone rang as he touched it, making him jump and slosh whisky onto his favourite rug, the one he'd bought in Tashkent.

'Sod it.'

He let the machine pick up.

'It's me again, Maidment. Look I—'

'Yes, what do you want?' His tone was brusque.

'I left you a message.'

'I've heard it.'

'I...yes, nurse, I'll only be a minute...I'm in hospital, not meant to use the phone at all today but I needed to talk to you.'

'About?' He didn't bother to ask why Maidment was in hospital or to wish him well. In fact it would be convenient if the old sod died, quite frankly.

'While I was being interviewed by the police they asked me some odd questions, very odd. Do you recall that you needed a new parking permit the first year I was secretary?'

'What? Have you received a blow to the head?'

'The permit – you needed a new one.' Maidment was insistent.

'You really do have the most ridiculous memory for trivia.'

'It was in August 1981. I need to know for sure.'

'I have no idea. Why?'

'Well, the police asked me whether I'd issued any replacements.'

The glass in his hand had grown so cold that his fingers turned white. He stared at them as he tried to ease his grip.

'What did you say to them?'

'That I might have done but couldn't be certain.'

'I fail to see the significance of this.'

'But the thing is they asked about *1981*.' The major's voice dropped to a whisper. 'The Hill boy vanished in 1982 so it couldn't have been connected with that.'

'Exactly.'

'But another boy disappeared in 1981, didn't he?' The voice was so low he could barely hear it. 'The boy whose remains they found earlier this year; his name was Malcolm Eagleton.'

Mention of the name ran like a shockwave through his body. The glass fell in slow motion from his numbed fingers and bounced on the carpet without breaking. He watched as the contents spilt out in a widening stain across his rug.

'Did you hear me? I need to know, did you have anything to do with his death?'

'I heard you. This is absolute nonsense. For heaven's sake, get a grip, man. Say nothing to the police until we've spoken face to face. When can that be?'

'They want to keep me in a week—'

'Call me from a payphone as soon as you're out of hospital

and we can agree where to meet up.' The ice was starting to melt. It would leave a water mark. 'In the meantime, don't bother phoning me again.'

As he replaced the receiver his hand was shaking. He really should get a cloth and mop up the spill but he didn't move. Part of his mind regretted the irreparable damage to a unique and valuable antique but even as it did so another part was calculating how quickly he would be able to leave all this behind and start afresh if he had to.

He cleared the answerphone tape and pulled it out to destroy. All the time his mind, usually so cold and logical, was spinning at the implications of what Maidment had said. He'd almost forgotten the Eagleton boy, considering him an early, clumsy mistake. It was Paul who had dominated his thinking for the past twenty-five years; Paul who had become idealised as the perfect boy in his fantasies; and Paul whom he had always considered his likely nemesis. Not silly Malcolm, who'd turned out to be such a disappointment.

There was now no question of returning the police call until he had spoken to Maidment but he would need a reason to explain why he'd ignored it. He was only just back from his long weekend. Perhaps if he went away again at once it would work as an excuse. But where?

The idea when it came to him brought a smile to his face. Not only would he be able to lie low for a few days he would also be able to indulge himself with his latest boy for as long as he liked. If time was running out and he'd have to move on, he reasoned, there was no longer any need to go easy on young Sam, was there? Once he'd finished with him it really didn't matter what happened next but it would satisfy his innate possessiveness to know that nobody else would be able to enjoy him. Decision made, he went in search of a cloth in an attempt to rescue his precious rug.

CHAPTER THIRTY-THREE

Hospital routine suited the major; an early start, a limited menu of meals that offered sustenance rather than a lottery of gastronomic experimentation and lights out at a decent hour. It was just like the army except that he had no responsibilities other than to get well. Of course, there was the disturbance of visitors to be accommodated, not that he'd received many in the thirty-six hours since he had been admitted.

Margaret Pennysmith had brought an extravagant basket of fruit that he knew she could ill afford and the gesture had touched him. Her visit had been far more enjoyable than he would have thought a month ago. She wasn't put off by the ward with its groans and the staring eyes from some of the other beds. And now that she knew him better she no longer indulged in the sort of mindless chatter that had previously passed for conversation. To his surprise they'd discussed current affairs and her opinions extended beyond a reprise of tabloid editorial. From a discussion of the continuing fighting in the Middle East they'd moved easily to the parallels with his own experiences when in the army. She was a good listener. When the nurse came to announce the end of visiting time they'd both been surprised and he'd found himself disappointed when she left.

She gave him a card. Inside he found not only her good wishes but also those of others at the church who still had faith in him, or perhaps who considered him forgiven. There were precious few names but the minister's was there, which meant that he should expect a visit later. He propped the card up on the nightstand next to the telegram from his son and his daughter-in-law in Australia. Nobody from the golf club had made contact. It saddened but did not surprise him and he was honest enough to know that his reaction in reversed circumstances would probably have been similar.

The doctors had kept the police away to give him time to rebuild some of his strength. They'd told him that they wanted to keep him in for up to six days but he thought that excessive even though he was now dreading a return to the house. Margaret had told him straightforwardly (he would have resented any pussyfooting about) that it had been vandalised. She and the friends who still believed in him had done their best to clean up but she confessed some of the damage was beyond their ability to repair.

No, he was in no hurry to go home. The time in hospital was almost a gift, a respite from an unfriendly world and an opportunity to think. The police would soon be allowed to visit now that he'd had a day of complete rest. Before then there was much to sort out in his mind. He could remember everything of the last interrogation. Each word had cut into him and awoken the guilt he carried. She was smart. Inspector Nightingale had virtually dismissed his involvement in Paul's death and that had thrown him off guard. None of his prepared defences had worked against her flanking assault. Her accusation that he'd somehow aided a serial child abuser and killer had taken his breath away even before his lung collapsed. If she were correct then no amount of good deeds could wipe out the guilt he must bear.

Was she right? His phone calls had been rash and worse than useless. With no facial expression to provide him with a clue he'd been left straining to detect guilt or evasion in tone alone. As a result he'd ended up analysing every word, every pause or quickly drawn breath. Even now he found himself replaying the conversation over and over again as he lay silently in his bed.

It was the replacement parking permit that disturbed him most. Locker keys were lost regularly but not stickers that attached to the inside of a windscreen. The only time they were loose was when they were newly issued, in August each year. Malcolm Eagleton was taken in August and killed. Even if he could persuade himself that Paul's death had been an accident the coincidences surrounding Malcolm's murder wouldn't go away. And if Malcolm had been taken by someone from Harlden golf club then there was only one man he knew for certain had been involved in Paul's death. Was it likely that two such men co-existed in a single golf club? He didn't think so and that meant that...

The major stopped his thoughts from spinning. There was one big question, he told himself, and these other concerns were a distraction. Was he in any way guilty, even inadvertently, of protecting a killer of young boys who'd gone on to abuse and slaughter more?

The question buzzed inside his mind, distracting him from the incidental noises in the ward. When DCI Fenwick had challenged him about his involvement in the other death he'd dismissed the questions easily. He was innocent and at the time could see no connection between Malcolm Eagleton and Paul's murder but in prison the invisible seeds of doubt had taken root and begun to grow. Prison contained so much pure evil that it had opened his eyes to the fact that seemingly ordinary people were capable of foul acts beyond his comprehension. In battle he had witnessed horror but he'd somehow linked it to the circumstance of war. He could believe that hostilities brought out the worst in people but not peace.

With hindsight he realised that his naïve faith in a fellow officer had been self-imposed. All his rationalisation about duty and loyalty had been so much icing on a bitter, dark cake of guilt that was of his own making. Percy had manipulated him very cleverly. He'd known that he would do him the favour of disposing of the incriminating items because of the hold he'd had over him since discovering his bigamy. Percy had used it well while they were still in the regiment together, to advance his own career and even, on one occasion, to block Maidment's own advancement. So a phone call asking him to help dispose of some embarrassing items before his wife returned had been a simple matter to accept.

Percy's thinly veiled threats to reveal his bigamy had been the real reason he'd remained silent despite the growing realisation that he had helped in the cover-up of the death of a child. And now the police interviews had stripped him of his protective self-delusion. When the lady inspector had started her recent attack he'd been without the armour of blind innocence. He groaned.

'Are you all right, Major? Can I get you some painkillers? You're perfectly entitled to them, you know.' The charming nurse paused at the foot of his bed, carrying a urine bottle undisguised by the cloth draped over it.

'No, I'm perfectly fine thank you, Nurse Shah.'

'There's no need to suffer discomfort.' She smiled at him in a way that brought a lump to his throat and he cursed the loss of control he kept experiencing.

'Really, no, but thank you.' He coughed to clear his throat and tried not to wince at the pain that lanced across his ribs.

Dear, oh dear, he needed to get a grip. There were important decisions to be made, and quickly. He'd given his word never to speak about Paul's death to anyone and he never had, not even to his wife, not even when he'd watched the press conference given by the boy's parents. Their grief had been terrible, his guilt suitably awful, but he had kept silent, telling himself that there was nothing he could do to bring the boy back.

Over the years the guilt had started to fade and with it the compulsion to reveal what he knew. It was precious little, after all. He'd never seen the body, only the boy's clothes. A bloody blazer and trousers weren't proof of death and they had been buried under tons of rubble and concrete before he realised their significance. At the time he'd thought their disposal foolproof, now he cursed the fact that he hadn't thrown them away at the municipal tip.

When he'd pulled the sack from his car boot and it had torn on the catch he had gone to find another. It had been a cloudy night and the lights for the club car park were on a timer to save money, so he'd walked to the kitchen in the dark, confident of the familiar route. He'd forgotten the builders' rubble that tripped him up and lacerated his palms so that his blood fell onto the new sack.

When he returned to the car he'd followed its interior lights, his own sight adjusted to the night. That's when he'd noticed the contents of the bag for the first time. The school crest on the blazer pocket was instantly recognisable, as were the splashes of crimson across it, to an old soldier who was used to seeing blood on a uniform. He'd pulled the jacket out to study and felt the sticky dampness of the felted fabric. One sniff was enough to confirm it was blood. His first reaction was confusion. He knew that there had to be a rational explanation but he hadn't been able to think of one.

He'd been asked to dispose of some 'embarrassing rubbish – so the wife doesn't see it'. He'd thought he was removing a kinky costume or sex toys. Confronted by the sight of bloodstained clothing, he'd put everything into the new sack and driven back to Percy's immediately. He was met at the front door and ushered straight into the study. The radio was on and he'd time to hear a news flash about a missing local boy before it was switched off. It had turned his thoughts to ice and made him decide that he had to be direct.

'Are you involved in that boy's disappearance? Did you give me his clothing to dispose of?'

Percy had simply nodded.

'Good God, man, what were you thinking? We must go to the police.'

'No. You don't understand. That boy, Paul Hill, was a nasty piece of work. He'd been blackmailing a friend of mine who was stupid enough to become involved with him. My friend brought him here so that I could persuade Paul to stop. He thought that my authority might impress the boy.'

'But he's missing and this blood... Is he dead?' He'd collapsed into a chair.

Percy said nothing.

'Is he?'

'I believe so, yes.'

'How did he die?'

'My friend said it was a terrible accident. Paul carried a knife, a vicious-looking thing, and he started showing off with it, to prove he wasn't scared, I suppose. I don't know how it happened but somehow he cut himself and then ran off. It wasn't a deep cut but about an hour later my friend was back here saying Paul had bled to death right on the edge of my wood.'

As he told his story Percy poured them both large whiskies; he'd thought it odd even then that his friend's hands weren't shaking.

'I promised to help him. He was an old comrade. There was no way I could abandon him.'

'Why on earth didn't you go to the police? It was an accident, they would've seen that. Your reputation is such that you'd be believed. It's not too late, we can still call them.'

'No!' Percy started to pace. 'It's not that simple. There's a man's reputation to consider, a decent man who's done a lot of good for this community. I've given him my word.'

'But he can explain. To do otherwise is madness.'

'You don't understand. I said that Paul was a blackmailer, what do you think he'd been blackmailing my friend about?'

'I have no idea but that doesn't matter, it will simply help your friend's case if the boy was a criminal.'

'My God, you are dense at times. Think, man! What is there between a grown man and a teenage boy that might give rise to blackmail?'

Maidment recalled the shock of those words, the rush of embarrassment and repulsion that must have shown on his face.

'Exactly. If it came out it would ruin my friend.'

'How old was Paul?'

'That's irrelevant. He was a teenager; a manipulative lying little bastard from a bad home who got what was coming to him and I simply will not let him ruin a decent man's life.'

'But it was an accident. The police will realise that when they examine the body; they have ways of telling.'

'We disposed of the body. What do you think they'll make of that?'

'You disposed of it? But that just looks guilty. Why?'

'It was a panic reaction. I accept that it's an odd way for innocent men to behave but it was my friend's idea and I went along.'

'You can explain all of that to the police.'

'You really are an innocent, aren't you? It's quite extraordinary for a man in your position. Anyway, I told you we disposed of it.'

'Dig it up.'

'Impossible, we burnt it.'

'What? But...but...' He'd been at a loss for words.

'Exactly. There is now no proof that his death was accidental. Do you really think the police will believe us?'

Maidment had thought for a long time. His whisky was

topped up and he finished the glass without thinking.

'We must still go to the police,' he'd said eventually.

'And tell them what exactly?'

'What you've just told me. It will be difficult, I accept, but there's no alternative.'

'What proof do I have to back up the story?'

'I'll support you, of course, tell them exactly what's happened.' Maidment had looked Percy in the eye to reinforce the strength of his offer. What he saw there made him shudder. Percy regarded him with a mixture of contempt and amusement.

'What does your word count for, Jeremy? If they knew the truth about your past, about your own little adventure with a girl who turned out to be underage—'

'She was not, not by the standards of the tribe. And I had no idea...'

Maidment shuddered as he remembered his own lame excuses. Percy had enjoyed his moment of cringing embarrassment, then said, so coldly it had made Maidment shiver, 'And anyway, why should I get dragged into this at all?'

'I don't understand.'

'Think about it. You arrive at my house late at night in a state. In the boot of your car you have a sack containing bloodstained boy's clothing with your fingerprints all over it. You won't find mine there, I wore gloves. As far as the physical evidence goes, and you know how our police just love "hard evidence", you're guiltier than I am.'

'But you'd vouch for me, surely.'

'Can't. I've given my word already. Much as I'd like to help you, old man, I'd have to stay quiet. Shall we call the police now? I assume you have an alibi for the whole afternoon and evening to put you in the clear?'

He hadn't. Percy's hand had hovered over the phone.

'Wait. I need to think.'

'Not so sure about the infallibility of our famed judicial system now, are you?' Percy had laughed.

'I don't know what to do.'

'It's simple, do nothing. I'll give you my word never to reveal what you've done and you must give me your solemn oath to do likewise. Go home, dispose of the bag, clean out your car and have a good bath before bed.'

'But a boy's dead.'

'By accident, not our fault and he's no loss to anybody, trust me.'

'His parents...they'll be devastated. They need to be told. All this uncertainty...'

'What can you tell them? The boy's dead but there's no body? I certainly can't do anything so it's down to whatever you think you can say, which is not a lot. You weren't even there when it happened. No, Jeremy, the best thing is to do nothing and keep quiet.'

He hadn't been able to bring himself to speak but had nodded and Percy had insisted they shake hands on their mutual pledge.

During his drive back he'd been terrified of being stopped by the police. When he saw the foundation hole at the club it had been the easiest thing in the world to drop the sack into it and throw a layer of rubble on top. Then he'd gone home, avoided his wife, vacuumed the car and taken a bottle of whisky into the bathroom with him. The next day his hangover had been so bad that he'd barely been able to think. Somehow he'd managed to get through the interminable meetings and a dinner in the evening, and so the first day had passed, almost easily. The following day was the same, then the next and soon a week of silence had gone by.

Weeks became months, months eventually years. He sometimes tried to tell himself it had been a bad dream but his conscience never allowed him to believe that. But he told himself so often that there had been no other way out of the problem that he had ended up believing his own logic. When it came, Hilary's illness had felt like a punishment for his sins, extracted from her. With her pain and slow, lingering death the guilt returned. He'd retired, giving up an occupation he'd thrived on to be with her. There had been hours of simply waiting by her bedside with only his guilt for company. He thought that he might have a breakdown but he'd survived; to escape into madness was a release he couldn't allow himself. Instead he'd waited, suffered with her and prayed.

When she died, at two o'clock on one sunny spring afternoon in her own bed, he had sat by her for hours. He told her then what he'd done and begged her forgiveness. Then he'd prayed for her soul, held her for the last long, long time, kissed her and made the phone call that took her away from him for ever.

By her grave he'd made a silent pledge to do good for the rest of his life in some poor penance for his sins and in the hope of avoiding hell so that he could, after his time in purgatory, be with her again.

'I really do think you should take some painkillers, Major Maidment.' Nurse Shah was standing beside his bed.

He quickly wiped his face and tried to smile. 'I was dozing. It was a bad dream, that's all.'

'Didn't sound like it to me. You don't need to suffer, you know,' she said as she walked away.

'Oh yes I do,' he whispered and closed his eyes.

'We've wheeled him into a side ward so you can have some privacy,' the nurse said.

Nightingale and DC Stock followed her into the room where the major sat up straight in the only occupied bed.

'Good morning, Major.'

He observed that she chose not to sit in the low visitor's chair, nor pretend an interest in his health. Unexpectedly, he started to like her.

'Good morning, Miss Nightingale.'

Neither of them had need for small talk.

'I have relatively few questions but they're important ones.'

He nodded an acknowledgement.

'I would remind you that this is a murder investigation, the victim little more than a child, no taller than five feet and one inch tall when he died. Whatever you might have heard or been told about Paul Hill you should not take at face value. Consider instead the motives of whomever it is you've chosen to protect and think very hard about that person. Can you be sure that they were telling the truth? Are they worth your good name? Do they deserve your loyalty?'

She paused to let the words sink in but he was ready for her. These questions, and others in a similar vein, had kept him awake all night. No, that wasn't correct. It was the answers that had prevented rest. In the early morning hours he'd finally stripped away comfortable layers of delusion to reveal the straightforward truth: he had been conned by a liar. He no longer believed that Percy had been protecting a friend but his own neck. He'd been a dupe, a fall guy too stupid to realise his mistake, but that didn't mean he was about to tell the police anything.

They were pretending now that they thought him innocent of Paul's murder but he suspected it was a ruse. Once he confessed to any knowledge they'd pounce on him, accuse him of killing the boy and have their case made. Percy would do what he'd threatened to do years ago and deny all knowledge while revealing his own crime of bigamy.

He'd been stupid enough to be fooled once in this affair and it wasn't about to happen again. Overnight he had decided to hold his tongue and settle the matter in his own way.

'My first question is simple. Do you know who killed Paul Hill?'

In the silence that followed they became aware of hospital noises, the clatter of trolleys, squeaky rubber soles on the linoleum and in the distance what might have been a muffled moan.

'Do you think this person is capable of other crimes against teenage boys?'

She was determined, he would give her that, but he evinced no indication that he had even heard her.

'Is there anything you can tell me that will help me find this man and make sure he's put away for life?'

Controlled too; despite the fact that she'd been forced to delay her interview she showed no emotion as she waited out the next pause.

'We know what happened in Borneo, Major. We have traced your "wife" – I suppose I can call her that. It was easy, she still uses your name and the regular payments from your bank account led us straight to her.'

Maidment stared at her in shock. Yet again she had managed to wrongfoot him.

'The crime of bigamy carries a prison sentence, you know, as does sex with an underage girl.'

'It was forty years ago!' he managed to say, though he was finding it hard to breathe.

'She didn't marry again, despite your money. Apparently, she never gave up hope that you would go back for her and your son. Who knows what she might do in revenge?'

He had to look away, unable to face the contempt in her face. If they already knew his secret did it mean that Percy had told them? Or had they found it by going through his bank statements? He didn't know what to do and found himself struggling to keep calm.

'What's going on here?' The registrar was standing behind them, looking at Maidment with consternation. 'I told you five minutes of *easy* questioning, not a full-scale interrogation. Nurse!'

Nurse Shah hurried to the major's bedside and lifted his wrist to take his pulse. The look she gave Nightingale would have made Maidment laugh if he hadn't been feeling so weak.

'He had a very disturbed night, Doctor,' she said, angling her body to break Nightingale's visual hold on her patient.

'You must leave,' the registrar ordered them.

'But this man has vital information related to a murder investigation. It is imperative that we question him.'

'Can't you see he's too ill to speak? I will not have him interrogated to the point of collapse again. Out.'

'But he's required to—'

'I don't care what he's meant to do, for whom or why. While he's in hospital he is my responsibility and it is my authority that decides when *and if* he can answer questions. You've done quite enough damage for today.'

Nightingale realised he wasn't going to back down and nodded to Constable Stock to go.

'We'll be back tomorrow, Major. Concentrate on getting better, won't you. We need you alive.'

Nurse Shah placed a protective hand on the major's arm.

In the car park outside DC Stock couldn't hold his tongue. 'Well, that was a total waste.'

Nightingale ignored the implied criticism as Stock's opinion mattered little to her. It was the sort of error of judgement that she'd learn to correct in time.

'It doesn't matter.' She walked to the driver's side of the car. 'Throw me the keys, I'll drive. His conscience almost betrayed him into breaking his word once. He may have stepped back from doing so but it won't let him rest. If he doesn't talk to us it's because he's decided to handle the matter in his own way. And we'll be there when he does. Get in.'

She found Cooper as soon as she was back in the station.

'Bob, I want the twenty-four-hour watch on Maidment to continue when he goes home. You're to supervise it personally. He's meant to be in hospital for another few days but I'm betting he'll check himself out early so be careful you don't lose him before you begin. I think he's going to lead us to our killer.'

CHAPTER THIRTY-FOUR

As always, the *CrimeNight* presenters were professional and determined to do everything they could to help the police. Fenwick was given twelve minutes of airtime. It had taken a combined BBC and MCS team two man-days to prepare – two working hours for every minute on air – but it was worth it.

Woven into the piece were references to the car Oliver Anchor saw burning the night Paul vanished and the abuse of Sussex boys in the early 1980s. He appealed to men who might have been victims to come forward, promising complete confidentiality. The culmination of the slot was an instruction for the writer of the anonymous letters to come forward.

The call-in number received fifty calls within thirty minutes and over one hundred by midnight. Many were from people who suspected neighbours or workmates of abusing children; every one was treated as if it might lead to Paul or Malcolm's killer. A few were from wives or girlfriends who knew or suspected that their partners had been abused as children. They rarely gave their name or address but the special counsellors Fenwick had organised managed to coax details from two for follow-up the next day. And three calls came from the possible victims themselves. A consistent feature was that they'd moved away from Sussex at the earliest opportunity.

One confessed to being an addict in drug rehabilitation for the third time; another was unemployed and about to be evicted from his home because of debt; and the third had just become a father and was so terrified that he might start to abuse his own child that he'd left his wife shortly after their baby was born and was living in a shelter for the homeless. As he listened to the delicate interviewing of each man Fenwick's anger grew. Not only had the abusers stolen the men's childhoods, they'd also ruined their adult lives.

The victims could tell the police little about the men who had abused them other than that Taylor had made the introductions. He was also the one who, in the words of Jeff, the frightened new father, 'broke them in' before passing them on to a range of clients, who were often masked and used aliases to protect their identities. Police appointments were made with all the victims for the following day.

Fenwick stayed in the incident room, on hand for any call that sounded particularly interesting. Shortly before one a.m., an officer signalled him over.

'This man says he sent the letters.'

'That makes the ninth tonight, Abby.' He'd been excited the first time but now the news was tarnished with past disappointments.

'But he knows details we held back. It feels different.'

'Very well.' Fenwick sighed and settled the headset and mouthpiece into a more comfortable position.

'This is Chief Inspector Andrew Fenwick, who is this?'

'My name doesn't matter. I saw your broadcast tonight. You mentioned my letters. Why do you need to speak to me?' The androgynous voice was muffled, as if the caller had placed a handkerchief over the mouthpiece.

A tingle of adrenalin bubbled into Fenwick's system at the question. A hoaxer normally bragged and made fresh claims; this was different. Fenwick gestured for the call to be traced.

'For the reasons I gave. We believe the man responsible for Paul's death may still be a danger to children.'

'You mentioned Bryan Taylor.'

'He's still a possible suspect.'

'You don't need to worry about him. Taylor is dead. He died a long time ago.' The speaker sounded more like a man this time.

'How do you know?'

'I saw him die, or to be more precise I saw him dying. Technically he was still alive when I left but he was hurt so badly there's no way he could have survived.'

'How was he hurt?'

'That's not relevant. If it's Taylor you're worried about you can relax,' the voice continued calmly. It *was* a man. Fenwick could hear traffic in the background but tried to ignore it as he concentrated on the words.

'Did he die as a result of an assault of some sort?'

Fenwick was aware that he was breaking all the rules – going straight for information rather than trying to establish rapport. He needed to slow down.

'Not exactly.'

'You haven't given me your name yet. What should I call you?'

'Don't try that. You were doing better before. Let's just keep it factual, shall we?'

'Was it suicide or an accident?'

'Neither. Taylor had no conscience and wasn't a clumsy man. He was stabbed in a fight. It was his own fault. He tried to take a knife from someone and managed to get hurt.'

'Did you witness this?'

'Yes.'

Fenwick chose his next words carefully.

'Was the fight with you?'

A definite sigh then.

'Let's just say that I was involved.'

'You killed Bryan Taylor?'

'No, I told you I wasn't there when he died and the stabbing was the result of an accident.'

'When and where was this?'

'I can't tell you that. It's irrelevant now anyway.'

'The details of a killing are never irrelevant.'

'They are in this case, trust me. Anyway, I only called to tell you to forget about Taylor. Goodn—'

'Wait! If you sent us the letters you'll know about the photograph.'

'Of the house and gates, you mean? Yes, has it helped? The house had a pool, by the way, I forgot to mention that.'

'It's not a good picture. The focus isn't great.' Fenwick tried to keep the excitement from his voice. They'd never disclosed the detail of the photograph publicly.

'What do you expect? It was taken in a rush.'

'On its own it's unlikely to help us, I'm afraid. We need more.'

'Like what?'

Fenwick could hear reservation in the man's tone despite the muffle.

'Names, an address, more details of what happened to Paul.'

'And you'll leave the major alone?'

'If we can find better suspects; but he was involved. We have physical evidence that links him.'

'I've seen his picture and I can tell you, he wasn't there on Paul's last day in Harlden. I'm certain.'

'Were you there? Come on, you know so much. I need to be able to trust you but you're not helping me.'

'I'm trying to, believe me, only...'

Fenwick held his breath.

'Yes, I was there but I wasn't really one of the abusers, the men that raped Paul.'

'But you saw it all. Were you spying on them?'

'That's as good a way of putting it as any. Look, I have to

go, it's late and I'm due indoors.'

'Wait, please. You must help me. It's a matter of justice, for Paul and perhaps for other boys too.'

There was a long pause. Fenwick could hear the sounds of traffic again despite the time so the Well-Wisher had to be in a built-up area, perhaps a city.

'I can't give you an address but I can give you descriptions. Smith, or The Purse, was the oldest, the others were fitter, bigger and tanned, as if they'd worked abroad. Alec had very pale eyes, almost white, and a tattoo of an octopus but I've told you that.'

'But you were close enough to see it. You were doing more than spying, weren't you?'

'I must go. I've given you more than you need to do your job.'

'I will do my job but you can help me do it better and quicker, please. We should meet. I can't make deals over the phone but there may be a way to keep you out of this, despite Taylor's death.'

An ironic laugh.

'I'm already out of it. You must do this yourself, Andrew.' It was definitely a man's voice, light and with no discernible accent.

'But I need your help. I may never be able to do this on my own.'

'You are never on your own. God will be with you and He will help you. Go in peace.'

The line went dead. He looked up expectantly for the trace.

'A payphone in central London.'

'Sod it! Get someone local over there right away. He might have left fingerprints or saliva this time.' Even as he said the words he doubted them.

Despite his success in drawing the Well-Wisher out from cover Fenwick felt deflated. If Taylor were dead he could save manpower and drop the search for him but he already knew that

Taylor hadn't acted alone. Maidment would never have protected a man like him. Despite the success of the programme he felt that he was no nearer to learning the identity of Paul's killer or being able to make a link to the murder of Malcolm Eagleton.

He sent most of the team home and waited out the early hours with the few who remained. In the lull he started to listen to the mass of less interesting calls. The programme had flushed out a mix of people struggling to disentangle real memory from what they'd seen or heard in the media: attention seekers, the genuinely helpful; the delusional; and the hoaxers. By three in the morning he felt that he was wading knee deep in the flotsam of public curiosity. Somewhere in the miles of tape there might be a point of detail that would prove crucial but he'd no way of knowing where and the unsatisfactory conversation with the Well-Wisher dominated his thoughts. He decided to go home.

In the empty hours driving on deserted roads he wondered who the caller had been – someone who worked at the house where Paul was raped? But why keep quiet? Maybe his silence had been bought? But if so, why break it now and why not simply give him the address where it had all happened? Fenwick puzzled at the riddle for the remainder of his journey and was no closer to solving it when he stumbled into bed and crashed out into a dark sleep.

The *CrimeNight* programme was deeply disturbing. The police knew that Maidment wasn't guilty and had an informer who might know enough to lead them to him. It was all very inconvenient and would require a change of plan. 'Smith' took a sip of whisky and swilled it around his mouth. He'd already drunk the meagre supply in the minibar when the programme had started so he'd made do with the little that was left as he watched it. It put the seal on a disappointing day.

The simplicity of his idea to go away, ignore phone calls and disappear up to London for a few days had vanished in the reality of dawn. There were things he had to do before leaving and they had taken him longer than he'd expected. Even though he knew that the house should be empty of anything incriminating he still felt compelled to check. All his records, financial arrangements and his own supply of child art were kept at a separate location; even his bank statements were innocuous as cash flowed freely within his hidden businesses.

By the time he'd reached London he had been in no mood to visit the house and booked into a hotel on Park Lane that promised luxury and anonymity until the morning. He'd switched on the television as a diversion but the sound of Paul Hill's name shocked him into paying proper attention. Other than the existence of the Well-Wisher the thing in the programme that worried him most was the intensity of the lead investigating officer. Fenwick. It wasn't a name he was familiar with and he hadn't arrested Maidment but it was a name he could not forget. Smith was good at reading people's characters and had a particular instinct for their weaknesses. Even through the medium of television he could sense obsession; Fenwick wasn't a man to give up. He would keep on searching for Paul's killer until he succeeded or retired, whichever came first.

And so he concluded reluctantly that he needed to change his plans. No, not change perhaps, merely accelerate. He'd always intended to spend some time abroad. It would be so much easier to pursue his interests away from the overdeveloped sensitivity of the West. There were still areas of the world where his particular habits were not considered abhorrent and were treated as a legitimate preference, not a crime. In certain countries even when things, very occasionally, went a little too far and there was some tidying up to be done, it was relatively easy to arrange. The boys he used were judged the lowest of the low, almost vermin. He liked to think that he was contributing to the prosperity of the local economy by his interest. Yes, he'd spent some very happy holidays exploring more exotic delights. The fond memories compensated for the inevitable sadness he felt as he realised he would have to abandon England, at least temporarily.

It was inconvenient to hurry one's departure, suggesting an element of panic that didn't sit well with his self-image. The sensible thing to do would be to buy a plane ticket first thing in the morning and then return to his house straight away to pack. But the idea grated; he'd come to London for a reason and the idea of running home with his tail between his legs made him angry. But he was in no mood for Sam now so what should he do?

Smith rang down for a bottle of malt whisky and more ice, and then paced the room as he considered his options. The one he favoured was to continue with his original plan. Visit William tomorrow, indulge in Sam for as much of the day as they could both manage and then make plans to spend several months abroad. If tracked down he could make a statement to a local lawyer, even see the British authorities if they insisted on visiting him but they wouldn't be able to extract him from the island paradise he had in mind. It was a place where the local officials were understanding and English a common language. Accommodation was cheap and came with domestic service in the fullest sense. He'd be able to live for a long time there without exhausting the offshore money he had put aside.

There would be no evidence to support his extradition. Once again he congratulated himself on insisting to Bryan that his real name should never be used in front of the boys and that they should be brought blindfolded to the house by a circuitous route. His one mistake had been to share Paul with Alec and Joe, sadistic bullies who cared nothing about whom or what they hurt as long as it was young flesh. It had been a rare lapse of judgement, one that he acknowledged but didn't dwell on.

He thought back to the much-regretted day when Ball had phoned to say that he and a friend needed some action while they were on leave in the UK and he'd obliged, wanting to show that he was able to supply whatever they required as well as he'd managed during his various postings. One call to Bryan and it was sorted. Only later, when Ball and his friend had already arrived, had Bryan called to say that the only boy he could find at short notice was Paul.

Until that point he'd had exclusive use of him as he always did with his favourites, unable to bear the thought of anyone else soiling their bodies. And Paul had been perfect, combining an older boy's lasciviousness within a childlike body. And what a body. Ever since, he'd been looking for another Paul in the faces of the boys he procured. Sam was the closest he'd found in many years and it was irksome to have to leave him so soon. On the other hand, the similarity had its drawbacks. Normally he could control his occasional outbursts but with Sam...well, it was very difficult and that made the boy dangerous.

He had a fantasy of taking him home, keeping him there in secret where they could enjoy all its facilities, even the pool. Some of his best memories involved boys in the pool – and some of his worst. Since Taylor's absence he'd had the discipline never to indulge himself at home.

He should have learnt his lesson when the Eagleton boy drowned. It had been an accident. Malcolm was like a fish in water and it had been easy to tempt him from the public baths with stories of his private pool. He'd brought him back one hot August afternoon while his wife was away on one of her interminable visits, plied him with ice cream, chocolate, and fizzy drinks laced with plenty of vodka.

Later, when they were in the pool together, he'd expected the boy to be drunk and compliant. He'd reasoned that if an oaf like

Taylor could seduce kids there was no reason why he, with his refinement, could not. But it hadn't been like that. The child had started to cry, really loudly, and he'd had to make him stop. He'd held his face under the water as a threat, that was all, to make him shut up, but he wouldn't so he'd done so again, and again. When the noise finally ceased he'd let the boy go and turned to leave the pool, worried about how to keep him from talking. Killing him hadn't entered his head but when he turned around and saw him lying on the mosaic tiles at the bottom of the pool he hadn't rushed to revive him.

Instead he'd poured himself a large Scotch. Later that night he had taken the body to the North Downs. The drive was the worst experience of his life, worse even than realising the boy was dead. He was convinced that he was going to be stopped and the car searched, as if guilt somehow radiated from him. But once again luck was on his side. He'd managed to bury the body, not as deep as he would have liked because of the chalk but deep enough and had then piled scree and rocks on top of the earth before turning for home with an easier heart.

He'd followed the news of Malcolm's disappearance closely. After an uneventful but intensely stressful week he'd gone away on holiday to Brazil, leaving a short note of explanation for his wife. On his return he resorted to using Bryan again but on condition that he could become involved in the financial side of the business. Bryan, full of ideas but without the money to support them, had accepted him as a backer and the enterprise had grown steadily. They had revolutionised Taylor's business quickly, extending supply, finding new markets, expanding into towns across Sussex at a remarkable rate.

It was all going very well; then Bryan introduced him to Paul Hill and for months nothing else mattered. His eyes misted. Paul had got under his skin like no boy before or since and his hunger to relieve that particular itch had driven his search for new boys for the past twenty-five years, culminating with Sam.

Would it be possible to have Sam flown out of the country to join him? He wondered whether he could persuade William to organise it for him, though it would mean revealing his destination and link him directly back to the house in London. But how else would he ensure Sam's exclusivity and his silence? He couldn't be left behind as a loose end. The only alternative was to pay William to sort it out; the man was a slug and would do anything for money – but could he really contemplate destroying the boy?

A knock at the door brought his whisky and fresh ice. For the rest of the long night, Smith worked his way down the bottle sipping steadily until, sometime before dawn, he made his decision and finally crawled into bed.

CHAPTER THIRTY-FIVE

The mood in the incident room was upbeat on Wednesday morning despite the early start. The whole MCS Choir Boy team, apart from Alison and her group who had more than enough to do, had travelled over to Harlden, eager to win their share of the fresh leads from the *CrimeNight* programme the evening before.

Most of the work would involve reviewing and following up the lower-priority phone calls but they didn't care – it was fresh evidence after weeks of working a dead case. There were three critical interviews with potential abuse victims. Fenwick would sit in on one with a man who lived in London and claimed to have been abused by Taylor. Specially trained interviewers from the Sex Crimes Unit would lead the questioning. He'd already been reminded in no uncertain terms that even if he found himself sitting opposite a six-foot-tall, sixteen-stone bricklayer with a BNP tattoo on his chest, the person they would need to reach and talk to was the damaged child inside.

Afterwards, he planned to visit the child protection squad who were watching the house Ball had visited and then drop in on the team from Camden who were trying to trace people who might have seen the Well-Wisher, as the phone box he'd used was in the middle of their patch.

Another of the men who had called *CrimeNight* lived in Edinburgh and would be interviewed locally. He asked Clive to fly up there if it looked promising. And the third caller was in Brighton. Nightingale planned to meet him that afternoon, after she attempted to see Oliver Anchor without his mother present.

Before they split up, Fenwick asked Nightingale and Cooper for an update on their progress. Nightingale told him about her interrupted interview with Maidment and her suspicion that he would try and contact the man he was covering for as soon as he could.

'Bob's organised twenty-four-hour surveillance on him, which will continue when he leaves hospital, and I'd like a tap on his home phone.'

'We should be able to have that approved with what we've got on him.' Fenwick made a note to himself to authorise the request.

'How about one for the hospital too?' Nightingale asked hopefully. 'If he's really wound up he may not wait until he's home.'

'I'll do my best but it's difficult in a public place, you know that. Will you see him again today?'

'If I can once I've been out to the Anchor place. Oliver left me a message last night. I think the television coverage got to him.'

'Good. If you need to, you can mention that others have come forward; it might help him to know he isn't alone.' Conscious of the advice he'd been given he added. 'Should you handle the interview yourself or do you need expert help?'

'I'll be fine. I had special training when I was on attachment to Brighton. Besides, I think I've built up a rapport with him.'

It was Cooper's turn to run through his interviews from the day before.

'Six down, three to go,' he said. 'One's on holiday, two haven't returned my calls. I've rung them back and will chase up today. Of the six I met with only Adrian Bush – or Bushy as he insisted I call him – knew the major. He was glad we'd dropped the murder charge; said he couldn't see the major murdering anyone, especially not a child. When I asked him if Maidment would cover up for a friend, he went a bit quiet but said he still couldn't see it, not for murder.'

'And you didn't have the sense that Bush was that friend?'

'No, definitely not. Moving on?' Fenwick nodded. 'Alex Cotton never served with Maidment. He lost an eye in the Falklands and the use of his left arm. He's pretty bitter but I didn't pick up any sense of unease from him and judging by his taste in calendars I'd say he's a hot-blooded hetero.'

'Vernon Jones, or Jonesy to his mates...'

'Hang on, you've had Bushy, now Jonesy, don't they believe in using given names in the army?' Fenwick asked.

'Oh, it gets better, believe me. Ernest Knight is known as...'

'Ernie?' ventured Nightingale.

'No, Milky, after the Benny Hill character, you know: *"Ernie, drove the fastest milk cart in the West"* – remember him?' Cooper grinned but both she and Fenwick looked blank. 'Never mind. Then there's Patrick Murray, known as,' he paused theatrically, waiting for a comment.

'Paddy,' someone ventured.

'Nope, Minty to his mates. I tell you, only Alex Cotton has kept to his given name.'

Fenwick glanced anxiously at his watch.

'Time's passing. Were there any revelations at all, Bob?'

'Not really. Cotton is a member of the golf club; Jones knew Taylor and didn't like him; Murray is a bachelor and a bit prim, if you know what I mean, but that's hardly grounds for arresting him, not in this day and age.'

'So who's left?'

'Richard Edwards, Ben Thompson and Zach Smart.'

'Well let me know if there's anything out of the ordinary. I'm going to see about the phone taps before I go up to London. I'll be tied up most of the morning but I want you to let me know the moment anything so much as mildly interesting comes up. My mobile will be on.'

Raised eyebrows greeted his remark; Fenwick was notorious for forgetting to keep his phone charged and then blaming others for not being able to reach him.

'Before you go, sir.' Nightingale raised a hand to stop him. 'Your phone conversation with the Well-Wisher. We're all dying to hear about it. Where did the trace take us to?'

'A public phone box in Bloomsbury, London. The Met sent out a team straight away but it was empty and the handset clean, so was the surround. They're following up locally but so far there's nothing new. It's a popular area with the homeless so there's a chance one of them saw something despite the time of the call.'

As he left he heard laughter break out behind him as someone threw something, and another said pointedly, at Cooper, '"A bit prim." What the bloody hell does that mean? Prim! You've gone soft you have. It's all your Doris's fault.'

'I've not gone bloody soft, you...'

Fenwick walked away briskly with a smile on his face, glad that the spirits of his team had lifted.

When work was assigned after Fenwick left, Nightingale needed a volunteer to cover a couple of hours' surveillance on Maidment because Stock had an emergency dentist appointment. Cooper, thinking that it would be as good a place as any to eat his lunch and read the paper, volunteered as long as he was relieved by three, because he needed to finish off the last of his interviews. Nightingale agreed at once, relieved that there'd be someone sensible in place until Stock returned. Cooper stopped by the canteen intending to buy a meat pie to top up the low-fat sandwich Doris had insisted on giving him for lunch but was tempted instead by a jumbo sausage roll and a slice of Dundee cake; he reasoned that the latter would be good for him because it contained fruit and nuts and they were healthy. He'd eaten the roll while driving out of Harlden and took the rest of his food with him to a seating area at the end of Maidment's ward.

After lunch the major was moved back into the main ward and chose to sit in a vinyl-covered armchair to read. Cooper was tempted to read himself and tapped the newspaper in his pocket, but he knew that he'd be asleep within minutes if he did. Instead he drank some water, made himself wait five minutes and then ate his cake. He counted to three hundred in an attempt to stay awake but then had to start pacing the corridor, studying the paintings in an effort to fill his last hour before Stock took over. After less than twenty minutes his back started to ache and he was forced to sit down. At two o'clock the first of the afternoon visitors began to arrive, just as Cooper was losing the battle with his eyelids

Sarah Hill looked at herself in the mirror and failed to connect in any way with the stranger she saw there. Another woman stared back at her: tall, middle-aged, scrawny-necked, with a lined face and empty eyes. The most you could say about her was that she was smart and wore new shoes. Had Sarah Hill cared about such things she would have noticed that the hair colour she'd chosen the week before was too dark for her now that she was older; that the trouser suit, whilst tailored, emphasised her lack of figure and that the blouse sat askew under the jacket. But she had no mind for such details. In fact she had little mind left at all. What remained was focused entirely on the deed in front of her. Inside the large black leather handbag she had her purse, house keys, folding umbrella and a five-inch kitchen knife.

Cooper just had to find fresh air. If he didn't he would nod off. The major didn't look as if he was going anywhere as he was still attached to a drip, happily reading his book, so it was as good a time as any for a stretch. He made a dash for the lift and then walked sharpish outside and round to the right where he'd noticed a wooden bench.

The sunshine and air perked him up immediately and he took a copy of the *Enquirer* from his coat pocket. They were still milking the Hill story. Their 'exclusive' with the kid's poor mum had given them page after page for days and when news was light they'd rehash it to fill a few inside columns. Today's piece was about Sarah Hill herself: 'a tragic story of love and loss'. Stock glanced at the headline and started to read the article despite himself.

Her life might have been blighted as the paper said but looking at the 'then and now' photos of her he thought she'd probably brought a lot of it on herself. All right, she'd been a bit of a looker when she was young but he reckoned there was a shrew hiding behind that smile. And her eyes gave him the creeps. Although they were startling they were too intense. He closed the paper with a shudder and looked around him. He'd had his five minutes and it was time to get back.

As he reached the hospital entrance a smartly dressed woman, with no taste, crossed in front of him. He angled his body away to avoid being hit by her large handbag and followed her inside. She paused to study the signs and he passed her heading towards the lift but by the time it arrived she'd caught up with him. He leant forward and pressed the button for the third floor. She did the same even though it was already lit up.

The woman was one of those people who stood too close, no respecter of personal space. She made Cooper uncomfortable. He glanced quickly at her profile but there was no need to rush his observations as her eyes were focused in the middle distance. Her lips twitched as if she were muttering silently to herself. It was enough to give you the heebie-jeebies and he took an unconscious step away from her. His movement attracted her attention and she turned to look him full in the face. The shock of recognition took him by surprise. What was Sarah Hill doing here when he'd just read that she had few living relatives or friends?

When the lift doors opened he stood back and allowed her to go first. Something, call it a policeman's instinct if you like, kept him a discreet distance behind her as she shuffled to the reception desk.

'Major Maidment, please?' she said in a voice that was normal enough.

'Melton Ward over there, love. He's on the left-hand side about halfway down. He's a lot better tod…' The nurse's voice tailed off as Sarah Hill turned and walked away.

Cooper was concerned now. The *Enquirer* quoted her as saying she blamed the major for her son's death. Whatever had drawn her to the hospital she wasn't here to wish him well.

He kept close, cursing the fact that it was just his luck to be on duty when a nutter came in to shout abuse at his suspect. He'd never minded breaking up disturbances but when a woman was involved he found it embarrassing, particularly if they turned out to be stronger than he was.

Mrs Hill was rummaging in her bag as she entered the ward. Cooper put it down to nerves. At the foot of the major's bed she paused and he looked up.

'Mrs Hill.' His voice was calm but Cooper was close enough to see the dread in his eyes. 'Good afternoon. Do sit d—'

'Don't talk to me, you despicable old man.' Her voice was low but visitors on either side glanced over just the same. 'You killed my boy but they let you walk free! There's no justice in this world.'

The words were louder now and a nurse at the far end of the ward started walking towards them.

'I didn't kill him, Sarah. You have my word on that.'

'Liar! My boy's dead because of you, yet here *you* sit getting the best of care, breathing God's fresh air. It's not right!'

'Sarah.' The major rose stiffly from his chair, a hand outstretched in entreaty.

'My Paul's dead and it's your fault!' she screamed. 'You're a wicked old man, a pervert and you deserve to die!'

Cooper knew that he had to say something but he hung back, afraid to make matters worse. Instead, he stood on the other side of the bed and said, with what he hoped was authority, 'Mrs Hill, let's just calm down, shall we.'

She ignored him, sobbing, trying to catch her breath and speak at the same time. When she looked down into her bag Cooper thought she was searching for a handkerchief. The unexpected sight of five inches of sharpened steel stunned him.

Mrs Hill swung wildly at Maidment, blinded by tears and fury. The blade missed but failure merely drove her forward and the major had nowhere to hide. He was trapped against the chair, a wall behind him, a mad woman in front. He threw himself backwards as far as he could. The knife glanced past his cheek and cut the saline IV drip leading into his arm. He pulled the stand in front of him to deflect the next blow and raised it to push her away. But she swayed to one side, almost onto the bed, and stabbed at his unprotected side. The tip of the knife nicked his arm and slid upwards, catching him again as it sliced towards his shoulder She pulled back, ready to stab, her whole attention focused on his unprotected neck. Cooper came to life and lunged across the bed, catching her around the waist as she raised her arm to strike. He grabbed her in a bear hug with one arm and tried to reach the knife with his other hand. The major was there at once and prised it from Sarah's fingers.

'Call 999,' Cooper shouted as he managed to cling on to the struggling woman. 'I'm going to need some help.'

'So now we're even,' Maidment said, his voice shaky as he dropped the knife onto the floor. 'Thank you, Sergeant Cooper.'

* * *

'Cooper saved the major's life? Well, there's sweet justice for you.'

Nightingale's reaction was typical as word went round Harlden station. Cooper was a modest man but by the time he'd returned to the detectives' room from making his statement, rumour had inflated the story to the point where the knife was more than eight inches long and Sarah Hill an amphetamine-fuelled giantess. Despite his natural modesty it was hard not to bask in the glow while he drank a strong cup of tea with extra sugar and accepted a home-made rock cake from one of the secretaries.

Although she'd been arrested, Sarah Hill was to undergo a thorough psychiatric assessment and it was Cooper's opinion that she would be sectioned as a result. For some reason he called Maidment to tell him and could hear the pain in his voice when he responded.

'I don't want her in some awful state-run establishment, Sergeant. If she has no money to pay for private treatment then I will see to it.' He kept insisting even though Cooper knew that he no longer had that sort of discretionary income. Something of his thoughts must have sounded in his voice because Maidment added, 'I can always sell a painting.'

Cooper knew how much that would pain him but he didn't miss his opportunity.

'That's a powerful guilty conscience you have there, Major Maidment. Why not do something even more valuable and tell us everything you know? Surely you owe it to Mrs Hill to help us.'

But once again Maidment refused to say anything and Cooper was left feeling increasingly frustrated by his obdurate silence.

Fenwick had managed to secure warrants for a tap on Maidment's home phone but not for Melton Ward and Cooper organised the surveillance rota, determined that one way or another the major was going to give them Paul's killer.

As soon as Sarah Hill had been arrested, Maidment decided to leave hospital, reasoning that the police would be distracted with her. The ward sister told him that he was putting his recovery, if not his life, at risk but he ignored her and the subsequent protest from the doctor on duty. His hand was shaking as he signed the hospital disclaimer but he left anyway.

DC Wadley, acting on direct instructions from Cooper, followed Maidment at a safe distance as he hobbled towards the taxi rank outside the hospital leaning heavily on a stick. Wadley was parked in a doctor's space by the entrance and was behind the wheel before the major had settled himself in a cab and closed the door. As he let out the clutch Wadley sneezed in nervous excitement. This was his first real piece of detective work since moving from uniform the previous week. The responsibility felt enormous, a fact that Cooper was relying on. Wadley kept telling himself that if Inspector Nightingale was right they'd have Paul's killer in custody within hours and that he'd be the one to make the arrest.

The Anchor family farmhouse was deserted when Nightingale arrived. She prowled around the outbuildings, keeping well away from the snapping dogs in their cages. There was nothing to see but dried mud, old tractor parts and cluttered work benches. Oliver wasn't there, despite his promise, and her spirits sank. She was probably wasting her time but was so keen to question him that she lingered in the yard anyway.

The sun felt good on her face. One of the feral farm cats must have had kittens. Three tabby bundles of fur with blue eyes were playing with an end of baling twine in the doorway to an old shed. She could see the mother half hidden behind a galvanised bucket. The cat stared at her unblinking, then decided that she was safe and returned to licking its back leg as part of a protracted wash.

'Oh, you're still here.' Oliver's disappointed voice broke her reverie.

'Of course, waiting for you. Where's your mum?'

'Farmers' market. We have a stall for things.' He was dismissive. 'Stupid stuff but it sells.'

'Where can we go to talk?'

Oliver's face had taken on a deep red flush. She thought that he was summoning up courage to tell her that he'd changed his mind about talking to her so she hurried on.

'I'm dying for a coffee. Do you want one here or shall we go into town?'

'I can make coffee, y'know.'

'Great.' The alternative choice never failed. 'I've got some biscuits in the car.'

His face brightened.

The kitchen was less tidy than when she'd first seen it. Dirty breakfast things were stacked in the sink and used tea mugs littered the table. Farmers' market or not it was obvious that Mrs Anchor was expected to do the washing-up. She was dreading Oliver's coffee but he was careful in his preparations, concentrating on each step. Nightingale started to question him as he picked up his first biscuit.

'Did you see *CrimeNight*?'

It was obvious from his face that he had and she continued quickly.

'We had an enormous response. Lots of people called in saying they knew Bryan Taylor and some of them even said that he'd assaulted them.'

Her words had the effect that she'd expected as Oliver's face started burning with shame.

'You weren't one of the callers, were you?'

'I never.' He shook his head shedding biscuit crumbs across his shirt front.

'It's a pity. It would have been much easier for you to admit things over the phone.'

'Things?'

'Yes, like telling us that you were one of Taylor's...special friends. I'm sure it was years before Paul disappeared. A strong man like you would have matured early. It probably stopped a long time before the burning car. Isn't that right?'

Oliver had lost interest in the biscuits and was staring miserably at his clasped hands.

'It almost doesn't matter if you don't tell me, you know. I'm aware of the basic facts, it's just the details I need now.'

'How d'you find out?' he asked her innocently. Nightingale kept any trace of triumph from her expression; he was all hers now.

'The police have ways of finding things out; it's our job. Of course, when we learn things indirectly,' she decided to rephrase, 'that is, when you don't tell us stuff yourself, we might get some parts wrong, and that's not good for you.'

'Why not?' It was barely a whisper and she had to suppress an unhelpful feeling of pity.

'Because people can be cruel. They say things that aren't strictly true – like saying that you actually enjoyed what you did for Bryan, for example.'

'I never!' Oliver brought his fist down hard on the table and the mugs jumped.

'You never what, Oliver?' Nightingale asked gently and held her breath.

'I never enjoyed it. Not ever.' He glanced at her and she exhaled slowly.

'I didn't think you did. But you need to tell me as much as you can in case there are other things that I've got wrong.'

He shook his head, eyes shut.

'Look, would it be easier if I just asked you questions? That way all you need to do is say yes or no. I'll need to take a few notes, though. You won't mind, will you?'

Oliver shook his head and gazed out of the kitchen window, a look of terrible sadness on his face that brought a lump to Nightingale's throat. She swallowed it away.

'So, you were eleven when you and Bryan started to become friends?'

'Nine.' His eyes were back down on his clenched fists. 'He was workin' on our barn. My job was to take him drinks without spilling.'

'And when did Bryan,' she paused searching for the right words, 'begin to become friendly with you?'

'Same week.' Oliver sighed with ancient wisdom. 'Said I was special. It had to be our secret. No one'd said I was special before 'cept Mum and that don't count, do it?'

'It's always good to hear the words from someone else. I imagine Bryan was nice to you?'

Oliver smiled. It was so pathetic that Nightingale had to look away briefly.

'He could do tricks; made an egg come out my ear once, a real one!' The magic of the moment was still clear in his voice. 'We were friends.'

'Of course you were, but he wanted to be more than friends, didn't he?'

Oliver nodded but said nothing.

'Oliver, you're going to have to tell me some of the details but what we'll do for now is I'll ask something and you can say yes or no. Why don't you have another biscuit?'

He took one automatically but then sat crumbling it to pieces. Eventually Nightingale lifted the debris from his fingers.

'Did Bryan touch you?'

A nod.

'Did the touches go to private places?'

Eyes half shut, another nod, barely noticeable, his cheeks aflame with shame.

'And did he make you touch him back?'

'Yeah.'

She could see tears in his eyes.

'You're doing very well, I'm proud of you. Did he make you do more than touch?'

There was a snuffle.

'I'm sorry, I couldn't hear that.'

'Yes.'

'For how long did this go on?'

'Don't know; till after school started.'

'Then what happened?'

'He picked me up one Saturday. Said I could help him, 'cept that there weren't no job.'

'It was more of the same?'

'Worse. He give me sweets and a toy but I was crying and he said I shouldn't 'cos I was special, and he loved me and the presents showed he did.'

'Did he ever give you money?'

'Once when he'd forgotten to buy sweets.'

'How much was it, can you remember?'

'Don't know; all his change, I think.'

Nightingale had to swallow to control her anger.

'Did you meet often?'

'Saturdays and when Mum was at market.'

'Just you and Bryan?'

He hesitated then nodded.

'Oliver, I need you to tell me the truth.'

'First it was me and him but...'

'Go on.'

'Just before Christmas he said we was going to see Father

Christmas. We went to a big house. There was a Christmas tree in the hall taller than Bryan.'

'Where was the house?'

'Dunno – he covered my eyes, said it was a secret.'

'Whom did you meet there?'

'The room was dark.' Oliver looked away, the tears stark on his face. 'Wasn't Father Christmas though.'

'Did this man have sex with you?'

Oliver flinched at her words then nodded.

'I need words.'

'Yeah.'

'How often did this happen?'

'Coupla times but then I got sick. Doctor came to see me. He...he said something to Mum.'

'He examined you?'

'I had this rash; it itched like mad. Mum thought it was the measles and he looked and then...he said something to Mum.'

'And afterwards?'

'Mum had a talk with me.'

'Did you tell her about Bryan and the other man?'

'Eventually. She don't let up, Mum.'

'I'm sure she doesn't. What did she do?'

'She went and saw Bryan and I was happy because I never saw him or the other man again.'

'Did she go to the police?'

'Don't know. She was so angry.'

'You were in the same year at school as Paul, weren't you?'

The change of subject took him by surprise and it took him some time to think.

'Yeah. He was younger than me 'cos I missed a year. We were friends. I looked out for him and him for me.' It was recited like a pledge.

'Is that what Paul always said?'

'Yeah. He was my mate.'

'What did you think when you saw him with Bryan?'

'I tried to warn him!' Oliver was distressed, the guilt obvious in his face.

'Wouldn't he listen?'

'Not Paul. He was smart, smarter'n me even though he was younger. Said he could look after himself. I tried to watch out for him, honest.'

The tears were back and she reached over and patted the back of his enormous hands. They were locked together in a tight ball of agony.

'I'm sure you did your best.'

'I really, really tried.' A fat tear rolled down Oliver's cheek, then another.

'Of course you did but the trouble with clever people like Paul is that they're often too smart for their own good.'

'Paul was special.' Oliver sobbed.

'I know and I'm sure you miss him.'

'Still do,' sniff, 'he was my best friend; never had another.'

She gave him some tissues and waited for the crying to quieten. When it did she picked up the questioning quickly.

'On the day Paul disappeared, you saw a car burning. Tell me about that.'

He wiped his face with his sleeve, leaving a slimy trail on the blue denim.

'It was Bryan's car.'

'Are you sure?'

'Certain positive. I knowed that car. I could see the number plate.'

'Did you go close to the car?'

Oliver looked up at the ceiling and blinked away a tear before shaking his head.

'Why not?'

'Men there watching.'

'Men? Who were they?'

'Couldn't see their faces. They had their backs to me.'

'How many men and what did they look like?'

'There was three of them. One was short; one sort of like a wrestler; I couldn't see the other man proper.'

'Why were they watching the car?'

Oliver leant forward and put his face in his hands. She could see tears trickling between his fingers.

'Please, Oliver, you have to tell me, for Paul's sake.'

'Just...give me a minute.'

Nightingale waited impatiently until Oliver wiped a hand over his face and looked at her. The raw pain she saw there made her wince.

'OK, here we go; I can do this,' he said to himself and nodded, a new look of concentration on his face. 'The car was burning hot. I could feel the heat where I stood and the trees were scorching.'

He made it sound like an excuse. Nightingale suddenly realised what was coming.

'Go on, I'm sure there was nothing you could have done.'

'There wasn't! If it had just been the men I'd a tried to get him out but it was too hot.'

'Get who out, Oliver?'

'Paul.' Tears ran unheeded down his face. 'There was a body in the front seat; it must've been Paul. It was all burnt, like it was covered in black paint.' There was an agonising pause then he whispered the final part of his confession.

'I ran away...I was really scared.'

'Other people must have seen the burning. I don't understand why it wasn't reported.'

'The track we went down wasn't there in those days. It was in the woods.'

'But the smoke would have been seen, surely?'

'Lot of stubble-burning. Used to be anyway, can't do it no more.'

'Did you go back afterwards?'

'A long time after. When I got home I...I can't remember what happened but I know I was sent away to a sort of special hospital. When I came back the car was gone, just black trees where it'd been.'

Oliver wiped his face with his sleeve again and finished his mug of cold coffee.

'Was Bryan one of the men watching the car burn?'

'Don't think so.'

'You're sure?'

Oliver nodded his head.

'I think I'd've recognised him from the back. I don't think he was there but I can't swear it.'

'What the hell's going on here!'

Nightingale and Oliver had been too engrossed in their conversation to hear Mrs Anchor's arrival.

'We're having the conversation that you should have had with the police twenty-five years ago, Mrs Anchor. Why didn't you come to us when the doctor told you what he suspected had happened to your son? At the very least you should have reported the burning car!' Nightingale didn't bother to disguise the disgust she felt. 'All these years you've left the Hills to suffer and who knows how many boys to be abused by Taylor and his pals.'

Mrs Anchor bit her lip but countered indignantly. 'Oliver was incoherent, in a terrible state when he came in. My only concern was for my boy. And anyway at the time, sorry dear,' she said looking quickly at Oliver, 'nothing he said made sense. He was hyperactive, screaming, we could barely restrain him. When the doctor arrived he gave him a sedative and then next day we agreed he should go to hospital.'

'But later, when you heard the news about Paul, you must have realised that Oliver might have witnessed something. Your husband reported seeing Taylor's car, for heaven's sake!'

Mrs Anchor sat down heavily in the chair at the head of the table. Her flush had gone and she looked exhausted.

'Oliver, go and find your father. He needs to come back early today, tell him.'

Nightingale watched as Oliver lumbered out of the kitchen obediently, his frame dwarfing his mother as she sat in her chair. To her surprise the farmer's wife took out a packet of cigarettes and lit one.

'I didn't realise the significance of what Oliver saw, not for several days.' She started brushing up the biscuit crumbs from the table automatically.

'Rubbish. What aren't you telling me? With something this serious don't imagine I won't find out. I'll get a warrant for his medical records if I need to.'

Mrs Anchor took a long pull and held the smoke in her lungs before exhaling.

'It's true. When Oliver went to hospital we were at our wits' end. I knew something wasn't right with the lad but I put it down to his earlier...trouble and the fact that he'd always been quiet. When he had his breakdown it really shook us – we had no idea he'd got so bad.

'The doctors gave Oliver a full medical examination when he was admitted. They discovered the signs of previous abuse. I told them that there'd been a difficulty in the past but it was over with. Problem was I'd never reported it and Arthur didn't know. Our GP was an old friend, married to my sister-in-law, so when he'd told me that Oliver had been abused I begged him to keep it quiet, not even to tell Oliver's dad. He knew us and that we'd never hurt Ollie so he said nothing for my sake and never reported it to the social or police like he should have.'

'If you'd only had the courage to tell your husband and the authorities about that abuse Paul Hill and Malcolm Eagleton might be alive today!' Nightingale's mind was filled with the image of the two boys grinning at the camera. 'This wasn't just about your family.'

'I know that now, don't you think I don't? But at the time all I wanted to do was protect *my* family; that's all that mattered. If the social had got involved then who knows what would have happened. They might have accused Arthur and taken Ollie and my other boys away. They almost did later when he went into hospital after Paul vanished.' She stubbed out her cigarette and lit another.

'Go on.'

'When they found that he'd been abused Arthur argued with the doctors, told them it was impossible. That turned out to be a big mistake. He ended up under investigation by social services, then the police.' Her voice faltered but she was made of stronger stuff than her son and remained dry-eyed.

'It was awful. Oliver was still on medication so he couldn't say anything to help us. It was a terrible few months. Then Oliver got a bit better and started seeing a psychiatrist. The story about Taylor came out. We were no longer suspects and when my son was well enough he was allowed home into our care.

'I'm sorry to say that I never gave Paul a thought in all that time. We were living through our own nightmare and I had no energy to spare for someone else's. After Oliver came home we never talked about what had happened. We hoped he would forget all about Taylor.'

'Of course he wouldn't! He's just bottled it up because you made it a taboo subject. Even now he's not really well, is he? He needs proper counselling.' Nightingale's tone was harsh.

Mrs Anchor looked at her defiantly.

'He's all right. He can cope with the world and we're here to look after him. He doesn't want for anything.'

'Except for friends his own age and perhaps even a relationship with a girl,' she said cruelly.

'You have no right to barge in here and form snap judgements, miss. You've got what you came for; don't lecture me in my own home and pretend that you care one jot for my son's welfare. He's our problem, not yours and we'll deal with it our way.'

'But he needs help, Mrs Anchor, particularly now he's managed to acknowledge what's happened to him. It was a very brave thing to do.'

'You're police not medical. Leave us alone.'

'He'll need to make a full statement at the station; will you bring him in or shall I take him with me now?'

Mrs Anchor stared at her defiantly but knew when she was beaten.

'I'll bring him in myself.'

'And if you try to change his mind I'll arrest you for obstruction. What's more I'll press for a custodial sentence; who'd look after your boy then, Mrs Anchor?'

Nightingale rose to leave, struggling to control her temper and to conjure up some compassion for the woman but Mrs Anchor had the last word.

'You should ask yourself why your colleagues didn't do more to find Taylor at the time. They had plenty of information, my Arthur made sure of that, but they never caught him. If anyone failed my son and Paul Hill it was you lot!'

Nightingale climbed into her car and drove away.

CHAPTER THIRTY-SIX

From the end of Nathan's second visit Sam had plotted how he could escape. At the age of eleven he'd considered himself mature enough to run away from what he considered a loveless and overcrowded home and now, his twelfth birthday unremarked and uncelebrated, he was confident that he was more than capable of surviving on his own.

He looked back on his timidity of only the month before with contempt. He had been stupid to consider this place a refuge, to believe William had any concern for his safety. All he was good for was earning him money, for as long as his looks and his body lasted. As soon as they vanished he'd be on the scrapheap, like Jack.

Thinking of Jack made him scared all over again. He hadn't realised that Jack had been Nathan's boy before him but looking back it made perfect sense. Jack hadn't been worked hard; he'd been given a room of his own, complete with a small bathroom like this, and for a while William had treated him as special. It was one of the reasons that Sam and the other boys had been indifferent to his suffering. They'd missed what was really going on.

Jack had never been one to muck about; a silent boy happy in his own company, they hadn't noticed as he withdrew entirely. It was only when he started to look ill that they'd wondered what was going on and had put it down to drugs. Previously, Jack had boasted about keeping himself clean, so there was quiet contempt when it became obvious he was in a bad way. Looking back on it all Sam realised that Jack probably hadn't been hooked, just badly hurt by Nathan. The reason for his long absences became obvious. And then he disappeared.

Sam rubbed his neck and looked in the mirror at the fading bruises. They were almost gone; he'd massaged in the herbal-smelling stuff William had given him every eight hours as he'd been told and it seemed to help. The other bruises, the ones that didn't show but hurt more, were still there and he knew that if Nathan did to him again what he'd done before he'd end up badly injured, maybe even dead. The thought made him cry at night but that wasn't what gave him nightmares. It was the choking. When he woke in the dark unable to breathe, with the memory of Nathan's hands around his neck, he was convinced that next time he was going to die. He'd been out of control during his last visit and it was only William's banging on the door that had stopped him.

Sam needed to escape. He'd tried opening the window but it was locked fast. Even if he broke it, one look outside told him he was too high up to jump. There was no fire escape, no drainpipe down which he could climb and his sheet and duvet tied together would leave him dangling high above the broken paving of the yard below.

He forced himself to recall every bit of knowledge that he had about the outside of the house from the day he'd arrived and including his two feeble attempts to escape. The sign above the door had said Madeira Hotel but the one in the window always read 'No Vacancies'. The hotel was a front. There were no guests: just the boys, a meagre staff and their masters. Before he'd been moved he had shared one of the larger bedrooms with three other boys on a lower floor. The windows were barred and the fire exits, left over from the days when it had been a hotel, were locked.

Back then he hadn't paid much attention to his surroundings and had no idea of the floor layout. Since moving up here he'd been stuck in his room. He knew he was on the fifth floor and that the other rooms were used by staff – cooks, barman and security – and by William who was rumoured to have his own rooms in the corner wing of the hotel. It was the worst floor from which to try and escape as there were always people asleep in their rooms between shifts. William liked to keep the staff together; it stopped them getting wandering feet, he said. Most of them were foreigners and Sam thought they were probably illegal immigrants.

As he lay in bed, he plotted. He was too smart to try and escape without a plan like before. He needed to create a reason to leave the room.

On the morning of the twelfth day in what he thought of as his captivity, he woke before dawn and went to relieve himself. As he flushed an idea came to him. If the toilet broke they'd have to let him out to go outside. He lifted the cistern lid and peered inside. The tank looked brown and scummy. There was a ball floating on top of the water with a lever attached to the inside of the flush handle. He tried the mechanism a few times, watching it carefully. The next time he flushed he held the ball down as hard as he could and noticed that the water flowed in constantly until the ball bounced to the top and somehow cut it off.

The joint attaching it to the lever didn't look that strong. Grasping the ball-thing he pulled hard, yanking it. It wouldn't break. He tried again, leaning back with all his weight. He felt something give but only a little. Outside his room, there were noises of people walking along the corridor as the house stirred into life. He put his radio on loud enough to disguise the sound of his efforts and carried on pulling. At one point he cut himself on a bit of metal but he ignored the blood, all his energy focused on breaking the ball from its mount.

The rattle of a key in the lock had him running back to his bed just in time, as one of the security men brought in his breakfast tray. He was on full cooked rations, plus toast and milk. The man left without looking at him. Sam wolfed the tepid food down, barely tasting it, aware that he'd need all his strength for his escape. As soon as he was finished he went back to the cistern. After what seemed an age but according to the radio was only ten minutes, there was a snapping sound and the ball floated free. He flushed and watched as the water kept flowing, filling the cistern above its normal level. His spirits rose with it. He was going to flood the bathroom! But when the water had reached almost to the top of the tank it stopped. For some reason, even though he could hear it pouring into the loo, it wasn't over-flowing.

Sam wanted to cry but bit down on his bottom lip instead. He forced himself to examine the tank again. There was a pipe leading from it, one he hadn't bothered with before. He had no idea what it did but he put his palm over it and watched with satisfaction as the water started to rise again. So that was it; an overflow for the extra water. For his plan to work he had to block it somehow.

He rolled up his sleeve, took a long piece of toilet paper and stuffed it into the escape pipe as far as it would go. He repeated the process three times, prodding the paper so that it went right down inside. When the pipe was full he stopped and watched as the water reached the top. It seemed to hover there for an age before the surface tension broke and it slowly started to dribble over the side and splash onto the floor tiles. Sam yelped in excitement and did a little dance, then sobered up quickly.

This was only the first step. He had to think very carefully about what to do next. There would be only be one chance of escape and he needed to take full advantage of it. He dressed fully for the first time in days, put on his trainers, brushed his teeth and hair, and stuffed the remains of his toast in his pocket. He picked up his radio and held it tight. Then he counted to one thousand, to give the water time to cover the floor, before he started banging on the door. It took a while for someone to come and it turned out to be the barman, Jan, woken from his sleep after a late night shift.

'What the fuck do you want?'

'There's a flood!' he said dramatically and pointed to the bathroom.

Jan stepped over to the bathroom and looked inside. As he bent down to inspect the floor Sam smashed him over the head as hard as he could with the radio. Without waiting to see the results he ran to the door, slammed it shut and locked it, pocketing the key. He took a second to get his bearings. The rest of the floor was quiet, doors shut. Behind him there was silence from his bedroom.

There were signs for fire exits at both ends of the corridor and he ran to the one furthest from William's rooms. It opened as he'd hoped. They might lock the boys in but he didn't reckon William would risk being burnt to death if the house went up in flames.

He ran down the concrete stairs, his footsteps light and soundless, looking above constantly for signs of pursuit but he remained alone. Each floor had its own landing marked with a number. When he reached level two he thought he heard a door open at the top of the stairs. He kept on running as fast as he could, knowing it would be useless to try and escape into one of the corridors as the doors at this level would be locked. He reached the ground floor and pushed open an emergency exit. It led to an area at the back of the kitchen.

Sam looked around wildly. There was no way out! Opposite the door were large rubbish bins taller than he was but there was no point hiding in there; that would be the first place they'd look.

He was panting with fright and forced himself to take a few deep breaths. Think, he told himself. If there are rubbish bins there must be a way for them to be collected.

He looked around the yard again slowly. There was a wooden gate immediately to his right. A sturdy padlock held an iron bar in place but the gate wasn't that tall, seven foot at most. Sam put his right foot against the wood and reached up so that his fingers touched one of the crosspieces that held the wooden planks of the gate together. He heaved himself up and almost made it but his foot slipped and he banged his knee hard. The little yelp he let out was more fear than pain. He was unaware of the tears on his cheeks.

He tried again: right foot high; right hand up on the beam; left hand beside it; he pulled and lifted his left leg quickly onto the locking crosspiece. The toe of his trainer found a grip and he leant his whole weight against the gate, then scrabbled up with his right hand so that he could grab the top and really pull himself up.

His breath was coming hard, his heart hammering inside his T-shirt, but he managed to lift his left hand next to his right and take his full weight. He was hanging onto the top now, his head high enough to see over the gate to freedom but the lower half of his body seemed to dangle, impossibly heavy. With a grunt of effort he heaved himself up so that his stomach reached the top of the gate and his face and arms hung over the other side. He was balancing on his stomach, the wood cutting into his skin where it took his full weight. For an awful moment he felt his body arch backwards, pulled by gravity down into the yard but he hunched his shoulders forward and regained his balance.

He hung there suspended, teetering without stability. Even though the gate wasn't high the ground beneath him seemed a long way off and there was no way he could swivel his body over so that he could jump feet first. If he fell he'd smash his skull on the pavement. For a long second he was pinned there by his own fear then the emergency exit door crashed open and one of the security men ran into the yard followed by Jan. The door swung back in a full arc banging into Sam's hand where he clung to the gate and obscuring him briefly from view. The man started over to the bins, giving Sam seconds in which to make up his mind. He grabbed the emergency exit door, pulled his upper body partway onto it and then brought his other hand up under his body.

With the angle of the door to help him he managed to lever his body full length along the top of the gate and then let his feet slide down the other side. He'd just managed to force all his body over when the security guard turned around and saw him.

'Oi, you! Stay where you are, you little punk. I'm going to kill you!'·

With that sort of encouragement Sam let go, landing heavily but squarely on the pavement in the service alley at the back of the hotel as the security man slammed into the gate. He heard him rattle the lock and then the thump of his foot as he started to climb over but Sam was off. He turned left away from the front of the hotel and ran down an empty side road. The street at the end was full of run-down houses from the turn of the century but Sam didn't notice. He'd spotted a busy road in the far distance with people and buses and he sprinted towards it.

Behind him he felt rather than heard the security guard land outside the yard but he didn't waste time looking back. The man grunted as he fell and there was no sound of following footsteps so he must have hurt himself. It was the bit of luck Sam needed and his spirits soared adding speed to his heels. He was going so fast that he didn't notice the dark blue Alfa Romeo pull up ahead of him and a man jump out. So when William's arm snaked out and caught him around the shoulders his feet left the ground as he swung helplessly in his grip.

Sam opened his mouth to scream but William's palm was already over it as he was thrust into the car as easily as a bag of shopping. The central locking clicked into place as he pushed himself up and scrabbled for the handle.

'Sit still.'

It was all William said; he wouldn't even look at him as he drove the short distance back to the wooden gates and hooted to be let in.

'Help me!'

'Shut it.'

'Help me!' Sam screamed again and again until a blow across the back of his head stunned him into silence.

William unlocked the car and the heavy hands of the security guard and a bleeding Jan grabbed Sam to pull him out. He pushed his whole body into the struggle against them but it was as effective as using a feather as a battering ram. As they re-entered the house one of the staff ran up to William.

'Nathan's on the phone,' he said urgently.

'I'll take it. And shut that up while I'm on the phone; he needs to learn the art of silence.'

A filthy handkerchief was thrust into Sam's mouth and a bag put over his head. He was carried up the stairs, his feet dragging on the threadbare carpet.

'Wait.' William's voice carried to them. 'There's been a change of plan. Put him in the lock-up; I'll be taking him out later.'

Sam was thrown into a small, bare room without windows and the door was locked behind him. He spent a long time screaming and beating the door but it had no effect and eventually, exhausted, he drifted into a fitful sleep.

CHAPTER THIRTY-SEVEN

Fenwick and the police specialist went over the statement from one of the self-confessed abuse victims together. They concluded that there was a good chance it was substantially truthful but it was sometimes difficult for victims of abuse to disentangle reality from their nightmares. Several more sessions of careful, sympathetic questioning would be needed before he could be sure he had a reliable witness for any prosecution.

But the good news was that the victim had identified Taylor from an array of e-fits put before him. He also described his car, knew the registration number and talked of a large house with ornate gates.

Fenwick needed fresh air after the interview and went out to buy a sandwich and fruit for a very late lunch, delaying his next visit as he ambled through St James's Park, his thoughts on the Well-Wisher and the identity of Paul's killer. He found a bench, finished eating and called Harlden, noting that the battery on his mobile phone was low again, though he was certain he'd charged it. His call was answered quickly and he was put straight through to the incident room.

'We've arrested Sarah Hill for the attempted murder of Jeremy Maidment,' Bob Cooper said in a deadpan voice Fenwick could tell was forced.

'Really?' He could do laconic better than anyone. 'Well, we knew she was unstable. Who saved him, or did he disarm her with a bedpan?'

'Well, I did, guv.'

'Good grief!'

'It's true, there are witnesses.' Cooper laughed.

Fenwick joined in but sobered quickly.

'Poor woman. She'll probably be better off in care but it's such a shame.'

'The major's not pressing charges, even though he's clearly at risk from her. Just as he's still refusing protection.'

'Guilty conscience.'

'He's decided to leave hospital already, against his doctor's advice. Nightingale thinks it won't be long before he leads us to the man he's protecting.'

'If it's likely to be today I must come back.'

'I wouldn't bother, there's no way he's going anywhere; he can barely walk. The doctors are furious with him for discharging himself and putting his recovery at risk.'

'Maybe he sees it as some sort of penance. If Nightingale's managed to wake his conscience the guilt will be eating into him worse than any physical pain.'

'So you do think he's a decent bloke then,' Cooper said with some satisfaction.

'I think he started out decent, Bob, and maybe he still is inside, but he's flawed. He's covered up for a child murderer and serial abuser. No amount of good intentions and charity work can ever compensate for that. A man is what he does in my book.'

'But surely the real bastards are the men that raped Paul and killed Malcolm. Watkins and Ball are accounted for, maybe three if you believe the Well-Wisher about Taylor...'

'Which I do.'

'But that still leaves this man Nathan or The Purse, whatever he calls himself; he's the villain I want to find.'

'Me too. I'll be going to Camden later to see what they've been able to find out about the Well-Wisher. By the way, who owns the land where the car was burnt? Has Clive posted a report on that yet?'

'Hang about; I'm in the incident room now.'

He could hear Cooper call over to one of the research officers.

'Yes, he gave an update this morning. It's owned by the council. They bought it as a potential waste-recycling site fifteen years ago. The previous owner isn't on the database, as it only goes back to 1995 but there's a search going with Land Registry. Shouldn't take too long to find the answer. Oh, and there's a message here for you or Nightingale to call Tom at the lab, says it's urgent.'

Fenwick used some of his precious battery for the call.

'Andrew, good. I've just spoken to Louise Nightingale; she had her phone off during a tricky interview apparently, but I'm glad you called because I've got some fascinating news.'

'Well, don't keep me in suspense.'

'You remember the blood Nightingale found in the copse, with the cigarette butts?'

'You've finished analysing it and got a match.'

'Don't spoil my moment of fun! I don't get that many.'

'Go on then, Tom, amaze me.'

'Nicolette made the breakthrough. She extracted DNA from the sample Nightingale gave us and then did something really smart. Rather than running it against all the databases she decided to check it with everything we've worked on for the Hill and Eagleton cases. And, yes, she found a match.'

'To whom; not Ball?'

'No, another of Paul's rapists.'

'What? It must belong to The Purse. Ball's dead; Taylor's meant to be dead; Watkins was in custody when the meeting happened… Do you realise what this means? Ball met The Purse the day before he was killed. He might even have been given the drugged whisky that killed him. But how was The Purse injured?'

'That, I'm happy to say is your job, not mine,' Tom said with relief.

'This is fantastic. Say well done to Nicolette for me, will you?'

'Of course. And well done Nightingale too. If she hadn't taken those samples you'd be none the wiser.'

Fenwick called her at once but had to leave a message as her phone was off. She'd delivered a critical link between the Choir Boy investigation and Paul Hill. The Purse was still alive and had been within a few miles of Harlden in the last fortnight. He might even have been responsible for Ball's death.

Fenwick had that strange feeling that came just before the end of an investigation, a sense of something vital about to happen. It was as if all the facts had sunk down within his subconscious and combined into a deep, mud-like goo, confused and without substance. But within that volatile mixture a process had been going on unnoticed, elements shifting, re-sorting, fitting together to create new ideas in an alchemy that was establishing the case's own DNA. Tom's news about the match had dropped into this seething mass and it was as if a chain reaction had started that would require very few further ingredients to complete.

If asked, of course, Fenwick would simply have said that things were coming together. He never revealed the subterranean workings of his mind to anyone.

As he walked back his skin prickled. He was hypersensitive to everything happening around him: the rush of tourists and early commuters; the smell of exhaust, sweat and stale food that hung in the heavy air; the casual brushing by of people too preoccupied to notice the man in their midst walking at a pace slower than the crowd.

When he reached Scotland Yard he asked for the man leading the surveillance of the hotel Ball had visited shortly before he died.

Ed Firth was younger than he'd expected from their

conversations on the phone. About thirty-five, tall and lanky with glasses, he looked more like a college professor than a detective, and yet he was in charge of the Child Crime and Protection Unit for east London. His team had taken over surveillance when the regular detectives became convinced the house was a brothel servicing paedophiles. Firth shook his hand briefly and then went straight to business. There was little humour about him and Fenwick sensed he cared too much about the victims he was charged to protect and rescue than was good for him.

'We've been able to establish for sure that the Madeira Hotel is actually a paedophile brothel and we've just managed to get someone inside. He's working there serving drinks and food but it's very hard for him to give us reports without rousing suspicion. Until this morning we hadn't heard a whisper but then our man called to say that one of the customers is different; there's a rumour that he might even be the owner.

'This man.' Firth passed Fenwick an eight-by-six black and white photograph. 'We don't know his name and he's only visited once since we've been watching. Do you know him? Apparently there's a special boy they keep for him that none of the other punters are allowed to use.'

Fenwick took time to study the picture. It showed a man in his seventies, slight, short, with thinning hair and a toothbrush moustache, leaving the house in an obvious fury. He didn't recognise him but asked Firth to send a copy through to Harlden so that they could cross-check it against their long list of interviewees.

'Do you know who the boy is that's reserved for him?'

'This lad.'

Firth handed him a shot of a boy looking out of a window on the fifth floor of the hotel.

'This is an enhanced version. He's been in that same room for as long as we've been watching the place and we're becoming concerned for his welfare. According to our source the boy tried to run away this morning; went over the back gate but they caught him. We don't know his name.'

'I do. He's Sam Bowyer, born in Cowfold, West Sussex, and he's only twelve. He ran away from home two months ago. Here.' Fenwick opened his briefcase and passed Firth Sam's slim file. 'Why are you concerned for him?'

'Look here – on the enhancement to the photograph. See the bruising?'

'Dear God; it looks as if he's been strangled. Why haven't you raided the place?'

'The longer we continue surveillance the more of the bastards we can capture on film and the more information our man can secure from inside. If we go in too early we may end up with a weak prosecution.'

'And meantime those boys in there continue to be abused, may even be murdered.' Fenwick tried to keep his tone neutral but some of his feelings escaped into his words and Firth flushed.

'Don't you think I know that, sir?'

'Whose decision is it when to launch an operation?'

'My boss, Head of Vice, and the CPS. They've a conference tonight as it happens. I'll tell them my concerns – again – but I don't think they're going to change their policy, which is wait and gather as much as we can.'

'They can't wait any longer. There really could be murder in that house, I wasn't playing with words. We're investigating a paedophile ring that's already resulted in two boys' deaths, maybe more. This lad could be next.' Fenwick picked up Sam's picture, his face was consumed with anger.

Firth looked at him strangely but Fenwick said nothing to explain the vehemence of his remark. How could he tell a stranger that the boy was so like young Paul Hill that he'd had a premonition of doom about him from the moment he'd first seen his photograph in the random pile of missing persons?

'I'll do my best but it would help if you could give me chapter and verse on the other cases.'

'Call this number, ask for Alison Reynolds. She can give you everything you need. And send copies of the surveillance photographs to her as well. She's knee deep in a swamp of pornography that would turn anybody's stomach and one of these men might just match the suspects we're trying to identify. While I'm here, can I look through the other surveillance pictures in case anything strikes a chord?'

By the time he left Firth they were on better terms, though the half hour he'd wasted on the photos had produced no shock of recognition. Outside the rush-hour traffic had built up and he debated whether to take a cab or the tube to his final appointment. The cars were nose to tail in front of him so he decided on the tube.

He changed onto the Piccadilly line and less than half an hour later was talking to Detective Sergeant Ben Woods at Holborn Police Station. If Woods was surprised that an officer of his rank would trouble to follow up personally on what he clearly considered a minor inquiry, he was too experienced to show it.

'We've been through CCTV footage from the area but there are places not covered, including the phone box itself. You're welcome to view them if you want to, sir, or you can take them with you.'

He pointed towards seven video cassettes, not as many as Fenwick had hoped for.

'I'll have a quick look here and then take them when I leave. What about the area; were there many people about?'

'Between one and one-thirty in the morning? Very few. We've put up notices requesting information and asked in the hotels and bars in the area but without success I'm afraid.'

'No one saw anything at all?'

'Nothing, sorry.'

Fenwick took the tapes into the equipment room feeling a fool. He didn't know why he still did this sort of thing, following up on detail when he could as easily have sent someone else. But he was in the area and he wanted an excuse to stay away from his office a little longer.

He considered the management side of police work a necessary evil. At MCS he'd discovered a civilian clerk keen to be more involved in operational policing and who relished acting as an unofficial administrative assistant for him alongside his secretary. Thanks to their efforts he had improved his reputation and had time to devote to his own priorities without it being noticed.

He had to accept that the other reason he was in London and not in Harlden was that Nightingale was handling the main investigation very well without him. He still felt guilty about his treatment of her at the start of the case and was trying to compensate by giving her space to prove herself.

He fast-forwarded each of the tapes in turn, slowing to normal speed every time a figure came into frame. After half an hour, with just a brief break for something that allegedly was coffee but could have been sump oil, he'd isolated five sections that showed the same man walking from Montague Place at the back of the British Museum towards Russell Square and back again between 1:20 a.m. and 1:39 a.m. The period that he was out of shot coincided exactly with the time of the phone call to *CrimeNight*.

Unfortunately none of the frames gave him a good view of the face and he could only estimate the man's height at around five six or seven. He found Ben Woods, who arranged for copies of the relevant sections to be made, and gave instructions that the originals should be sent to the Met forensic lab to be enhanced urgently.

'Is there much around that area?' Fenwick asked as he sipped another mug of poisonous brown liquid.

'Nothing that's open at that time of night; a few shops, a pub on the corner but the landlord saw nothing. There's a church a bit further up and a refuge for the homeless in Huntley Street but again they close their doors well before one.'

'Anyone sleeping rough that you could lean on?'

'Sleeping rough – yes, there's plenty doss in the gardens around there this time of year, but lean on, no. They're out of it by that time of night and even if they did see something we'd be the last to know. We've got your details if we do hear anything though, sir.'

Fenwick waited for a couple of stills of the best frames then left. It was just after seven and the weather was perfect. Blue sky, an occasional cloud and enough breeze to freshen the air without chilling the bare arms of office workers who were lingering in sunny spots outside pubs sipping their beer and iced drinks.

On impulse Fenwick started walking towards Russell Square. He cut past the children's hospital thinking that for all the good it did there were too many youngsters hurting on the streets of London beyond its reach. At the square he stared at the phone box on the corner as if willing the Well-Wisher to materialise. Instead a beggar tried his luck for the price of a cup of tea. Alerted by the smell Fenwick turned around before the man spoke.

'Spare change, guv? Ain't had a cuppa today.' From the smell on the man's breath he suspected that the man hadn't had a cuppa for years and doubted whether any money he gave would get near a teabag.

Fenwick's colleagues would have been surprised to learn that he kept loose coins in his pocket for random distribution: charity tins, beggars, young people sleeping rough. It was something of a lottery whether the recipient received twenty pence or a pound or some number in between because he never looked at what he passed over, but he invariably gave something. The man in front of him looked sixty but was probably nearer forty, worn down by years of rough living. By chance he received seventy pence. Fenwick was rewarded with a knuckle to the man's forehead, a gesture of gratitude too servile for him to receive comfortably. He made to move on but then paused.

'Is this your patch?' he asked the man, not sure of current vernacular because he'd been away from the sharp end of community policing for too long.

The vagrant looked startled at being spoken to but then glanced at the silver shining against his grimy palm and nodded.

'Some weeks, yeah, but I likes to move on. Roving sort, me.'

'Is it a popular area?'

'Fair. There's a Mission up the road there. Comes in 'andy when there's nuffin' else.'

'Only as a last resort?'

'It's dry,' the man spat the word out, 'an' they insist on a bath.'

'Ah, it's Salvation Army.'

The man scratched his head, sending a waft of fetid air towards Fenwick who kept his face neutral.

'Nah, they wear regular togs. They let us smoke, an' there's a TV but an evening without a snifter, well...' He made to nudge Fenwick with his elbow. 'It's a longun, in't it.' He gave him a friendly grin that betrayed the result of years of lack of basic dentistry.

'It is indeed. Have you seen this man around here?'

The friendly smile vanished to be replaced with a look of caution. Fenwick rattled the change in his pocket but it had no effect. He pulled out a pound coin. The caution stayed but the man licked his lips as if he could already taste liquor. He glanced at the photograph.

'Mebbe. Not very clear, is it?'

'Take a closer look.'

The A4 paper was taken from his hands and studied.

''E looks familiar. It's that coat more'n anything. I've seen it around.'

'Locally?' Fenwick added another pound to his own palm. The vagrant nodded. 'Any idea whereabouts?'

'I'd be lying if I said yes, mister, but I've 'elped, 'aven't I?'

'A little. Look, if you can suggest someone else who might know him and take me to them I'll give you the money.'

There was a split second of hesitation.

'Jacko. Has a berth in the park over there. C'mon.'

The park was a scrap of lawn and a few bushes with benches dotted along a path in need of weeding. There was a bundle of bedding on the farthest bench and it was towards this that they headed. As they grew closer the bundle moved and took on a vaguely man-like shape.

''Ere Jacko, bloke's got dosh if you can tell 'im this geezer's name. No 'arm telling; e's not one of us.'

Jacko grunted and sniffed. He said something Fenwick couldn't make out.

''E says money first.'

'No, name first then money and there's a fiver in it for you if he cooperates.'

The bundle of rags muttered something that sounded suspiciously like '…'kin rozzer' but he ignored him. The two men mumbled to each other for a while as Fenwick inspected a nearby bush and tried to manage his impatience.

'Gi'us the pic then,' his helper snorted and Fenwick passed it over. There was more grunting then Jacko said, quite clearly, 'Reckon it's Peter up at the Mission. He dresses like that.'

Fenwick gave out his meagre rewards and followed their directions to the Mission on Gordon Square Gardens. When he got there he saw that it was jointly funded by a group of churches including, Methodist, Catholic and Anglican. On the board outside the opening times were given as 7:30 p.m. to 11 p.m. in summer and 4 p.m. to 11 p.m. in winter. The door was locked and the windows blank so he pressed the bell to one side. Nothing happened. He tried again, for longer. Still nothing, yet when he bent and looked through the letterbox he was certain he saw movement.

'Police,' he shouted through it.

Bolts were drawn back and a chain rattled. A fresh-faced young man with a crewcut smiled at him cheerfully.

'Sorry, we get so many trying to come in at all times of day and night that I'm used to ignoring the bell. I'm Charles, Charlie to my friends; part of the cleaning crew.' He stuck out his hand. Fenwick shook it and felt the calluses.

'Detective Chief Inspector Fenwick,' he said. 'Is Peter here?'

'Peter?' Charlie frowned. 'Oh, Father Peter. No, he won't be here until after Evensong. Can I help you? If it's about the *CrimeNight* programme, we've already told a colleague of yours that we can't help. I'm sorry. Is there anything else?'

Fenwick was pleased that the locals had been as thorough as they'd claimed but decided to test out the picture anyway.

'Yes. You can tell me whether this is someone you know.' He passed the still over.

The recognition was obvious on Charlie's face but it was quickly replaced with a look of confusion.

'Is something wrong?' Charlie asked.

'No, but we're keen to talk to this man and confirm his identity.'

'I see, well, perhaps it would be best if you, er, talked to one of the brothers. I'm just a volunteer.'

'But I think you know this man, Charlie. Look, he's done nothing wrong but it's essential I meet him. He could be of great assistance to us in a murder inquiry.'

Charlie looked even more flustered.

'Well, I don't know.'

'I'm sure that the brothers would expect you to cooperate with the police when we're trying to help someone. And as I say, Father Peter has done nothing wrong.'

Charlie started nodding before he opened his mouth.

'It's not a very good picture but I'm fairly certain it looks like Father Peter. Is he all right?'

'As far as I'm aware. Why shouldn't he be?'

'He's so dedicated,' Charlie replied. 'He works all hours, sometimes in very rough areas. It doesn't matter what time of day or night it is, he's always out there.'

'So why the locked doors?'

'Here, you mean? For security, sadly. This is only one of the shelters we run and we can't staff it all day. Some of the others are open twenty-four hours. That's where Father Peter will be, at one of them but I couldn't tell you which. All I know is he'll be here around eight to check everything's all right, then he'll be off to St Olaf's; that's his real passion. It provides temporary home and help for young runaways. Peter campaigned for it and champions it within the Church. They can look after almost forty now, get them cleaned up, well fed and, if necessary, encourage them into treatment. It's up near King's Cross Station. He may be there – would you like the address?'

'Please.'

Charlie scribbled it down and handed it over. Before he closed and locked the door he picked up a tin from inside.

'Would you care to make a donation, Chief Inspector, while you're here?'

Fenwick handed over a ten pound note and cursed the fact that he felt guilty instead of virtuous. He always did.

CHAPTER THIRTY-EIGHT

News of Sarah Hill's arrest travelled across Harlden faster than a bush fire. It became the topic of conversation in shops, pubs and sitting rooms within hours. Opinion was again evenly divided between those who were glad that she was out of harm's way at last and others who thought it a shame that she'd failed in her attempt.

Under the cover of its smokescreen Major Maidment slipped out of hospital and away home. As he arrived at his front door it was immediately apparent that Margaret Pennysmith hadn't exaggerated. The downstairs window was boarded up, his front flowerbeds were denuded of plants and the vestiges of graffiti marred the perfectly pointed brickwork. Inside, something foul had been pushed through the letterbox and cleaned away with disinfectant. The smells of both lingered in the tiny hall. He had deliberately not told anybody that he was returning home. The fridge was bare but a note on the table informed him that there were casseroles and pre-prepared vegetables in the freezer.

'Thank you, Margaret,' he said out loud, deeply touched, and crawled upstairs for a hot shower.

As he sat in the hot stream of water, willing the deep-seated aches from his beating into submission, he went over the plan for what he knew he had to do. Even though he was certain that the confrontation wouldn't result in a physical encounter, psychologically he would prefer to feel in better shape before he made his journey, so he decided to telephone to make an appointment for the following day. He dried himself carefully and dressed in his loosest clothing, shunning the dressing gown behind the bedroom door as too louche, despite his injuries.

There were ten messages on his answering service. The first three were abusive but the fourth was from someone called Jason MacDonald, asking him to call back to discuss 'some important information' he had. He'd never heard of the man so he deleted it. Messages five through eight were also full of anonymous hatred; nine and ten were again from MacDonald. This time he introduced himself as a reporter from the *Enquirer* and Maidment's remarkable memory dragged up the photographic impression formed by the glimpse of headlines he had seen in that paper on the day of his release from prison. There was no way he wanted to speak to the man who'd exploited Sarah Hill so cruelly.

He put the smaller of the meals that had been left for him into the microwave to defrost and turned on the oven to heat it through as he didn't trust the micro-thing to cook it properly. Then he picked up his hat and walking stick and made his way gingerly to the phone box at the end of the road beside the castle wall. His phone might be tapped; it was the sort of thing that Inspector Nightingale would think of. He knew the number he needed off by heart and dialled. It rang for a long time, then the machine demanded that he leave a message.

'This is Jeremy Maidment. Percy, if you're there please answer the phone.'

There was the sound of the handset being picked up.

'I wondered if you were going to call. You're out, are you?'

'Yes. I'd like to see you – tomorrow if possible.'

'No can do, old chap. Tonight's your only option, say around seven?'

'That's not terribly convenient. How about the day after?'

'No, I won't be here. It's now or never; make up your mind.'

Maidment decided at once.

'Very well, seven o'clock it is.'

They both rang off without pleasantries that would have been hypocritical. The major realised that he was in no fit state to drive and booked a taxi for six-thirty before returning to the house where he forced himself to finish preparing a meal he didn't want but knew he had to eat.

The food refreshed him and it made him think. If he suspected that his phone might be tapped shouldn't he also acknowledge that he could be being followed? He'd seen no one on his journey home but then he'd been concentrating on being as inconspicuous as possible. Maidment stood up from the table, wincing as his back and ribs protested at the movement, and eased his way to the bay window at the front of the house. All but the side panes of glass had been boarded up so his view was obscured.

Cursing mildly under his breath he climbed upstairs, pausing on each step to catch his breath. From behind the curtains of his bedroom window he peered up and down the road. It was empty except for the usual line of parked cars. Most he recognised as belonging to his neighbours but there were three that he did not. From where he stood he couldn't tell if any of them were occupied but they might be. He decided to take no risks. Despite the protest from his body, he forced himself to walk back to the phone booth. This time he took the local directory with him and made two calls. The pavement back to the house seemed to stretch on for ever but he made it eventually.

He hobbled to his favourite chair and almost collapsed into it as the clock on the mantel chimed three quarters. He closed his eyes. The cushions felt so comfortable that he knew immediately he would fall asleep so he sat up again and set his watch alarm for a quarter past six, time enough to wash up the supper things and be ready to leave at the appointed hour.

* * *

Cooper decided to work late. Doris was out at a whist drive so he wasn't expected home and he was frustrated with his lack of progress. Despite days of hard work he'd had no luck in finding Nathan/The Purse. He'd tried cross-referencing the names to the nine army acquaintances of Maidment that lived locally without success. Two still had to be re-interviewed: Ben Thompson and Richard Edwards. Zach Smart had returned his call that afternoon, full of apologies for not coming in to the station to make a statement as he'd promised. He was just back from holiday, he explained, and invited him round immediately. His open, cooperative response half convinced Cooper of his innocence even before he saw him. By the end of taking his statement he was sure that he could cross him of his list of potential suspects, not least because he had proof that he had been in Germany in 1981 and away on holiday in September 1982. Cooper had left and called Ben Thompson immediately. There was still no reply so he'd driven round to his house and chatted with a neighbour who confirmed that Thompson was out. That left Edwards. His calls during the day had gone unanswered yet again and this time he wasn't able to leave a message. He thought it odd, then told himself that the machine was probably full.

Edwards lived a few miles outside Harlden. Perhaps he should take a quick drive out to see him again. At least it would be something to do and it would stop him feeling so useless. Cooper glanced at his watch. It was past his teatime and he always worked better on a full stomach so he decided to visit the canteen first and stop off at Edwards' place on his way home.

He managed to buy the last steak and onion pasty, and there was a slice of strawberry gateau left as well. Consequently, he was in a contented, if sleepy mood, when he strolled back to his desk. It was almost six o'clock and he was inclined to forget his earlier idea and go straight home. When his phone rang, he cursed. It was the operations room.

'We've got Stock on for you, Bob.' Cooper sat up straight and put his coffee down so that he could pick up a pen. Stock was one of the officers he'd put on surveillance duty.

'Cooper,' he said when he was switched through.

'It's me, guv. Maidment's been out and about.'

'Where is he now?'

'Back in his house but he's used the phone box at the end of the road twice. That's suspicious, isn't it?'

'Could be.' Cooper scratched his stomach ruminatively and suppressed a belch. 'What was he wearing?'

There was a pause as Stock digested this unexpected question.

'Well, normal stuff I guess.'

'Outdoor clothes, not a dressing gown?'

'No, he was properly dressed but he was walking very slowly, leaning on his stick. The second time I thought he was going to collapse.'

'Even so, he might be going out again later tonight. You call me straight away if he moves. I might still be here. You've got my direct line as well as my mobile, haven't you?'

Stock confirmed that the numbers were programmed into his phone and rang off. Cooper dialled Nightingale's office then her mobile but there was no reply. With a feeling of disbelief he called her home. The answerphone had time to click in before she picked up. In the background he could hear jazz playing softly as he told her about Stock's call.

'He suspects a tap,' she said, 'and the call must have been significant for him to walk to the phone box. Do you think he's arranged a meeting?'

'I don't know, maybe, but Stock said he didn't look well. I would have thought that he'd wait until he was feeling better. I know I would.'

'So would I but he may be desperate. He's held his silence for so long he's bound to be impatient now he's out. Tell Operations that they're to call you *and* me if he makes any move at all.'

Cooper replaced the receiver. He was wide awake again and didn't want to go home but neither did he want to sit and stare at his computer screen. That left only one option. He'd drive out to Edwards' house, have a mooch around and try to talk to his neighbours. It would be as well to be careful though. Edwards was the highest-ranking officer on Cooper's list, a lieutenant-colonel, and seemed beyond reproach. People like Edwards tended to be well connected and inclined to complain at any imagined slight. The more he thought about it on his drive out of Harlden, the more comfortable he felt about the plan he was following: a low-key amble without raising any alarm. In retrospect, it was a great pity that he left exactly when he did, as photographs from London arrived on his desk less than five minutes later. Had he seen them, subsequent events would have turned out very differently.

The evening traffic was surprisingly light and he made good time. The local church clock was striking half past six as he drove into the village where Edwards lived. He passed the local pub, making a mental note to himself to return for a chat once he'd nosed around. It sat opposite a small village green with an ornamental pump and a row of pretty alms cottages on the far side. Edwards' house was at the top of the hill above the village, set well back behind a stone wall and elegant wrought-iron gates. Cooper parked beside the village green within easy walking distance of both pub and house.

The gates were pulled to but not locked. Beyond them a gravel drive led to a late Victorian double-fronted house and then went beyond it to an enclosed area of garden. There was no sign of a car but then there was a double garage to one side of the drive so that didn't mean anything. The house looked deserted but he pushed open the gates anyway so that he could wander around the grounds. In his pocket he had a copy of the blurred photograph that the Well-Wisher had sent but at any angle he couldn't make the picture match the ironwork before him.

His footsteps crunched on the drive. Halfway up it security lights, set too early for the summer twilight, flashed on, startling him. He felt conspicuous and was about to turn back when the hall lamp in the house came on, shining from the fan light above the door. Before he could knock it was flung open and a voice that could have cut glass called out.

'You're bloody early!'

He stepped onto the stone porch and looked at the man silhouetted against the light.

'Excuse me?' he said, recognising Edwards as his eyes adjusted.

A look of surprised arrogance crossed the man's face and he moved to push the door closed. Cooper's size nine blocked his way.

'You're Richard Edwards.'

The man glared at Cooper's foot.

'Get away from my house before I call the police. I am in no mood to buy from a door-to-door salesman.'

It was the voice of a man who expected to be obeyed but the arrogant tone merely served to annoy Cooper.

'I am the police, sir. We met last month, don't you remember? Detective Sergeant Cooper, Harlden CID. Maybe you received my messages.'

The look of calculation crossed the man's face so quickly that Cooper couldn't be sure that he'd seen it – but his pulse quickened.

'I'm Edwards, but now is not convenient, Sergeant.'

'I thought my messages made it very clear that I needed to see you urgently.' His voice was firm.

Generations of Sussex yeomen had produced Robert Courtney

Cooper and he wasn't about to be ordered around by some jumped-up retired officer. He studied the man in front of him deliberately. They were confronting each other eye to eye and Cooper was not a tall man. Edwards had thinning straight hair that once might have been sandy and affected a prissy moustache that concealed a fleshy mouth and helped to distract attention from a weak jaw. But he was fit, with a precise bearing and well-tailored clothes.

'May I come in?'

Without waiting for an answer Cooper pushed his way over the threshold into the hall. There were doors to the right and left and a curving staircase on the far wall with a passage running past it to the back of the house.

'This is extremely inconvenient, Sergeant. I'm expecting guests and have already told you that I cannot see you tonight. I could meet you later in the week.' Edwards pushed out his bottom lip, Cooper noticed, when he was annoyed. It made him look like an ageing, spoilt schoolboy.

'I won't keep you long. A few questions now and we can continue another time. Shall we make ourselves comfortable?'

Cooper instinctively turned towards the sitting room they'd used on his previous visit and was inside it before Edwards could stop him. In the centre of an ornate rug were a trunk and two large suitcases, packed, labelled and strapped. He took a step closer.

'Off on a trip are we, sir?'

'Yes I am, which is another reason why I'm very busy. If you insist on asking your wretched questions we can use my study.'

Cooper barely heard him. His near sight might be a bit dodgy but his distant vision was perfect and he'd seen the date and destination on the labels. Years of being in the army had conditioned Edwards to being precise in the direction of his luggage. He was leaving the country the following day.

Cooper's mind was racing as he walked down the passage towards the study. If Edwards meant to leave within twenty-four hours, why had he suggested a meeting later in the week? That wasn't the action of an innocent man with nothing to hide. And he was going to a part of South-East Asia that Cooper knew from bitter experience didn't believe in extradition.

Coincidence? Hardly. By the time Cooper pushed open the study door he was sure of two things. Number one, Edwards was guilty as sin of something and, two he was in deep doo-doo. He was alone in the home of a man who might well be a killer, hell-bent on fleeing the country and nobody at the station knew where he was. Nervously, he slipped his hand into his jacket pocket and fumbled for his mobile phone, cursing the fact that he didn't automatically keep the wretched thing on because he hated its intrusion.

'Why don't you take a seat over there, Sergeant?' Edwards pointed to a chair on the far side of an elegant fireplace. He was walking towards it when pain lashed across his shoulders, forcing him to his knees. Another blow struck his skull and the lights went out.

Edwards studied the man at his feet and noted the trickle of blood running from his nose onto the rug.

'Blast, I've always liked this rug,' he said, as he used luggage straps and string to tie Cooper's legs at the knees and ankles, and then to truss his arms tightly behind his back.

The wretched man might already be dead but he doubted it. Just to make sure, he pulled back an eyelid and watched as the pupil reacted to the light. Good. He had never intentionally killed someone and he didn't want to start now. His plan, constructed in the time it had taken Cooper to study the luggage labels, was to take him, trussed up, out into the woods after Maidment's visit and then tell William to deal with him sometime after he'd left the country. He'd have to find another method as the poker was part of an antique set of which he was rather fond. He took his weapon to the kitchen and washed it carefully before returning it to the fire rack. Then he found some duct tape left over from sealing his trunk and placed a strip over Cooper's mouth, pressing down firmly. He used the rug to drag him behind the sofa next to the window so that he would be out of sight for Maidment's visit. He would have to use this room as he wouldn't have time to move the luggage from the sitting room and he didn't want his next visitor to realise how quickly he intended to leave the country.

It really was rather vexing the way people kept interfering with his arrangements. At least he could rely on William. He would be on his way already with the boy. The thought made Edwards shiver. One more time, he promised himself, here in the house and maybe even in the pool, which he'd been heating ever since he'd returned home that morning. And then, well, he'd leave Sam to William – literally.

His instructions for delivering the boy had been clear and the arrangements, to put him in a secure location in his woods, left his address uncompromised as even William didn't know where he lived. William was to leave Sam in the ice house and lock him in, making sure both doors were secure using keys he'd left in the lock. The boy should be drugged, not senseless because where was the fun in that, but enough to make him compliant. For safe measure he'd told William to tie his hands as well to make him easier to deal with. Edwards planned to collect Sam as soon as he'd got rid of Maidment, bring him back here for the rest of the night and then put him back in the ice house again for William to collect. He hadn't been precise on this point but he thought William would have the sense to realise that whatever he found would have to be dealt with so that there could be no risk of the boy ever revealing what had happened to him.

He knew that he was running a risk but it was a slight one given William's cooperation, and he felt he deserved one final session of unconstrained pleasure. It was so difficult now that what were ludicrously called 'sex holidays' were classified as a crime. Ridiculous; sex was all right for the wretched Club 18–30 yobs who boozed and screwed their way through cheap Mediterranean resorts in orgies he thought far more disgusting than his refined behaviour.

He only ever gratified himself in private and he chose beautiful boys, ideally in that delightful pre-pubescent stage when their flesh was as smooth as rabbit skin, the necks narrow, holding their heads above them like flowers just opening to the sun of experience. Paul and Sam were perfect specimens. What he engaged in with the boys was quite the opposite of the sweaty, grunting, alcohol-fuelled couplings that were ridiculously considered 'normal' sex.

He shuddered, feeling chilled. Moving the lumpy sergeant had made him perspire. It wouldn't do to greet Maidment in disarray as it was his intention to get rid of him as quickly as possible and to do that would require rock-hard composure and confidence. If he could continue to count on the man's guilty past and elephantine sense of honour to bind him to silence then the major would live. If not, well, it would be sad but inevitable that he did not. Another little job for William.

He used the downstairs cloakroom to freshen up, splashing his face with cool water and combing the long strands of fine hair back carefully over his scalp.

At seven o'clock exactly the doorbell rang and he led Maidment to his study, their habitual meeting ground.

'Whisky?' He waved the lead crystal decanter towards him.

'No, thank you.'

'You don't mind if I have one? It's been a bugger of a day.' He noticed Maidment wince at his choice of words, or maybe it was in response to pain from his battered body. 'You look terrible, old man. Is that the result of the beating you took from those girls? Bloody hell. Mind you, I've never believed them to be the weaker sex. Just shows I was right all along. Come on, a snifter won't do you any harm.'

'No, thank you. I'm not here for a chat, Edwards.'

He was surprised at the abrupt use of his surname from someone of lower rank.

'You know why I've come.'

'I really don't think I do. Why don't you enlighten me?'

Edwards took his drink to the other side of the fireplace nearest the door, from where he could see both Maidment's chair and the sofa behind which he had concealed the policeman's unconscious body. It was completely hidden in the gap between the wall and the back of the sofa, with the curtains that framed the window cutting off any chance of a side view. He relaxed a little.

'Paul Hill,' Maidment said.

'Go on.'

'You killed Paul Hill.'

Edwards threw back his head and roared with laughter.

'My God, Maidment, you are so stupid. I swore that I hadn't twenty-five years ago and I swear it to you again now. I promise you absolutely that I did not kill Paul Hill.'

'You what?'

Nightingale leapt up from the table in fury, knocking over her wine glass in the process. Clive calmly picked it up and mopped at the spreading stain with some kitchen roll.

'...Then get on to every taxi firm in the book and find out which one picked him up from the golf club and where they took him.'

She slammed the phone down and ran her fingers through her hair in exasperation.

'They lost him. I can't believe it...they lost him.'

'How?' Clive knew her well enough not to try and sympathise.

'He took a taxi to the golf club, paid it off and went inside. To be fair to Stock he decided to go in to check where he was and that's when he realised that Maidment had gone. Otherwise he'd still be sitting there in blissful ignorance; what a cock-up.'

She went to pick up her glass of wine, noticed that it was empty and drank from his instead.

'I'd better let Fenwick and Cooper know, then I'm going to have to go in. I know there's little I can do but...'

'Of course, I'd do the same.'

She bent down and kissed him quickly.

'Sometimes it helps that you're a copper too.'

He just nodded and rose to go.

'I'll leave you to it. Call me when you can. If things are going to get lively it might be a good idea for me to go and help Alison tonight after all.'

Nightingale nodded absently, acknowledging his departure without hearing the words and was on the phone before the door closed behind him. Cooper wasn't at the station and there was no answer from his home so she was forced to leave a message on his mobile. She had no better luck with Fenwick, despite having told everyone to contact him the moment anything happened. She was forced to leave him a message as well. In a foul mood, feeling very alone, she scraped the remains of her supper into the cat's bowl, picked up her car keys and slammed the flat door behind her.

CHAPTER THIRTY-NINE

Nightingale tried Cooper's radio on her short drive to the station without success. When she rang his home number a second time a familiar male voice answered and she breathed a sigh of relief.

'Bob, thank goodness!'

'No, it's his son. Dad's out, so's Mum. Can I take a message?'

'Just ask him to call me as soon as he gets in, can you? It's Louise Nightingale. Tell him it's urgent.'

'Is everything all right?'

She could hear the edge of concern in his voice and forced her own to be calm.

'Just the usual but it's important I speak to him.'

Nightingale waited impatiently for the security gates to the police car park to draw back then skidded into the space reserved for the superintendent and ran up the steps two at a time. She really wanted to find Cooper. She needed him as a sounding board as she made decisions on what to do to minimise the damage of Maidment's disappearance and find him as quickly as possible. She might be the senior officer but Cooper's experience was worth as much if not more than her rank and she was honest enough to acknowledge it.

She stopped by Fenwick's office but it was deserted, so was the incident room. DS Robin was in the CID room when she entered at a run.

'What's up? A problem?'

She noticed the gleam in his eye and realised that he'd love her discomfort. She didn't care.

'I'm looking for Bob Cooper, have you seen him?'

'He was in the canteen when I came back at six but that was an hour ago. Haven't seen him since, come to think of it. Probably at home.'

'No, he's not and I need to reach him urgently. Do you know the pubs he might visit between here and home?'

'Some, yeah.'

'Good, then start calling them to see if he's there.'

Robin picked up a well-thumbed telephone directory without another word. He was a fan of Cooper's though he thought the sergeant's support of the trumped-up bitch who'd been promoted over them both an error of judgement. But if Bob was in a spot of bother and she was out for his blood he'd do whatever he could to find and warn him.

While Robin started phoning Cooper's usual haunts Nightingale scanned his desk in the hope of picking up a clue as to where he might be. He was probably somewhere enjoying a pint, she told herself, but that didn't explain why he was out of touch with his surveillance team. He'd told her he was going to work late. Supposing he'd found something while working alone and had decided to follow up without her.

A memory of his botched arrest of Chalfont came back to her. They'd meant to be working that case together but he'd decided to handle the arrest himself. She'd never challenged him about it, believing that he'd learnt his lesson the hard way, but now she wished she'd made it more of an issue at the time. A worm of worry wriggled its way into her stomach and refused to go away.

Some half-finished reports sat on his desk. She scanned them quickly and as rapidly discarded them. Beside them lay some notes in his handwriting:

~~Adrian Bush (Bushy)~~
~~Alex Cotton~~
Richard Edwards – called again still no answer
~~Vernon Jones (Jonesy)~~
~~Ernest Knight (Milky)~~
~~Patrick Murray (Minty)~~
Ben Thompson – away for another week?
~~Zach Smart – called in seen him – not him~~

Cooper had become obsessed with these names, if this is what he'd been working on before he went out it might help to find him.

In the privacy of her tiny screened office away from Stock's curious ears she rang Zach Smart. A few minutes later she replaced the receiver certain that Bob had been worrying at the list while he waited for Stock to report in. She was about to dial Edwards' number when her own mobile buzzed on her desk.

'Nightingale.'

'It's Fenwick. Have you found him yet?'

'No, Robin's checking the local pubs right now but—'

'Why? The major's hardly likely to be meeting the man he suspects is a killer in a bar.'

'Sorry, I meant he's looking for Bob. As far as the major's concerned we're working our way through the taxi firms. No joy yet. He was last seen at six-thirty going into the golf club; that was thirty-five minutes ago. Apparently he walked straight through and into another taxi out the back.'

'What's this about Cooper?'

'I can't find him. He's not here or at home and he's not answering his mobile…'

'Surprise, surprise. He's probably in the pub somewhere.'

'Maybe, which is why Robin is checking them but he said he

was going to work late. What if he's stumbled into something?'

'Bob's too experienced to do that. He may look a bit of a lumbering old sod but he's street smart.'

'I know, it's just that…'

She couldn't bring herself to admit the feeling of unease in the pit of her stomach.

'Woman's intuition?'

'Don't mock, Andrew.'

'I'm not.' His voice was immediately serious. 'If you think something might have happened to him then you should do everything you can to put your mind at ease but don't slacken the search for the major.'

'Of course not. By the way, where are you?'

'Still in London so I'm unlikely to be back for at least an hour and a half even if I set off now – unless I order a helicopter. Should I?'

'There's no need, really; I've got it all under control. Operations have sent out a message to all patrols to look for the major and we'll be through checking the taxis within half an hour.'

'Have you spoken to Quinlan?'

She hesitated.

'Not yet.'

'You should call him and agree how you'll work together until I'm back in Harlden.'

'But I'm on top of things; I really don't need him to get involved.'

'With all of this and Bob out of the picture you need him. I know you'll do a good job but this could become too big for you to handle alone. Remember Maidment had a service revolver. If he's protecting an army buddy he might have one as well. You were thinking of asking for firearms to be on standby, weren't you?'

'Well, I…yes, eventually, when we found the major. Look, Andrew, I can manage.'

'Nightingale, I'm SIO and I'm telling you to call the superintendent. This is not a negotiation.'

'Yes, sir.'

'Right, I'm about five minutes away from cornering the man I think is the Well-Wisher and I'm certain that he knows who Maidment is protecting. As soon as I've got what I can from him I'll call you and assess whether I need to hitch a 'copter ride back. Also, you should have received a photograph from the Met of a man they think owns the house in London that Ball visited. It might be The Purse; check it out and remember, call me any time you need to. Good luck.'

He broke the connection, leaving Nightingale to stare at her phone. She took a deep breath then called Superintendent Quinlan. His home number was engaged. That would be Fenwick who'd obviously decided not to trust her. What was he saying? For once, Nightingale didn't waste time speculating. Finding Cooper was more important. She dialled the number next to Edwards' name, waited while it rang unanswered and replaced the receiver. Quinlan's line was still busy so her next call was to Operations. She spoke to the officer in charge.

'I need you to put out a bulletin, a search for Bob Cooper's green Volvo estate, registration number RCC 157. Yes, it's personalised. A present from his wife, I think. And there are some addresses that patrol should concentrate on first; ready?'

Quinlan had been in the middle of a rare supper at home when Fenwick interrupted him to explain what was happening with the Maidment investigation.

'It's all very well delegating operational responsibility to Nightingale, Andrew, but it's your neck on the line as SIO.'

'I realise that.'

'If I were you, I'd call the ACC. At least you'll be able to say you consulted with your boss if this goes pear-shaped.'

'But that's just flannel. He can't help me and anyway, what's happening is down to me. If something goes wrong, and I don't see why it should, I'll be the one to carry the can; that's only fair.'

Quinlan sighed and Fenwick imagined him shaking his head in exasperation.

'It's your career.'

'Yes it is. And with that in mind I have a favour to ask you. Would you mind supervising Nightingale for me while I'm...?'

'Aren't you at the station?'

'Not exactly. I'm in London.'

'What the bloody hell are you doing there?'

Fenwick told him, his words falling into an increasingly incredulous silence.

'I intend to leave here as soon as I can and make my way back to Harlden. I'll see if I can borrow a helicopter.'

'No! For God's sake, don't do that. It will only draw attention to your damn fool errand. Good grief, Fenwick, will you never learn? Of all the times to go off on one of your tomfool escapades...'

'Things were quiet when I left and I've had plenty to do here.'

'That might just turn out to be your epitaph.'

'But I—'

'Quiet, let me think.'

Fenwick held his tongue.

'Right, here's what we're going to do.'

His use of the word 'we' and his automatic instinct to help reminded Fenwick of how lucky he was to have an ally like Quinlan.

'Your only possible saving grace is that the ACC insisted on you taking personal responsibility for tracking down the Well-Wisher. That's what you're doing. If you can find him, make him talk and turn him into a first-class witness for the prosecution, you might just escape from this mess with your career intact. Stay up in London. Don't rush back. If needs be, you can say that I insisted on stepping in here. After all, this was my case once and I have an interest in seeing Paul Hill's killer in jail.'

'Thank you. And Nightingale?'

'I'll call her now and say I'm on my way in. You just concentrate on getting a good result in London.'

The pain in Cooper's skull was intolerable when he opened his eyes. It was so bad that he thought he was going to be sick so he shut his eyes against the fear of choking. He must have passed out because the next time he opened them the sky outside was growing dark. Any movement, even blinking, was agony, so he lay there, trussed up like a Sunday chicken, and tried to think. It was difficult. As well as the nail-like stabbing in his head, his shoulders, arms and hips were burning with pain as his body protested its restraints.

I'm too old for this. The thought filled his mind. It angered him that he should have put himself in such a position, walking in on a suspect without back-up. He wouldn't be missed for hours yet and even when he was no one at the station would know where to find him. *What a plonker.* The pain in his head wouldn't ease up, not like on the movies when the hero was up and fighting within seconds. He lay there feeling as sick as a dog and bloody stupid.

In all probability he was going to die. *And serve you right,* he told himself. He was terrified. The realisation that he might very well be a coward at the hour of his death made him livid. Not that it was a subject he'd previously dwelt on as he wasn't that sort of bloke but when he had thought about it he'd imagined himself noble and calm, not shit scared. *What would the Zebra do?* he asked himself, to no avail because there was no way

Fenwick would have got himself into such a predicament in the first place.

But thinking of his boss helped. They'd been good mates, he decided. What he felt for Andrew went beyond respect; there was deep affection and a determination not to let him down. Well, he'd done that right and proper, hadn't he? Cooper shook his head in self-disgust and the wave of pain pushed him back into unconsciousness.

The sound of two men having an argument roused him. He recognised the voices at once.

'...don't want palming off with one of your whiskies, dammit; I want to know the truth.'

'Oh, Jeremy, Jeremy, what a fool you are. The truth! As if truth is an absolute that I can pluck out of the past and present as solid fact. Don't be ridiculous.'

'I will not be fobbed off, Edwards. I'll ask you again, did you or did you not kill Paul Hill?'

'No, I damned well did not.'

Cooper was shocked into full consciousness by the force of truth he heard in Edwards' words. He shut his eyes against the pain of the electric light and tried to concentrate.

'If you didn't, then who did? I demand an answer.'

'Sit down, for God's sake, Jeremy.'

Cooper felt the weight of someone on the sofa behind which he was concealed. It nudged him into the wall a fraction and he tried to roll his knees over so that he could hit the back. It was impossible and the effort made his gorge rise but in moving he felt something slide from his pocket to the carpet behind his back. It was his mobile phone. If he stretched out, the tips of his fingers just brushed it but not enough to push any of the buttons. As Edwards and Maidment continued to argue he strained towards the slippery metal object, swallowing down the vomit at the back of his throat, until he was able to get his thumb around the bottom corner and flick it closer to his palm. His hands were virtually numb but he clenched and unclenched his fists, forcing the blood to flow, glad that his gag prevented him from screaming in pain as it did so. Finally, he had the phone in his hand. He proceeded to fumble with his useless fingers in the hope of switching the damn thing on.

'You want to know about the day Paul Hill disappeared?'

'I do.'

'And if I tell you, what will you do with the information?'

'That depends on what you say.'

'But you can't go to the police. You gave your word.'

'I gave my word based on what you told me. If that was a pack of lies then I have every right to break my silence.'

'It wasn't a pack of lies. I think you'll find that you will have to hold your word. And if you don't, with your past, who do you think the police will believe?'

There was a brief silence and Cooper imagined Edwards sipping his drink while Maidment tried to decide what to do. He must have nodded his acceptance of Edwards' terms because he carried on, sounding satisfied.

'Very well. What happened on 7th September, 1982? Paul Hill did come to this house that day. Bryan Taylor brought him in his car. It was a regular arrangement. Oh, for God's sake, don't look like that, Jeremy. The boy was a tart, a nasty little prostitute who preyed on men. He was no innocent lured into the life, trust me; he had a fully developed sexual appetite and a voracious demand for money.'

'This is quite disgusting.'

'In your opinion, maybe, but not everybody agrees with you. Homosexuality isn't a crime and I can assure you that this was consenting, yes indeed.'

'He was a child, Percy, a boy of fourteen. I've seen his photograph, he barely looks twelve.'

'Looks can be deceptive and in his case they were. Anyway, I do nothing that the Greeks did not do. Boys used to be married at that age in older civilisations. With your classical education surely you appreciate that.'

'Nothing excuses child abuse, Edwards, nothing.'

Maidment's voice contained all the anger that Cooper could feel roaring in his insides but it was blinding him to the danger he was in. If Edwards was prepared to kill a policeman, and Cooper was certain that he was, then another man's death would mean nothing.

'My God, you can be pompous. Oh take that "disgusted of Cheam" look off your face; you're hardly Snow White. Shall I continue?'

'Go on, you've started so you might as well continue.'

'Paul and Bryan arrived. It was a blistering hot day so we all had a swim. Things got a bit out of hand. Bryan always was uncouth and clumsy. Anyway, Paul ran off into the changing rooms and we decided it would be best if Bryan took him home early.

'I swear to you, the last time I saw Paul he was dressed in his school uniform and sitting in the front seat of Taylor's car.'

'What happened next?'

'About half an hour later, just as we were sitting down for an early supper—'

'So it wasn't just you and Bryan with Paul; there were others! No wonder things got "out of hand" as you so delicately put it.'

'Grow up, Jeremy. It was nothing heavy, just some fun. Paul wasn't harmed in any way.'

'According to your definition of harm. Poor little blighter.'

'Now just hold on. That little bastard doesn't deserve your sympathy. Sure you won't have a whisky? I'm dry.'

'No.'

There was a clink of bottle against glass and a splash of soda, then a sigh as Edwards took a deep swallow.

'Where was I? Ah yes, about half an hour later – I was in here as it happens – I saw Bryan's car pull up at the old gates. They've gone now – antique but some idiot smashed into them last year and ruined them. I waited a moment but he didn't drive in so I went out. He was slumped in the driver's seat, barely conscious. There was blood everywhere. Taylor told me that there'd been a fight in the car and Paul had pulled a knife. He took it off him but not before the Hill boy had stabbed him.'

'Where was Paul?'

'Somewhere back in the woods where Bryan had left him.'

'You're saying he killed Paul in self-defence?'

'Exactly, though Bryan was in a bad state and it was hard to understand him. We kept asking him where he'd hidden the body but he just mumbled something about the woods.'

'And Paul's blazer and trousers, how did you end up with those?'

'They were lying in the footwell of the passenger seat. Bryan didn't explain how they got there. I opened the gates and we managed to manoeuvre Bryan and his car around the side of the house out of sight. Joe, one of the men staying with me, was trained in field medicine, so he saw to Bryan while I tried to tidy up the car. I put Paul's clothes into a sack and placed it by the dustbin to dispose of later, then I went to help with Bryan.

'He died around seven o'clock. Joe thought it was a wound to the liver, enough for him to bleed to death.'

'You didn't take him to hospital?'

'Don't be stupid. There was nothing they could have done for him. Joe told me it was a mortal wound.'

'How did you dispose of his body?'

Cooper listened to the silence, knowing the answer already and willing the major to leave while he still could.

'How?'

'We put him in the car and drove it to some wasteland at the edge of my property. There was a fair amount of stubble-burning going on; early, I know, but it had been a good harvest. We set fire to the car and burnt the body.'

'Dear God... But bodies don't burn away to nothing; I've seen the aftermath of enough mortar fire to know that.'

'Good point. We moved the remains of the wreck and of poor old Bryan later when they'd cooled down. They're buried on my land somewhere where no one's going to dig them up by accident.'

'So how did I end up with a bag of Paul's clothes? It doesn't make sense.'

'Because I forgot about the damn things!' Edwards snapped, obviously annoyed. 'I was sitting down to a well-earned snifter and switched the radio on as a bit of a diversion.

'You can imagine what I felt when they announced the disappearance. I nearly had a heart attack. We'd taken Bryan at his word but what if he'd just dumped the body and there was something on it to link him back here? It was then I remembered the clothes. I couldn't just drop the sack in my bin and I didn't want it here overnight in case someone had seen Bryan and Paul together and then reported seeing the car at my house. And I didn't want to risk a trip in the car with search parties crawling all over the place.'

'So you called me and I took all those risks.'

Edwards laughed.

'But of course. I knew you'd feel obliged to help me out and anyway, it wasn't so much of a risk for you as you'd been nowhere near the boy. I was sure you'd have some sort of alibi.'

'I didn't, as the police have demonstrated to their satisfaction. You dropped me in it and have done nothing to help me prove my innocence whatsoever.'

'I can understand you being angry, old man, but it's all in the past now. You're out of prison; they have no real evidence against you. You'll be fine.'

'My reputation has been ruined, my friends have deserted me, there are suggestions that I might be asked to resign from the club. And you call that fine? I think not, sir, I think not.'

'So what are you going to do?' Edwards asked his voice strangely unconcerned.

Cooper held his breath as he waited for the major to speak.

'I don't know.'

Operations rang Nightingale at 19:16 to tell her that a patrol had found Cooper's car parked in a village less than two minutes walk from Edwards' house. She told them to stay where they were and called Quinlan at once. He was already on his way to the station and ordered her to do nothing until he arrived, other than alert the firearms unit of the location.

Less than ten minutes later they were sitting in his office with the head of the firearms team on speakerphone. It was agreed that two of his officers would reconnoitre Edwards' house. One would pretend to be making routine police inquiries while the other looked around outside. Once they reported back a decision would be made on how to proceed, in particular whether and how to enter the house.

Nightingale stood up as soon as the call finished.

'Where are you going?'

'I have to be there. I won't do anything stupid.'

Quinlan regarded her indecisively.

'It's Bob Cooper we're talking about, sir.'

'Very well.' Quinlan nodded. 'But we'll be quicker in my car.'

Edwards' phone rang, breaking the silence. He ignored it; he'd already had a message from William to say that the 'package' had been delivered and that he'd be back to collect it whenever he received instructions to do so. Cooper tried again to ram his knees into the sofa but his legs had gone numb and he could barely move his body. There was the faint clink of ice in Edwards' glass then nothing. He heard Maidment sigh and then the sound of Edwards standing up.

'If you want my advice, it's to keep schtum. Paul Hill wasn't murdered by me. In fact he wasn't murdered by anybody if Taylor killed him in self-defence. This will all blow over again like last time and life will return to normal.'

'Not for me it won't.'

'No, I can see that. But shopping me for a crime I didn't commit won't help, will it?'

Cooper managed to press a button on the phone. He couldn't be sure whether it was a different one or whether he kept repeating the same number as he had little feeling in his fingers. It was clear to Cooper that Maidment would never persuade Edwards to do the right thing but he seemed blind to the fact and continued to try to use moral suasion to convince him.

For Cooper, bound and gagged, virtually immobile, their heated discussion brought thinking time but little hope. He was certain that Edwards would have to kill him to allow his escape from the country. The only question was whether he would murder the major as well. It appeared that he didn't want to, otherwise why would he be wasting time in a futile debate? He doubted that it was sentiment that stayed his hand. More likely it was worry that the murder might be linked to him combined with the practical difficulty of overcoming the major and then having to dispose of two bodies.

Both men were becoming angry. They were virtually shouting at each other now and he thought that if Maidment had been fit they would have come to blows. Their row was interrupted by loud knocking from the front door.

'Who the devil's that at this time of night?' Edwards turned to Maidment. 'Were you followed here?'

'I made certain that I was not.'

The last of Cooper's hopes crumbled. The knocking came again.

'I'd better go and see who it is. Stay here.'

Edwards left the room and pulled the study door to behind him. Cooper heard Maidment stand up, walk over and open it. There was the sound of muffled voices from outside but he couldn't hear clearly enough to distinguish words. The front door banged shut and Maidment returned to the sofa. Cooper's latest attempt to hit the back of it with his knees failed.

'Who was that?'

'Oh, nobody.'

'It looked like the police and I thought I heard them mention that sergeant's name, you know, Cooper.'

The sergeant in question shouted out against his gag and almost choked.

'You eavesdrop now, do you, Major? A dirty habit.'

'Not as filthy as some I could mention.'

'Look, I'm getting weary of this. Let me explain to you again the simple facts of the matter. One, Paul Hill was a prostitute; two, yes, he was slightly underage but not much; three, I did not kill him, nor did I see him killed. Taylor was the guilty party and Taylor died. Four, I disposed of Taylor's body and car but I didn't kill him either. I accept that technically that's a crime but not a significant one. It's time to leave Paul Hill and Bryan Taylor dead and buried in the past where they belong.'

'What about Malcolm Eagleton?'

'Who?' Cooper could hear Edwards choke on his whisky from where he was lying.

'The boy who vanished a year before Paul. The one whose bones the police found some months ago.'

'Why on earth should I have known him?' More chinks as the ice slid towards his lips and back.

'The police mentioned him when they were questioning me. Then separately they asked me about a replacement parking permit in 1981. I only issued one and that was to you. I put two and two together.'

'I really don't see the connection, old chap.' Edwards's voice was muffled, as if he'd turned towards the fireplace.

'So you deny that you knew him.'

'Absolutely.'

To Cooper, world-weary, experienced and confined to using only his ears, the difference in Edwards' tone when he answered Maidment's questions was obvious. Edwards had told the truth about Paul Hill but was lying about Malcolm Eagleton. He wondered if Maidment had noticed it too.

'If I went to the police—'

'I'd still deny everything; say that I had no knowledge of Hill or Eagleton and that you were trying to frame me to escape your own guilt. It's your blood and fingerprints they have, remember, not mine.'

'You'd do that?' Maidment was aghast.

'Of course, I'd have to. Don't be shocked, most people would do the same.'

'Why should I perjure myself and risk my good name further for a piece of filth like you?' Maidment stood up and took a step towards Edwards.

'I had so hoped that you wouldn't do this, Jeremy.'

Cooper heard Maidment gasp and sit back down with a thump that knocked the sofa to one side. By straining his neck Cooper had his first view of the room. All he could see was part of the floor, Maidment's feet in sensible brogues and from Edwards' knees downwards. Ignoring the hammer blows in his skull and the fire that lashed across his shoulders and down his arms, Cooper managed to wriggle a few inches on his buttocks so that he could push the top of his head against the curtains that were blocking the rest of his view until he could see almost all of Edwards. He was standing with his back to the fireplace with his whisky glass in one hand and a revolver in the other. Belatedly Cooper realised that he was no longer holding his phone and that he was probably sitting on it.

'What the devil are you doing?'

'I had hoped that you would cooperate but it appears that you aren't going to.'

'So you're going to kill me? How do you propose to get away with that?'

Maidment stood up and took a step forward.

'No, Jeremy, don't rush me. Stay where you are.' Edwards drained his drink and put the glass on a side table.

'Put that thing away, Percy, for heaven's sake. You always were a lousy shot.' It was a good attempt at bluster but Cooper could hear the tremor in his voice.

'Even I won't have a problem at this range. Here.' There was a thud as something landed on the sofa. 'Oblige me by tying your feet together with that tape, would you.'

'No, I damn well won't. If you're going to kill me, do it like a man.'

'Very well but not in here. We'll step outside if you don't mind.'

Maidment stood up and took a step towards the fireplace.

'Stay there, Jeremy, that's as close as I need you.'

'What about the noise?'

'Good point. Can't be too careful.' Cooper watched Edwards pick up a brocade cushion from a chair.

'Now, if you'll just—'

An electronic version of Vivaldi's 'Spring' from *The Four Seasons* echoed around the room. Beneath Cooper's posterior there was a curious vibrating sensation. Maidment and Edwards looked at each other and automatically felt for their mobile phones but the noise wasn't emanating from either of them. It was coming from behind the sofa.

'What the—?' Edwards stepped over to glance down at Cooper and laughed. 'Ah, it's my sleeping policeman. I should have realised. I'll be with you in a minute, Sergeant,' he said grinning, 'don't go away.'

He was still laughing when Maidment lashed out with his walking stick and flung himself to the floor. Edwards brought his gun round and fired but missed the moving target. Maidment was already hunched on the rug, swinging wildly with his cane as he crawled towards him.

Edwards fired again and chipped the marble of the fireplace behind Maidment's head. The ricochet thudded into the wall above Cooper's shoulder. As Edwards squeezed the trigger a third time Maidment rolled into him, shaking him off balance so that his arms went out automatically to steady himself and the shot went wide. With his left arm Maidment grabbed Edwards' calves in a rugby tackle that toppled him to his knees but he couldn't shake the man's grip on the revolver.

Maidment brought his right hand up to block Edwards's gun arm and pushed it away from his head. He groaned in pain as the damaged muscles in his chest were forced into action. Another shot ricocheted off the side table and into something soft. Maidment had survived so far against all the odds but what strength his adrenalin had given him was fading rapidly. His breath caught in his throat and the pain in his lungs told him that he'd done terrible damage to himself from his recent injury.

He had both hands tight around Edwards' gun barrel, trying desperately to keep the muzzle away from his head. Edwards was clawing at his fingers with his free hand. He felt one snap but there was no pain. Maidment held on, willing the gun away with all his dwindling power. Slowly, remorselessly, the barrel lowered towards his left eye. It shook, wavered, but he felt Edwards' finger tighten on the trigger as the gun inched closer to his face. Maidment had no more strength, nothing left to deflect the bullet ready in the chamber. He was going to die. In desperation he bucked his body beneath Edwards, trying in vain to shake him off as he felt the finger close tight and he heard the preparatory click of the hammer.

'Police!'

The firearms unit burst into the study as another shot drummed into the floor next to Maidment's ear. Edwards put up his hands as soon as he saw the rifle aimed at his chest. His arms were pinned behind his back in seconds. Maidment struggled to rise but collapsed back to the floor, his head soaked in blood.

'Take it easy,' an officer said and held him down gently.

'Thank you,' Maidment murmured, ever the gentleman. Nightingale ran into the room and knelt beside him.

'Where's Bob?'

'I believe you'll find Sergeant Cooper behind the sofa. I do hope he's all right.' Then he fainted.

Two officers pulled the sofa away from the wall as Edwards was handcuffed and led out of the room.

'Bob!' Nightingale was at Cooper's side instantly. She pulled the tape from his lips as carefully as she could and removed the rag from his mouth. 'Thank God you're alive.'

She turned and shouted at the door.

'Get the paramedics now! We have an injured officer in here.'

'I'm sorry, lass, I let you down. I should never have come on my own.'

'Don't talk. We'll get you to hospital and sort everything out later.'

Nightingale bent down and kissed his forehead, pretending not to see the tears in his eyes.

It was very dark in the cellar, so dark that Sam couldn't see anything in front of his face. He didn't know what time it was and wondered how long it had been since William locked him in here. He struggled again with the rope on his wrists, ignoring the pain, until he felt it give and he was able to move his hands more. By wriggling and twisting them he was able to pull the rope up over his thumb and then, agonisingly, slowly over the knuckles of his right hand. After that it took him less than a minute to remove his bindings.

Despite the warmth of the evening outside, it was cold underground and he was dressed only in a T-shirt and jeans, his feet bare since they'd taken his shoes after he'd run away. He shivered. He needed to stay warm until someone came for him. Sam tried jumping and running on the spot. It worked for a while but his head began to spin and he had to sit down to stop himself from fainting. He felt weird. William had left him with a bottle of Coke with a straw but it had made him feel sick so he'd stopped drinking it.

Where was he? William had put a sack over his head and a gag in his mouth, and then carried him from the car. It hadn't taken more than five minutes so he must still be somewhere in the woods he'd seen as they had driven down the track, but where? He tried again to explore his prison, remembering to count his paces this time: fifteen from where he'd been standing to the rough wood of the door. He pounded on it, shouting until he was hoarse. Nothing. When he leant his ear against it he couldn't hear anything from the other side so perhaps is was too thick. No wait, maybe there were two doors. Yes.

He tried to remember the sounds that had accompanied his imprisonment. When they'd reached this place he'd heard the jingle of keys, a creak and then they'd gone down some stairs.

William had paused and then there had been a change in the air. He could have been opening another door. The idea made him feel worse.

Fifteen paces. He put his right hand out as far as it would go along the wall to the side of the door, facing in towards the room he paced after it. Ten paces and he reached a wooden shelf of some sort. His fingers explored. After a few inches there was an upright, then another one. He counted twenty before he touched the chill stone of another wall. With his other hand he skimmed the surface of the shelving. The rows were close together and every one of them was divided into boxes too small for books. Where on earth was he?

Instead of panicking he turned ninety degrees along the next wall. This too was covered in wooden shelving. His fingers groped on and recoiled suddenly as they touched something cold and slimy; glass. It was a bottle. He pulled it from the shelf and felt along its length to where the neck narrowed and foil capped the end. Wine; he was in a wine cellar.

The thought made him feel better. He wasn't in some derelict building or abandoned mine shaft. The wine had to belong to someone. William had keys; he would come back; there's no way he'd just leave him here. But supposing it was an abandoned cellar? It was suddenly very important to know how many bottles were stored there. Sam searched, then searched again.

Only two bottles; nothing else. Maybe the cellar was no longer used. The thought made him whimper. Had he been thrown out like Jack for a reason he didn't understand? Sam started to cry, the sound echoing in the dark as he began to realise that he had been left there to die.

CHAPTER FORTY

Nightingale rang Fenwick with news of Richard Edwards' arrest as soon as she'd seen Cooper safely to hospital and into the care of the registrar.

'Edwards has already found a lawyer, and an expensive one too. He's claiming entrapment and police assault, would you believe it? His first line was to deny everything but fortunately we had the surveillance picture you'd sent from London. As soon as he saw it he shut up and hasn't said a word since.'

'Well, I've got some news that's going to help even more. The Met has just raided the house here; they waited until peak commuter time and bagged six clients as well as the staff. I'm confident one of them will identify Edwards if they're offered a deal.'

'That's brilliant; why don't you sound pleased?' All Nightingale could hear in Fenwick's voice was disappointment.

'Sam Bowyer wasn't there, neither was the manager, a man called William Slant. They left together at five-thirty and Slant lost the tail the Met had on him on the M23. They have no idea where Slant went but I'm leaving the search to them; they have the resources and it was their case. I've been on to Brighton though, to let them know and they want to cover the Sussex end of the search, which is fine by me.'

'They'll find Sam, don't worry.'

'Maybe, but we were so close to getting the boy. If the Met had only moved in earlier...'

'Look, don't sweat it. You did all you could...Oh, OK,' he heard her talking to someone in the background. 'Sorry, I've got to go. Round two with Edwards and I'm going to enjoy this.'

'See if you can find out about Sam. I'm going to interview the man I'm certain is the Well-Wisher, then I'll be coming straight back.'

'Good, because I think we may need our star witness to make the case of murder against Edwards.'

He broke the call, his relief at the outcome marred by guilt that Bob Cooper had almost been killed. Why hadn't they realised that The Purse was actually Percy, another stupid army nickname for Edwards? No doubt there would be some fall-out because Cooper had ended up in a deadly situation, though if, as he suspected, Edwards was behind Choir Boy, the praise would outweigh criticism for everyone involved. But no matter how many times he reminded himself that he should be celebrating, all he could think about was the fact that Sam was still missing and that he hadn't been there to arrest Edwards personally. There was no reason why he should have been; after all, he'd insisted on putting Nightingale in charge of the Paul Hill investigation and his decision had been vindicated by her performance. Even so, his mood darkened as he hurried through the crowds.

According to a call from Charlie at the Mission, who had spoken to one of the brothers after Fenwick left, Father Peter was taking a service at a church just south of Euston Road.

Evensong was underway by the time Fenwick arrived so he slipped into one of the ancient pews at the back to wait. He tried to concentrate on the service but instead he found himself biting the skin at the side of his thumb as he worried about Cooper and Sam in equal measure. After the final blessing Father Peter disappeared into the vestry and Fenwick walked briskly down the aisle after him.

When he entered the cramped room only the curate was there.

Father Peter had gone, rushing on to St Jerome's where some potential new residents for his hostel had arrived in need of persuading to come in off the street. The curate pointed out the location of the church on Fenwick's *A to Z* and he left, trying not to curse the priest on the basis that it would be bad luck.

St Jerome's was on the far side of Clerkenwell, a short taxi ride away or a twenty-minute walk at a fast pace. There wasn't a vacant cab in sight so he forced himself into a jog. He could hear a church bell somewhere striking eight.

He paused on Farringdon Road at the corner with Saffron Street and rang the hospital to which Cooper had been admitted. Nightingale had said that the paramedics at the scene were pretty certain his skull wasn't fractured but he wanted to be sure. He was told by a nurse, whose mood matched his own, that Cooper was being X-rayed and it could be hours before they would know for certain how he was. And when they did, she informed him with some glee, he wouldn't be told anyway because he wasn't family. He broke the connection, swore creatively and rang Cooper's home. Of course there was no one there. Doris and their son would be at the hospital. He left a message wishing Bob well and asked that they call him on his mobile as soon as they had any news.

Then he called the hospital again, conscious that he hadn't asked about Maidment. This time he ended up with a receptionist who, on hearing that he was a senior policeman, was far more helpful. The news wasn't good. Maidment had been admitted with a newly punctured lung, an ear that had been virtually torn off by a bullet and other suspected internal injuries. He was in the operating theatre and his condition was described as serious. Fenwick broke the connection confused by his feelings. Like Cooper, he couldn't help but warm to Maidment; his bravery and common decency was beyond doubt. But he'd protected a child molester and murderer for over twenty-five years and had left Paul's family with uncertainty that had driven his mother insane. Maidment might have been a hero once but, if so, he was a deeply flawed one.

There was one other call to make and he knew this number by heart so he continued his brisk walk as he dialled. Quinlan was in his office in buoyant mood. Richard Edwards, Purse or Percy to his mates because of his whistling ability (though none of the younger members of the team had ever heard of the real Percy Edwards), was under arrest for the attempted murders of Maidment and Cooper, giving them time to work on wider charges.

'Thank you for giving Nightingale cover. I'm sure it made a difference.'

'I did very little. By the time I called Firearms I discovered you'd already been on to them and after Cooper's car was found everything happened like clockwork.'

'I'm glad to hear it. I don't want a screw-up now. Nightingale will obviously be focused on the murders. Can you make sure she liaises with Clive and Alison so that we cover the Choir Boy angle as well?' Fenwick was unaware that he was effectively giving orders to his old boss and missed the significance of the laugh as Quinlan answered.

'Of course. Mind you, once Edwards sees the evidence we have against him it wouldn't surprise me if he tried to do a deal; a lighter sentence in exchange for his full cooperation.'

'We have ample evidence for attempted murder, child prostitution and paedophilia but we don't have him for murder. And that bastard deserves everything the system can throw at him; we owe it to Paul, Malcolm and God knows how many other families.'

'I agree but pursuing the other charges would be a lot easier. And without the Well-Wisher it will be difficult to make a case against him for Paul and Malcolm's murders, so a plea isn't as disgusting a solution as one might think – particularly if he gives us the names of some of his associates. Unless you find the Well-Wisher and bring him back as our lead witness for the prosecution I expect CPS to consider a deal if it's offered.'

'I'm going to do my best but I think the Well-Wisher's a priest.'

'Damn.'

'Exactly; but still, I'm going to try and extract a statement.'

'You need to,' Quinlan said in a tone that recalled their earlier conversation and his implied criticism of Fenwick's 'London jaunt'. 'By the way, I haven't contacted the ACC yet – thought you might want to.'

'No, I'd like Nightingale to do that. She should have the lion's share of the credit.'

'If you insist but he's bound to want to speak to you. I don't need to tell you that he'll expect a bloody good explanation for why you were where you were at such a critical time.' With those cheery words Quinlan finished the call.

Fenwick reached St Jerome's and was ushered into the back of a large, dimly lit church. Father Peter sat in a front pew with two teenage boys. Only the murmur of their voices reached him but he thought that he could detect an element of capitulation from the lads so he waited for their conversation to finish. He struggled to identify and shift the grey mood that had settled over him despite his team's success. To his relief he realised that his feelings had little to do with missing out on the arrest; he was genuinely glad for Nightingale and more confident than Quinlan was of being able to persuade the ACC that his journey to London was appropriate. It wasn't worry about his career that was eating into him, it was a sense of something being out of alignment despite the successful conclusion to two major investigations.

As he waited he tried to identify what was wrong but it eluded him. It wasn't just because he needed Sam Bowyer to be found for his own peace of mind; there was something else.

'There you go, mate.'

The whisper startled him and he almost jumped as a plastic beaker of strong tea was passed over his shoulder by a thickset man who looked about forty, with a scraggly beard and fingernails engrained with dirt.

'That's for waitin' and not interruptin' 'is work. In my book that makes you OK, even if you are a rozzer.' He spoke quietly with a thick East End accent. 'Name's Gerald, Gerry to me mates.'

'Thanks, Gerry. I'm Andrew Fenwick,' he replied in the same hushed tone and watched as the man settled in a pew beside him.

'Cheers, Andy.' Gerry clunked beakers and took a slurp of tea that was more audible than his words. One of the boys by the altar looked back over his shoulder.

'You encouraged them here?' Fenwick waved his cup in the direction of the huddled group.

'Yeah, a good catch t'night, so's to speak.' He grinned, revealing blackened teeth.

'How did you persuade them?'

'Not too difficult. They're not hooked yet, not the young 'un anyway. Got him off a bus this mornin', would you believe. Conductor was about to throw 'im to the police for dodging his fare but I paid it for 'im and took 'im to the Centre. Problem is, that older lad; 'e's already headin' downhill and 'e's a bad influence on the other. That's why it's taking Peter so long.'

'Why do you do this?' Fenwick had to wait for his reply while Gerry choked noisily on the contents of his lungs. He hawked and was about to spit then remembered where he was and took an audible swallow instead.

''Fing is, Andy, Father Peter saved my life. 'Ad TB, didn't I, was nearly gone with it but 'e got me into a clinic and Bob's yer uncle. Took me over a year to get better, and I didn't touch a drop the whole time. By the time I was out I reckoned I could do wivout it, and that's when he offers me this job. It's not much and I'm a bit old for it now.'

'How old are you, if you don't mind me asking?'

'Twenny-nine.' Fenwick's face remained steady. 'Young enough to remember what it's like for them poor kids but I'll need to move on to saving older souls soon. Kids don't relate so well to me any more.'

'They did,' Fenwick said gently and pointed towards the boys. 'How many do you reckon you've saved?'

'It's not me as saves 'em. Andy. That's Father Peter. I just catches 'em; Gerry the Catcher, I am. 'E's the one as works the miracles. Not that we always win. For every five I brings in, four ends up back on the streets. Can't make the change, see, but Peter never gives up. There's some bin in 'is shelters more'n ten times and 'e still welcomes 'em back with a smile and a hot meal. Only the real troublemakers are barred, those as peddle and pimp are kicked right out. 'E may be small but he's bloody tough, s'cuse my French.'

'You said "his shelters". Aren't they run by the Church?'

'Churches. Yeah, that was part of the problem 'e put right. We had Missions competing, squabbling yer could say. Then 'e comes along, only just ordained and as fiery as they come, so I'm told. Before my time but the story's done the rounds so we've all 'eard it.

'In 'e comes, no mor'n twenny-something and takes each of the Missions to task. Says they need to work together not against each uvver. Took 'im a few years but one by one he wins 'em over. Now it's all organised, wiv a joint governin' board, proper fundraisin', links to the socials and probation, like. You mention it, he's sorted it.'

'All his own work?' Fenwick tried to keep the scepticism from his voice but didn't quite succeed.

'No need to be sarky. 'E's not a saint and I ain't about to make 'im one.'

'Sorry, Gerry. It's just that you made him sound almost too good to be true.'

'Well, 'e's not perfect – 'as a wicked temper for one thing – but I swear, wivout 'im you'd have dozens of lads dead now that are leading decent lives, and 'undreds wasting away on the streets instead of 'aving a chance to make their way in the world. 'E's a leader, see. 'E may be small and quiet when 'e's not fired up, but my Lord, you should see 'im when 'e wants to get sommick sorted. No stoppin 'im then.'

'Gerry!' A clear tenor voice rang out from the front.

'Can you take Reg and Ben along to St Olaf's? I've called ahead and they're making room so don't take any nonsense when you get there. Then tomorrow, sharpish after breakfast, pick them up and bring them over to me. We're going to do the tour.'

'Righyerare, Father. Come along then, you lot. You're in luck you are, best grub around at St Olaf's. See yer, Andy.'

Gerry ferried them out. Fenwick picked up the empty beakers and stood up.

'Don't worry, Chief Inspector, I'll come to you,' Father Peter said as he walked slowly down the aisle.

Fenwick would have preferred it the other way. It was lighter near the altar and gloomy back here with the door closed. The first thing he noticed was that Father Peter was indeed short, no more than five foot three; the second was that his thick wavy hair was entirely grey, despite the youthfulness of his voice. It made it hard to guess his age. Then when the dim light fell on his face he noticed the scar. It ran from under the outer edge of his left eye in a vivid diagonal down to the corner of his mouth, which was lifted in a permanent half smile that was ironic rather than sinister.

'So you know who I am?'

'Of course, Charlie made sure of that. Good of you to come to me.'

Fenwick's hand was taken in a grip far stronger than he would have expected. He noticed that the priest didn't look at him but kept his gaze on the crucifix above the altar.

'What can I do for you?'

It was a light, pleasant voice.

'I'm looking for a man and I hoped you might be able to help me.'

'That's a rather menial job for someone of your rank, isn't it?'

'This is a very special person.' He pulled out a slim Dictaphone and slipped in a mini-cassette of the Well-Wisher's call to *CrimeNight*. 'Do you recognise this?'

He pressed the button and a disembodied voice filled the nave.

'It sounds muffled. I'm very sorry but I can't help you,' Father Peter said and rose to leave.

'Please; perhaps these photographs will help.' Fenwick passed over the stills from the CCTV camera and waited. Father Peter's body stiffened but still he said nothing.

'It is you, isn't it, Father? The recording and these pictures. You're the one who's been trying to tell us that Major Maidment is innocent. Please sit down. I could ask you to come to the station at Holborn or in Harlden, and it may come to that, but I'd rather be civilised about it.'

With obvious reluctance the priest sat down, his body angled away from Fenwick towards the altar. His eyes went back to the ornate crucifix upon it.

'Eighteenth-century silver. It means we have to keep the church locked when no one's here. It would be gone in a minute if we left it unattended. I want to sell it but I haven't been allowed to. The proceeds would fund at least three months' costs at all the recovery centres.'

'Why wasn't it a popular suggestion?'

Father Peter laughed. It was a surprisingly bitter sound.

'The cross was a gift from a noble family to whom I'm meant to be grateful and remember in my nightly prayers but I'm afraid there are so many others more deserving that they come well down my list.'

'They were benefactors of their time, I imagine.' Fenwick found himself drawn into debate despite his best intentions.

'Hah! It was self-glorification not charity that motivated gifts like that. Far better to have given money to the poor who were dying of malnutrition on the streets around their grand houses.'

Fenwick changed the subject quickly.

'Is this picture of you, Father?' He pushed the CCTV stills in front of the priest again but Father Peter continued to stare at the cross, his back rigid. 'Please, sir, we're talking about the future of men's lives here, about justice and retribution. You must help me.'

'There is no must about it, Andrew. I have my work here. It's what God called me to do and it takes precedence over the future of a couple of well-to-do men who will be elderly by now and who've had more in their lives than the boys sleeping in St Olaf's House can ever hope for.'

'That is not your judgement to make, surely. The Church isn't above the law in civil matters.' Father Peter remained silent. 'Very well, as you've brought God into this I shall also use his name and ask you this: Why did God let me find you? Why has He brought me here to this place if He didn't expect you to help?'

The priest simply shook his head then lowered it as if in prayer. Fenwick bit his lip and took hold of his temper. His lack of patience had always been an Achilles heel.

'I appreciate that what you've learnt may have been in the confessional, even from one of Edwards' other victims; a boy who ran away to London and whom you saved perhaps? Could you at least give me their name?'

'Edwards?' There was a softening in the priest's shoulders and his head came up.

'That's the name of the man who abused Paul Hill and his friend Oliver Anchor, plus many others.'

'Edwards,' Father Peter said, as if Fenwick had resolved one of life's mysteries. 'And he abused many boys?'

'We're still piecing the evidence together. Now that there's a name and face we hope to reach other victims. So far we may have found four.'

'So you don't need evidence from me to make a case.'

An admission. Fenwick tensed.

'Maybe not to make the case for abuse but for murder, yes, and to confirm finally what happened to Paul Hill. In order to give his mother, father and grandmother closure, what you know might be very valuable.'

'Paul's grandmother is still alive?'

'Very much so,' Fenwick chuckled. 'Quite an old lady.'

'You've met her?'

'Yes. She's living with her son and his new wife and family in Harlden.'

'Really? It's a funny world.' Father Peter flexed his shoulders and rubbed his neck. 'Well, I'm sorry, Chief Inspector, but I cannot tell you anything about Paul Hill.'

'We want to find his remains so that his family can bury him. Father, please, you have to help us.'

'I shall pray for his family, I've done so for many years but that's all I can do. I'm sorry but you've come on a wasted journey. I don't wish to be rude but I have to go along to St Olaf's now. I want to be sure those boys are settling in.'

'I could insist that you accompany me, sir.'

'To what end? It will make no difference.'

Fenwick knew he was right. Nothing he could say would change this man's mind. He stood, an admission of defeat.

'Goodbye, Andrew.'

Father Peter walked to the door. Fenwick followed him, shook his hand briefly in farewell and stepped out into the London dusk. A few paces down the street he stopped suddenly and turned, catching Father Peter unawares as he watched him go. Even in the dying light his eyes shone with a remarkable inner glow.

CHAPTER FORTY-ONE

Fenwick hailed a taxi and directed the driver to Victoria. It wasn't until they'd reached Parliament Square that it hit him.

'My God,' he said aloud.

'You what, guv?'

'We need to go back to St Olaf's, in Turk's Head Yard, as quick as you can.'

'It's your money.'

The cabbie shook his head as his belief in the universal stupidity of passengers was confirmed yet again but executed a neat three-point turn.

There were flashing blue lights outside the shelter. An ambulance was parked in front with its rear doors flung wide. The front door to the building was open and Fenwick stepped into the hall. Ahead of him to his right there was shouting, the sound of a boy screaming. He was filled with superstitious dread for Father Peter and was about to run forward when a lad no more than twelve made to bolt past him and outside. Fenwick caught him neatly around the waist and lifted him off his feet.

'Where do you think you're going?' he asked, avoiding the wildly swinging fists. He recognised one of the boys from the church.

'You're Reg.' Involuntarily, his arms about the boy tightened briefly. Here at least was one boy who didn't need to disappear again into the night.

'Let me go!'

'There's no hurry – why don't we go and find someone in charge.'

He was encouraging a reluctant Reg inside when Father Peter rounded the corner. Their eyes met and in that instant the truth passed between them but all Fenwick said was, 'Reg was having second thoughts. Where would you like him?'

'In there.' The priest pointed at the dining room. 'I'll be with you soon as I can. One of the boys had an epileptic fit and hurt himself. It's upset the others but we'll get him off to hospital and things will soon settle down. I should go with him really.'

'Not this time, Father,' Fenwick said quietly but with clear authority. 'Send someone else.'

Fenwick went into the dining room with Reg to make sure he didn't run off. The boy looked exhausted, world-weary, very unlike the smiling school photo he was sure graced a missing person's file somewhere and maybe a living-room wall. Reg looked as if he was still inclined to bolt given the opportunity so Fenwick decided to treat him as he would Chris when he was in need of coaxing out of a sulk.

'I'm ravenous,' he said and found a tin of biscuits on the serving counter. Reg watched him, torn between rebellious silence and hunger. Hunger won.

'Here.' Fenwick gave him the tin, then rescued it quickly as five biscuits disappeared in thirty seconds.

'You an Arsenal fan then?' he asked, pointing to the cannon on Reg's grubby T-shirt, two sizes too big for him. He could see the remains of bruises on the boy's bare arms and had to work hard not to reach out to hug him.

'Yes.'

'Who do you think's the best Arsenal player of all time?' It was enough to catch the boy's attention, particularly as the biscuit tin appeared in front of him again.

'Thierry Henry, of course. He was magic.'

'Ever seen him play live?'

'Nah, only on the telly.'

'I have, when they beat Man U at home a couple of years ago. It was amazing.'

Reg's eyes were alight with curiosity.

'You really did?'

'Yup. Are you old enough to understand the offside rule?'

'I've been watching since I was five,' Reg said with pride and puffed out his chest. 'S'easy.'

When Father Peter found them the remaining biscuits had been broken into pieces and arranged on one of the Formica tables. Henry was half a jammy dodger. Fenwick and Reg jumped at the opening of the door and the priest burst out laughing.

'You both look so guilty! Come on, Reg. You can take what's left and share them with your friend. Andrew and I need to talk.'

'We'll catch up later, Reg,' Fenwick called out. 'I've got a mate who might be able to get you a ticket to Highbury. I mean it.'

Reg scuttled off with one of the helpers.

As the door snapped shut a wave of exhaustion crossed the priest's face but it was gone quickly. In the bright strip lighting Fenwick could study his features clearly for the first time. He stared at the remarkable, unmistakable eyes.

'Did you give yourself that scar, Paul?'

The priest didn't bother to hide his surprise.

'How did you guess?'

'You were cursed with beauty so it would be impossible to disappear unless you did something about it. How old were you when you realised you had to do it?'

Father Peter released an enormous sigh.

'Fourteen; I did it almost immediately. I hated my face so much it actually felt good despite the pain. I dyed my hair too but the roots kept on showing and it nearly fell out. I used the cheapest stuff, you see.'

'That's the reason for the grey now?'

'No,' he tried to smile, 'that's natural. God's gift to me when I was twenty; came almost overnight.'

'Will you tell me about it now?'

'What will happen?' The priest didn't sound anxious, more curious.

'I really don't know,' Fenwick said. He had no idea what he would do after he took Paul Hill's statement.

'Well, at least you're honest. Would you mind if I got us something to eat? The kitchen's just through there and I'm famished. You must be too, despite the biscuits.'

In the spotless kitchen they looked in the fridge and found eggs, butter, tomatoes and microwave chips in the freezer.

'Tomato omelette and chips in fifteen minutes – how about that?'

'Perfect,' said Fenwick. 'I'll make us some tea.'

The priest talked as he worked at the stove.

'How much do you know?'

'Assume nothing; start from the beginning.'

'The beginning? No, there's no need for you to understand why I turned out to be a nasty, lying, perverted creature. Just accept that's how I was by fourteen. I don't blame anybody for it but myself.'

Fenwick didn't argue but disagreed within his silence. With a suffocating, neurotic mother and an ineffectual father more concerned with money than his son's welfare, he could see why he had been perfect raw material for Bryan Taylor's seduction.

'I met Taylor when I was in the Scouts. He assisted with the troop and said I could earn money helping him in his business. One way of making money led to another.' Paul's face twisted in self-disgust.

'How old were you?'

Paul leant his head back, as if resting his skull on the top of his spine. Once again a look of utter tiredness crossed his face to be wiped out with one of determination.

'I must have been eleven. I'd only just joined Scouts, I know that. It didn't take him long to spot my weaknesses.' He cracked the eggs into a bowl. 'Water or milk?'

'Pardon?'

'Do you like your omelettes with water or milk?'

'Er, milk, whatever. Thanks.' Paul's calmness was disconcerting.

'At first Bryan kept me to himself. It was tame stuff he wanted, not like...Edwards, that was his name, wasn't it?'

It was a rhetorical question. Fenwick knew that Paul would never forget it now that he knew.

'But then Bryan wanted more: photographs, films, you name it. There was no Internet in those days but he must have made a fortune from the images of me. I got a fiver after each session and considered myself lucky.

'It went on like that for a long time. I was only one of his boys but unlike the others I didn't grow hair in embarrassing places and my voice refused to break. Then one day Bryan told me that a friend of his had seen my picture and liked the look of me. Would I meet him? I said, no way. Bryan was one thing; it almost didn't count with him any more but with some other bloke, well, that was different. There's sliced bread over there and some sort of spread in the fridge if you don't mind.'

Fenwick moved to obey. He watched the priest, beat and season the eggs carefully, then add a splash of milk, and was moved by the quiet acceptance that flowed from him.

'Throw me the spread if you've finished with it. Thanks. Where was I? Oh yes, Bryan's friend. Eventually, I said I'd meet him when he offered me twenty pounds, an absolute fortune in those days. But I wanted to back out when he put me under the blanket in the boot of his car. It stank of petrol fumes and my face was rammed up against the saddle of my bike. But by then it was too late. I was locked in.

'He drove around so that I lost all sense of direction. When we arrived I could see big gates from the edge of the blanket and there was the sound of gravel under the tyres. He presented me to Edwards as if I were a prize. The man actually ran his hands over me, like you see people do when they're buying a racehorse. Then he told me to...well, it doesn't matter. I earned my money and I didn't cry, not once.'

Paul beat the eggs viciously and took too much care slicing some butter for the pan.

'Is this Edwards?' Fenwick showed him the photograph taken by the Met the previous week.

Paul gasped and looked away quickly. He nodded and gripped the edge of the stove until his knuckles were white.

'Was Edwards a bully?'

Paul coughed to clear his throat.

'A sadist. He liked it most when you screamed. He wanted to see tears but I never gave him that pleasure. He almost killed me once but Bryan stopped him. Choking, that was his thing, until you couldn't breathe and your eyes felt as if they were going to burst from their sockets.'

He sniffed and stopped talking, unable to continue.

'How many slices?' Fenwick asked, buttering the bread. 'Two, three?'

'Ah...just one, thanks. They'll need it all for breakfast. I suppose you want to hear the rest of it.'

'Just about the way you disappeared.'

'Of course you do...well...Bryan took me to Edwards' house more than once but the last time there were two other men with him. I think they were ex-military; Edwards certainly enjoyed bossing them around. As soon as I saw them I wanted to leave. He scared me enough but these two were really hard men, younger than him, very strong. I was terrified just looking at them and I tried to run away but...they got me. They got me...' His voice died away, leaving the noise of sizzling butter in the echoing kitchen.

'Go on, if you can. Just the basics.'

'Right...the basics.' He tried to laugh but it was pitiful. 'Well, the basics are that they stripped me, threw me into the swimming pool and raped me, one after another. I tried to get away...I had a knife in my school bag and I thought if I could reach that I could slash them...or me. I would happily have died.'

Fenwick could smell burning. He went over to the stove and turned off the gas before guiding Paul gently towards the table. He could feel the man trembling under his hands as he eased him into a chair. Paul lowered his head into his palms and said nothing. At some point someone entered the kitchen, took one look at the tableau and left.

'Can you continue?'

Paul remained silent. Fenwick felt completely unequal to the task he faced. He hadn't had the special training they handed out these days and he wasn't equipped to deal with the agony stripped bare before him.

Minutes passed and neither man spoke. Then Fenwick's stomach rumbled loudly and it broke the tension.

'I promised you supper.'

'Never mind that. Are you OK; can you tell me the rest?'

'I'll give it a go.' The uninjured side of his mouth lifted to match the other in an attempt at a smile.

'Afterwards...after they finished...I could barely walk. Bryan was furious with them. Things had got out of hand, you see, and he was scared. Perhaps he was also concerned for me.' A look of amazement crossed Paul's face. 'I hadn't thought of that before. I've always put his behaviour down to a desire to preserve his own skin but who knows?

'He helped me dress and they half carried me somewhere. I was out of it; all I can remember is that it was a basement, dark and cold. I passed out. The next thing I remember was standing by his car. I refused to go in the back with my bike so he put me in the front passenger seat. Bryan was angry but he still collected his money from Nathan – I mean Edwards. I wasn't meant to see. He must have thought I was too traumatised to notice but I wasn't. He had over £200 and he offered me £20. The thought of him making all that money out of my pain filled me with rage. The more I thought about it the more it consumed me.

'We drove back the usual way, on narrow lanes through the wood. Before we reached the first houses he pulled off the road into a clearing and told me to get in the back. I refused. Looking back, I think I must have been hysterical. He put his hands on my shoulders. Bryan never hurt me, that wasn't his thing, but his touch after everything else that had happened pushed me over the edge. I hit him, again and again, and he slapped me with the back of his hand; only once but it was enough to knock my head against the dashboard.

'I fell into the footwell next to my duffle bag. It's a cliché but I honestly don't know how the knife ended up in my hand. I started slashing at him with it. He swore and grabbed my wrists really tight but I wouldn't let it go. I thought that if I did I'd die. We were struggling close together when I fell against him.

'It was an accident, it really was.' Paul looked at him with his giant blue eyes and Fenwick wanted to believe him.

'I felt the knife push against something firm, then it gave way, whatever it was, and the blade slipped in. I let go and sat back. Bryan and I just stared at it, the silly plastic brown handle sticking out from his stomach. Then he pulled it out and blood went everywhere. He started screaming and I got out of the car.

'My trousers and blazer were covered in blood so I took them off, threw them somewhere and grabbed my duffle bag. Bryan was crying out for help but I ignored him. My sports kit was in my bag and I put it on. Bryan started the car. I slammed my door and went round to get my bike. I just managed to pull it out and close the hatchback when he put the car into reverse. It almost knocked me over but I rode away. I never looked back, I just kept on cycling until I fell off but I didn't get far.'

'Where did you go?'

'As it turned out I was on a bridle path parallel to the A23. I couldn't cycle for long because I hurt so much so I pushed the bike. It was growing dark when I found a barn and fell asleep. When I woke up it was almost light and I was scared. I didn't know what to do. I'd stabbed a man and run away. The idea of going home was impossible.'

'But surely you knew your parents would forgive you. They loved you and you'd been provoked beyond endurance. Your actions might have led to a man's death but I doubt there's a jury in the land that would have convicted you.'

'Maybe, but that's not how you think when you're a terrified kid with a guilty secret. I couldn't face all…that coming out. My life was ruined. You have no idea, Andrew, how self-loathing can eat away at a child's confidence. I was convinced that I was as guilty as Cain and would be despised for ever. I decided to keep running. I had chocolate in my bag, my twenty pounds and the camera my parents had given me for my birthday, together with a few school books.

'I kept to the footpaths and didn't see anybody though I heard voices calling once. When I came to Oliver's farm I realised where I was. I waited until Mrs Anchor went out. I knew that she left the back door unlocked so I didn't even need to break in. I filled a bag with food and the money she kept on the mantelpiece. Then I looked for clothes. None of Oliver's would fit me but she was quite small so I took two pairs of jeans and some shirts and socks.

'I was feeling a bit more confident so I went into her bathroom for a wash. She had this dye shampoo – a blonde tint – and I used it, then stole some soap, a towel and a toothbrush.'

'Where did you go?'

'North. I was still hurting quite bad so I could only travel a little each night. In woodland somewhere on the North Downs I found this caravan. I needed shelter so I broke in. While I was there an old man came in. It was his place. I thought he'd be angry with me and call the police but he didn't. He wasn't quite right in the head and lonely I think. Jim – that was his name – insisted on cooking me his "special" as he called it: tinned frankfurters, fried with tinned sweetcorn. I was so hungry I ate every scrap. He took it as an absurd compliment and asked me to stay.

'He wasn't after anything but company and a bit of appreciation. It was so refreshing. There was no television, just an old radio. I slept most of the time. But on the third day Jim became ill; I think it was a bad bout of flu. I couldn't leave him after he'd been so kind to me so I stayed and looked after him, making him drink plenty of fluids, trying to coax him into eating something.

'The van was stuffed with food. It looked like he bought in bulk so there was plenty but little choice. I can't stand tinned sweetcorn to this day. By the end of a week he was well enough to get up and then he started to potter around. On the Saturday – that would be twelve days after I ran away – he went into the local town. It was market day and he wanted to buy us a treat, he said. He came back with a newspaper.' Paul paused. His eyes filled with tears. '"Is this you they're writing about, lad?" he asked me. I could only nod. I was so ashamed. He'd thought the best of me, you see, and it was all there, the terrible things they were writing about me.

'I burst into tears and he comforted me. Then he made me go and wash. He'd bought me new clothes in the market and some trainers. He was so kind and he didn't want anything, nothing. While I got dressed he cooked us a special supper, fresh steak, new potatoes and tinned tomatoes and there was Coke too, just for me. We neither of us had much appetite but we ate anyway. Afterwards he asked me what I wanted to do. "Stay with you," I said, but he shook his head. "Much as I'd like that, my lad, you can't. You need to go back to your parents. I'll take you." Well, of course that was the last thing I wanted. So I lied. I told him that I'd do it in my own way. He was a decent, trusting old man and he believed me.

'He washed my old clothes and while they were drying by his stove he made me sandwiches for my journey. Then we went for a walk in the woods and he told me about the son he'd left behind years before in Cyprus when he finished his National Service and returned to the UK. "I think about him often," he told me. "He'd be a grown man now and I keep wondering what he's made of his life. I don't wish that on your parents for anything."

'Back at the van I packed my things. I needed an extra bag and we strapped that behind the bike seat. He stuffed an envelope in my hand as I left. I opened it later that night. Inside was £50 in five pound notes and a picture of Jim. Here he is.' Paul opened his wallet and took out a dog-eared black and white picture. It was so worn that the face was a pale blur.

'A few years ago I went back. I was too late of course. The van had gone and when I asked around nobody had heard of him. He must be dead by now, he was over seventy when I met him, but I still look for his face when I walk the streets.'

'Is that why you became a priest?'

'No! Jim was as atheist as they come. The reason I'm a priest is because of Father Richard. I ended up in London eventually. I'd dyed my hair and the new clothes from Jim were enough to keep me looking neat. On the way I made sure I travelled in public only outside school hours and hid out of sight the rest of the time. Of course, as soon as I reached London it didn't matter that I was about in daytime. I was just another runaway living on the streets. By then I looked nothing like my neat school photograph and the weather had changed. People aren't nearly as observant in the rain. Have you noticed that?'

'Yes, all the time. It's a real pain in my job.'

'I can imagine but it helped me. In London I became invisible, particularly after this.' He touched his scar. 'I did what a lot of runaways end up doing, servicing middle-aged men around King's Cross and Euston. Within months I was out of my skull on crack and giving most of what I made to the dealer who ran us. By the time I was fifteen I worked all the time just to make my fix and I started to starve. Any money I managed to get went on drugs not food. I began to steal, even from charity shops. They were easy targets, or so I thought. I was caught in a Save the Children outlet. Ironic, don't you think? The woman there was all for calling the police and charging me but one of her customers stopped her. That was Father Richard. If he hadn't been in the shop who knows where I'd be now – probably dead.

'He took me straight to hospital. I had blood poisoning. I said I was Justin Smith and that I was a runaway. I refused to name my parents. Nobody recognised me. When I was admitted I weighed five and half stone, what little hair I had left was streaked blond and my complexion had gone. If someone had put my school picture next to my bed no one would have known me.

'I almost died. I was in hospital for over a month. Father Richard visited me most days and he was waiting for me when I came out. He found me a place at a rehab centre where I spent the most agonising months of my life, even worse than in the hospital. Crack is almost impossible to give up and it tortures you as you try; horrendous. But I beat it; I won with his help.

And then Father Richard found me a place in a refuge where they encouraged me to go to back to school. I had a lot of catching up to do but lying there in the centre, realising that I'd been killing myself, had shocked some sense into me.

'The thought of a future was more scary than dying but I decided that nothing in life, not even in my life, should be a complete waste. I never touched drugs again, or drink or cigarettes. I studied and helped out at the refuge. Then Father Richard asked if I would go to church. I didn't know what to say. I still had my street cred, you see, because I'd nearly died and the scar made me look tough. Going to church would wreck my rep so I resisted for months. But at Christmas when I was sixteen I finally gave in. I went to the carol service, then midnight mass. Father Richard was so pleased that I went back the following week and the next.

'I wasn't a convert, it wasn't anything that obvious. It was just that I'd found a place where I wasn't being judged all the time. I took my GCSEs two years late but I got seven and that encouraged me to try for A levels. I passed three. I was nineteen, too old to be staying in the refuge but there was a church hostel where I was allowed to help out for board and lodging.'

Paul stopped. His eyes were clear again, his emotions back under control. Fenwick stood up and made the tea he'd started almost an hour earlier. When they had mugs in front of them he asked Paul to finish his story. He knew it was none of his business but he was filled with curiosity to know whether Paul was a true Christian or just willing to try to be because he was grateful to Father Richard and the Church.

'What else is there to say?' Paul took a long swallow of tea and rested back in his chair with a sigh. 'It was after my A levels that I decided to try for the priesthood.'

'Excuse me for asking but how did you come to believe?'

Paul gave him a look that penetrated to his soul.

'Ah, the question of the rational man. You'd be surprised how many people ask it. My answer won't help you, I'm afraid. It was very simple. I woke up one morning and I knew. I knew that God existed, that He'd been calling me for a long time and that I'd been too deaf to hear. It was as if my ears were opened and I heard His voice.'

Fenwick shook his head.

'I told you my story wouldn't mean anything to you. Everyone has to find God their own way but one thing that helps is leaving space for Him in your life.' He paused, waiting for Fenwick to respond and when he didn't he smiled.

'Try going to church more than once or twice a year. It's a start.'

Fenwick felt embarrassed. Somehow during Paul's monologue they'd swapped roles. He had walked into the kitchen in command, ready to arrest the priest if necessary, now he almost stood accused. He cleared his throat noisily, trying to work out what to say next and was saved the trouble when his phone rang.

'Andrew, it's Nightingale. Traffic have just found William Slant's car in the village below Edwards' house. No sign of him but it looks as if he might have taken Sam to meet Edwards.'

'Any sign of the boy?'

'No. We've searched Edwards' place and all the outbuildings and he's not there. We're starting on the woods but it's dark; it will take us at least twenty-four hours to work through them, even superficially. And Edwards isn't talking, at least not yet.' He could hear disgust in her voice.

'What is it?'

'The fucking bastard!' He'd never heard her use the word before. 'He's suggested he might just recover his memory about William Slant if we offer him immunity from prosecution.'

'No way!'

'Exactly but...' She paused and he could hear a deep intake of breath. 'He said that Slant's journey involved "tidying up loose ends". Andrew, he's virtually admitted that Sam is in serious danger and that we need to move fast.

'It's over three hours since Slant left London. We're checking motorway surveillance but so far we can't find anything. Of course Sam might already be dead but—'

'We can't assume that!'

'I know.' She tried to calm him down. 'But Edwards isn't going to break. It's his information and immunity or Sam's life. That's the trade.'

'Dear God!' Fenwick covered his eyes with his hand and tried to think. 'Even now he thinks of the boy as his property.'

'Quinlan's suggested I call the ACC – in fact he thinks that's what I'm doing right now.'

'Don't do that. He'll cave in; maybe he won't offer full immunity but it'll be pretty close. There's no way he'd want Sam's death to be seen as his responsibility.'

'I know; that's why I rang you. You're the SIO. It should be your decision and if you decide to call Harper-Brown I'll understand but—'

'Enough, Nightingale, let me think. I have to think.' He shook his head to clear it. 'I'll call you back in five minutes.'

He broke the connection to find Paul watching him.

'Another boy lost?'

'Maybe but not if I can do anything about it. Sam Bowyer.' He opened his briefcase and passed the school photo to the priest, who blinked in disbelief.

'It could be me.'

'Almost; except for the eyes.'

'And he's been abused by Nathan, I mean Edwards?'

'Almost certainly and now he's disappeared. An associate was taking him to meet Edwards – we think – but now we can't find him or Sam. The boy could be anywhere. Did Nathan have a favourite place that he took you?'

'The pool, or a bedroom in his house with mirrors if the weather wasn't good.'

'We've searched his premises; the boy isn't there.'

'Then I can't help you.'

Fenwick watched the second hand on the dining room clock click round knowing that he had to call Nightingale or the ACC. There was no point in delay. He shivered.

'I know, it gets cold in here; it's because we're in the basement. With the ovens going its fine but—'

'What did you just say?'

'With the ovens on the place is war—'

'No, before that, the bit about being in the basement.'

Paul looked at him in confusion.

'That's all I said.'

'No, there was more, before that,' Fenwick leapt up and started pacing in frustration, 'when you were telling me about your last day.'

'But that was at the pool and then later with Bryan in the car.' He frowned in confusion.

'And in between?'

Paul's face cleared.

'The cold room where they locked me up while they decided what to do with me.'

'And you're sure it wasn't in the house or one of the outbuildings?' Fenwick was standing over him, urging him to remember.

'Positive. I can remember the walk; it was through the woods.'

'How long did it take?'

'I don't know, it was so long ago...'

'Think, damn you!' Fenwick bit his lip. 'Sorry, Father. I didn't exactly mean...but there's a boy's life at stake. This is very, very important.'

'I know, I want to help but...I was barely conscious.' He

screwed up his face with the effort of memory. 'It was through the woods and we lost the sun so I think we went into a dense stand of trees. And there was a stream we walked by, not big, and stones, mossy stones. Alec almost fell.' He looked at Fenwick in triumph. 'I don't think it took them very long to carry me there; find the stream, it must be close by.'

'What did the place look like?'

'I was blindfolded but I know it was built of stone and very cold; he was using it as a wine cellar.'

'Maybe an old ice house? It would be in keeping with the rest of the estate.'

'Possibly but your searchers won't hear the boy if he's in there. It had double doors and was a long way underground. It might even look derelict by now; they'll miss it in the dark. I don't...'

But Fenwick wasn't listening. He was already on the phone to Nightingale telling her to intensify the search in the woods along a stream she would find there, to look for any building, no matter what condition it was in and to search it, not rely on calling out for the boy. When he'd finished Paul was staring at him, his expression once again calm.

'You didn't tell her the source of your information.'

'No.'

'It would have been easy to. Why not?'

'I would have had to explain about you.'

Paul looked at him in wonder.

'So you haven't yet made your decision, Andrew. Thank you, I thought it would be inevitable.'

'Bryan Taylor died.'

'I know, as a result of a fight with me. I pray for forgiveness many times every day.'

'Your parents have lived with the uncertainty of your disappearance for a quarter of a century.'

'That is deplorable but not a crime. You see, the problem is that if I told them I was alive they would destroy my work. My father's too weak to keep the knowledge to himself and my mother too unstable to handle it. She'd come storming in here, the press would follow, the story about Bryan would come out and I might well end up in prison. If you choose to put me there that's one thing, that is God's will, but I will not go there because I have a mother who loves me too well. And before you mention my grandmother, she already knows I'm alive, I made sure of that.'

'She told me about your visit to her in hospital.'

'Did she now?' Paul was surprised. 'She must have trusted you.'

'I didn't believe her.'

'Ironic. But the night is moving on, Andrew. You're needed back in Sussex. What is it to be?'

Fenwick was in time to catch the last train to Harlden from Victoria. He edged back into a dusty seat and let go a sigh that he seemed to have been controlling for the whole of his life. He was emotionally and physically drained. He had finally solved the riddle of Paul Hill's disappearance and thanks to his strategy his team had arrested a man who was behind one of the most organised paedophile rings in southern England; a brothel had been closed down and a supply line of child pornography disrupted if not destroyed. But instead of feeling elated the success left him saddened to his core and facing the worst dilemma of his career.

A good man's fate was in his hands and while his duty as a police officer was clear it was, for once, at war with his sense of what was right. The unexpected conflict ate into him. He closed his eyes and tried to think of a way to resolve his problem but it was impossible. He had no choice but to decide a man's future and only the breathing space of his journey home in which to do so.

His gaze fell to his hands where they lay loosely on his thighs. For a fanciful moment he imagined Paul's liberty in his left hand and the sentence that society would pass on him were the truth ever known in his right. Revealing it would be a brilliant coup. It would put the seal on a high-profile, successful investigation and remove any hint of criticism for his visit to London. It would also help his promotion prospects, maybe even make him the favourite candidate. The fingers of his right hand started to curl subconsciously as if he were plucking advancement from the stale air. Then he clenched both fists tight before releasing them slowly, letting the futility of his thoughts float free. His problem remained and its solution he knew would be a defining moment in his life.

The train rattled on as it gathered speed, swaying over points, flashing past stations that were closed for the night, taking him towards a time in the future when the decision would have been made.

He had always considered himself a man who could make difficult decisions, had even thought it one of his strong points, but now, when really tested, he realised that he was no Solomon. So he did what he always did when his brain refused to work: he pulled out a notepad and opened his pen. At the top of a fresh sheet of paper he wrote down the question that had been circling in his mind like a child's riddle without answer ever since he'd discovered the truth: *When is a murderer not a murderer?* The words confronted him, unhelpful. The crime he'd solved was murder after all, not some petty misdemeanour.

With an audible grunt of frustration he ripped the page from the pad and screwed it up, stuffing it into his pocket so that his thoughts shouldn't join the litter on the carriage floor. His watch ticked past eleven as he smoothed his palm across a fresh page, preparing himself. Half an hour later he almost missed his stop because he was concentrating so deeply on what he was doing.

The house was quiet when he let himself in. Ignoring the meal ready for him in the fridge, he poured himself a small whisky and took it into the study, closing the door behind him. While the computer booted up he sipped his drink and reread his notes. As soon as he'd typed up everything he was going out to join Nightingale in the search for Sam but he needed to have the record straight first and was impatient to finish.

He tapped in his password, opened the word processing package and started to type. The first words struck him as melodramatic and he deleted them several times before deciding to leave them in:

'THE ENCLOSED ENVELOPE IS TO BE OPENED IN THE EVENT OF MY DEATH, BY SUPERINTENDENT QUINLAN OF HARLDEN DIVISION, WEST SUSSEX CONSTABULARY EVEN IF HE HAS RETIRED. IF HE SHOULD PRE-DECEASE ME, THE ENVELOPE IS TO BE GIVEN TO INSPECTOR LOUISE NIGHTINGALE, ALSO CURRENTLY OF HARLDEN DIVISION. SHOULD NEITHER OF THEM BE AVAILABLE TO RECEIVE THIS, FOR ANY REASON, IT IS TO BE DESTROYED UNOPENED.'

He signed the page and started on the note itself, typing quickly. He didn't share the view of some of his colleagues that the roles of enforcement and judiciary should be combined when needs must in order to protect society. In his opinion no one had the right to be police, judge and jury. As a consequence he found himself struggling with a deep sense of uncertainty as he finished his confession and the defence of what he had decided to do.

His actions were so out of character that part of him wanted to rip up his words, file a regular report and pass the whole business over to CPS. Yet he knew that that would be wrong. Only he had met Paul Hill, watched him work with the runaways and listened to Gerry's testament. For whatever reason, he was the one to find the man who'd been the boy the world thought long dead. It would be egotistical to think that he had been chosen for the task but the decision that followed the discovery had fallen to him and he had taken it, not easily or willingly, but because he had no other choice.

If he was completely wrong in his assessment of Paul Hill, if tomorrow or some day soon he were to die – his silence guaranteed – then it was essential for a statement to be left that would allow justice to be done. But he couldn't rely on just anybody because he might die for other reasons. So he was leaving his documented conversation with Paul Hill in an envelope for the people he trusted most.

It was half past twelve when he finished typing. His eyes were sore and the whisky had given him a headache. He was addressing the envelope to his solicitor when his mobile phone rang.

'Fenwick,' he answered.

'Andrew?' Louise Nightingale sounded tired but elated. 'We've found him alive.'

'Thank God.' His mind was too drained to register anything but relief.

'He was where you said. We missed the building the first time because only the roof shows above ground and it was smothered in brambles and ivy, but when we reached the end of the stream I had the search party double back. You were so insistent that we'd find it, I took the risk.'

'You did well.'

'Aren't you pleased? Without you we'd never have found him. Sam would have died; he was already suffering from exposure when we reached him. You saved his life.'

No, Paul saved his life, he thought as he pulled the last printed sheet of his statement from the printer.

'Andrew! What's got into you? Look, we all want to know

how you got the information. It was from the Well-Wisher, wasn't it?'

'I can't say.'

'You're kidding me! The ACC won't let you get away with that even if Quinlan's inclined to. You're going to have to come clean. It's crazy not to. Your star's riding high for a change; don't throw it away by turning inscrutable. It will really piss Harper-Brown off. Make the most of your moment.'

'I've said all I'm going to say, Nightingale. Be grateful we have a result; enjoy the night but leave the interrogation of me out of it.'

'Hey – all right.'

'Is Edwards talking now?'

'Would you believe the bastard's still trying to negotiate. He's asked if he pleads guilty to child abuse and admits to the manslaughter of Malcolm Eagleton, will we give him a reduced sentence.'

'What did you say to him?'

'That the best we could do is tell the judge he was cooperating fully and that if he could give us names of other paedophiles it would help his case considerably.'

'Good.'

'He's adamant he didn't kill Paul though, won't budge. I've had another chat with CPS. They think we have a strong case for the abuse and a good chance on Malcolm Eagleton's death but ironically they don't think we have enough evidence to charge him with Paul Hill's murder. With the other charges Edwards will be inside for the rest of his natural life, however cooperative he is, but it still feels wrong to leave Paul unavenged, don't you think?'

'Sometimes that's just the way things are,' Fenwick said carefully.

'You amaze me. I thought you'd be on to the ACC first thing in the morning demanding more resources to finish this off properly.'

'Not this time. I think we've done enough.'

There was a pause. He knew that he'd surprised her for the second time that night and perhaps one day he might explain. Fenwick peeled off a stamp and stuck it to the envelope that he would post first thing in the morning.

'Well, if you think so,' she said eventually. 'It would be a lot easier all round to focus the prosecution where we know we can get a result, unless you've persuaded the Well-Wisher to talk of course.'

'He talked but he can't help us.'

'Why not? You need him to, Andrew; a lot of your credibility was riding on finding him.'

'Thanks for reminding me but, believe me, the Well-Wisher's testimony won't help us charge Edwards with Paul's murder.'

'So your trip to find Paul's killer was a waste of time,' she said dismissively.

'No; nothing in life need ever be a complete waste, Louise, not if we can help it.' He licked the flap of the envelope and ran his finger along the edge to seal it.

There was a long silence, which she broke with a sigh.

'You're keeping something from me, Andrew, I know it. But I can also tell that you're not going to reveal whatever it is. You could trust me, you know, you can always trust me – whatever it is.' She sounded so sad.

'I know, Nightingale; I know. You're a good friend – and that's the reason I don't want you dragged into something that could...' He was about to say 'damage your career' then realised that she'd never let him rest. 'Never mind. Forget it.' The words sounded final.

'Right. Well in that case I'd better let you catch up on some sleep before all hell breaks loose. You sound exhausted, not yourself at all. It's been some day, hasn't it!'

'That's one way of putting it,' he replied. 'Goodnight, Louise.'
'Goodnight, Andrew, and try to sleep well,'
'Do you know, I think I shall.'

Fenwick switched off the light and put the sealed letter on the hall table to post in the morning. He showered quickly, sloughing off the city's corruption, scrubbing his skin pink. Then he found some old pyjamas left over from when he used to wear them and a blanket warm from the airing cupboard. He padded on bare feet along to the children's bedrooms.

Bess was fast asleep, lying on her back with her arms spread wide; confident, smiling, happy even in sleep. He kissed her lightly and walked along to his son's bedroom. Chris had burrowed down under the covers as usual, with barely a strand of hair showing. Fenwick lay down carefully beside him on top of the duvet, draped the blanket over his legs and his arm across his son. He was asleep in moments. Chris didn't stir but in the morning, when Fenwick woke with the aches of a strange bed in every one of his vertebrae, he found Chris curled up against his chest fast asleep. He was smiling.

EPILOGUE

Orderlies were taking down the last of the Christmas decorations as Jeremy Maidment and Margaret Pennysmith came out of the lift on the third floor of the general hospital. A passing nurse recognised the major and paused in her bustling passage to speak to him.

'Major Maidment! My, it's good to see you up and about again. How are you?'

'Mustn't grumble, Nurse Shah,' the major said, trying to lean less heavily on a substantial walking stick. He'd been out of a wheelchair less than three weeks and the short walk from the disabled parking bay had made his legs shake.

'Well, lovely to see you.'

'She was nice,' Margaret commented. 'Now, which way is Camellia Ward? That's where they've moved Hannah. You sit here, Jeremy, while I go and find out.'

She went over to the nurse's station, walking almost briskly despite her arthritis. It was still there in the twinges of her joints and the winter weather made it worse, but for some reason it didn't seem to get her down quite as much these days. *Because I can't dwell on it while Jeremy needs me,* she told herself.

'We're here to see Mrs Hill, Camellia Ward,' she explained.

'Down there to your right.' The nurse pointed helpfully.

'How is she today?'

A look of caution crossed the nurse's face.

'You're not family, love; I know because they're off skiing and she won't let us call them.'

'I'm a very good friend though,' which was true. A strong bond of affection had formed between the two women after their meeting at the day centre and they'd seen each other regularly until Hannah became poorly after Christmas.

'Well, she's awake and has had some lucid moments today,' the nurse said in a way that made Margaret's spirits fall, 'but with pneumonia we're naturally cautious. The ward sister may be able to tell you more.'

But she wasn't there. A young trainee directed the major and Miss Pennysmith towards Hannah without volunteering any comment. She was in the bed closest to the nurses' station and the major, now an expert on hospitals, hoped that Margaret didn't realise the significance. But one look at Margaret's face told him that she did and he squeezed her arm briefly. They mustered smiles and approached the patient.

Hannah Hill lay propped up on pillows, a transparent oxygen tube in her nose and an IV drip stuck in her arm. She looked like a raggedy doll, discarded carelessly in a cot that was far too big for her, but when she opened her eyes and saw them her face lit up with a wonderful childlike smile.

'My dear,' she said, her Londoner's voice a pale imitation of itself, 'this is lovely. And you've brought the major; what a treat.'

It was obvious to her visitors that the brief welcome had exhausted her so they started chatting in a way that meant she only had to nod or speak the odd word to join in. At one point an orderly came along and offered to show Margaret where she could find a vase for the silk flowers that she'd brought, leaving the major and Hannah alone together.

'I wanted to say something to you, Jeremy...something important, before I go.'

'Ssh, you mustn't talk like that, Mrs Hill.'

'Hannah...and don't shush me...I know what's what and I'm all right with it.' She paused and took a few gulps of air. There were tiny bright spots of colour on her cheeks but her lips were almost blue. 'I read about what you did...with Paul's clothes...'

'Please, I...' The major could barely speak and looked away, deeply pained.

'No, listen...it's important... What you did was...dumb...I'll give you that, but...you don't deserve to go to prison.'

'The court will decide that, Hannah, though it's very generous of you to say so.'

He too had his hopes, at least for a shorter sentence. For some reason, after he'd admitted his part in the sorry affair and volunteered to act as a witness against Edwards, Chief Inspector Fenwick had argued strongly in his favour with the Crown Prosecution Service. He had no idea why Fenwick had chosen to act as his advocate because the man refused to return his calls, but he was intensely grateful, in a way that only added to his burden of guilt. Now here was dear Mrs Hill, close to death and trying to make him feel better; it was too much.

'Generous my ar...m.' She stopped again and pointed wordlessly to a plastic tumbler with a straw by her bed. Maidment raised it to her lips and held it for her while she managed a few sips. 'Thanks...get...very dry. Now listen, I've told Margaret but...she don't believe me, so I'm going to...to tell you too.' She closed her eyes briefly and he watched in concern as her chest heaved. After a few minutes she opened them again and fixed him with her remarkable bright blue stare. 'My Paul ain't dead. No...don't look at me like that...he's not.'

'I wish that were true, I really do, but...'

'That man they've arrested...did he say...he did it?'

'Well, no, quite the opposite in fact.'

'And did you...believe him?'

'Yes.' He nodded; he was certain that Edwards had told the

truth about his part in Paul's death when he confronted him. 'But there were others...' He couldn't bring himself to go on. Why torture her with the nature of Paul's murder.

'No buts...You mustn't carry...this guilt...about Paul... It's not right.' She chuckled, a disturbing chesty rumble deep in her throat. 'For Margaret's sake.'

The last words were barely a whisper. A nurse came by and looked at him sternly, then lifted Hannah's wrist to take her pulse.

'You're overexciting her. If you can't be more considerate you'll have to leave.'

'Sorry,' he mumbled.

'My fault,' Hannah mouthed but the nurse didn't appear to hear.

Margaret returned at that moment with the flowers in a vase and their previous conversation, such as it was, resumed.

'Once this silly trial is over and Jeremy is allowed to travel I think I've persuaded him to go to Australia and visit his son.'

'Smashing.' Hannah grinned, her eyes closed.

'And I'm hoping that Margaret might join me. She has a nephew in Hong Kong, you know, and we could stop off on the way.'

'Marvellous.'

'But it's a lot of money, I don't know if...'

Hannah's eyes snapped open and she glared at her friend.

'Family's important, Margaret!'

'Mrs Hill?' Nurse Shah came up to the bed. 'Your priest is here, dear.'

'My priest?' A look of confusion crossed Hannah's face but Jeremy and Margaret missed it as they rose to leave.

'We should be going. I'll call tomorrow to see how you are and maybe stop by again if they're allowing visitors.' Margaret bent down to kiss her friend's cheek, as soft as a baby's. 'Goodbye, my dear. God bless you.'

There were tears in her eyes but she determinedly kept her voice steady.

''Member what I said,' Hannah admonished the major as he took his leave. 'Family.'

He bowed to her, too polite to argue, and placed his free arm solicitously around Margaret's shoulders as they walked away.

They could see the priest sitting in the small lobby by the lifts at the end of the corridor ahead of them.

'It's odd,' said Margaret, dabbing her eyes with a lace-edged handkerchief, 'all the time I've known her she never struck me as religious. Still I'm so glad she is, particularly now...'

Neither of them was inclined to finish the thought. Nurse Shah passed as they made their slow progress towards the lifts.

'Goodbye, Major, look after yourself,' she called out, as cheerful as ever.

He nodded his head to her in acknowledgement.

'Major Maidment?' the priest asked standing up.

'Yes, Father. Forgive me but do I know you?' He stared at the uncomfortably familiar face in confusion.

'No, sir, you don't but for a while now I've wanted to meet you. I believe we have a mutual friend in Andrew Fenwick.' He stretched out his palm and Maidment grasped it automatically. 'No hard feelings, eh? Let the past be behind us now.'

'I beg your pardon?'

But the priest was gone, striding eagerly towards Camellia Ward.

'What the devil was that all about, Margaret?'

'I've no idea but he was quite young despite the grey hair. Pity about that terrible scar.'

They sat for a moment in the chairs by the lifts so that the major could summon strength for the final stage of their journey to the taxi. He was dreading the medical examination scheduled for the following week to assess whether he could keep his licence. A life dependent on the uncertainty of public transport and the favours of friends was an indignity he had hoped to avoid.

As they waited for him to recover the lift door opened and a man walked out. He was in his early thirties, handsome in a foxy sort of way and smiling as if he had a secret the world would love to share. The major stood up slowly and the movement caught the man's attention. His smile widened and took on a malicious cast.

'There you are,' he said, walking over to them. 'I tried your home but the neighbour said you were out visiting a friend in here.'

'And you are?' Maidment asked frostily, gathering his energy to walk past.

'Jason MacDonald of the *Enquirer*; perhaps you received my phone calls.'

'I have no desire to speak with you, now please move aside. We're leaving.' He took Margaret's arm.

'If you like, Major, but I really wouldn't do that if I were you.' He didn't bother to hide the implied threat in his words. 'I would have thought you'd have wanted to put your side of the story.'

'I am unable to talk about anything to do with the forthcoming trial, you must know that,' the major said with disdain.

'Oh, but I'm not interested in the trial, Mr Maidment,' MacDonald said, his smile revealing too many teeth. 'It's your family I want to talk about.'

'What does he mean, Jeremy, your family? What do they have to do with this?' Margaret clutched his arm more tightly.

'Nothing; they're in Australia out of harm's way,' Maidment said firmly but he was looking at MacDonald with growing unease.

'Oh, you mean your second family; your illegitimate son and daughter-in-law.'

'Jeremy! What's he saying?'

He couldn't meet her eye. Maidment felt his legs going and sat down abruptly. Margaret let go of his arm and folded obediently into another chair as MacDonald towered over them. He took a step closer, lowered his head so that it was inches from Maidment's face and said in a voice that made people at the reception desk turn around, 'I was doing some background for the trial. Unfortunately for you, some of your old army buddies can't hold their drink despite years of practice. It's amazing what friends will say in an attempt to protect you, quite amazing. It's going to make a great story.'

Maidment looked up at MacDonald, trapped by his words, waiting for the inevitable. Margaret clutched at his arm.

'It's your Indonesian wife and family that I want to talk to you about, Major. The fifteen-year-old girl you married, impregnated and abandoned so that you could return to your cosy life here. I don't know whether there's a statute of limitations on bigamy but that will hardly matter after my editor and I have finished with you.' Spittle from his lips flew into Maidment's eye and he wiped it away. 'There's one thing neither of us can stand and that's a hypocrite.'

'Jeremy?' Miss Pennysmith dropped her hand and stared at him, willing him to rebut the story as a fabrication but Maidment could only shake his head.

'I'm so sorry, Margaret, so very sorry.'

'So, you don't deny that you're married then?' MacDonald asked, triumphant. 'Good, because your long-lost family is waiting for you at our offices along with my photographer. Shall we go and join them?'

Maidment closed his eyes and bowed his head. Beside him he heard Margaret's first sob of dismay. He realised that whatever the outcome of his trial, this was to be his true punishment: the vestiges of his reputation shattered beyond repair; his past conduct laid bare for public condemnation; and worst of all, the possible loss of the companionship of a woman he had grown to regard with deep affection. He took a deep breath and turned towards her.

'I have to leave now. You should go home; I'll call you later and try to explain.'

Margaret Pennysmith burst into tears. He tried to hold her hand but she shook it away.

'Very well then,' he said to MacDonald and stood up, squaring his shoulders. 'We had better go.'

Behind him in the quietness of Camellia Ward, Father Peter was unaware of the vengeance that had been visited on the major, brought about because of his silent defence of the indefensible. He was focused entirely on the tiny bundle in front of him, small as a child and as vulnerable. Her eyes were closed, her breathing laboured but she seemed peaceful. He was too used to death to be anything but aware that she was already on her final journey and he started to pray silently.

An orderly stopped by with a cup of tea and his soft words of thanks caused her eyelids to flutter open. Hannah Hill took a few moments to focus but when she did and saw him her face came alive with pure joy.

'Paul,' she said, her eyes bright, her smile wide.

'Gran,' he whispered, barely able to speak but his expression reflected her own delight.

A stranger passing at that moment would have had no doubt that they were related.

'I hoped you'd come... How did...?' Words failed her as the breath caught in her throat.

'A friend called me.'

'Friend?'

'A man called Andrew; you've met him.'

She shook her head slightly, an indication that the reason he had found her was of no consequence.

'I'm glad.'

'So am I, Gran.'

They sat wordlessly as he held her hand and watched the faint signs of the rise and fall of her chest. Eventually, she asked, 'Will you stay…you know…till the end?'

'Of course, that's why I'm here.'

Her smile deepened and she closed her eyes. About them the business of the ward continued in its steady rhythm. At some point a nurse drew the curtains around their bed and another cup of tea arrived. Outside it grew dark. Hannah's breathing was barely perceptible. It was as if she were falling into a deep, deep sleep. There was no desperate struggle for air, just a gradual decline with each shallow breath. Paul prayed.

At some time around midnight he found he couldn't ignore the effects of the tea any longer and hurried down the hall to the cloakroom. When he returned her eyes were wide open, searching for him; her mouth was moving rapidly as if she had a critical message to share.

'I'm here,' he whispered, 'don't worry.'

Her lips opened and closed but he couldn't make out what she was trying to say with such urgency.

'I'm sorry, what?'

'Come…funeral,' she repeated. 'Say mass.'

'I can't be there, not on the day. It—'

There was an infinitesimal shaking of her head that cut across anything he was about to say.

'Remember…' Her fingers clutched his hand in a surprisingly strong grip. 'Family's important.'

Her last words were no more than warm air against his ear but they sank deep into his heart as her eyes closed, and lay there, a burden he could not shake no matter how hard he prayed.